It All Started... takes you through hidden parts of Disneyland and exotic locations in Walt Disney's history. You will finally meet the mysterious Blond-Haired Man, first seen at the bedside of one of the world's most beloved entertainers in the first book of the *Hidden Mickey* series, *Sometimes Dead Men DO Tell Tales!* What was included in the set of instructions he was given by Walt just before he died? Is there more to the Hidden Mickey quest than we were already shown? What is the real power of the red heart-shaped diamond that mysteriously came from the depths of the jungle?

Lance Brentwood, the spoiled bad-boy of *Hidden Mickey*, finds himself in an unfamiliar position – alone and at loose ends. Staying with his Security job at Disneyland, he goes back to the scene of his crime. Now, in an ironic twist of fate, Lance is the one at the receiving end of a .44 Magnum.

When Lance awakens in an unknown location, he learns that the legacy Walt set in place is more far-reaching than he had ever imagined. He is given one cryptic clue and finds that his entire destiny lies in it's decipher. Can Lance earn the trust of the Blond-Haired Man's daughter, Kimberly, or does the feisty beauty have plans of her own? The intrigue heats up when Lance has to team up with Kimberly as the two embark on an even wilder quest to unravel Walt Disney's final clue and ultimately find the very treasure that helped Walt build the greatest entertainment company in the world.

As the Blond-Haired Man's chauffer, Daniel Crain was content to sit on the sidelines and live the easy life. Seeing a chance to up the stakes, Crain will stop at nothing to step into the position of power he feels he has been deprived. The only thing he sees standing in his way is Lance–and what appears to be a growing attachment between Lance and Kimberly.

Who will win the battle for Walt's legacy – the one man determined to preserve it or the other man determined to destroy it? In what seems to be a no-way-out situation, Lance discovers there is far more to the Legacy of the great showman, Walt Disney, and is thrust into a life-or-death race to un the Master Storyteller wants someone to find.

For Lance, *It All Started*…

HIDDEN MICKEY 2

IT ALL STARTED...

Aaron L. Lagunas

BY
NANCY TEMPLE RODRIGUE
DAVID W. SMITH

2010
DOUBLE-R BOOKS

DOUBLE-R BOOKS ARE PUBLISHED BY
RODRIGUE & SONS COMPANY
244 FIFTH AVENUE, SUITE 1457
NEW YORK, NY 10001
WWW.DOUBLE-RBOOKS.COM

COPYRIGHT © 2010
BY NANCY RODRIGUE AND DAVID W. SMITH
LIBRARY OF CONGRESS NUMBER TX 7-309-599
WWW.HIDDENMICKEYBOOK.COM

HIDDEN MICKEY 2: IT ALL STARTED...
VOLUME 2, 1ST EDITION 2010, 2ND PRINTING 2011
SECOND BOOK IN THE HIDDEN MICKEY SERIES

PAPERBACK ISBN 13: 978-0-9749026-3-0
PAPERBACK ISBN: 0-9749026-3-2
EBOOK ISBN 13: 978-0-9749026-6-1
EBOOK ISBN: 0-9749026-6-7

COVER DESIGN BY JEREMY BARTIC
  WWW.JEREMYBARTIC.DAPORTFOLIO.COM
COPYRIGHT © 2010 BY DOUBLE-R BOOKS
WWW.DOUBLE-RBOOKS.COM
PENDANT DESIGN BY NANCY RODRIGUE
COPYRIGHT © 2010 BY NANCY RODRIGUE
WWW.AWESOMEGEMS.COM

PRINTED IN THE UNITED STATES OF AMERICA

*I would like to dedicate this book
to my husband Russ Rodrigue. He has
read every word I have written; he has
offered support every step of the way; and
he has been there for almost every book
signing and appearance I have made.
His behind-the-scenes work has been
invaluable to me. Thank you from the
bottom of my red diamond heart!*
Nancy Temple Rodrigue

*I dedicate my efforts in this book to
the two women most important in my
life: My wife, Dr. Kerri Smith, who has provided the means for me to do what I enjoy
doing, and my Mother, Donna Winchester
who has always faithfully supported
me and my projects.*
David W. Smith

Disclaimer

Dear Readers,

Writing the first novel in the Hidden Mickey series, *HIDDEN MICKEY: Sometimes Dead Men DO Tell Tales!,* was an adventure for both of us. No one could have predicted the interest and success that the novel has enjoyed in its first year of publication. From Disney fans to Mystery/Adventure fans, *Sometimes Dead Men DO Tell Tales!* has found a following among almost *all* who have read the book! Yet, this is just the start. To us, the book was our way of sending readers on a nostalgic—if not just plain fun—adventure as they visited places in Disneyland, relived their youth, and shared in the common goal of keeping Walt Disney's legacy alive. *HIDDEN MICKEY 2: It All Started...* has turned out to be every bit as much fun for us to write...and, we hope, as much fun for all who read it.

For the best experience, we recommend readers begin with *HIDDEN MICKEY: Sometimes Dead Men DO Tell Tales!* before moving on to this second book in the series. However, this novel stands on its own. Many questions our readers had after reading the first novel are answered in this book. Yet, this novel poses several new questions. We can happily say that these will be answered in the next book in the series *HIDDEN MICKEY 3 Wolf! The Legend of Tom Sawyer's Island.*

So, sit back, get comfortable, and dig into the quest for Hidden Mickeys!

Best Wishes,
Nancy Temple Rodrigue
David W. Smith

PROLOGUE

Saturday, July 27, 2002
11:30 P.M.

Lance looked up from the frosted window before him, knowing he had discovered something truly incredible, monumental. He interlocked his fingers behind his head, consciously willed his breathing and heart rate to return to anything under one hundred beats per minute, and gazed up at one of the few remaining lit bulbs feebly lighting the subterranean cavern that he had stumbled upon. Lance thought of all the rumors, the myths that surrounded Walt Disney. Some said he was abducted by aliens, others claimed that he was cryogenically frozen, others still maintain that he was alive, never aging, and hanging out with Elvis like a pair of 'lost boys' in their own private 'Neverland.' Looking back at the window and the blinking red light within, it became very apparent that only a thick pane of glass was all that separated him from one of the world's greatest entertainers.

A million thoughts flooded his mind, subjecting him, he supposed, to a phenomenon similar to that of someone about to die—seeing his life pass before his eyes. He didn't like what he saw. He had been such an idiot in what he had done to his friends Adam and Beth, how he had let his needs—no, his greed, he aptly corrected himself—turn him into a…a…. Lance groaned and shook his head in disgust. He couldn't even come up with a word bad enough to describe himself, as the thought of pulling a gun on his friends and threatening to shoot them for whatever had been in the sealed room returned to him.

He knew they had found Walt's Treasure. He was sure of it. The heavy door that had been the final puzzle to the treasure's discovery had been locked, but was now opened. In the chamber outside the one in which he now stood he had found a broken and empty crate. All this testified to the fact that someone had figured out the clue to the locked door.…

"Sunnee holds the key."

Four words that had sent him on a wild goose chase to Idaho while Adam and Beth either had known the answer or had figured it out.

"Sunnee holds the key."

Walt's favorite dog, a Chow, the one he had given to his wife Lillian for Christmas, was named Sunnee. This he had found out while in the Lapwai Library, after he had fathomed himself the fool and was led by Beth to the Nez Perce Reservation in Idaho where Walt's wife had lived as a girl.

Lance started pacing in front of the mysterious cylindrical machine that took up half of the room, unable to stand still. He just couldn't connect the dots. He understood the journey that Walt, the world's greatest storyteller, had taken them on, which had ultimately led them to the Disneyland ride Pirates of the Caribbean. There they had found the map with the red **X** that had led them to the secret chamber entrance behind the ornate headboard in the Captain's Quarters. The secret chamber had, in turn, led them to the locked door and the final, obscure clue. But what was it about the Pirates ride that connected the clue to the locked door?

Lance still tried to make sense of the clue: "Sunnee holds the key."

Sunnee, a dog, holds the key.

A dog holds the key.

Standing next to the machine that continued to puff small whiffs of white ice-cold air out of a small metal exhaust tube at the base of the metal box, Lance suddenly drew in a sharp breath of air and came to an abrupt stop. He knew the answer. It had literally dogged him all the way back from Idaho.

Picturing one of the most recognized scenes in the Pirate ride dark and silent above him—the jail scene where three hopeful pirates were locked behind metal bars—Lance suddenly had the same epiphany that Adam and Beth must have had weeks earlier.

The pirates were trying to lure a dog that held in its mouth a metal ring from which a long key dangled and shook every time the dog moved his head.

"Sunnee holds the key."

That dog with the seemingly knowing smile, Lance knew, had been there in plain sight ever since the ride opened in 1967.

Lance started pacing again, excited by his new discovery. "That key must have been THE key," he said out loud, his voice overloud as it echoed back from the concrete walls that housed the machine he had found. "The man really was a genius!" He stopped pacing and looked down at the frosted window where, behind the glass, he had recognized the man who had set this whole thing in motion with his diary, the clues, and the places in his history. His mind started running through all the ramifications of this discovery, his discovery. Yes, Adam and Beth had probably found some treasures of financial merit left by Walt. Lance could only imagine what might have been found in that wooden crate he had come across earlier. But this…he turned again to the machine and the window. THIS was huge! What price could be put on this discovery? His heart sped up again as his mind began to race. What would be the outcome, he imagined, the impact if this incredible discovery was ever to be revealed to the public?

He ran his hand through his hair, not even re-alizing he knocked off his Security hat in the process, as he began pacing again. This was big. "I knew it!" he shouted up at the dimly lit ceiling. "I always knew it would be big!" Lance thought back to his friend Adam; Adam never looked at the far-reaching possibilities of their quest. Adam thought small and compact and orderly. Lance had believed in something far bigger. But this discovery.... Glancing back at the machine, he was transfixed by the process that brought him here and the ramifications of this incredible discovery. It trumped anything he could have possibly imagined.

With a grin of triumph, Lance strode over to the blinking red light illuminating the little window. As he stared at the fog of condensed water that obscured his view of Walt, his smile faltered. A similar fog began to fill his mind, obscuring details that were really only hazy outlines.

"What in the world do I do now?" Lance asked himself out loud again, hoping that the sound of his own voice would somehow miraculously reveal a logical course of action.

"**Push Here**"

He looked down at his hand, at the forgotten piece of paper he had been holding since he discovered it on the ground and just now had thoughtlessly thrust through his hair.

"**Push Here**"

This small piece of paper, torn out of Walt's secret diary, had actually been the final clue—no, the final task—Lance concluded. It had fallen onto the floor in this secret chamber who knows how long ago...a chamber that only Lance knew about. He had searched and found the remnants of adhesive tape on a lone button on the side of the main console. He was certain which button the paper referred to. Yet, he was not certain as to what his next course of action should be.

"What do I do?" he repeated softer, as he

walked over to the dusty panel of buttons and switches and stared at that single, black button.

"You do absolutely nothing."

Startled, Lance swung around at the deep, resonant voice which came from a dark corner of the cavern. Before he could react, Lance saw the concrete door—his only exit—close with a distinct and final Bang! The wooden crate that he had hopefully propped in the opening to keep the door open was reduced to a scattering of ineffective splinters. As the already-dim lights in the cavern flickered on and off, Lance felt as if his whole world had been pulled out from under him.

A blond-haired man, probably in his mid 60's, stepped away from his dark observation point. An odd smile creased his lips. It was a smile that revealed a man of confidence and faint surprise as his green eyes looked Lance over. In his hand, the stunned Lance now saw a shiny, chrome-plated .44 Magnum.

"You do absolutely nothing."

December 14, 1966

"It all started with a moose." His boss had used these words right before he was dismissed. They weren't his final words, but the young blond-haired man knew these would be the words he would remember as he hurriedly left the hospital room. The instructions he had been given, the little black diary that needed to be placed, contacts he needed to make, all blended together with the grief he felt as he walked through the white hospital corridor. "It all started…," he murmured to himself.

Coming toward him from the opposite end of the hospital hallway, he felt the eyes of Walt's secretary settle on him as he continued toward the exit. Passing her, he offered a short, non-committal nod. He knew her by sight, of course, but she would have no idea who he was. It had always been that way and always would. He would have liked to have seen the painting she carried under her arm, but that would have meant a conversation. That would not do. The anonymity worked to his advantage. And, with the huge task Walt had given him, it was vital that he maintained it. Head down, he wiped the remnants of a tear from off his face. There was too much to do right now. He would grieve later in private. He didn't have time now.

As he headed to his home in the Fullerton Hills, the blond-haired man's emotions seemed to match the gloomy December afternoon. It was as if the sky was beginning to mourn the loss that the world would soon experience. He slowly pulled into the large, circular drive of his house. It was a large home, too large for the young, single man he had been then, but Walt had insisted. "A man should never neglect his family for business. There's room to grow here. Trust me. You'll need it. In more ways than one," Walt had chuckled mysteriously.

Much earlier, as Walt was overseeing the final construction details of this fine house, he called the younger man to his side. At the confused look on his face, Walt had handed him a different set of blueprints retrieved from the trunk of his car. Spreading them out on the floor of a huge room on the third story, Walt began pointing out the designs, diagrams, schematics, monitors, communications, and mechanics represented by specific symbols and codes, some of which the blond man recognized, others were as foreign to him as Egyptian hieroglyphics. As the large, curled pages were turned, his boss's cryptic ideas began to become clear to him.

Walt was silent for as long as it took for it all to sink in. He watched as the stunned confusion on the young man's face gave way to comprehension and acceptance. As the blond-headed man turned back a few pages, he silently ran his finger along a diagram, then advanced to a different page and nodded. Walt knew he had chosen well—the man next to him was as fastidious and meticulous as he himself was. The green eyes that turned from the blueprints back to Walt were now wide and excited. "This is amazing," he smiled. "You've thought of everything."

"I always try to," Walt responded, with a sly, knowing smile etched on his face. "I always try to."

Now, years later, parts of those blueprints were spread out on the large black oak dining room table, softly illuminated by open floor-to-ceiling windows and a large crystal chandelier hanging overhead. The prints that had specifically pertained to the alterations of his house had already been utilized and put away. Now it was time for the secondary, the most crucial part of the design to come into play. He glanced over at the black diary and the manila folder he had taken from Walt's hospital room. Both were now sitting on the matching sideboard against the wall.

For a moment, a small smile creased his face. Looking at the little black diary, he imagined for a moment how the few pages within would someday drastically change someone's life. He knew the book would eventually have a similar effect as that of a treasure map—only with far-reaching consequences.

The man knew the book would likewise preserve the legacy of the man he had come to love like a father. That thought, the pending loss of Walt from his life, eroded his momentary smile.

His wife had met him at the door, her unasked question answered in the sorrow she could see in his eyes. He took her in his arms for a quick embrace. "We knew it was coming," he softly told her as she began to cry. "But, it doesn't make it any easier, does it?" he whispered, kissing her forehead.

Seeing her distress made it difficult for him. *There is too much to do right now*, he reminded himself. He tried to hide the emotion in his voice as he made his first call. There was only one thing he had to say to every person on his short, but important, list. Grief aside, shock aside, they all would know what to do.

"It's starting," he said with muted reverence into his phone to the first person on the list. He hung up and started dialing the next number.

CHAPTER 1

Lance stared at the gun now pointing at him. *How ironic*, flashed through his mind. He had held a similar weapon against his friends not so very long ago. The moment of surprise passed for Lance. He looked from the gun back to the panel of buttons and switches. His fingers curled around the yellowed paper in his hand, feeling it crinkle. Slowly, he put his hand into his pocket, leaving the message hidden from view. The stunned surprise he felt gave way to questions. Did the blond-haired man know about the final clue? Had he somehow followed Lance from New Orleans Square into the chamber? Would he try and take this amazing discovery for himself? Was Lance going to be left in the lurch again?

As the questions continued to bombard his mind, Lance found himself becoming strangely calm. And in this calmness, he found his anger again. Anger at his own actions. Anger at Adam and Beth for taking the treasure. Anger at this unknown man for thwarting him yet again.

The blond-haired man's eyes went from being confident to being wary as he saw the change come over Lance's handsome face. He had expected the sight of the gun to stop the discoverer in his tracks. He had expected someone who would do as he said. Now he was not so sure.

"Step away from the instrument panel," he instructed Lance, motioning with the barrel of the Magnum.

The dim lighting caught on the shiny surface of the gun. Lance's eyes were involuntarily drawn to it. But his response was not what the blond-haired man expected as he saw Lance's eyes narrow in indignation and his lips become a firm, narrow line.

Realizing Lance was not stepping away from the machine as he was instructed, and knowing what was coming, the blond-haired man tried one last time. "I wouldn't do that if I were you," he warned.

Lance was beyond warnings. The idea of coming so far and being stopped was too much for him. Without another thought, he swirled back to the console and, with a resolute fist, punched the lone black button.

At Big Thunder Mountain, the high-speed roller coaster designed to look like a runaway mining train, Lance's security guard partner, Mani Wolford, or more commonly called Wolf, had just broken up a fist fight between two teenagers. They were arguing over who would accompany their companion, an eighteen-year-old girl, home now that the Park was closed. Heavy into their argument, they hadn't noticed she had walked off with the costumed cast member who had just finished his shift on the ride.

After escorting the angry, panting youths to the front gate, he warned them that if they decided to continue their juvenile tirade on Disney property, they would be escorted home in the back of an Anaheim P.D. Cruiser. Wolf returned to his last patrol through New Orleans Square. Not finding Lance waiting for him, Wolf resumed his sweep, covering the same ground Lance had gone over an hour before. His intense blue eyes took in every detail, looking into every nook and cranny for guests hoping to be overlooked and getting the dubious bragging rights that they had spent the night in the Magic Kingdom.

Finding no one, Wolf pulled his walkie-talkie from his belt clip and called for Lance. "P-1 to P-3. P-1 to P-3," Wolf called into the black box. Surprised he couldn't get Lance on their security channel, he repeated the call, then shrugged and put the device back on his belt. As he strode past the entrance to Pirates of the Caribbean, he instinctively looked toward the underside of the bridge that took guests over the Pirates queue area and transitioned them from Adventureland to New Orleans Square. He flashed his light in one dark corner and turned to leave. He then noticed the Cast Member Only door off to the left, under the stairs leading up to the Disney Gallery's Collector Room. It was slightly ajar. Not too unusual this time of night, he thought, as cleaning crews should be entering soon to start their work. Still, he felt he needed to check it out.

Pushing the door fully open, he stepped from the ornate wrought ironwork of New Orleans Square into the white, unadorned utility corridor of the cast members' backstage world. Unlike the corridors found throughout Disneyland's younger—and larger—sister park in Florida, where there are an abundance of underground corridors so a costumed cast member of one Land, say Tomorrowland, would be able to travel unseen by the public to another part of the Park without disrupting the look and feel of a different land, there was only this one large corridor that led down into the lower levels of the Pirates of the Caribbean attraction. Wolf was dwarfed within this corridor as it was large enough for trucks to drive down and make deliveries. There was a cast member restaurant located at the end of this corridor, as well as areas that were used for storage for various retail shops located above, inside New Orleans Square.

Wolf stood still for a moment after the door clicked shut behind him and let his keen hearing do his work for him. He could see numerous doors on the right side that lead to different parts of the Pirate ride. Further down and to the left was an opening that led to the back side of the Jungle Cruise that served as safety exits in case of a break down and the guests needed to be escorted safely off the attraction. He could hear no movement anywhere in the corridor or coming from the Jungle Cruise backstage areas.

Satisfied no one had snuck into that corridor,

he returned to the walkway between the Pirate ride and Tarzan's Treehouse. Making sure the door was firmly shut behind him, he made his way back through the silent Adventureland, nodding a brief hello to Anne, the Lead cast member of the Jungle Cruise who had filed her last report and was headed to the lockers and home. Wolf fell into step with Anne as she headed toward Main Street.

"Hey, have you seen Lance Brentwood, Anne?" Wolf asked, hoping she might have run across his partner. He knew that Anne, like many of the other female cast members, never missed Lance if he was in their vicinity. His good looks and easy-going personality was a magnet for most of the ladies working at—and visiting—the Park.

"I wish," Anne said, knowing he was partners with Wolf on most closing nights. "If you see him, let him know I'm still waiting for that phone call."

"I'll be sure to warn him…I mean, tell him," Wolf deadpanned.

Grinning, Anne slapped him on the shoulder as they walked out of Adventureland toward Main Street U.S.A.

As a small, hidden door on the panel flipped open, Lance turned back to the blond-haired man with a smile of triumph on his lips once more. His confidence faltered when he saw the reaction of the other man.

The gun was lowered as the blond-haired man rolled his eyes and shook his head. "I wish you hadn't done that," he stated flatly with an audible sigh, stepping back into the dark corner from which he had emerged.

"Why not?" Lance demanded, trying to peer into the darkness. "Answer me! Why not?"

But before there could be a reply, a thick cloud of blue gas sprayed out from a nozzle behind the hidden door. In vain Lance tried to wave it away as he backed away from the odorless gas. Within seconds the spray stopped, but it was too late for Lance. His eyes rolled back in his head and he silently dropped to the floor like a rag doll no longer wanted by a petulant child.

It only took moments before the blue cloud dissipated. Counting to a slow ten and seeing the seconds tick by on his watch face, the blond-haired man stepped back into the cavern. Knowing the air was now safe, he pocketed the white handkerchief he had placed over his nose and walked up to the inert Lance. He gently nudged Lance with the toe of his shoe. Disgusted, he slowly shook his head side to side. He answered Lance's final question. "Because I now have to carry you out of here and I don't really feel up to it tonight."

He stepped around to Lance's shoulders and, bending down, gave an experimental tug. He shook his head again and muttered, "It would have to be the tall one. Why couldn't it have been the girl? She looked a lot lighter." He eyed the distance to the hidden door from which he had entered, across the chamber from Lance's entry point, and gave a sigh. *Better get to it*, he told himself, *the door won't get any closer*.

Just as he reached under Lance's shoulder the man heard a sound coming from Lance's belt. "P-1 to P-3."

Knowing people would now be looking for Lance, he felt a surge of adrenaline push him to move faster.

With much groaning and straining, the blond-haired man managed to get Lance out of the chamber and into a different sterile white corridor than the one Wolf had just patrolled. Pulling a lone key out of his pocket, he securely locked the door behind him. Leaning against the door marked 'No Admittance' in order to rest his laboring heart, the man pulled out a cell phone and pushed number two. "Daniel, meet me at the junction. I need your help."

His hands barely shook as he put his phone back in his jacket pocket. Knowing his symptoms, he now pulled a little metal canister out of his pocket and unscrewed the cap. Placing one white pill under his tongue, he waited a minute for it to dissolve.

I'm too old for this nonsense. With a determined effort, he grunted as he hefted Lance's shoulders again, and backed down the silent, unused corridor.

Beth Roberts was happy today, giddy almost. She was back working at Disneyland. It had been five years since her abrupt leaving—she now refused to refer to it as a 'firing' no matter what the official record said. She was back with Adam rebuilding their relationship. She and Adam had made an incredible discovery not far from where she was currently working on the Pirates of the Caribbean ride. Adam was busy sorting through the ramifications of their discovery and setting up scholarships for the elementary school in Marceline, Missouri, and continuing his work as a General Contractor and Developer.

She had picked Pirates as her first assignment once Disneyland accepted Adam's and her offer to display some of the rarer and historically fascinating items that had been found along the way in their Hidden Mickey quest in exchange for her getting to work any of the rides she wanted. The first bronze nametag—presumably worn by Walt Disney himself after the Park opened, the matching Mickey Mouse watches from the 1930's, four never-before-seen animation cels from Snow White, an original Opening Day ticket to Disneyland, and some of the handwritten notes from Walt were all on display in the Opera House alongside the set-up of Walt's office from the Burbank Studio. Only she and Adam knew that the animation cels had been found carefully hidden inside Walt's desk in that same display. *How* she and Adam came to possess such items was never accurately disclosed. An obscure discovery at some garage sale in Missouri was their story…and they were sticking to it.

Beth, dressed in her Pirates costume, had smiled when she entered the Wardrobe Department the first time to pick up what she would be wearing. This 'official' costume the cast members wore wasn't too different from what she had purchased at a costume store back when she, Adam and Lance realized they would have to jump from one of the boats within the ride to continue the quest the diary had begun. *It just felt better to be in a 'real' one*, she thought to herself as she had laced up the low-cut bodice.

She thought of Lance often, especially here in Pirates. Her natural cheery disposition and kind heart refused to let her turn against him. Yes, he had stuck a gun in their faces and demanded the final treasure for himself. But, she just couldn't bring herself to believe he would have actually shot them. That wasn't her Lance. She couldn't talk to Adam about it and that really bothered her. Adam's heart had grown cold when his best friend pulled that gun and fired that first shot that had narrowly missed them. He hadn't forgotten and he hadn't forgiven. Beth didn't know if he ever would. So far, Beth hadn't run into Lance since she started working at Disneyland again. She wasn't entirely sure he was even still there as a security guard as she hadn't had time since her orientation training at the Disneyland University to ask anyone about his whereabouts. Knowing Lance's financial problems, Beth knew he had to work somewhere, do something. She had no reason to believe he would quit his job at the Park.

Beth stifled another sigh as she helped load a boat of guests for their trip through the world of Pirates. She had just gotten used to having Lance and Adam back in her life after Adam had broken up with her five years earlier and broke her heart. While she was ecstatic about having Adam back in her life—and in her heart—her tall, easy-going verbal sparring partner was gone.

While she had fallen in love with Adam again, it was Lance with whom she shared a deep friendship. She missed having him call her Captain Obvious or Shrew. She missed having him show up randomly at her apartment, raid her refrigerator, and then throw his six-foot-two length on her small sofa for a nap. She even missed his fun and not-so-subtle flirting with her, always saying how he would treat her like the 'pampered queen' he often called her if she would only leave Adam. Though she had never felt a level of romantic attraction for Lance and the simple fact she had always loved Adam—even when she hated him—Beth really missed Lance's character. In a word, Beth always felt comfortable around Lance. She smiled at that memory as the next boat pulled into the loading dock.

Yes, she missed her friend and hoped for all their sakes that he was able to work out his personal demons.

Beth was surprised toward the end of her shift by the appearance of a tall, dark security guard who had come in through the exit of the popular ride. He stood quietly in the little-used second exit gate out of the feeble light of the flickering lanterns that bathed the exit dock in ambient shadows. Because of the darkness of the interior, she couldn't clearly see who it was. She felt her heart skip a beat. *Lance?* Since she was on the opposite side of the boat flume and loading dock of Lafitte's Landing, the name for the Pirates of the Caribbean loading area, she could only keep doing her job and wait.

Her suspense was short-lived. Matt, the cast

member helping guests disembark, went over to see what the visitor needed. The security guard pointed at Beth. After a brief conversation and after the two now-fully loaded boats were whisked along the conveyor belts toward the ride's interior, Matt called Beth over. Not knowing what was up, Beth turned to her loading partner, Kirk, and asked if he could load her side of the dock for a moment. While it was a challenge to fill two five-row boats simultaneously, Kirk just smiled and told her, "Sure, take your time."

After the next two boats came to their abrupt stop and the guests filed off, Beth stepped up upon the texture-coated bow of the empty boat and crossed to the exit side of the dock. As she got nearer, she was disappointed to see it was not Lance. She wasn't sure who this man was. She had seen him before in the Park, but like the so many of the other nine-thousand employees that worked in the Magic Kingdom, she had not had the opportunity to officially meet him.

The nametag on his uniform said 'Wolf'. Beth was instantly intrigued as she had heard Wolf was a favorite topic backstage amongst the female cast members—almost as popular as the name of Lance. But where Lance was outgoing and friendly, Wolf was more of a mystery. None of the women really knew anything about him. And that really captivated them, drawing them to want to learn more—and see more about the tall, dark-haired employee. Beth remembered seeing him during the employee Canoe Races held each summer where he paddled on a men's team with his wet shirt plastered to his muscular body. Beth had seen at that moment another reason why so many of the female workers had an interest in Wolf.

And now, he had just sought out Beth.

She could feel the scrutiny of his sharp blue eyes even before she reached where he was standing. He was analyzing her. But not as a man might size up a woman in whom he was interested. No, this was different.

There weren't many preliminaries. Wolf got right down to business. "You are Beth Roberts, right? Friend of Adam Michaels and Lance Brentwood?"

Nice teeth, she thought to herself as she folded her arms over the scalloped, scooped blouse of her Pirate costume and smiled. *Striking eyes*.

Wolf, expecting an answer, was unsure what to do when she took her defensive posture and then smiled as she looked him over. She then stuck out her hand toward him.

"Hi, I am Beth. Nice to meet you, Wolf."

Now remembering his manners, or, actually the lack of them, he took her rebuke in good form. A smile transformed the sharp angles of his good-looking face as they shook hands. "Sorry. Yes, nice to meet you, too. I am worried about a friend and hoped you might have some information that could help."

Beth relaxed a little. The last time Security had come looking for her, she had been fired. "You must mean Lance, as I can't see how you would know Adam."

Sharp woman, Wolf thought. "Yes. I only

refer to Adam because of how highly Lance had spoken of you two. I know you were all friends."

Beth glanced over her shoulder. She really needed to get back to work. This interview was getting a little too long and Beth didn't want to keep Kirk double-filling boats much longer. She certainly didn't want to get into trouble in her first position back. "So you are worried about Lance?" *Join the club.*

"Yes, as a matter of fact," Wolf told her. "He is missing."

Beth hesitated. She knew Lance had gone off to Idaho on her false lead, but he should have been home months ago. Did he give up and go back to his family in Boston? Did he think that she and Adam would turn him in to the police for trying to abduct them? No, he knew that would raise too many questions about what she and Adam had discovered in terms of the treasure they found under Pirates of the Caribbean...and neither she nor Adam wanted to explain how they became owners of so many lost historical treasures they had found while following Walt Disney's lost diary—not to mention the fortune of gold and gems they found at the end of their quest! She shook her head at the thought, frowning. Lance wouldn't do that. He had been too adamant about his parent's lifestyle when the trio had flown to the island of Tobago to continue their search. Maybe he got a different job, or moved to a different city to start over. She shook her head, focusing back on Wolf's statement, "He is missing."

"I don't understand. How long has it been since you have seen him?" Beth didn't know how much to tell this stranger.

Wolf sensed her hesitancy and filled her in a little on some of the details she probably did not know. "You may or may not know that Lance is my Security partner. We were closing the Park three nights ago. I was called away on a disturbance and I haven't seen him since. I wondered if you might know where or how he is."

Beth bit her lip, thinking. "Lance always did like to keep people guessing. Are you sure he didn't just take off with some of his friends?" Beth asked with a little smile, thinking she could just as easily had said 'girls' instead of 'friends' but decided not to go there. When her smile was not returned, she continued, "I supposed you have done the obvious like calling him or stopping by his townhouse?"

Wolf gave a short nod. "Of course," not mentioning that Lance had lost his townhouse a couple of weeks ago. Wolf had helped him move into a small apartment. "His car is still in the parking lot, in the same place, and covered with dust." Wolf hesitated and let his revelation sink in, before adding, "And he never clocked out that night and has not clocked in since."

Beth's eyebrows shot up. "That is serious." Beth ignored the issue of the time cards and stated, "Lance never lets his cars get dirty."

Wolf was silent, waiting for more. Beth shrugged. "I'm sorry, but I can't tell you anything. I haven't…I haven't seen Lance in a while. We had a little, uh, falling out."

Wolf saw a wave of hurt pass over her eyes. She'd never make a good poker player. He knew she was telling the truth, and he knew it was bothering her. "Well, thank you for your time."

Wolf turned to go, but Beth called him back. "Wolf? Umm…I hope everything is all right. Could you let me know, please?"

He gave a curt nod and strode through the exit as silently as he came.

Beth watched until he rounded the corner and was out of sight. Her feelings were mixed with worry for Lance and Adam's cold-hearted dismissal of Lance as a friend. Beth stood in place as she watched Wolf retreat toward the exit. With a sigh, she turned to go back to work.

Wolf walked slowly through the quaint, narrow streets of New Orleans Square, his mind working over the disappearance of his friend while his eyes darted back and forth looking for anything amiss. A small group of teenage girls stopped him and asked if they could take a picture with him. Stifling his immediate response of 'No,' he remembered his Disney training and gave the girls a wide, if insincere, smile as they clustered around the dark, handsome man. The one chosen to take the picture grumbled as he walked off before she could have her picture taken with him.

By the time he reached the New Orleans train station, his personal cell phone vibrated. Pulling it out of his uniform's pants pocket, he glanced at the caller ID. Walking over to the empty exit ramp, he answered the phone. "Yes, boss?" Wolf listened intently to his instructions, a wave of surprise crossing his face. *Ah, that explains it*, he thought to himself. "Consider it done," were his only other words as he snapped the small phone shut.

When the steam train, the *Ward Kimball*, pulled into the station greeting dozens of guests with its ringing bell and a loud hissing of steam, Wolf waited until the engineer had gotten the train to a complete stop and was waiting for the 'All Aboard' call from the conductor. He walked up the ramp and asked the engineer if he had a Phillips screwdriver he could borrow. Knowing there was always a full set of tools handy at all the train stations, Wolf was soon on his way.

As Wolf headed toward the cast member entrance to the Pirates ride, he suddenly remembered the night Lance had disappeared. The door he was walking toward had been open that night. Now, thanks to the phone call, he knew exactly where Lance had gone.

And now—he needed to cover it up.

For two days, Beth had thought about the security guard's appearance at her work. She could tell he was worried about his friend and disappointed she couldn't help. Thoughts of Lance went swirling through her mind. Was he all right? Was he in trouble? After what he did to them, should she even care?

She gave a sigh. She had another hour to work before her shift ended. She was meeting Adam and his parents for dinner later that evening. Ever since Wolf had talked to her two days earlier, she had been bombarded with ques-

tions about him from her female co-workers who
had seen her talking to the mysterious man. Unfortunately, she couldn't tell them much. She had
gotten the distinct impression that Wolf was more
of an observer than a talker. And all of this had
done nothing to keep her from dwelling on the
possibility that Lance might be in trouble—
whether physically or emotionally.

When Beth's shift was over, she headed
down the corridor under Pirates of the Caribbean
that led to the backstage walkway where she
would cross over to Main Street and head to the
lockers where she could change out of her costume and go home. Her steps slowed as she
neared the door within that corridor that would
take her behind the scenes of the Captain's Quarters where she knew the secret door to the hidden cavern was located. *Had Lance gone back
there?* she wondered. Perhaps he had fallen
down the dark, steep steps and was lying there
hurt at the bottom. Maybe he got himself locked
inside somehow and couldn't get out....

Her imagination was making her heart speed
up. *Calm down*, she told herself. *Lance is a big
boy and can take care of himself.*

Then why was his Security partner looking for
him? Why has he been gone for days? And without his car?

Without another thought, Beth looked around
to make sure she was alone in the corridor. Passing a locked door marked 'No Admittance,' Beth
found a door labeled 'Captains Quarters.' She
pulled open the door and stepped into the darkness of the rocky passageway. She heard the fa-

miliar music of the Pirate ride and the screams of guests as they plummeted down the first waterfall. She quickly ducked into the side passage that led directly into the Captain's Quarters, the grisly remains of the pirate captain still upright in his ornate bed, magnifying glass in hand to study the big red **X** on the map spread over him.

Beth smiled in the darkness. *It sure was easier to just walk through the door than having to jump off the moving boat without being seen!* The jump had been terrifying, but tremendously fun.

As the threesome had done before, Beth timed the boats so she could slip unobserved behind the huge headboard. When it was again clear, she pushed on the red **X** on the map. Going back behind the huge gold and red headboard, she saw that the secret panel she, Lance and Adam had previously discovered was now open. Crawling in, she found the stairs and turned on the small flashlight all the cast members carry in their costume. She was relieved not to see Lance sprawled at the bottom of the stairs.

Going up to the door that had held their last clue 'Sunnee holds the key,' she was surprised to find it was now shut. She knew that Adam had closed the door just far enough to make it look as if it was locked. She knocked on the door and called for Lance. Not sure what to expect, she was again relieved to hear nothing. She then shone her flashlight over the door and briefly hesitated on the small dent that the first bullet Lance had fired had left on the metal plate that surrounded the keyhole. Shaking off the bad memory of when she and Adam were held at gunpoint by Lance down in this secret room, she immediately swung the light lower to look at the brass plate which had the final clue etched on its surface. She looked for the words 'Sunnee holds the key.'

To Beth's surprise, the brass plate was no longer there. She jerked the light back up to the keyhole. With the exception of the dent from the bullet, the brass faceplate was bright and shiny. She also saw there was no longer any keyhole in the middle. A solid piece of matching brass had been put in its place.

Beth took a step back, her mouth open in surprise. The plaque with the clue was gone and the keyhole had been removed.

The final clue to their quest had been completely removed.

No one would ever be able to open that door again.

CHAPTER 2

Lance's head was pounding. Eyes closed, his hand came up to rub his temple. When that proved to be ineffective in relieving the pain, Lance turned onto his side in an attempt to come to his feet. Instead of feeling the cold, hard cement of the cavern floor, his hand encountered a cool, smooth softness. He forced one eye open. Instead of the darkness of the cavern, his eye immediately shut at the painfully intense brightness pouring in from a leaded glass window.

"You should probably take that a little slower," came a soft, feminine voice from somewhere in the room.

"If I were any slower, I would probably be pronounced dead," Lance murmured as he rolled back in the bed and covered his eyes with an arm.

The responding laugh from the same feminine voice brought his mind instantly out of the fog enveloping it. Even though his arm laying across his eyes didn't move, he became alert. He wasn't in Disneyland any longer, that much he knew. He tried to listen to hear how many were there,

39

surrounding him. Under the covers, he felt for his Security belt. The huge Mag flashlight they carry had many uses, protection being one of them. Only it wasn't there. Neither was his uniform. He found his chest was bare and he had on some kind of silk pajama bottoms.

"He's awake. Sort of." The sound of a click told him the woman had just phoned someone. "Try opening your eyes again," she suggested. "The headache should be clearing by now."

Ok, I'll throw back the covers, jump out of bed, and run out of here, Lance plotted in his almost-foggy mind. *I'm pretty good at outrunning girls*, he smiled. Plan firmly in mind, Lance bolted upright in bed. It was working brilliantly until the vertigo hit again. He slumped back with a groan.

"Well, that didn't work, now did it?" the voice smiled at him, obviously enjoying herself. "It's all right, Mr. Brentwood. You are among friends.... More or less," she added in a muted undertone.

Lance managed to open one eye again. He focused on a shapely pair of legs emerging from a knee-length light yellow linen skirt. His practiced eye traveled down the legs to the pink-tipped toes peeking out of jeweled sandals. "I heard that," he said to her toes, moving his arm in an attempt to find out what the rest of her looked like. Yet another brilliant plan was thwarted when the door to the room opened and the toes stepped back, out of sight. He felt disappointed.

"Ah, Mr. Brentwood," said a deep voice, one that he had last heard over the barrel of a gun.

When Lance tensed again, the feminine voice reported, "He seems to be having trouble with the headache still and apparent vertigo. He wants to bolt but can't focus yet."

"Thank you, dear. You can go for now. I'll call you if I need you."

With a flutter of linen and a small whiff of subtle perfume, the door clicked shut again. *'Dear?'* Lance repeated to himself. Maybe she was older than he thought....

"Do relax, Mr. Brentwood. I can feel your tension across the room."

Slowly this time, Lance came to a sitting position. Waiting immobile for a moment, he found the vertigo was gone. Cautiously he opened his eyes, letting them adjust to the brightness. He glared at the blond-haired man who was leaning against the wall of the room looking very relaxed. He didn't see any gun pointing at him, but that didn't mean it wasn't close by or on the blond-haired man's person.

As if reading his thoughts, the blond-haired man's hands came slowly up, palms out. "I am unarmed, Mr. Brentwood, as you can see. I do apologize for the gun, but, as we were both dealing with unknowns, it was necessary, as you will no doubt find."

Lance let his words work around his mind as he reached for the silk robe lying across the bed at his feet. Slowly, pulling it over his bare arms and chest, Lance tried to figure out which question to ask first. "Where am I?" he decided to ask.

"In my home," the man responded casually, moving an arm around the room.

The response did not come close to satisfying Lance. *Ok, so it was going to go like that,*

Lance thought. "And if I ask sixty questions, do I get to guess on the right answer?" he shot out angrily. "Where am I?" he repeated, this time in a forceful tone revealing his frustration.

The hands that had dropped to the man's side came up again to pacify Lance. "I know you have many questions, as do I. You will find there is a Need-To-Know basis on both our parts. Please be patient and I promise that everything will be answered."

That wasn't satisfactory for Lance. "Am I a prisoner here?"

That seemed to surprise the blond-haired man. "Why, no! You are our guest. In fact, we have been waiting for you for a long, long time." He paused as if thinking on his words, and then added, "Well, we have been waiting for *someone*...," the man trailed off.

Before Lance could work that out, the man pointed to a pile of clothes on the mahogany dresser. "You might be more comfortable in those. Please join us downstairs in the dayroom once you are dressed. Kimberly and I will be waiting. Oh, and Mr. Brentwood, I am quite aware of your ability for rappelling, but please don't jump out the windows," the blond man grinned, sweeping an arm toward the two windows on the far wall. "Without the proper equipment, it's quite a drop from this high up." The man turned and opened the door behind him.

Lance held up a familiar shirt in his hands. These were his clothes. Not his Security uniform or even the clothes from his locker at Disneyland. To add to his confusion, these clothes had been hanging in the closet in his apartment.

As he watched the door click softly shut, Lance wondered what he had gotten himself into. He didn't hear any locking mechanism so he assumed he was not confined to the room and indeed was free to join his...captors? He didn't really know what to call them.

Taking off the robe, he took his time pulling on his shirt. After changing into a pair of his slacks that had been neatly folded on the dresser, Lance walked over to the window where sun filtered in through expensive lace drapes. Pulling the curtain to one side, he looked out over an expansive garden, lush with manicured lawns, colorful flowers, a white gazebo and a five-tiered marble fountain that served as a centerpiece of the grounds. Lance saw that the window was not two but three floors up, in truth making any attempt at escape a very real hazard to his health. A feeling of resignation swept over him while at the same time, a curious—if not cautious—feeling of intrigue was pricking at his consciousness. He pulled on a pair of his Italian loafers and took a deep breath before heading out the door...and into the unknown.

"So, tell me again about finding the clue 'Lilly Belle'. Was it you or Mr. Michaels who figured out where to go? Who devised the plan to rappel into the warehouse?"

"What difference does it make who did what?" Lance was getting exasperated. The blond-haired man had been asking question after question on his and Adam's search for the hidden items Walt had left behind. "I figured out some clues. Adam figured out others. Ask Adam!"

"I am not interested in Mr. Michaels. His part is essentially done. You, however, came back to the cavern. Why is that, Mr. Brentwood?"

Lance paused here, his eyes narrowed. The blond-haired man seemed to know everything about their search yet he seemed to know nothing about their quest. He was familiar with the diary somehow. Why didn't he do the search himself if he knew about the diary? Why was he not interested in talking to Adam? What about Beth? There had been no mention of her so far. How did he know Lance came back to the cavern? Did he know he, Lance, had no idea what the final clue was and wasn't even present at whatever treasure was found by Adam and Beth? Or was that what it was all about—this odd man sincerely wanted to know where the treasure was and what was in it. Should he tell the mystery man that he didn't know what the treasure even consisted of and that he had just stumbled, literally by accident, into the cavern where he found the machine holding what he assumed was a cryogenic Walt Disney?

Now Lance was second guessing even himself. Was it really Disney he found? Who else knew about the cave under Pirates of the Caribbean? Or, was it that he knew too much? This last thought made Lance especially nervous. What would happen to him if that was indeed the case?

Lance's usually cool demeanor was starting to crack again. He wanted some answers himself. "If you knew about the diary all along, why didn't you look for the treasure yourself?" he demanded.

"You know, if you keep getting mad and defensive, we are never going to get anywhere," the man coolly said. "Please, Mr. Brentwood. Sit down and relax," the blond-haired man requested, leaning back tiredly in an elaborate tapestry-covered wingback chair. Lance reluctantly sat in the chair opposite the man. For the first time, Lance scrutinized the man carefully as the older man reached over and picked up the Waterford tumbler sitting on the teak table beside him. Lance pegged the man closer to seventy years old. Although he retained a blond color in his hair, making Lance imagine a Scandinavian lineage, the man's skin was aged and his hand shook slightly as he held the small glass of amber liquid. Lance didn't think the older man would put up much of a fight. However, there was a sense of confidence or, at least, a cardinal knowledge that the man displayed, that added to the intrigue Lance was experiencing. Lance was mad, but he was also curious.

Taking a small sip of his brandy, the older man glanced over to the young woman who was frowning at him from across the room. She had come into the room during the questioning and quietly taken a seat on the other side of the room from Lance and her father, listening. Her displeasure seemed to have something more to do with his choice of beverage than anything included in the dialogue that had been taking place since she came in.

"I am only having this one drink, Kimberly, my

dear," the blond-haired man explained placidly, correctly interpreting her expression. He turned his attention back to Lance before Kimberly could reply. "Mr. Brentwood, I need to know some things before I tell you what you want to know."

Lance felt he was being put off yet again. He angrily jerked up from his seat and stormed to a window overlooking the vast green yard he had viewed earlier from the room two floors up. From their conversation he had learned they were somewhere in Fullerton, apparently a very exclusive portion of the Fullerton Hills. From this vantage point, he could see far beyond the property and below into the Valley. But he wasn't interested in the views. He wanted answers, and he wanted them now.

The blond-haired man noted Lance's defensive posture. He looked over at Kimberly for affirmation. She nodded. "All right, Mr. Brentwood, all right," he said with a sigh of resignation, if not a sense of surrender. "If you would please take your seat again, I will attempt to answer your questions."

Lance slowly walked back to his chair, not saying anything. He would hear them out, and then he would leave.

The blond-haired man took a deep breath, as if gathering his thoughts for a final solution to a difficult problem. He knew he would lose Lance if he did not reveal some important facts. He had waited such a long time for someone to enter that cavern, to find Walt. This was Walt's wish…his command, really. Now he was about to reveal a secret that he had kept for over forty years—a secret he had revealed only twice: Once to his now-deceased wife, and, only recently, to his only off-spring, his daughter Kimberly.

He just hoped this was not a mistake.

"Mr. Brentwood. Lance, if I might?" On receiving Lance's reserved nod, he continued, "Thank you, Lance. You are wondering about the treasure hunt you and Adam went on. You are wondering how much I really know and what I want. Correct?" At Lance's curt nod, he went on. "Yes, I do know everything about the diary and your treasure hunt. I know where you went and what you retrieved. What I do not know are some of the particulars on *how* you arrived at your answers and some of your actions to find the hidden capsules. That is why I was questioning you so carefully. I needed to know your involvement as compared to Adam's involvement. Why *you* were in the search. What *you* hoped to get out of it. What were *your* contributions. Unlike you, I do know what Adam and his Beth got in that small chamber. I know the value of each item. So you see, Lance, I am not a treasure hunter. The items that were found by the three of you do have worth, both financially and historically." After a brief pause, he added, "Especially those that Adam and Beth found in the outer chamber of the cavern. I also know that Beth has been able to use her new-found notoriety and Disney historical contri-butions to get her job back at Disneyland." The blond man leaned forward in his chair toward Lance. "I, on the other hand, have no need of that relatively small treasure. I have something of far greater value...both intrinsically as well as extrinsically."

Lance felt his heart skip a beat. Just days earlier he felt he had lost out on any significant treasure Walt may have left behind, and, more importantly to him now, he had destroyed his friendship with Adam and Beth…something he now understood was of so much more value than any monetary find. There were still reservations in his mind regarding this blond-haired man as the memory of the shiny pistol being pointed at him inside the cavern under Pirates of the Caribbean at Disneyland was still fresh in his memory. Yet, his own recollection of pulling a gun on Adam and Beth not so long ago made him wonder if this man was, perhaps, offering him a second chance.

At something.

The man continued to explain, "What I need to know is, what are *you* capable of handling?" He became slightly amused at the bewildered expression he had just invoked on Lance's face, but continued.   "Because, Lance, I need you to understand very clearly that this treasure hunt for the Hidden Mickeys, as Walt liked to call them, is not over."

Lance felt as if he were under the effects of that blue gas again. A wave of incredulity crossed his mind as he tried to comprehend what the blond-haired man had just said. "It's not over?" What did that mean? And he referred to Walt as if Walt himself personally told the blond-haired man about the Hidden Mickey quest. After the experience he, Adam, and Beth had been through—

after what he had put both of his friends through—
Lance couldn't possibly believe there was more to
this incredible venture.

When the blond man paused in his lengthy
explanation, Lance waited silently, stunned at
what this man was telling him; he now was literally
sitting on the edge of his chair, waiting for more.
When no more was forthcoming, Lance knew he
needed to say something. But, what? There was
so much now to contemplate. One thing, however, kept coming back to Lance's mind. He decided to voice it first. "So, if you are not looking for
the treasure, *what are you doing?"* Lance paused
for a moment then added with a slight hesitation,
"And what do you want from me?"

The blond-haired man glanced once more at
the woman sitting diagonal from the two men. She
again nodded for him to continue. "I am not seeking the treasure because I am, well, for lack of a
better word, the Guardian."

Lance frowned. Although he had no clue as
to what the older man was going to tell him, this
was definitely not on his "top-ten" list of guesses.

"The guardian? The guardian of what? The
treasure? Some other treasure?" Lance queried,
holding his hands out from his sides.

The green eyes of the older man peered
steadily into Lance's brown ones. He shook his
head. "No." A somber look fell across the man's
face before he finished, "Of Walt."

The man saw even more questions in
Lance's eyes. "Yes. Literally of Walt," he repeated and then continued, "And I am ill…very ill,"
he looked over at the woman in the room with res-

ignation. She couldn't disguise her sadness and he choked on his own emotion, cutting his sentence short.

The woman stood, coming over to her father, and for the first time since the two men began their discussion, spoke: "And now my father needs a replacement." She placed a hand on his shoulder where he lovingly put his own aged hand on hers.

"Me?" Lance's eyes were big, looking from Kimberly to her father, and back again. He hadn't recognized the resemblance before, but now he saw it clearly. Same green eyes, blond hair—though hers was several shades darker. Both were tall and with striking facial features that indicated some strong bloodline. His realization of their relationship had his mind racing again.

"I didn't say you, Lance," the blond man quickly gained control of his emotions and pushed himself up out of the chair to stand next to his daughter. He held his hands up in front of him. "It might be you, might not," the blond-haired man replied cryptically. "Certainly you, Adam, and Beth are persons of interest. There is much to be done before a successor is named and trained." He paused, carefully considering his next few words. "Pardon my use of theatrics, but whomever we choose must prove worthy of the task," the blond man stated, and then solemnly added, "And be willing."

Lance took a deep breath, holding it for a moment then letting it out very slow, very deliberately. Somehow finding himself on his feet, Lance sat back down as he watched as the man's daughter now stepped forward, seemingly to take over for the moment.

"Your Hidden Mickey quest was the start, Lance," she said with a pleasant smile. "You and Adam had a good start, but required a third party, Beth, to finish. We would like to know how well you yourself can do."

Lance thought over her words. "So I need to figure out some clue by myself? Is that what you want?"

"That's only part of it, Lance. We know you are intelligent. That isn't the point. How far are you willing to go? How committed would you be? Who would you trust? How much are you willing to give up protecting the legacy?"

Lance thought again about his pulling a gun on Adam and Beth and flushed. How much further would he have gone to claim that unknown treasure? Did this blond-haired man and his daughter know about the gun? Were they testing him now?

He got up to pace the room. This seemed to be a puzzle that had an increasing number of pieces. "I have seen the chamber under Pirates. It is safe to assume that it is not public knowledge? And that I am here only because *I* am the one who found Walt?" He paused and got an affirmative nod from each of them. "You said you are the guardian of Walt. You talk about commitments and legacies and being willing to give things up. What is involved in all of this? I think I need to know more before saying Yes or No to your offer."

The blond-haired man smiled. "I haven't

made you an offer yet. You are sounding more and more like the lawyer your father wanted you to become."

Before Lance could challenge this personal information, Kimberly looked at her watch and broke in, "If you both will excuse me, I need to get to work. I am Princess Belle today," she explained with a grin and a curtsey.

"You work at Disneyland?" Lance exclaimed, surprised. "How come I have never seen you?" He didn't add that he would have surely noticed someone as beautiful as she. "Doesn't Belle have brown hair?" he added as if a random, side thought.

"Oh, I have seen you. Many times," she answered with a broad smile. "But you were usually surrounded by younger girls. I probably seemed way too old for you!" With a quick laugh, she went over to kiss her father good-bye.

Lanced watched Kimberly move to her father's side, seeing her now with an inquisitive—if not an appreciative—eye. She was far from being too old. *I know I wouldn't have thought that*, he thought to himself.

"Have a good day, my dear. Oh, I would like you to check out that rumor floating around New Orleans Square. We need to see how serious they are about the additions."

"Will do!" she replied brightly, and headed out the door.

Lance stared at the empty doorway, unaware he was doing it. The room felt empty now that she had gone. Her father silently watched him. He knew Lance's reputation. When their eyes met moments later, each wisely said nothing.

1964

It was a beautiful spring in Disneyland. The jacaranda trees were in full bloom and keeping the street sweepers busy as the fragrant purple blooms fell. The tulips planted in the Hub at the end of Main Street and in front of Sleeping Beauty's Castle gave a vibrant contrast with their vivid yellow color. The two men stopped on the drawbridge of the Castle, leaning over the railing to watch the two swans slowly swim by. One of the men was much older, wearing a non-descript black jacket and a floppy-brimmed hat that drooped over his well-known face. He paused in the instructions he had been giving the other man, who had been busy scribbling every word in his notebook. The other man's blond hair shone in the bright sunlight. He had no need to shield his face. No one knew him or his name. He and Walt had worked hard to keep it that way. Even Walt's private secretary Louise didn't know this man.

Also unknown to others—even to Walt's older brother Roy—second only to Walt, this blond-haired man was the most powerful man at Disney-land.

When the swans swam under the drawbridge and out of their sight, Walt turned back to the man and studied his face a moment. Knowing Walt's ways, the man stood quietly and finished a thought in his notebook. A tour guide, dressed in her trademark plaid outfit and matching black felt cap, approached with her group of tourists. She held her riding crop in the air as she walked, the tour group's identifying blue triangle hanging from its end. She would go through the first archway in the Castle and tell them the story of Sleeping Beauty, then lead them through the diorama of the fairy tale inside the Castle.

Walt turned away as the group approached, not wanting to be interrupted at this time. He had a lot to go over with the younger man. When the guided tour was far enough away not to hear and recognize his familiar voice, Walt looked over toward the wooden fort entrance of Frontierland and its neighboring Adventureland. He would need to head over to the Jungle Cruise next…. Abruptly Walt turned back. The man raised his pen and waited. Walt saw the gesture and smiled to himself. He had chosen wisely.

"You know, Disneyland is a work of love. We didn't go into Disneyland just with the idea of making money. You know that, don't you?"

The pen stopped moving when he realized the question was aimed at him. "Yes, Walt. I do."

Walt regarded the other man's face again and nodded. "Yeah. I think you do. Probably better than anyone else here. That's why I am working so hard to preserve all this. Follow me."

They started walking toward Adventureland. Walt stopped every now and then to pick up some scrap of paper or test the strength of the railing around the Tiki Room. When he was satisfied, he continued walking. "When you believe in a thing, you need to believe in it all the way, implicitly and unquestionable. We both believe in Disneyland. Do you know what it will take to protect all this for the future?"

His companion smiled. "Faith, hope, and pixie dust?"

Walt tilted his head back and let out a loud laugh. A coughing spasm hit him next, causing him to grasp one of bamboo-like railings next to them. "Wish that would go away," Walt murmured as if to himself. "But, it won't...." He chuckled again. "That was a good one! Yes, it will. But, more realistically, it will take a life-long commitment, a lot of work, and eyes in the back of your head." Walt searched the younger man's face. "You up for it?"

The younger man looked at the well-loved face of his boss. This was no time for jokes. "Yes, I think I am. I know I am," he corrected with a determined finality.

Walt nodded. "Yeah, I think you are, too." He glanced around to make sure no one was close enough to overhear. "You and I are both realistic enough to know that neither one of us will live forever—at least, not in this form." Walt ran a hand down his side. "Well, I do want to live forever...." He paused to gather his thoughts before speaking again. "You know what I have been working on for years. Well, the pieces are falling into place very nicely, if I do say so myself. I'm rather pleased with these Hidden Mickeys I have placed. And then I came to realize that I was being somewhat narrow-minded. I was just thinking of myself. I came to realize that I needed to think of you and your future. Now, you're a young man with your whole life ahead of you." Another cough shook Walt. "Darn cough…. Like I was saying, you never know what is coming and you will need to be prepared for your eventuality." He paused and gave a fond smile. "Hopefully, for you it will be a lot longer than I was given. I set in place another arm of the quest. If you get to the place and time that you need a successor like I do, use this." Walt reached in his jacket and pulled out a white, unsealed envelope. He looked at it for a minute as if he didn't want to have to relinquish it and all that it meant. "I don't need to explain all the particulars. You will look them over later and will understand. Place them where you will."

After handing over the envelope, Walt started walking toward Frontierland. He was silent until they reached the Rivers of America. He waved to the pilot of the stately white steamship, the Mark Twain, as it chugged by. When he resumed talking, his voice was softer, showing the emotion behind his words. "All this has to be protected," he said with a broad gesture of his arm that took in the whole Park. "I have to be protected. Thirty, forty, fifty years from now, I want to see what my Park has become." He turned back to the blond-haired man. "You understand what I am saying?"

The notebook was closed. "You will, Walt," he promised. "You will."

2002

Hours later, Lance was dismissed. Head spinning with the enormity of the task ahead of him, he sat quietly in the back of the black Cadillac as the blond-haired man's chauffer drove him back to Disneyland and his waiting car. Lance began taking in all the things that the mysterious man had told him: "First and foremost is the protection of Walt." "Your name will never appear on public records again." "No one will know who you are outside of your Security job—which you should keep, by the way." "You will never attend a Board of Directors meeting." "Your name will never appear on any stock certificates." "You have to keep your finger on the pulse of the Park." "Make sure all future clues are kept in place within the Park." "Monitor current medical breakthroughs." "You will have the deciding voice on certain changes within the Park."

Daniel Crain, the man behind the wheel, surreptitiously watched Lance in the rearview mirror. He could see different emotions float over Lance's face as he thought over all he had been told. When their eyes happened to meet in the mirror, Daniel offered, "If you need any help or suggestions, just ask. I've been in this for years."

Lance just nodded vaguely and looked out the window as they traveled down Harbor Boulevard.

Taking the silence for affirmation, Daniel saw his chance to add, "I'm part of the family, you know. Yeah, me and Kimberly, well, we would be glad to assist in any way we can."

Daniel felt a wave of satisfaction when Lance's eyes swung to the mirror again at the mention of Kimberly's name. He could see Lance did not miss his reference. Daniel heard a lot as he drove his boss around as there was no partition between driver and passenger. Yes, Lance can have his little plans. He, Daniel, had his own— and he was not about to have this newcomer interfering with them.

The two men traveled the rest of the short distance to the employee parking lot in silence. Stopping at Lance's dust-covered 1989 Jaguar Vanden Plas, Daniel gave him a smug salute and sped off, the rear tires spitting gravel back at Lance.

Muttering something unpleasant under his breath, Lance turned to his Jag. He gave a short sigh. He still missed his sleek, black Mercedes. And his townhouse…and his lifestyle—all of what he had before his father cut him out of his trust fund. He shoved the thoughts of his father to the back of his mind as he reached for the keys in his pocket. As he inserted the key in the door's lock, he heard the Mark Twain's whistle. He could tell from the sound that the paddle-wheeler was approaching the loading dock. *Kimberly is working at Disneyland today.* The sudden thought stilled his hand. Ignoring the not-so-subtle reference from Daniel Crain, Lance brought her lovely green eyes to mind and wondered how she would look as a brunette dressed as Belle.

With a smug smile of his own, he relocked his

Jag and turned toward the employee shuttle bus that would take him to the entrance. As he rode, he planned what he would say. "Why, hello there, Miss…Miss…." Lance's mouth went from a smug smile to a confused frown. What was her last name? As he thought back, he realized he had never learned the blond-haired man's name. Three days in their house and he never thought to ask.

Lance's smugness returned. *There is more than one way to skin a cat*, he thought. *Even a lovely green-eyed cat*. He even whistled a little tune as he turned toward Personnel. Misty would be working today. Petite, raven-haired Misty. She would be very happy to see him.

Ariel's Grotto was a lovely spot nestled between the Matterhorn Mountain and the Tomorrowland entrance. Statuesque King Triton rose majestically, looking as if he was carved from the faux granite that formed the rock pond, water spraying out from the tips of his trident and his hand extended out to the waters he commanded. Sweeping ferns gave the garden a lush, almost tropical feel, shading the grotto like a Pacific Island paradise. At the end of the curving walkway that meandered around the pond under the carefully manicured trees, a rock formation made to look like Ariel's undersea hideaway was the spot used by many of the princesses for their Meet-and-Greet sessions with adoring children. They would pose for pictures and sign countless autograph books, smiling and beautiful in their royal costumes. Sometimes their prince would be in costume as their escort, regally leading them by the arm to their next location or "backstage," as cast members of the Magic Kingdom would call the behind-the-scenes areas of the Park.

It was here that Lance found Kimberly in her flowing gown of gold, her hair now brown and wrapped around her fair head, held in place by a circlet of gold. His breath caught in his throat at her beauty and it wasn't just her elegant costume or her surroundings. Kimberly possessed a natural beauty and poise that could not be disguised by makeup or a costume. She didn't see him standing toward the back of the crowd, busy as she was with taking pictures and answering questions about the Beast and why he wasn't there with her that day. Mesmerized, he couldn't take his eyes off the lovely sight in front of him.

When the assisting cast member announced that the princess was through for the day and needed to get back to her castle, a groan went up from the crowd, including one from Lance as he joined in their disappointment. Kimberly gave a final wave and hugged one little girl who was dressed in a much smaller version of Belle's gown, telling the little girl how beautiful she looked. Smiling, Lance watched Kimberly start walking away, still under her spell. With a self-deprecating laugh, he shook his head and remembered why he was there.

His long stride caught up to her as she passed Snow White's Grotto. He knew there was an employee-only door just inside the Castle and she would disappear through there. He had to say something fast. "Why, if it isn't Miss Kimberly Bryan Waldron." Not the best line, but it was all he could think of.

Kimberly recognized his voice and came to an abrupt stop. Not realizing she was no longer beside him, her assistant kept walking until he reached the door. On looking back, Kimberly gave him the 'all right' signal, that she would be just a minute. She gave Lance a beautiful smile, one that melted something deep inside him. "Oh, very good, Lance! You discovered my full name! I wondered if you noticed the oversight at the house."

Rocking back on his heels, Lance returned her grin. "It takes a lot to pull one over on me," he told her.

"So, did my father tell you? No, don't tell me," her golden-gloved hand came up to his lips, silencing any reply he would make. "He wouldn't do that. You had to do some detective work, didn't you? Snooping at the house? No, you wouldn't do that. What would you do?" She was playing with him, but he didn't care. He could see the amusement in her eyes. "Ah, Personnel then. Was it Misty? She always spoke highly of you. Yes, it must have been Misty. Am I correct?"

Lance wanted to test something. "It could have been Daniel. We did have time to chat in the car on the way over here." He saw a momentary tightening of her lips and something flash across her eyes. He wasn't sure what it was, but it certainly wasn't love.

Her outer composure didn't waver. "No, it wouldn't be Daniel who told you. It had to be

Misty. So, what are you going to do with this monumental discovery?"

That set Lance back a step. "Do?" he echoed and paused. "I just know who you all are now and who I am dealing with." He paused, searching for more of an explanation. "A name to go with the face," he shrugged, a modicum of bravado seeping back into his voice.

"Well, I do congratulate you, Lance," she bowed her head as if bestowing a blessing. He should have been warned by the gleam in her eye when she looked up. She turned to leave, and then turned back abruptly, one hand raised. "Oh, one little thing, Lance. I was given my mother's maiden name." When she saw a smug smile return to Lance's face, she could see the wheels working in his brain. She decided to burst his little bubble. "And they were married out of the country. Good luck with that!" With a laugh, she disappeared through the waiting door to take her backstage for a break before her next appearance.

Lance stood rooted in the same spot, looking at the closed door as people walked around him to enter the Castle or to stop at Snow White's Wishing Well. He thought back to all the times that Adam had tried talking to girls. Lance grunted a self-deprecating laugh as he wondered if this was what Adam had felt like every time he had been shot down.

A bright red 1967 Mustang GT Fastback pulled up in front of the mansion, its white racing stripes glittering in the bright sun. The 427 engine had announced its arrival long before the actual car came to a skidding halt. The owner of the car reached behind his driver's seat as the blond-haired man approached the car. Handing his boss the brass plaque, Wolf asked, "So, Lance was here?"

The older man ran a hand over the words etched on the plaque. 'Sunnee holds the key'. It seemed like a lifetime ago since he had helped put the plaque in place and then waited and waited for its discovery. Wolf's words brought him back to the present. "Yes, yes, he is fine," was his distracted reply. "I'd ask you in to join me for lunch, but I know you have to get back to work."

Wolf nodded briefly. He knew there was another reason for his summons than just the delivering of the plaque. As was his nature, he waited patiently.

Looking off into the distance, the blond-haired man contemplated his next words. He had never liked this part of his assignment. "I realize Mr. Brentwood is a personal friend of yours." He paused and, as expected, received no answer. "You now know about his discovery of the secret chamber. Kimberly and I believe Mr. Brentwood might very well work out to be my successor, and, as you are already friends with him, that would work out well for you. However," he paused again and sighed, looking away from the intent blue eyes fastened on him, "however, if he doesn't work out, we both know he already knows too much. As he is your friend, will you still be able to carry out your assignment? Will you be able to use your, how shall we say, 'special talents' to re-move him from the scene?"

"I already promised Mr. Disney that I would protect him. The same promise was made to you when Walt introduced us. I will not go back on my word." Wolf's breathing was very shallow. He knew his words were honest and true. He just hoped he would not be called upon to back them.

The personal reference to Walt stilled his boss for a moment. He knew not to question the issue of Wolf's age. Wolf appeared to be thirty years old—he *always* appeared to be thirty years old—yet he recalled a personal conversation with Walt Disney that happened well over thirty years prior. There were some things that had arisen over the years that the older man simply did not question. Seeing Wolf standing quietly, staring at him, brought the blond man back to their current conversation. He understood Wolf's position and could sympathize—to a point. Personal feelings had never and would never be allowed to interfere with the grand purpose with which they had both been entrusted. "I know I can count on you, Wolf," he finally said, meaning it. "If worse does comes to worst, do you know how you would handle it?"

Wolf thought for a moment. A small smile came across his serious face. "Off the cuff, I think I do know where he could be taken. Actually, he might actually enjoy it…eventually…once he got used to the transition, that is." The smile disap-peared as quickly as it came. "But, I don't think it will come to that."

"Let's hope not, Mr. Wolford, let's hope not. Stick close and be there if and when I need you."

"Yes, sir." Wolf knew he was dismissed and slid back into the black leather driver's seat. As the engine roared to life, Wolf shifted his four-speed top loader into second and sped down the long driveway. He really hoped Lance didn't muck this up.

Days later, Lance was expected back at the mansion. Before he arrived, Daniel came out to the garden to tell Kimberly her father needed her in the library. She felt a mild irritation when Daniel accompanied her into the room and took a chair to take part in the discussion. He gave her a warm smile, secure in the knowledge that she wouldn't challenge him in front of her father.

Busy studying a couple of faxes that had just come in from the Park, the blond-haired man didn't notice this little byplay. "Oh, there you are, my dear," he smiled as he looked up. "Thank you, Daniel." When Daniel didn't take the hint and leave, Kimberly's father let it go. The important matters would come later, after they were alone. "So, now that we have all had a few days to think, tell me what you think of Mr. Brentwood."

"I don't like him," Daniel stated, leaning forward in his chair.

Choosing to ignore Daniel as if he wasn't even there, Kimberly directed her comment to her father. "He's very handsome."

Looking over at the rude noise Daniel made, her father continued, "That's not what I meant."

Kimberly gave her father a smile. "I know," she laughed for a moment before becoming serious again. "I think he might prove worthy. He is certainly intelligent enough and seems to have a disposition that would suit…. But," she paused, frowning.

"But what?" her father prodded.

"But what if he doesn't work out? What then? He knows too much already."

Daniel decided to try and find out a little more himself. "What exactly does he know?"

Daniel was ignored again. The blond-haired man paced the area in front of his expansive desk. "Yes, there is that problem, isn't there? Well, not to worry too much about that. I have an inside man already on that job." He made a grimace and clutched at his heart.

"Who is…," Daniel started to ask.

The answer of this startling revelation was lost to Daniel as Kimberly instantly rushed to her father's side. "Daniel, you can go. Now."

"But I can help."

Kimberly didn't even glance over as she placed a small white pill under her father's tongue. "Now." The order was abrupt and final.

With a glare at the two people in the room, with no look of compassion or care, Daniel strode from the room and headed for the kitchen, wondering who it was the old man had mentioned.

"Are you feeling better, Dad?" Worry was etched on her face.

She made sure he settled into the tufted leather chair behind the desk. He always felt more at ease behind his desk, surrounded by his papers and bulletins. The tightness was loosening. Color was coming back into his pale face as he patted her hovering hand. "Yes, yes, my dear. It is passing." He looked up into her worried face. "I wish I could say it was over now, but we both know better. I have been trying to prepare you for this eventuality for quite a while now."

Closing her eyes, Kimberly rested her forehead against his clammy one. "I know, Dad, I know," she whispered, her voice full of the emotion she was trying to contain. "It just doesn't make it any easier."

As if she was a little girl of five again, and not a grown woman of thirty, he pulled her into his lap. "Well, if it makes you feel any better, I don't like it either," he tried to joke, his arms around her. "There is so much to do, and I don't want you to have to do it alone. I always wanted you to have a normal family life. Children. Cooking. A career. Traveling. Whatever you wanted. Your mother gave up a lot to be with me."

"Mom loved you more than life itself. She didn't see it as a sacrifice."

"I know that, my dear. I was lucky. But you...you have a whole wonderful life ahead of you. You're what? Fourteen? Fifteen years old now?" He was glad to hear her chuckle at that. "I just don't want you to have to be anonymous."

Kimberly sighed and snuggled deeper in his arms. A lone tear escaped her eye and streaked her cheek. "Can't I have both?"

His hand stroked her golden hair, a gesture he used to use when she couldn't sleep as a little girl. "It is possible. It would take the right man," he said slowly, thinking. "I never intended for this to be put on you," he admitted.

"I know, Dad, but I want it. I can do it! It's been my whole life. I...I want to meet Walt. I want to see this through!"

"Forty years and I still miss him," was the quiet response.

They sat quietly for a moment, each with their own thoughts. The tightness was coming back to his chest, but he ignored it like he had been doing for months now.

"Well, we have Lance and Daniel so far. And, if need be, we could always take a second look at Adam."

Her head shot up. "Daniel? You have got to be kidding."

He shrugged. "He has been with me for a number of years and has proved quite loyal. Not the brightest bulb in the Christmas tree, but I think he could be trained...eventually."

Kimberly closed her open mouth and shook her head in disbelief. She wasn't going to get in this argument with her father right now. If things worked out like they both thought it would, it would be her decision and hers alone. Her throat tightened again, and she couldn't have spoken anyway.

"Now, I need you to get off my lap so I can get some papers organized. Lance is due here any moment, and this isn't the picture I would like to portray." With a playful push, he got her to move to one of the burgundy leather wingback chairs facing his desk. She didn't fail to see that his face was still ashen white. Glancing out of the window, seeing a Jaguar pull into the circular drive, he hit one of the buttons in the panel on the desk.

"Yes, boss?" came the sound of Daniel's voice, raspy through the intercom. "Do you need me?"

"Yes, Daniel. Could you please bring us some tea and show Mr. Brentwood in here, if you would. I see he just pulled into the drive."

Kimberly hid a smile as she heard a muttered, disgusted, "tea…," through the intercom before the button was released.

Lance and the Limoges tea service were brought in minutes later. Daniel went to stand behind Kimberly's chair after he had set down the fragile service. Lance saw her eyes slightly roll upward at his gesture, and stifled his smile behind a cough.

"Welcome back, Mr. Brentwood," the blond-haired man started. "We have a lot to cover. You'll excuse me if I am not too quick on my feet today. I am a little under the weather. There is a room I would like you to see. It itself will answer many of your questions. I call it my War Room. You shall shortly see why."

Daniel's ears perked up at this revelation. He had been trying unsuccessfully to get into that locked room for two years. Now would be his chance to see the one of the secrets that had eluded him so far—what it was that Lance apparently had seen that no one else had. As the other three people in the room stood and headed for the library door, Daniel quietly fell right in step behind them. It was only the turning back of his boss to retrieve his tea that foiled his plan.

"Ah, Daniel, I see you are still here. Good.

Good. Could you please hand me my teacup?"

"Yes, boss." With an inward groan, Daniel went back to the desk. He hesitated as he looked at all the flowered cups that had been placed there. Which one was it? He thought for a split second and picked up the cup and saucer closest to the pot. "Here you go, sir." He handed the cup to his boss and gave him a one-sided smile.

The blond-haired man looked into his flushed face. "Are you all right, son?"

"Yes, yes, no problem."

"Very good." Turning back to the group, he slowly walked in front of them. "Let's get started then. Oh, Daniel," he called over his shoulder, taking a sip of the lukewarm tea, "could you please bring the car around? I need to show Mr. Brentwood something later. Thank you."

Daniel stopped in his tracks and watched the backs of the three people as they entered the elevator that would take them to the third floor and the War Room. All three, as they turned to face the front of the elevator, avoided looking into his face—each for their own reason.

His eyes narrowing, Daniel gave a small smirk as he noticed his boss taking another sip of his tea, grimacing at the bitterness, as the doors of the elevator closed them off from his sight.

Lance tried to stand with his mouth closed as the enormity of the room and its function seeped into his overloaded brain. Monitors. There were floor to ceiling monitors covering an entire wall of the room. A bank of telephones. An old-fashioned gold and ivory telephone set off to the side covered with a large glass dome. Copy machines. Fax machines. A holographic map of Disneyland with certain pinpoints blinking red—including the points of the quest from Walt's diary that he and Adam had figured out. Those were other Hidden Mickeys, he had just been told. *Protect them. Protect Walt.* There was Walt's chamber under Pirates, lit up by night-vision cameras as bright as if it were sitting in the middle of Main Street. Another map—this one of the world with even more flashing pinpoints of light in Africa, Europe, the Caribbean, the Pacific and South America.

"So that's how you knew," he muttered, more to himself than to the other people in the room with him. "Incredible."

He was about to ask a question when there was a crash of porcelain behind him and a shriek from Kimberly, "Daddy!" He spun around to see the blond-haired man slowly crumple to the carpeted floor, Kimberly right with him.

"It's his heart," she told him. "It's been worse lately."

Lance pulled out his cell phone. "I'll call 911."

"No!" The voice was stronger than either of them would have expected from a man in his condition.

"Daddy, let him call!" Kimberly pleaded.

A white, bloodless hand reached up to her beloved face. "No, my dear. It won't do any good this time." He pushed away the Nitro tablet she was trying to give him, the grimace on his face showing the intense pain he was in. "It won't do.

I can tell. You know what to do next. Lance," he called, weaker now. "Lance, listen to me!" The stricken man reached out to Lance, holding his wrist. Lance felt the cold, clammy fingers grip him with a resolute grasp. "You missed a clue already. Walt just about handed it all to you on a silver platter, but you missed it." He was getting excited now, wheezing in the effort to speak and get this out before it was too late. "You had it all along."

Lance waited, torn between calling an ambulance, worry for the man in front of him, and wanting to shake him for his foolishness in letting them do nothing but watch him die. "I had what all along? I don't understand."

The voice was so weak now. They had to lean in to hear him. "The next clue. You've had it all along." The effort spent, his duty done, he gave a last smile to his shocked daughter, closed his eyes and his grasp fell limp.

"It wasn't time," Kimberly cried. "It shouldn't have been now! I'm not ready."

Lance tried to take her in his arms, unsure of what he could or should do. She pushed him away. "No. There is no time for that now, Lance. You have to go. I...I have to make a call. No one else is supposed to see this room. You have to go!"

He looked at her with a disgusted amazement on his face. "Your father just died and you are worried about some kind of propriety!?"

Her green eyes flashed. "Don't judge me, Lance. There is more going on here than you know about yet. I have been trained for this moment for years. We knew it was coming," her voice caught, but she fought down the emotion threatening to devour her. "I know what I have to do. It is the only way. Please," she softened her voice, "Please, if you want to help me then you have to go."

"I don't want to go." Lance was adamant. "I want to help you here, now."

She could see the concern in his eyes. "I know you do, but you can't. Not yet."

"But, what did he mean about the last clue? I don't understand."

"That I honestly don't know, Lance. That is something you are going to have to figure out. And I hope you figure it out soon for the sake of all of this," her gesture took in the room, her father, and Walt. "Please, Lance, just go."

In a futile gesture, Lance raised his hand toward her but let it drop. Without another word, he turned and walked from the room. Looking back, he saw that Kimberly had followed him as far as the doorway. He was hoping she would call him back. But, with a soft click the door was shut and a bolt was pushed into place, locking the War Room. With that gesture, he knew that he, too, was locked out—locked out until he could figure out what it was that he missed, what it was that he had all along.

Forgoing the elevator, Lance headed down three flights of thickly carpeted stairs, his mind spinning.

"You had it all along."

He had work to do. And, he suddenly knew at that moment…for him…it all started….

Once the Jaguar was safely off the property, Kimberly picked up the nearest phone on the desk. Composing herself as she dialed the well-known number, she heard it ring twice before a deep voice answered, "Yes, boss?"

Emotion flooded through her when she heard both the words and the voice. Her eyes filled up as her throat tightened. "It's me," was all she could whisper.

There was silence from the other end for a few, long moments. There was only one reason for the daughter—not the father—to be calling. "It happened?"

Not able to talk, Kimberly nodded into the phone.

Understanding the silence, Wolf told her, "I'll be right over. Please don't touch anything. I know what to do."

"Thank you," she whispered and hung up.

CHAPTER 3

"**Y**ou missed something.... You had it all along.... You missed something.... You had it all along."

These words kept playing over and over in Lance's mind. What was it he missed? They finished the quest. Adam and Beth had gotten the treasure—whatever it was.

"You missed a clue."

Lance mentally went over each step of the journeys he, Adam and later, Beth had taken as they followed each of Disney's obscure clues. Marceline. Kansas City. Golden Oak Ranch. The Studio. Back to Marceline and Kansas City. Disneyland. San Francisco. Tobago. And back to Disneyland again. He went over each clue and its logical next step. How could they have possibly missed something? And even if they did, didn't their discoveries still take them to the conclusion of Walt Disney's "Hidden Mickey" quest?

Was it in the small treasures Walt left along

the way? The first gray capsule had given them the stock certificates to the railroad. There was nothing else there. The abandoned building in Kansas City? They found the engraved WED and figured out where the hidden capsule was stashed. Was there something else in the ruins of that room? The entire building just needed a good, stiff breeze to come tumbling down. No, the gray capsule had to be the only find there with its Alice script and the Laugh-O-Gram business card.

Lance found himself pacing back and forth in his small living room. Could it have been in the old garage in Kansas City? The studio in Burbank? The Golden Oak Ranch? Lance ran a frustrated hand through his hair. The Ranch was huge. Was there more to it than the guest house where they had found the WED carved in the attic? No. Mario, the groundskeeper, had known Walt personally. He would have told them. He had been waiting for someone to come along for forty years. No, it is for certain he wouldn't have let them leave if there had been something else of this much importance.

What about Manny at the Studio? No, it couldn't have been him. He didn't even know what they were looking for. He had shown them Walt's empty office. Walt's desk had been moved to the Opera House at Disneyland and it had given them the unpublished animation cels from *Snow White*. Tobago? Were they supposed to have searched the whole island? The movie *Swiss Family Robinson* had been filmed at Barcolet Bay. The crew had stayed at the Blue Haven Hotel. The clue pointed specifically to Jeremy B. But,

Jeremy had been dead for many, many years. If there had been something else connected to Jeremy, they would never learn what it was.

No, none of that fit. After seeing the War Room, Lance realized the blond-haired man had been aware of almost every step of their journey. What he didn't know, he was able to fill in by questioning Lance. It would be ridiculous to think that a man's dying words would be something impossible to attain. This man had spent his entire life protecting Walt and his legacy. His last words would certainly be true.

There just had to be something they overlooked in the clues and treasures that they already had in their possession.

Without any idea of what he may have missed, Lance decided to go to the only place he could think of that might trigger some lost thought or message or *something* to tell him what they had overlooked. Standing in the quiet lobby of the Opera House on Main Street in Disneyland, he studied the items of Walt Disney's history that Beth had on loan to the Park in exchange for allowing her to have her job back. Lance ran his hands over the edge of the glass case; the metal frame was warm from the fluorescent bulb that illuminated the case from under each side. He paused in his scrutiny to think of his old friends. If the lobby had been empty, he probably would have banged his forehead against the wall. Instead, he gave a deep sigh—one that was echoed by a trio of teenage girls who had followed him into the building.

Unaware of the girls' longing looks, Lance stared unseeing at the display in front of him. How in the world would he ever be able to justify pulling a gun on them and demanding the unknown treasure for himself? It hadn't really hit him hard until he was exhausted in Idaho and on his subdued flight home to California. He knew who Sunnee was by then, but at that point, it didn't seem to matter. He thought about how he hadn't even returned to the hidden cave under the Pirates ride for over a month after that fiasco. How he had taken the hated gun and thrown it into his little wall safe. The force he had used had been so great that it scattered the few important papers he still possessed. He remembered the stock certificate and a white envelope had fallen out of the safe. He had grabbed them up off the floor and threw them back in the safe before slamming the door shut, vowing never to open it again.

His eyes narrowed as he thought back on his documents in that little safe. What was there? There were the worthless lease papers for his Mercedes—the one his father had taken back. The stock certificate for the Atchison, Topeka and Santa Fe Railroad was a minor prize that he and Adam had found early in their quest and that he had forgotten to return to Adam after having it evaluated. His birth certificate. A few valuable coins he had collected. A letter from an old girlfriend. A copy of his grandfather's will that had been invalidated by his father. Just those few things and that white envelope that had fallen to the floor. He looked away from the display of

Walt's office, over the heads of the patient girls who now smiled encouragingly at him. What was in that envelope? Another letter? Maybe, but he didn't think so. He couldn't remember seeing any writing on the front and knew that it hadn't even been opened. It had been curled. He recalled that it hadn't stayed flat at first. It was like it had been rolled up in something....

Something hard and plastic and gray...yes!

"That's it!" Lance exclaimed out loud. "That has to be it!"

The three girls looked around, confused. They couldn't see what in the world he was talking about. They just knew it had nothing to do with any of them. Their theory was further validated when Lance suddenly turned away from the display that had oddly held his interest for so long and strode quickly out of the ornate building. The girls gave each other a disappointed pouty-face look and decided to go ride Space Mountain.

"That has to be it," was Lance's mantra as he drove home, banging his palms against the steering wheel while impatiently waiting at red lights. He zoomed around slower drivers invoking more than a couple honking horns and dirty looks which he would have seen had he taken the time to glance at the cars he passed. "That has to be it," he caught himself saying again as he slammed the shift into park and shot out of his Jag.

"Hand the envelope to Manny, Mo, or Jack if you can't find it." That had been part of the clue that led them to the Burbank Studio and then to the Opera House at Disneyland that had Walt's original desk on display behind a large plate glass

window. But he and Adam thought they had figured out the clue and hadn't needed to open the
envelope that was part of the find at the Golden
Oak Ranch. They simply tossed the envelope in
the back of his car after discovering the Grant
Deed to the guest house and another page that
had been torn out of Walt's diary. *Wow*, he
thought unbelievingly, *this find was almost treated
like trash.*

Once home, Lance quickly spun through the
combination dial of his safe. Trying to avoid
touching the gun as much as possible, he pulled
the white envelope out from under the still-scat-
tered documents inside. He stood carefully examining it as he held it in his hands. Only this time
he held it with a touch of reverence.

Taking the envelope into the kitchen, he
pulled a paring knife out of his messy utensil
drawer. With his heart pounding in his chest, he
took the knife and put it gently under the back flap.
Licking his dry lips, he started making a clean slit
across the top of the envelope. He retrieved two
sheets of paper from inside and set the envelope
on the table as he unfolded the first page and
started reading:

*"Well, boys, if you are being handed this en-
velope, that means two things: 1) I am no longer
here having fun setting this up, and 2) the person
or persons who handed it to you needs some help
in figuring me out. Don't we all? Ha ha.*

*"I hope everything in my studio is going well.
I know you all are doing your best to keep things
on track. I chose well and I know you will carry*

on to the best of your combined abilities.

"Since you know I plan things out pretty well and pretty far in advance, this letter probably doesn't come as much of a surprise to you. Please help the bearer of this missive as best as you can without interfering or asking too many questions. You know me too well to do that, anyway. They have a mission to fulfill and the contents of this envelope are designed to help them on their way. You have your work to do and they have theirs.

"Forgive the secret nature of this, but it is something very important to me. I am sure they already realize how important this is, so give them any help they might need. I don't think this is too difficult to figure out, but then, who knows all this better than I do?

"Give them the attached paper and your promise of help in case they can't figure it out. Tell them to get busy and that 'this trip inspired the first Hidden Mickey in film. Look for El Lobo and tell him WED sent you.'

"I wish I could be there with you all seeing how everything we started is working out. Keep up the good work, boys!"

Lance again read through the letter Walt had written to whom he assumed were Walt's dedicated animators. He knew about the "Nine Old Men"—the most loyal animators who had stood by Disney through the bulk of his career. Recognizing Walt's handwriting from all the clues and the pages from Walt's diary that he, Adam and

Beth had originally found, he smiled to himself as he held the letter. Walt thought of everything, even to the point of offering help if the discoverers of his long-hidden diary got stuck on following his clues.

Pausing for a moment, the papers now resting in his lap, he looked sightlessly out of the kitchen window next to him. He, Adam and Beth had finished the first set of clues that the diary had set in motion. He realized that Adam and Beth had found some kind of treasure in the small closet-like room under Pirates. The blond-haired man had confirmed that actuality. However, it was he who had found that hidden button recessed in the floor that they must not have seen. That button revealed an even larger room and the cryogenic chamber. Was that the point of the quest the diary had sent them on? To find the treasure and then the chamber and its famous resident? Lance could picture Adam discovering whatever was in that small wooden crate and in his haste, probably because he was nervous—as Adam tended to be—he missed completely the whole purpose of the quest: *Walt.* Yes, he had the treasures that had been found along the way, but he hadn't seen the grand reward. Now Lance sensed he was holding what appeared to be another quest set in place by Walt. *However*, he thought, *wouldn't this quest also lead right back to the chamber where Walt was?* But, what would be the point of that? Why had the blond-haired man been so adamant that Lance had missed something? He had said the search for the Hidden Mickeys was not over. Was this envelope part of the grand plan of becoming the Guardian? Or, were these clues set in motion by Kimberly's father all along? Perhaps when he began having heart difficulties and sensed his pending demise, he put the envelope in with the original clues Walt left. No, that couldn't be. This note was also written by Walt, Lance was sure of this; it could not have been hidden after Walt was…. Lance pictured Walt's face within the machine's glass window.

As he pondered these thoughts, he glanced at the slightly-yellowed envelope sitting in front of him on the table. Walt must have wanted to insure his eventual discovery. Perhaps Kimberly's father was only aware of the envelope, not its contents. Lance shook his head. He felt a mild headache coming on. But he couldn't put his mind to rest.

What if the envelope had been opened and the clue in Walt's desk had never been discovered? What would have happened to the ending of that quest? Or, perhaps this clue circles back and leads the discoverer right back to Pirates of the Caribbean and the secret chambers…which would make sense if Walt wanted a backup quest.

His mind was spinning as he went over the same ground. There were so many questions and fewer and fewer people to answer them. The blond-haired man was gone now, his daughter distraught. She didn't seem to know about the envelope nor what her father had meant. Maybe Daniel Crain could help? Lance made a sour face. He wasn't sure what Daniel did or didn't know, but he sure wasn't going to ask him at this point to find out....

Well, I'll just have to follow this clue myself and do the best that I can, Lance decided, taking up the papers again to study the second sheet he hadn't looked at yet.

Like the first page, the second sheet had the Disney Studio's logo on the top. It was unlined and the clues, as Lance could see that they were clues, were listed top to bottom on the right side of the page. The left side held a line apparently for writing in the answer to the clue. He counted nine lines in all. Two of the lines, in the third and fourth positions, were off-set a little from the others. Lance wasn't sure if this was done on purpose or was because of the fact it was hand-drawn. "Time will tell," he muttered to himself as he began reading the clues.

As he read the first clue, he smiled to himself and looked around for his car keys. It looked like he was going back to Disneyland.

Lance made a photocopy of the second page and took this with him to the Park. He didn't want to risk either damaging or losing the original pages as they had both been written by Walt. As he looked it over again, he felt the excitement like he had felt earlier in May, back when Adam and he had run the Mouse Adventure race through the Park. This would have fit right in with what they had to do back then during the exciting scavenger hunt the Park hosted twice a year.

He looked across from the Main Street plaza, over toward the Fire House. Up above the Fire

House was Walt's private apartment—where Adam had found Walt's diary in the first place. Instead of remembering Wendy, the curvy cast member who had been on duty that day and who had later accompanied Lance on a few very memorable dates, Lance thought about Adam and how much fun they had had on their adventures together. He again wondered if Adam would ever forgive him. Knowing Adam as well as he did, he told himself, *probably not for a long, long time.*

The shadow that had crossed Lance's eyes passed as he knew he had to get to work. There would be some time, some way in the future to make it up to Adam and Beth.

"Lance? Is that you? I haven't seen you in ages!"

At the sound of his name, Lance turned to see Julia smiling at him. His face broke into its customary grin. Julia worked at the Haunted Mansion as a 'Ghostess', greeting people in dead-pan seriousness at the entrance. Her bubbly personality was the exact opposite of the character she was supposed to portray. Lance had taken her out a few times, and once they had even danced the waltz in the Ballroom Scene of the Mansion, dancing in and out of the ghostly residents, when the ride had been down for maintenance. She was now making it obvious she would like to go out again.

He could see she was dressed for work in the formal, somber costume of the Mansion, so he chatted with her for a few minutes without answering any of her subtle questions about seeing him again. A pair of green eyes that belonged to another beauty kept appearing in his mind's eye, and this was proving to be very distracting as he tried to talk to Julia.

When Julia couldn't put off heading to the Mansion any longer, she gave a good-natured 'see you later, Sweetie' to Lance and hurried to her assignment. She gave one backwards glance before rounding the corner and was disappointed that his dreamy brown eyes weren't following her. *I'll get you next time, Sweetheart*! she promised herself with a smile. She had had too much fun with Lance to give up on him that easily.

Lance's attention was once again on the paper in his hand. He read and reread all the clues before filling in any of the answers:

_____	107 Main Street
_____	1st Completed Building
_____	Down, down, down, down
_____	You need a magic feather
_____	Holiday Hill
_____	31 Royal Street
_____	1964 World's Fair
_____	Richfield Oil sponsor, better have a C ticket
_____	Kiss-O-Meter copyright date

"This trip inspired the first Hidden Mickey in film. Look for El Lobo and tell him WED sent you."

Lance's photographic memory came to his assistance once more. From all the research he had done with Adam, Lance remembered reading that the first completed building when Disneyland was originally built was the Opera House. After writing that on the second line, he slowly walked down Main Street looking for addresses to the different shops. This proved to be more difficult than he expected. Hardly any of the buildings had actual addresses on them. By the time he located a street address of 217 on the final building called the Refreshment Corner, it showed he had gone too far. He did realize the desired store would be on the same side of the street. Retracing his steps, he came to the huge, curved arch of the Crystal Arcade, the words spelled out in white lights. He wondered how he could have missed the address—it was on both sides of the marquee—107. He wrote in 'Crystal Arcade' on the first line.

He now headed to New Orleans Square to see what was sitting at 31 Royal Street, hoping it was a restaurant. His stomach was starting to growl at the sweet smells coming from the Candy Palace that he had already walked by twice, the sugary aroma intentionally pumped through small round vents located at knee level from the candy kitchen.

He smiled when he saw the number 31 was over the entrance to the Blue Bayou restaurant. Applying the full power of his smile to a hostess at the reservation desk whose nametag identified her as Kerri, he managed to get a table right away. Ordering a bowl of clam chowder from the server, Lance munched on the sourdough rolls that were set quickly on his table. Set in perpetual dusk, the Blue Bayou sat on the edge of the well-known Pirates of the Caribbean ride. Sounds of the bayou that drifted across the dark water mingled with the sounds of boatloads of guests embarking on their journey into the world of pirates. A flash from a camera would light up the surroundings briefly, only to dim to nothing and leave the flashing fire-flies to be the only source of light around the bobbing houseboats. Croaking bullfrogs and distant screams of riders going down the waterfalls inside the attraction mixed with the dim clatter of silverware and plates being set and removed and the constant, soft murmur of people eating inside the restaurant.

Being a gregarious sort of person, Lance was unused to dining alone. Yes, there were many wistful glances being thrown at him from numerous female diners—some of which were thinking they would like to change his solo status, or at least, spend time on a dark ride—or any ride—with this most handsome man. But these glances went unseen by Lance as he was intent on looking at a piece of paper sitting next to him on the table and eating his meal. Not once did Lance even glance around the restaurant or make eye contact with any of the handful of ladies in the place. Lance did look up from his bowl one time, looking up only at the ceiling and then he cast a longing look at the boats of the Pirates of the Caribbean which drifted by. This place, this ride especially, held many memories for Lance: some good, some very, very bad. He supposed he was keeping himself in a self-imposed exile, punishment for his reprehensible actions. As he returned his attention to his steaming bowl of clams and broth, he figured he would eventually get over it, and *probably far sooner than he ought.* He smiled as he remembered the quote Beth had said to him once. For just a brief moment, the image of Kimberly flashed in his head, her soft green eyes crying over her father, and overshadowed his memory of dear Beth. For some reason, the woman had him transfixed; he was driven to solve the clue this time, not just for himself, but also to somehow help her. He hoped that the image of Kimberly crying over her dead father was not going to be his last memory of her.

Refreshed by the meal and leaving alone—much to the regret of a few of the ladies that were still seated around him in the Blue Bayou—Lance turned his attention back to the quest at hand. He had no idea what 'Holiday Hill' meant nor the reference to a 'Kiss-O-Meter'—even though he did like the sound of that one, and he knew there were at least two attractions that were brought into Disneyland after the World's Fair in 1964.

Knowing there was a display of the old ride tickets inside the Opera House, he headed back to Main Street and wondered why he didn't think of that while he was standing there earlier. The ride tickets used to be required to enter the different rides and attractions at Disneyland. From 'A' to 'E', each ticket had a different monetary value and was only good for certain rides. The 'A' tickets were only ten cents and were good for the vehicles that traveled up and down Main Street, like the Omnibus, and were also good to ride the Carrousel in Fantasyland. The 'E' tickets were for the best rides. Depending on which decade you came to the Park, you would see new rides printed on these premium money-green-colored tickets: Jungle Cruise, Pirates of the Caribbean, the Matterhorn Bobsleds, the Monorail, the Submarine Voyage, or Space Mountain.

Lance found the glass-enclosed table that contained various Disneyland memorabilia. He located the spread of vintage Disneyland tickets, an information plate describing the various tickets, their historic beginnings, and when they were finally discontinued completely in 1981 in favor of unlimited Passports. Lance concentrated on the rides listed on the 'C' tickets shown in the display. Most of the dark rides in Fantasyland were on this white-colored ticket in the middle of the ticket book. Rides like Mr. Toad's Wild Ride, Peter Pan, and Dumbo, in addition to the Autopia car ride that had a queue entrance in Fantasyland as well as Tomorrowland. Beth's old ride, the Mike Fink Keel Boats, was no longer running, but it was recorded for posterity on the 'C' ticket as well. He looked back at the Autopia attraction printed on the 'C' Ticket—the cars that could be driven by children and ran on a track to keep them within the confines of the ride.

With a smile of satisfaction, Lance said to himself out loud, "Now, what other ride could possibly have been sponsored by an oil company?" Lance tapped the glass top then pulled out his paper again and wrote 'Autopia' in the second line from the bottom.

He had another thought about one of the answers and left the Opera House on Main Street. He headed north up toward the hub in front of Sleeping Beauty's Castle and proceeded to weave through groups of people toward the drawbridge of the castle which led directly into Fantasyland. He gave a tip of his imaginary hat to the Partners Statue of Walt and Mickey holding hands, displayed in bronzed glory in the center of the Central Plaza Hub. Lance walked around the center garden and casually glanced at the smaller bronze statues that all faced inward toward the Mickey and Walt Statue. He paused just for a moment, looking all around the circular walkway, noting for the first time how appropriately each of these other characters that Walt had created—or had embellished with his brand of story-telling—all were turned toward the middle, all facing Walt and Mickey; all literally looking up to Walt as a child would look up to his father or mother. Lance smiled, nodding his head as he thought he understood the subtle reference the Imagineers had intended when designing the hub's layout.

Crossing the portion of Main Street that curved around the front of the castle, Lance walked across the drawbridge, under the dark arches of the Sleeping Beauty Castle and into the noisy bustle of Fantasyland. Peter Pan's Flight was the first, most popular ride on the right; a few steps further was Mr. Toad's Wild Ride. Going around the glittering white Carrousel, he could hear its calliope playing a traditional carnival tune as horses galloped around in a circle to the delight of dozens of happy children sitting on their gallant steeds. He approached the bobbing, soaring elephants of the Dumbo ride, watching the smiling gray elephants with outstretched ears as wings. Holding more children, some with parents, they all flew around the mouse, Ringmaster Timothy, who stood upon a shiny mirror ball in the center of the attraction. Lance stood quietly near the exit as the gray pachyderms made their wide circle, going up or down at the whim of their young pilots. He now wasn't watching the circling ride vehicles, however. He was watching the ride operators as they walked along the line of waiting, eager guests. After asking how many would be riding, they would hand the youngest member a black plastic feather, telling them they would need this 'magic feather to make Dumbo fly.' The feathers would be collected as the guests entered their elephant and then handed out to the next group waiting at the gate.

Turning away from the ride, Lance pulled out the paper and looked at the fourth line clue: 'You need a magic feather.'

On the first of the off-set lines, Lance wrote 'Dumbo.'

Lance now had five out of the nine answers he needed. With a sigh, he headed back to Main Street and the City Hall. The large sign identifying the City Hall also had smaller letters spelling the word 'Information.' It was the one place guests could find answers to questions and also served as the Park's Lost and Found department. *Adam would have had it all planned out rather than all this running back and forth*, he realized as he ran up the few steps into the cool interior of the ornate building.

He was able to find out, with the help of an old map behind glass on the wall, that 'Holiday Hill' was a mound of dirt that eventually became the site for the Matterhorn Mountain. It had also been named 'Snow Hill', the helpful cast member,

Joe, informed Lance. "It was a popular place in the mid-1950's for picnics before the massive renovation of Tomorrowland and the addition of the Matterhorn," continued Joe, a tall crew-cut, red-headed young man. "I guess there were lots of trees and picnic tables up on the hill." Looking around to see where the other cast members on duty were, Joe then added with a smiling whisper, "And places for making out."

That reference brought Lance around to asking about the Kiss-O-Meter, which drew a blank look at first from the young worker. Then he got on the phone and called someone. After much pausing and an "I'm not kidding," some old placement chart was found. "It's in the Penny Arcade!" was the triumphant response. Not seeing an equal response out of his guest, the cast member added a reserved, "Really…," as Lance had a look on his face that said, "I don't believe you."

Joe stood there for a moment, shrugged his shoulders, and said, "It was some sort of game in the Penny Arcade…I guess."

With a "Thanks for your help," Lance left the City Hall building and headed back up Main Street once again, turning into the brightly lit entrance of the Penny Arcade and past Esmeralda, the talking bust of a robotic gypsy woman who promised to reveal his future for a quarter. However tempted to see what Esmeralda saw in his future, he passed on her clairvoyance and walked into the Arcade, looking around at the various coin-operated machines that lined the walls of the room and older, more antique-looking machines that were lined up in the center of the room. The Penny Arcade still held machines that dated back to the 1920's. For a penny, you could look into the view screen and turn a crank to watch an old, black and white silent movie. For twenty-five cents, you could turn a handle and make a marionette of Pinocchio dance from his strings. And, backed against the wall, near the corner leading into the Candy Palace, for ten cents, you could squeeze a bright silver handle and it would tell you the power of your kisses.

Smiling, Lance stood in front of the tall, bright machine. Every ten spaces up the scoreboard had a light bulb to tell you if your kiss was only a ten and 'Amateurish,' or a forty and 'Intoxicating,' or all the way up to one hundred and 'Dynamite.' The last poor soul who tried it had left the machine lit in the humble number thirty spot and would forever be known only as 'Amorous' or until some other individual tested his or her kissing fortitude; at least it wasn't in the negative ten spot and known as 'Frigid'! Lance looked at the red heart on the top of the machine that enveloped a kissing couple. He would guess from the look on that man's face that he ranked at least a ninety and was 'Devastating.'

Glancing back at his quest sheet, Lance looked at the faceplate of the machine and quickly spotted the copyright date of 1940. He entered that number on the last line of the page.

"I'd like to see how you rate," a woman's voice whispered in Lance's direction as he finished writing the date on his sheet. Standing beside him, a tall, slender blond woman wearing a lime-green tank top and a short denim skirt was looking at the machine...more specifically, looking up at top 'Dynamite' level.

Lance turned and looked at the woman who appeared to be in her late twenties. "With my luck, I'd probably end up on 'Lukewarm'," Lance told her with a laugh.

"Oh, I don't think so," the woman purred, turning her head to look at Lance. "I'd like to test your luck."

Lance didn't know what to think of the pass the woman was obviously making. Normally, he would have played along, gotten the woman's phone number, and looked forward to having dinner with her. Now, with his preoccupation with the quest, the seriousness of what had happened to him, his thoughts of Kimberly and her dad, and the task at hand, Lance found himself looking at this situation differently.

"I guess we may never find out," Lance told her with an apologetic look on his face. He saw the woman's disappointment; her frown was more of a surprised pout. Lance was sure she had seldom, if ever, faced rejection. "Sorry," Lance muttered as he turned and walked toward the arcade entrance.

He didn't even look back.

Out on Main Street again, Lance held the sheet of clues under the bright sunlight. Standing near the curb so as to not block traffic streaming down the sidewalk or down the street, Lance looked over the remaining clues. He was left with only one open answer—the 1964 World's Fair attraction. It would be either Great Moments with Mr. Lincoln, or It's a Small World. Wait, weren't the dinosaurs in the diorama from the Fair also?

The answer sheet now looked like this:

> Crystal Arcade
> Opera House
> Alice in Wonderland
> Dumbo
> Matterhorn
> Blue Bayou
>
> _____
>
> Autopia
> 1940

Looking down the answer sheet, Lance tried to find a starting point on how all these answers related to each other. Two were buildings on Main Street, one was a restaurant, at least four of them were rides here in Disneyland, two were animated movies, one was a location out of the country…. He shook his head. That wasn't helping. He could see no reason for putting them together that way. It had to be something else. Time frames? *Alice* and *Dumbo*, if they were talking about the movies, came out in 1951 for *Alice* and 1941 for *Dumbo*. The Matterhorn Mountain here in the Park was built in 1959; the Matterhorn in Switzerland…well, that wouldn't work. The Opera House and the Crystal Arcade were there in 1955 when the Park opened. The World's Fair was 1964. No, the years were all over the place. There had to be another angle.

Looking again at the placement of the words, he wondered why the third and fourth lines were offset. There had to be a reason for that. It couldn't have been just a typographical error. Walt had a reason for everything he did.

Staring at the answer sheet, Lance thought he saw a pattern emerge. He decided to insert It's a Small World in the remaining blank to see if completed the idea he was forming. When he lined the words up the way the blanks were spaced, he took the letters down in a straight line and came up with the answer:

Crystal Arcade
Opera House
A**l**ice in Wonderland
D**u**mbo
Matterhorn
Blue Bayou
It's a Small World
Autopia
1940
'Columbia 1940'.

Smiling to himself again with a new sense of purpose and direction, Lance left the front of the Penny Arcade and headed for Frontierland. The Sailing Ship Columbia was docked in Fowler's Harbor, off the main track of the Rivers of America when it was not being used for guests or being used in the nighttime show, *Fantasmic!* Lance stood on the old Keel Boat dock that was now used as a smoking area for guests, and looked up at the tall, red backside of the ship, its name proudly displayed in golden letters. There were white-framed windows that opened into the display of crew quarters that would have been standard on the ship in 1787 when she sailed as the first American ship to circumnavigate the world.

As Lance stood pondering how a ship that had sailed in 1787 would figure in a clue dated 1940, a familiar voice sounded at his side. "I could smell your cheap cologne all the way into Critter Country."

Lance turned to greet his Security partner. "Hey, Wolf! It was hand-mixed for me in Italy, as you well know."

Wolf was unimpressed. "Now, why in the world would I know that?"

Lance looked surprised. "Because I told you, like, a month ago."

"You are assuming, yet again, that I actually pay attention to anything you tell me." When Lance could come up with no reply and was still staring at him, Wolf asked, "You take up smoking?" as he indicated the dock that was designed to look like it was made out of rough-cut logs. Lance was standing among several people who were obviously using the dock to relieve their cravings for a smoke.

"Hardly," Lance laughed, but then he broke off. He hesitated to say more. He trusted Wolf completely, but wondered how much of this quest he should share.

"You haven't been around much," Wolf told him, leaving it up to Lance to tell him any of the particulars if he so wanted.

Knowing Wolf as well as he did, Lance knew this was Wolf's way of saying he had been missed and he was curious. "Yeah, I...I...um, have a project that came up suddenly." He indicated the Columbia with a tilt of his chin. "I'm just trying to see if this ship holds an answer that I need."

"Do you need to get inside? Do you need to see the museum below deck?"

Lance slowly shook his head. "I don't think so. Now that I think about it, this ship's design is set in the wrong year. I need something with the name Columbia in 1940 that is associated with Walt Disney."

"Columbia University? Columbia Pictures? The Columbia River?" Wolf counted off, his monotone sounding a little like the computer "HAL" from the old motion picture *2001: A Space Odyssey*.

Lance let out a breath. "I hadn't thought of all of those. I need to do more research at home, I guess."

"Does this have anything to do with all the places you went with Adam earlier this year?" Now Wolf was really curious as to what Lance would tell him. He knew that Lance had come back from his last trip to Idaho alone and was a changed man. Even after Wolf's brief conversations with his boss and with Beth Roberts, he still didn't fully understand what had happened, and this was the first time he had actually seen Lance since he went missing a week ago. He would like to know how far Lance was involved with his own boss, how seriously he was taking all of this. Knowing the old Lance, Wolf was hoping he wasn't treating it like a game. There was too much at stake—both for Walt's sake and for Lance's.

Lance was silent and looked his security partner in the eye. He saw trust, curiosity, and strength in the blue eyes that stared back at him. *Sometimes you have to take a chance*, he told himself. "Tell you what, Wolf," he finally said, "why don't you come over after you get off work tonight and I'll tell you all about my trips with Adam and Beth. I think I may need your help, if you are willing." *Well, not all about my trips*, he corrected himself silently. *Some things will have to remain a secret for now.*

Wolf gave a curt nod and picked up his walkie-talkie that beeped. Lance knew Wolf was now needed in another part of the Park. After checking in, Wolf gave him a brief, "I get off at eight o'clock. I'll be over around nine. See you then."

Lance watched as Wolf strode off toward Adventureland. He felt relief mixed with anxiety—relief that he may have a partner again and anxiety that he was choosing the right partner and doing the right thing.

Time will tell.

Columbia, 1940

It was all starting to wear on him. He was tired. Exhausted, really. The strike at the Studio was going on and on. This trip through South America, urged by his friends Rockefeller and Whitney, had been for two reasons: A goodwill trip between the United States and Latin America, and a filmmaking venture. The animators that were still at the Studio were finishing up *Dumbo,* and

Fantasia had just been released to mixed reviews. He was even forced off his boat in the Panama Canal to attend their premiere of *Fantasia* at a theater there in Panama. There was just no time to relax and recharge.

Still, the trip had been creatively fruitful. The DC-3 that took the group into Chile had become the inspiration for a future short film about a little mail plane he would name Pedro. There would be two films that would blend humans with animated characters.

The Studio and money. Two things always on his mind, eating at him, adding to the pressure and the worry. And his worries were half of that of his brother, Roy, who worked almost daily to keep the Disney Enterprise from going bankrupt.

He was recognized and welcomed everywhere he went. Thronged, more like it. He would put on a gaucho hat and serape, speak the few Spanish phrases he knew, and when those ran out, he would stand on his head to entertain the vast amount of people who came to see him. But thoughts of the Studio kept coming back. The betrayal he felt because of the strike at the Studio.

He just had to get away to be by himself. He needed some quiet.

The chance came when their boat stopped in Columbia. With a small group, he commandeered a launch and traveled about thirty miles up a river deep into the jungle. The lush beauty of the tropical rainforest calmed him. Hanging vines. Calls from hidden creatures. Blooms of exotic flowers. Dark, murky waters that hid potential dangers unseen below a placid, calm surface.

At his request, they pulled into a clearing, tying up the launch on the roots of a huge tree emerging from the ever-moving green waters, waters that would eventually find their way to the mighty Amazon. Lowering a gangplank, they made a cheerful camp with a carefully-watched fire that kept the insects at bay and was used to prepare a simple meal. As dusk fell, the native guides recommended they stay the night rather than attempt to run the river in the darkness. Some of the men were a little leery of the noises emerging from the dense undergrowth as the night became more pronounced. Not Walt. He turned his back on the fire and walked to the edge of the clearing, peering into the shadows, his imagination running full speed. One of the guides brought him a tumbler of tequila. "Go no further," he insisted, as Walt finished off the liquid in one long drink and handed the tumbler of ice back to the man before turning back to the trees. "Please, Mister, come back to the fire."

Walt barely heard him. His mind was active, fertile; as fertile, he thought, as the lush soil that bore the weight of each step he took. He stopped and looked back at the guide who stood with a bewildered look on his face, holding the glass tumbler in his hand. "Don't worry. I'm just going for a smoke. I'll be all right," he assured the man. Looking out to the west, Walt pointed toward the silhouette of a raised hilltop, a black mound seen against the backdrop of deepening twilight. "See that big rock formation?"

"El Lobo? Sí."

"Is that what it is called? El Lobo? Well, I'm

just going as far as El Lobo. You go back to the fire. I'll be right back." It was not a request. It was an order.

The guide held back from trying to issue any further warnings and gave a shrug. "Sí, Señor." He didn't like it, but had no choice.

Walt welcomed the darkness as he walked away from the bright, warm light of the fire. He could hear a muted argument going on in camp and knew it was about him and his safety. *Let them argue*, he told himself. *I need this*.

The moon was cresting full above the tall foliage that surrounded the clearing where the camp fire blazed in the distance. A single beam of moonlight cascaded through branches illuminating the area as Walt reached the rock formation. Standing about ten feet tall, the rocks seemed to form a crouching wolf, staring straight at him, standing next to the river's edge. He ran his hands along the jagged rocks that were the 'teeth' in the open mouth of the wolf-like shape. His smile faded as his thoughts inevitably returned to his Studio. "What am I going to do?" he whispered to the wolf, shaking his head in frustration. Walt reached into his pocket and pulled out a small hard pack of cigarettes from his pocket, thumping the top half of the box against his palm. After a cigarette appeared in the open top, Walt took the cigarette out by his lips, sliding the slender smoke from the box. Reaching into his other pocket, he took out his familiar chrome-plated Zippo lighter and flipped the lid open. Turning the flint-wheel once, the lighter emitted a two-inch flame, illuminating Walt's face and hands. He held the flame in front of his face and stared intently into the flickering flame. "How are we going to go on? I don't want to have to close," Walt said out loud, this time speaking into the flame as if it were a crystal ball that could reveal an answer to his question.

He was startled by a deep voice that came out of the forest. It wasn't the voice of any of his friends. "Walt, you don't need to worry about your future. Your studio will survive just fine. You will even find the money for your little Park. It will become a reality."

The unlit cigarette dangled between loose lips before he unconsciously let it fall to the ground. He looked around for a moment, still holding the Zippo as a miniature lantern. He turned around, searching for the voice. Was it a voice? Yes, definitely he heard the words spoken. It was not an alcohol-induced hallucination as he had only the one drink. Suddenly, a stiff breeze blew across the jungle floor, rustling leaves and branches, and, to Walt's dismay, blew out his Zippo lighter, allowing the twilight to consume him.

Walt was now confused. He tried lighting the Zippo, but the wind kept blowing out the weak flame. He closed the lighter with a loud snap and listened to the sounds around him. Was one of his friends playing a trick on him? "Who's there? Show yourself. How do you know about my Park? No one knows...."

He broke off as a dark shape...a hand, he thought, as he squinted in the dim moonlight trying to identify what had actually emerged from the trees. Clouds moved in, riding the sudden wind and now obscured the moon. He was bathed in complete darkness. He again squinted his eyes, trying to see better, unwilling to take a step closer. Was it a hand? It looked wrong, but it had to be a hand because it was holding something…something that dangled in front of him.

"Take this! Safeguard and protect it. It will be far more important to you than its face value," the voice told him. "It will show you things…about your little magic kingdom…about your heart's desire. But, remember this: How you get it is up to you."

Extending his hand with hesitant trepidation, Walt reached out for what appeared to be a pendant on a heavy gold chain. The moon decided to peek through the moving clouds again and reflected off the object; a blood-red glow seemed to radiate from a heart-shaped stone at the end of the chain. Flashing gold circles could be seen behind the gemstone. Could this be a red diamond, the rarest of all diamonds? Even in the dim moonlight, colors of the rainbow flashed from its red depth.

Walt forgot about the unknown voice. He was mesmerized by the brilliant stone turning slowly in front of his eyes. His free hand came up to touch the red fire. For a moment, Walt felt a strange emotion course through his body. His fingers caressed the stone with a slight tremble. As his fingers touched it, a vision streaked through his mind's eye. Blinking, he was not sure if the moonlight was playing tricks on his eyesight or the minimal alcohol was having an effect. Suddenly as his vision became clear, he could see a pink and white turreted castle and there were swans floating peacefully in the surrounding moat. Across the lowered drawbridge, he saw scores of happy children streaming toward a slowly turning carrousel filled with white horses.

"That's it!" Walt whispered. "That's it!"

Just as suddenly, he was rocked back by a wicked gust of wind that swept down from the north, swirling around the area in which Walt was standing. Not wanting to lose the pendant in the freakish windstorm, he put it protectively in his pocket; he went behind the nearest tree for shelter from the leaves and debris that gusted past him. Shielding his eyes from the dirt, he could make out a bright light that suddenly lit the glade he was in. Then, as quickly as it came, the wind and the light vanished.

Somehow, some way, he knew he was alone again. What had just happened? Who was that? Why? He rubbed his forehead in confusion as he made his way back to the quiet camp, stumbling now in the darkness. Not wanting to talk to anyone, he soundlessly found his sleeping bag next to the subdued fire. As his mind went over the wonderful vision still in his head, he fell asleep. It was a deep, peaceful, restful sleep—the sleep of one who had finally been given answers to his many questions.

Upon awakening in the misty, damp morning, he was greeted with a pounding headache and many anxious looks from his companions. The pain of his headache worked against the sharp images of his vision. Did he really see what he thought he saw? It was probably just one of his friends joking around. *Wow, what a dream*! he finally decided with a laugh. Saying nothing to the others, he silently vowed never to touch tequila again.

Standing next to the cold firepit, Walt stared unseeing into the ashes. It had seemed so real. He couldn't shake it off. *Better than seeing pink elephants*, he told himself, smiling slightly, trying desperately for it all to make sense. *Magic Kingdom. I like that.*

Unthinking, Walt's hand went into the pocket of his trousers. He let out a gasp when his fingers touched the heavy gold links of the chain. Glancing around, he could see that the others were occupied with loading their impromptu camp back onto the launch. He pulled the chain partway out of his pocket. When the sun hit the curves of gold and the brilliant red stone, his heart sped up.

Without a word to the others, he jammed the pendant back into his pocket and hurried back to the glade where he had heard that strange voice. Assured now that he was alone, Walt carefully removed the pendant once again. Holding it up in front of his eyes, he examined the beautiful object thoroughly. It was indeed a heart-shaped red diamond. It had to be since he saw the colors of the rainbow in every facet. "It was true!" he whispered. *Ancient*, was his next thought as he examined the way the gold was crafted; the patina gave the precious metal the appearance of age— great age. As he turned the pendant around, the back of the setting came into view. What he had thought were three circles was actually an outline in a shape that was unmistakable to him. *Mickey!* he smiled to himself, *a red diamond with a hidden mickey*. The familiarity of the shape relaxed Walt after the confusion of the apparent vision he had the night before. Reaching out his hand, his fingers outlined the shape of Mickey's ears. His finger touched the brilliant red heart and the same emotion as last night coursed through him once again. Not fighting it this time, he let the thoughts and pictures flood through his mind. This time he saw an elegant triple-decked paddlewheeler, all in white, slowly making its way up a winding river in the wilderness. A Native canoe, full of laughing people, came next. He could see two native guides in the front and the back of the canoe, their paddles deep in the river's water. A log raft named Becky pulled away from a wooden dock and headed for a cave-filled island....

As Walt's hand dropped from the stone, the vision vanished. "How could they know?" he whispered out loud. The words he had been told came back to his mind. *How you get it is up to you.* He couldn't answer the 'who' or the 'how' right now. There was too much to consider. But he believed one thing: This vision of his future would come true!

Hoping to get at least some kind of an answer, he placed the mysterious piece of jewelry back into his pocket and turned his attention to the surroundings. The rock formation of the crouching wolf was more defined but looked decidedly different in the bright sunlight that had finally burned off the river mist. He didn't pay much attention to the rock formation. He was studying the ground around the trees from which the heart-shaped pendant had emerged. He was looking for footprints, bootprints, tire tracks, anything that made sense.

There were no footprints to be found. All he found in the dust, however, was the unmistakable shape of paw prints. Big paw prints…that led part-way into the jungle and simply vanished.

CHAPTER 4

"**W**hat do you think, Wolf?" Lance asked after he had explained his plan. Wolf had kept his word and came over to Lance's apartment as soon as he had gotten off work and could drive over. Sitting in Lance's living room on opposite sides of a black leather sectional, Wolf admitted, "I think you are definitely going to need some help," while secretly thankful Lance had come to him for assistance. It would be better for both of them if Lance was able to complete this mission successfully.

Knowing nothing of Wolf's ulterior motives in helping him, Lance forged ahead, telling him about the clue that he claimed was left behind by Walt Disney himself. To help support his argument, Lance displayed the handwritten note that talked about the El Lobo and Hidden Mickeys...and he showed him the list of clues that had formed the word "Columbia." He thought that he would need something to augment the degree of interest by showing Wolf the note and the handwriting that was unmistakably written in Disney's own hand.

Wolf seemed mildly intrigued by the clue "Colombia" and the handwritten note. He seemed more enthusiastic—if anyone could call Wolf enthusiastic about anything—when Lance asked him to join him on a trip to the South American country. It was THAT Colombia that Walt was alluding to.

At least that was what Lance was hoping Walt was alluding to.

Lance and Wolf were glad they didn't have to follow Walt's entire trip in South America to find what they needed to find. From their research, they knew Walt's trip had been exhausting. Argentina, Chile, Peru, Ecuador, the Panama Canal. The trip had been fruitful, though. Not only was it a successful goodwill tour, the two films, *Sauldos Amigos* and *Three Caballeros*, were a result of the trip, each earning attention from the Academy Awards.

After changing planes in New York at 10:00 p.m., their fourteen hour flight was nearing its end. As they were flying over the Pacific Ocean to make their approach inland, they were impressed by the beauty of both the coastline and the inner land in the brilliant early morning light. The sparkling blue of the water turned into vivid greens of the mountainous areas. It was no wonder why Columbia was renowned as one of the most beautiful countries in the world.

A large country with a population of almost

forty-three million people, Columbia bordered Brazil, Venezuela, Panama, Peru and Ecuador. In his research, Lance had learned that in the early 1500's, Columbia was invaded by the Spanish who found a wealth of gold buried in its fertile ground. Increased taxation by Spain to fund its wars finally led to uprising and revolt. But it wasn't until 1819 that Simon Bolivar and his armies finally defeated the Spanish and formed the independent Republic of Gran, which included Columbia, Panama, Venezuela and Ecuador. Early in the twentieth century, all the partners withdrew from the association and Columbia was on its own in 1905. Intrigued by the gold discovery, Lance wondered what they would discover at their trail's end.

After all the experience of his extensive journeys with Beth and Adam, Lance made all the necessary plans for this excursion. Wolf was settled back in his seat, his stoic face showing neither boredom nor excitement. He had done plenty of traveling himself and would judge matters as they arose. He did have a question for Lance he had forgotten to ask.

"Lance? Tell me…," he broke off when he saw that both of the flight attendants were hovering around their seats again and Lance's attention was diverted. Wolf could see some of the interest was being directed his way, but ignored it in his usual manner. At different times during this all-night flight, he had privately wondered just how many pillows, snack bags, ear phones, and drinks Lance could handle. When Lance was handed a third drink and the attendants finally remembered there were other passengers onboard to attend, Wolf took the cocktail from him, downed it in one gulp, crushed the plastic cup, and set it back on Lance's tray table. At the amused look on Lance's face, Wolf explained shortly, "It's only 5 a.m. We don't need you tipsy."

"'Tipsy'?" Lance repeated, letting out a laugh. "I didn't think you would even know that word, let alone use it!" He waved off Wolf's concern. "I know, I know. The girls are just being friendly. What was the drink this time?"

"I have no idea. I didn't even taste it. I wanted to ask you something. What was the Hidden Mickey reference in the clue you showed me? Something about it being the first one? I never did hear the explanation of that."

Lance glanced around to see where the flight attendants were and to check the surrounding passengers. Most of the other passengers were either reading or were asleep. Pretty sure he wouldn't be overheard, he still lowered his voice when he answered. "Can you hear me if I talk like this?"

Wolf didn't show his amusement. *If you were whispering from the front of the plane, I could still hear you*. "Yes, I can hear you fine," he said out loud to Lance.

"Okay, good. I just didn't want anyone else to hear. Anyway, when we first read Walt's diary, he said he would be sending us on a search for Hidden Mickeys. We, of course, thought he meant the ones like you find hidden around Disneyland— you know, the three circles that make up Mickey's head?"

Wolf nodded. He was used to being stopped while on duty at Disneyland and asked if he knew where this or that Hidden Mickey was located. He had finally had to memorize a few just to make the guests happy.

Lance continued. "We quickly found this was just a metaphor for everything he had hidden. Some of the prizes he had left behind really were Mickey somethings; others were not. So, I wasn't sure if this part of the clue would turn out to be an actual Mickey or not. Turns out it was. I found it in only one of the reference books that you saw. It was one of the main reasons I knew which Columbia Walt meant. The first time a hidden mickey appeared in a film was in the 1945 animated short film called *Cold Blooded Penguin*. It was a part of the film *Three Caballeros*. There was even a picture of that scene in the book I had. Mickey is seen painted on a sand pail belonging to Pablo the Penguin, who is the star of that film."

Wolf just nodded again when Lance finished. He had always been impressed by how thorough and detail-oriented Walt was, how one idea of his could be taken and grown and developed into a lasting phenomenon.

They were both silent as the plane began its descent toward the airport, lost in their own thoughts.

Once they had landed, they had a connecting flight to a nearby coastal village. Their spacious jumbo jet was replaced by a small ten-seat commuter/cargo plane. The helpful and attentive flight attendants were replaced by Wolf who now found he needed to stow both of their bags. Jockeying for position on the runway, their small plane was dwarfed by its larger cousins. After three jarring bounces, they were once again airborne and heading back toward the coast at a much lower elevation. They crossed a few rivers and wondered which was the one they would be taking in a few hours.

Once they landed and cleared a rather relaxed Customs, Lance came across his first obstacle: He didn't speak the language. He had become complacent in the former travels as English was all that had been needed. Now in a small town away from the commercial and tourist centers of the bigger cities, he was faced with a string of local taxi drivers who had no idea where the certain harbor was that held their reserved boat. Repeating the name slowly didn't help any more than showing them his itinerary. After watching Lance and the driver getting more and more frustrated, Wolf stepped in and easily gave directions. Both Lance and the taxi driver were visibly relieved as their luggage was thrown into the trunk and they settled into the back of the cab.

"I didn't know you spoke Spanish," Lance commented as the taxi sped off from the airport clearing in a cloud of dust.

Wolf gave a small smile as he looked out the window. "You never asked."

Used to the quiet moods of his Security partner, Lance grinned. "True. Anything else I should know that might come in helpful?"

Wolf pretended to be deep in thought. "I can also speak Lakota, French, some Italian, and can start a fire with two sticks and a piece of string. Is any of that helpful?"

"Seeing how remote this area is, the fire might come in useful. Lakota? What is that?"

"My people. I am Lakota."

Lance grabbed the armrest of the car as the driver made a sharp turn, seemingly on two wheels. "That would explain the fire thing then."

Wolf just smiled and made no further comment.

Moments later the cab came to a screeching halt in front of a small marina. Some of the signs were in English and grandly proclaimed "Tropical Jungle Excursions" and "See the Amazon." From his research, Lance knew the slow-moving river in front of them was nowhere near the actual Amazon River, but it was considered a tributary of it. Wolf was in a deep discussion with the taxi driver over the exact amount of the fare. The driver apparently had forgotten that the dark one spoke Spanish. The two men came to a reluctant, but almost mutual, agreement. Lance wondered what exactly Wolf had said to the man as the driver muttered something that sounded rather unpleasant under his breath after tossing their bags onto the pavement, slamming the trunk of his cab, and speeding off again.

"What did he just say?" Lance asked Wolf.

"'Have a nice trip'," was Wolf's steady response.

Lance's eyes narrowed. "Really? I didn't get that from his body language."

"I didn't think it was necessary to add *where* he thought our trip should go...."

Lance broke out in a wide, easy grin. "Yeah,

I kind of thought that was the case. See if you can find…" he broke off to consult his travel itinerary, "a Jorge. He is our skipper into the wilds of the tropical jungle, as it said in their brochure online."

Wolf gave a noncommittal grunt and quickly found the location, their guide, and their manner of transport. Both men stood on the dock a moment and stared at it. Humphrey Bogart wouldn't have taken this boat.…

"You already pay?" Wolf asked him.

"Yeah," Lance muttered flatly.

"Great."

"Yeah. Well, we wanted an adventure."

"Wasté kte sni."

Lance looked over at him. "What did you say, Wolf?"

"I said 'it won't be good'."

Lance gave a laugh and slapped him on the shoulder. "Well, it won't get any better the longer we stand here and stare at it. Ah, this must be our intrepid guide."

Jorge emerged from the shack that served as his 'Safari Office.' Dressed all in khaki, he did give the air of a Jungle Explorer. Fortunately for Lance, he did speak English. "Welcome, amigos, to Columbia!" he declared, his arms spread wide in greeting.

Lance sincerely hoped he wasn't expecting a hug.

"You misters ready for your jungle cruise?"

Lance wanted to make sure of their destination first. "You know for sure where El Lobo is located? It is on this river?"

"Oh, sí, Señor Brentwood. El Lobo is a famous landmark in this region. Many…umm, I am not sure of right word. I would say many de tribu come to see El Lobo. You ready go now?"

Lance looked to Wolf for translation, but Wolf had an odd look on his face. He didn't look exactly worried, just suddenly alert, and there was a tenseness that appeared around his mouth.

"Anything wrong, Wolf?"

Wolf's sharp blue eyes cleared as his head snapped around. "No. It should be fine," was his vague reply.

Jorge had already tossed their abused baggage onboard the *Niña*, as he had affectionately named his small boat. The two men sucked in their doubts as to the seaworthiness of the *Niña* and followed their bags in a more orderly fashion.

As the small Evinrude motor coughed and sputtered to life, Lance glanced around for life vests. Amused, Wolf watched for a moment and then reminded Lance, "We're not in California any longer."

As the jungle quickly enveloped them, Lance had to agree, swatting at some buzzing sound that seemed to find him irresistible.

"Must be a female mosquito," Wolf grinned over at him.

Lance waved his hand over his ear again. "I see they don't seem to be bothering you at all."

Wolf's eyes narrowed. "They wouldn't dare."

Lance gave up on the ineffectual waving he had been doing since they left the dock. He was starting to relax and appreciate the lush greenery around them. "You know what this reminds me of? The Jungle Cruise back home. Walt must have been equally impressed by the sights. It is beautiful."

Wolf looked curiously into the water. He wondered which part of the Amazon or its tributaries had the flesh-eating piranhas. It would have been interesting to drop some of their lunch into the water and see the result. *Purely educational*, he told himself with a smile.

The two friends knew from their research on Walt's trip that they had about thirty miles upriver to travel. The day was a balmy eighty degrees, not a cloud in the sky—when they could see the sky through the jungle canopy that sometimes spanned the moving waters.

Knowing it would be hours before they reached their destination and not feeling a need to chat at the moment, all three men were lost in their own thoughts. Lance, invariably, turned to remembrances of Adam and Beth. How could a journey such as this not bring them to mind? If Adam had been the one who discovered their destination, they would have had more specific, detailed information about the area. Beth would have loved the beauty of the jungle and commenting on every parrot that screeched overhead or on the variety of flowers that bloomed profusely. He hadn't nicknamed her Captain Obvious for no reason. He gave a silent sigh as he trailed a lazy finger in the water as they motored along. Then, remembering, as Wolf had done, that piranhas were native to South America, he hastily pulled his hand back into the small boat.

Wolf maintained a contented, even look on his face, but his mind was working around the word that Jorge had been unable—or unwilling—to translate. Wolf knew the translation, and it bothered him some. *Witch doctor* would be the closest English words. He knew the wolf was important in many cultures' beliefs and the fact that the rock formation they were seeking was called El Lobo, or The Wolf, all worked to make him wonder what exactly they would find at their journey's end.

Jorge was also thinking of de tribu, only he wasn't particularly worried. He had four religious medals fastened securely around his neck. There was also some garlic, two silver bullets, and a string of juju beads in the boat, just in case….

In the jungle, when darkness falls, it falls quickly. Lance had decided to take their journey on the river right after they arrived, rather than spend the night at one of the small motels in town and get a fresh start in the morning. He was hoping their journey would end before sundown and avoid spending the night in the jungle, but, if they did, they did. There were enough supplies to keep them fed and hydrated and warm. Jorge didn't seem to mind one way or the other. If their trip took two days instead of one, he would get double the fare.

In time, the *Niña* pulled into an almost-imperceptible cove. There was so much underbrush and moss hanging from the trees that Lance and Wolf were surprised when there was actually a sturdy post in place with which to tie up the little boat.

Jumping to shore, Lance looked eagerly around. He didn't see any formation that might be worthy of being called El Lobo. In fact, he didn't see any rock formations at all. Walking away from the river they had traveled, he could hear the sound of running water coming from another direction. He turned to ask Wolf his opinion, but he could see that Wolf was apparently listening to something else. Turning his head this way and that, Lance couldn't detect any unusual sound. Wolf was standing completely still, his head up and tilted to the side as if he heard something very faint. Lance saw his nostrils flare briefly.

"You just sniff the river, man? That's probably not a good idea here," Lance offered with a smile.

Wolf turned back to Lance, looking at him as if he couldn't at that moment remember where they were or why they were there. That look passed in an instant. "No, I was just listening to the sounds coming from the jungle." The statement in itself was true, but his eyes said something different.

Knowing Wolf wouldn't tell him anything unless he wanted to, Lance let it go. They were so close now that he was excited to get moving. "So, which way do we go? I think I hear another river or stream or something over that way," he offered, pointing vaguely to the west.

After conferring in Spanish with Jorge, Wolf nodded. "You're right. Let me grab the flashlights and the shovel while Jorge gets a fire going." He paused, glancing up at the sky. "Are you sure you don't want to wait until morning? It will be dark soon."

"No, let's get going. If we don't find what we need, we can come back in the morning. If we do find it today, we can go home tomorrow," as he slapped another mosquito against his neck.

"Is the jungle losing its appeal for you already?" Wolf teased.

"Something like that," Lance muttered as a shriek from a parrot sounded close by.

There was a faint path leading away from their clearing through the jungle. The men could tell others had made this journey since Walt's time. That made Lance all the more certain they were on the right path.

With Lance taking the lead with one of the flashlights, Wolf brought up the rear. Jorge had no desire to go see El Lobo. He got paid whether they came back or not. Wolf could hear the whisperings of a breeze as it filtered through the jungle canopy. Only...he wasn't sure it was a breeze. He felt his heartbeat pick up a bit.

Lance's flashlight played over the huge formation in front of them. He was fascinated by the rocks and the fact that he was in yet another place where Walt himself had walked decades ago. Knowing how he and Adam had found the clues before, he got to work making a systematic sweep over the entire formation with his flashlight. He was going to ask Wolf to lend a hand, but, on turning around, he could see that Wolf had company.

Wolf stood tall and wary as the dark figure emerged from the depths of the jungle. Their eyes locked as the older man slowly approached the dark, tall man. He got within twenty feet of Wolf and stopped. Squatting down, he made a show of lighting the torch that was pulled out of the cloth pack he carried on his back. The flint sparked and caught, and suddenly the clearing was bathed in light. In the flickering, waving light, the stranger was much older than Wolf had thought at first. Lines appeared deeply etched in his face. His black eyes were cloudy, a whitish film covered the left eye completely. He was dressed in worn, loose clothes. There was nothing remarkable about his outfit except for the decoration that hung around his neck. The necklace was made from teeth—sharp canine teeth. Wolf recognized them as wolf teeth.

Knowing they had been followed for the last ten miles of their trip, knowing he was now being scrutinized, Wolf said nothing. Out of respect for the other man's advanced age, he would let de tribu speak what was on his mind.

He was inwardly surprised when the man spoke to him in his native language. "Wóciciyaka wácin."

Wolf answered him in English. "Then speak. Wóglake."

De tribu was unfazed by the English words. "Tukténitaŋhaŋ he?"

"Does it matter where I come from? I am here now."

"You have been here before."

Wolf's eyes widened. That was the only indication of the surprise the words invoked in him. "You are wrong. I have never made this journey."

De tribu saw the look that passed quickly over Wolf's dark eyes. "Watohal."

Wolf's demeanor almost fell with that one word. The future?

But the tribal healer was not through with Wolf. He switched to Spanish. "Debe proteger el corazón."

"Protect what heart?   ¿De qué estás hablando?" *What are you talking about?*

The older man pointed at Wolf with his blazing torch. "No puede caer en malas manos."

Wolf didn't move when the torch was thrust at him. "I don't know what you mean by 'wrong hands'. I am just here with my friend." He switched back to his Lakota tongue. "Wo iyokihi mitawa sni." *Not my responsibility*, he spoke clearly and slowly.

"Iye tawci un." *It will be*, was the prophecy spoken just as clearly and just as slowly. De tribu advanced two steps toward Wolf. He seemed hesitant to approach any further. Lowering his voice, he switched back to Spanish, "Yo se que eres."

I know what you are.

Wolf lifted his head and straightened his shoulders. Pride emanated from him. He glared at the older man, daring him to continue.

De tribu didn't take the challenge. Now was not the time. "Ekta gni." *Go back.*

Wolf snorted at him and turned his back. This

man was dismissed. Wolf had no further use and would listen to no more. Now was not the time.

Recognizing the gesture, the older man went to the stream and, with one grandiose gesture, doused his torch. By the time Lance's eyes adjusted to the sudden darkness, de tribu had vanished back into the jungle.

Lance, who had remained uncharacteristically quiet through that fascinating interchange, looked from the dark jungle back to Wolf for an explanation.

"What was that all about? Who was that? What did he say?"

"He said 'Yo se que eres'," repeated Wolf flatly.

Lance just stared at him for a moment. "Yeah, that's what it sounded like. But what does it mean?"

"He wished a good journey," Wolf muttered, glad of Lance's inability to speak Spanish.

Lance was going to mention body language again, but, by the dark look on Wolf's face, he decided to let it go for now. They did have a long plane flight home. He would find out more at that time.

"That's nice," Lance commented dryly. "Do you think you could help me look for the clue now?"

At Wolf's blank look, Lance knew the interview with the stranger had affected Wolf profoundly.

"Walt. Clue. El Lobo," Lance reminded him.

Silently, Wolf nodded and moved toward the rock formation. As he began a search pattern over the rough surface, Lance noticed Wolf's eyes were narrowed and angry. Now his curiosity was really piqued.

Minutes later, Wolf asked, "What is it we are looking for exactly?"

"That's been the problem all along. We never know for sure. The most common find were the initials WED. That turned out to be our indicator."

"You mean like these?" Wolf pointed his flashlight low on the clearing side of the rocks.

Eager, Lance ran around to where Wolf indicated. "Yes! That has to be it! Why don't you start digging right there?"

Knowing Lance's propensity to avoid both laborious work and getting dirty, Wolf rolled his eyes and reached for the shovel Lance helpfully handed out to him. The tip of the shovel bit into the fertile, dark earth. It seemed like mere moments before the tip of the blade struck something hard. Hoping it wasn't yet another rock, Lance swung his flashlight over the freshly-turned dirt. Wolf moved aside more of the loamy soil. The small beam of light caught on a different color— gray.

Excited, Lance motioned with his light for Wolf to keep digging. Smiling to himself at his partner's lack of manual exertion, Wolf carefully continued to unearth what turned out to be a wide, flat plastic container. Since this was the first time Wolf had been in on a find, he felt some of Lance's excitement override his disturbing interview with de tribu.

When the container was sufficiently clear of dirt for Lance's approval, he reached into the hole to retrieve it. "This is shaped like the capsule we found inside Walt's desk in the Opera House," Lance told Wolf. They had found twelve hand-painted animation cels from *Snow White* inside that capsule. Some of those cels had been part of the parcel Beth and Adam had loaned to Disney-land to get her job back. *Well*, thought Lance, feeling generous at this point, *they were welcome to them*. Whatever was here, whatever was to come, he hoped it would have meaning and value to him.

Wolf broke into his train of thought. "Is this what you usually found?"

Staring at the gray capsule in his hands, Lance had actually forgotten Wolf was there with him. "What? Oh, yes, it is. Do you want to open it here or when we get back to the harbor?"

Wolf raised one shoulder in an uninterested shrug. His attention was diverted again. His eyes were busy scanning the jungle. "It's your call," was his distracted comment.

Lance looked back at the prize in his hands. He really didn't want to open it here or in their im-promptu camp. "Why don't we just stash it in your pack and open it in private later."

Wolf silently took the capsule and didn't even glance at it as he put it in his backpack. He seemed on the alert again, tense.

When the capsule disappeared from his vi-sion, Lance's attention turned to his partner. He noticed Wolf's wary stance. Knowing Wolf's rep-utation on the job of finding every person trying to hide out in the Park, Lance wondered what was making him edgy. "Is everything all right, Wolf?

You look as if you expect poisoned arrows to come flying out of the jungle," he teased.

After a final, searching look into the darkness, Wolf turned to lead them back to camp. "I don't think they use arrows any longer."

Lance's eyes got wide when he realized what Wolf had just said. They walked a little faster over the dark, rocky path as it wound its way back to Jorge and his welcome campfire.

When the two friends emerged from the jungle, Jorge anxiously looked from one man to the other, saying nothing at the troubled look on the dark one's face. Knowing this jungle, knowing what might lurk in the depths, his hand involuntarily went up to caress one of the medals hanging from his neck. His lips moving in a silent invocation, he motioned the others to the food he had warming over the fire. Lance, his good mood returning at the mention of a hot meal, chatted with Jorge about the river, his life here, and if he had ever made any trips to the Amazon itself. He didn't notice Wolf wasn't eating or taking part in their conversation.

After Lance and Jorge had retired to their sleeping bags to try and get some sleep before dawn arrived, Wolf stayed on guard. He sat with his back to the fire, not letting the brightness affect his night vision. His blue eyes never stopped moving. When all movement ceased from the two sleeping bags, when their breathing evened out, Wolf stood from his place near the fire. Eyes narrowed, he left the small clearing and silently blended into the darkness of the jungle.

Four days later, a travel-weary Lance let himself and Wolf into his apartment. His plans of getting home early were dashed by a tropical storm that blew in over the Pacific and stopped all air traffic for two days. Once the storm cleared, the airport became a clamoring mass of people all trying to get home.

As Lance sprawled tiredly across his sofa, he could see Wolf idly thumbing through one of his research books that needed to be returned to the library. "Don't you ever get tired?" he asked Wolf.

Wolf raised one shoulder in a half shrug. "Not really. Must be superior breeding," he kidded.

Lance chuckled. He had used that same expression on Adam when Adam had trouble grasping the intricacies of rappelling. "That must be it," he agreed, groaning as he got to his feet and heading to the kitchen. "Gosh, I'm hungry."

That earned a smile from Wolf. "You just ate on the plane—and on the way home from the airport."

The reply was muffled as it was coming from inside the empty refrigerator. "That was two hours ago. I really need to go grocery shopping," he said more to himself than to Wolf.

Glancing at the wall clock, Wolf told Lance, "I need to get going. I really don't want to watch you waste away from hunger."

Lance was surprised. "Don't you want to be here when I open the capsule and see what's inside? We did decide to wait until we got home, you remember."

Wolf looked out the window of the small

apartment toward the tiny, rectangular pool in the center of the complex. A few children were splashing noisily in the shallow end. "I appreciate the offer, but this quest is something I think you need to do."

"But you went all the way to Columbia with me. Why would you do that if you weren't really interested in it?"

Wolf just shrugged a shoulder again. "Because you asked me to go. In case you needed some help—as you did," he said with a smile. He wasn't sure what Lance would have done with the language problem. Probably pulled out some dusty Latin phrases and tried those.

"And I was glad you were there. I was thinking you might want to work along with me to see where it goes." Lance was surprised at Wolf's answer. He found all this fascinating. Apparently Wolf didn't share the enthusiasm.

Wolf's eyes looked far away. "I need to go home for a few days. I need to speak to my father about something. I have an on-going situation of my own to deal with."

"About that old man in the jungle?" Now Lance was really curious. Wolf didn't talk about his family much. Okay, ever…. And when he took off he would be gone for days at a time. "Want some company?"

Not answering Lance's questions, Wolf headed for the door. "In case you end up at the Park again tonight, as you always seem to do, be careful. It is going to be very foggy tonight."

Frowning, Lance looked out the window. The sky was completely clear. "But…."

"Doka," Wolf told him with a raised hand.

Lance raised his hand in like manner. "What is that? Good-bye?"

Wolf gave a small smile. "We don't say good-bye. Doka means 'see you later'."

"Doka, Wolf. Thanks!"

Through the window, Lance watched his Security partner walk across the apartment complex to his waiting Mustang GT. Suddenly feeling lonely and contemplative, Lance wondered why Wolf wasn't even interested in seeing what the gray capsule contained. His thoughts returned to Adam and Beth and how excited they were on every discovery. "To each his own," he muttered.

He glanced at the telephone and wondered if he should call Kimberly to see how she was doing and to let her know that he was back. He looked out the window again and crossed his arms. Did she even know he had been gone? If she was her father's daughter, she probably did. He was being tested, he knew that. Once he opened it, should he tell her about the capsule and what was in it? Did he really trust her? She had literally pushed him out of her house after her father suddenly died. Why didn't she let him help? What was she hiding? Did she know about that strange old man in the jungle?

There were more questions than answers at this point for Lance. And he wouldn't find out anything standing there staring out the window. Pushing his prodigious hunger out of his mind, he grabbed his suitcase off the recliner and took it into the bedroom. Pulling closed the thin drapes at the one window in the room, he opened the zipper of his travel bag and pulled out the eight-inch long gray capsule.

Just like the capsules they found on their first journey, this one was likewise securely sealed at one end to protect it from the elements. It took most of Lance's strength to pry off the two-inch tall and six-inch wide end cap. The seal had done its job admirably, and the contents were dry and intact as Lance upended the capsule. Three sheets of paper fell out and fluttered to the bed. The smaller sheet was easily recognizable as a sheet torn out of Walt's diary. The second sheet was a five-by-seven-inch piece of white animator's paper. The third, protected between the first two sheets of paper, turned out to be a lone animation cel. Lance carefully picked it up by its edges.

The painted drawing on the clear sheet was a highly detailed, intricate wooden box with a large, red heart as its clasp. Plunged through the heart was a finely drawn golden dagger that had three jade green stones at the top of the hilt and the ends of the handle. Lance frowned as he stared at the cel. "Kinda gruesome," he muttered, not recognizing the drawing. There were swirls of blue and green in the face of the box, and a glow had been drawn around the entire box. "I should have kept some of the cels Adam got. At least they were recognizable from *Snow White*... Hey, hold on a minute...." He gently set the animation cel on the bedspread and went into the living room. Taking up one of the research books he had been using, he used the index in the back to find *Snow White*. Quickly turning through the pages of stills from the movie, he found a full page shot of the Evil Queen. There in her hands was the same box that was on the animation cel in his bedroom. "Okay, it is still gruesome," he smiled as he read the story of the Evil Queen telling the huntsman to bring her Snow White's heart in that box. "Gosh, I hope that isn't a hint of what's to come...," he mumbled as he returned to the bed-room.

He next picked up the diary page and read what had to be another clue: "**You don't need to go to France to find this royal wolf's castle.**" Momentarily thinking about a certain French for-eign-exchange student he had met in college, he was somewhat disappointed he might not have to make a trip to France. He might not know how to speak Spanish, but he had found plenty of ways to be extremely fluent in French!

The last piece of paper proved to be a tinted drawing. He wasn't sure if it was drawn by Walt or not as it was not signed. The drawing was of three coats of arms, or shields, sitting side-by-side in a row. The first one was a solid, dark blue with three fleurs-de-lis—two on top and one centered below the other two. The middle shield was a lit-tle more elaborate. Sitting on an off-white back-ground were three standing birds, blue with white breasts. Coming up from the lower left side was a dark blue chevron that held three fancy crosses. The third shield was the one that caught Lance's eye. It was an even darker blue background than the first shield. Three gray stars were at the top edge. Under the stars was a large white animal standing on its hind legs, furry tail upright behind it. To Lance, it looked like a wolf, as might be suggested by the clue that accompanied the drawing. All three shields were on a soft pink background, the top of the pink had wide serrated edges, but was incomplete. Lance gave a half-grin. *I guess you didn't want to tell me exactly where to go, now did you, Walt?*

Lance decided to go get something to eat before starting to figure out what the clue and the drawings meant. There was an inexpensive Chinese restaurant just down the street. The leftovers alone would keep him fed for a couple of days. Humming "Whistle While You Work", he drove off in his dusty Jaguar.

A black Cadillac was parked five stalls down from Lance's. As the Jag headed in the opposite direction, toward the main street, the side mirror of the Caddy was adjusted to watch the car's progress. Smiling to himself, the driver bided his time to make sure the Jag didn't suddenly come back for some reason. Just as Lance settled into the red leather seat of the restaurant, Daniel Crain was using a well-worn lock pick to let himself into Lance's apartment.

Going to the window in the living room, he did a quick check to make sure Lance wasn't somehow walking up the curving sidewalk. Daniel looked around the small living room and attached kitchen. The black leather sofa was the most dominant piece of furniture. A medium-sized TV stood on a low oak bookcase filled to the brim with leather-bound volumes. Not interested in the furnishings, Daniel headed for the desk in the corner of the room. Careful not to disturb anything, he poked around in Lance's desk drawers, looking for bank statements or something he might be able to use against Lance later. When he heard footsteps on the walk outside, he hurried to the side of the window and peered out. He relaxed when the person kept walking past Lance's section of the apartment complex. Going back to the desk, he hesitated, not remembering if the checkbook was on top of the pile of papers, or where the gold letter opener he had examined had been placed. He swore out loud and wondered why he hadn't paid more attention to the details. He put it back to the best of his knowledge. After finding nothing to interest him, Daniel pushed the chair back in place and headed to the kitchen.

He figured Lance would have a safe somewhere considering what he had overheard from his boss. Rich people always have safes. *Or, former rich people*, he snickered, remembering what he had heard about Lance's fall from grace. Opening every cupboard, he only found the usual mess in the usual kitchen. Lance obviously wasn't a gourmet chef. Neither did he have a safe hidden in the kitchen.

Irritated that he was finding nothing of interest, Daniel made his way into Lance's bedroom and smiled when he saw the three items Lance had left on the bed. He made a clicking noise with his tongue. "Tsk, tsk, tsk. My, rather careless, aren't we? Leaving out important items like this!" Forgetting to look further for a safe, he concentrated on the things piled on the bed. He moved the drawing of the crests off to the side to get a better look at it. Taking a small digital camera out of his jacket pocket, Daniel snapped a picture of each item so he could analyze them later. He glanced at the luggage tag still hanging off of Lance's bag. "Columbia! So that is where you went. My, for a penniless beggar, you do get around, don't you?"

Happy with his discovery and certain he had left no traces, Daniel knew it was time to leave. Going back into the living room, he resisted the strong urge he had to steal or break something. Daniel gave a final look around the small apartment, laughing at the size and furnishings. "Hot shot lawyer," he sneered, and left, quietly closing the door behind him.

Lance came back from dinner carrying a large paper sack filled with white take-out boxes from the Chinese restaurant. Along with the happiness he found in having a full stomach, he had also gotten an interesting fortune cookie. "Love and prosperity will soon be yours." He pulled it out of his pocket to read it again as he walked over to his desk. He was actually surprised when he tripped on something. The leg of his chair was angled in such a way it didn't go all the way under the desk. That was odd, as he was sure he had pushed it completely under in that small room. Every inch of space helped....

He fixed the chair with a mindless shrug and headed for the bedroom to look over the clue again. He had thought more of the French foreign-exchange student than the clue during dinner and needed to get his mind in Clue Mode again. He stopped in the middle of the room when he saw the three items spread out on the bed. He knew he had placed them in a neat pile. Didn't he?

He stood with his arms folded against his chest, staring at the bed. He was *pretty* sure he had left them neat.... Maybe it was jet lag? It had been a strenuous trip.... Everything was still there. He couldn't see anything missing.

Get some sleep, Brentwood. You're getting paranoid. And no more saké shots, he told himself as he headed for the bathroom to get ready for bed.

CHAPTER 5

Lance identified the animation cel as coming from *Snow White*—even though he wasn't sure yet why it was included or if there was some clandestine meaning he hadn't as yet figured out. The three shields were very non-Disney in appearance, so he figured he would need to do some research in heraldry and probably wouldn't need the Disney research books any longer. Since his mother had done some genealogical search of his family name about ten years ago, he recognized the shields from that standpoint. Now he just needed to find whose shields they represented and how they may have been connected to Walt Disney.

Returning the Disney books to the library, he found the research librarian was available and willing to help—especially when he showed her the copy he had made of the drawing. Without too much searching, she first identified the shield on the far left as being the national coat of arms of France. Then, at Lance's beaming smile of thanks, she got to work on the second two.

Lance, however, was thinking of the clue "You don't need to go to France to find this royal wolf's castle." Maybe Walt was telling him to ignore the well-known coat of arms and concentrate on the other ones? He could only make guesses at this point.

His attention was then brought back to the librarian who was now frowning over her books. "I don't understand the other two," she muttered, more to herself than to Lance. "I would call it 'Argent, on a chevron sable between three martlets sable, three crosses crosslet.' The birds are probably martlets—they shouldn't have legs, though—but I can't find three of them facing that direction, with or without the crosses. The wolf...I'm pretty sure it is a wolf.... 'Sable, a wolf, or three mullets argent in chief.' The wolf is passant...walking and looking to the left. But why the three stars? There's no mantling....no crest...they seem incomplete....and then there's the tincture or colors...are they true or were they colored over? I don't understand the blazon...." She looked up to Lance, who was making no sense out of what she had just told him. He could see by her eyes that she was excited about the research, the chase. "You see," she continued, "any coat of arms can be drawn in different ways, yet all of the styles are considered equal." Seeing Lance's blank look, she tried to clarify. "Let's say you are printing something on your computer. You can type the same letter in many different styles, or fonts. But, it will always be the same letter. It is the same for the shape of the shields. They can look like these shields in your drawing, or they can be a different shape, yet all point to the same lineage."

Lance smiled at her. "You lost me at the word 'passant'."

The excitement in her eyes dimmed a little when she saw her audience hadn't kept up. "I'm sorry!" she said brightly. "I just love heraldry and searching for family lines, as you can probably tell. How soon do you need your answer?"

Yesterday, Lance thought to himself. "There isn't a tremendous rush, but I am anxious to learn about the other two, especially the one with the wolf. There might be a lot riding on it."

The librarian's eyes sparkled. "Oooh, that sounds fascinating. Can you leave the drawing with me and come back tomorrow?"

Giving her a grateful smile, he said, "Tomorrow it is." As he started to walk away, he suddenly remembered something. "If it might help your research, see if those other two shields have anything to do with either Walt Disney or royalty."

"Certainly," she said as she turned back to her computer screen with a new gleam in her eyes.

"**S**orry, Lance," he was told the next day. "I couldn't find anything on those two remaining shields. I could find pieces of each one on other shields, but nothing as you have them drawn. Are you sure the drawings are correct? The first shield is so easily identifiable."

Lance just shook his head. "No, that's the way I received them. And I have no way of checking with the one who drew them."

"The only connection I could make with Disney and royalty, as you mentioned, might be the Beast in *Beauty and the Beast*. The prince was turned into a huge wolf who could walk upright, but that's kind of a stretch of the imagination. Sorry, it's the best I could do."

Disappointed, Lance thanked her for her time. As he drove away, the librarian's reference to *Beauty and the Beast* kept coming back into his mind. The Beast lived in an enchanted castle. Lance was pretty sure the story took place in France. But the clue said he didn't have to go to France to find that castle. Where else was there a Beast's castle? Any of the other theme parks around the world? Anaheim's Disneyland had Sleeping Beauty's Castle. Walt Disney World had Cinderella's Castle. Paris? No, that was also Sleeping Beauty. Tokyo? Like Paris, the time-frame would be all wrong. Besides, it, too, had Cinderella's castle.

That's too bad, Lance thought with a grin. *I wouldn't mind having to go to Tokyo—even if I can't afford it!*

As he continued driving, he tried to think of some place inside Disneyland that might have the Beast's Castle. Storybook Land Canal Boats? *Oh, please, not again!* as his head slumped briefly against the steering wheel at the red light on Orangethorpe. He and Adam had ridden the little boats over and over trying to decipher one of the clues last time. The incredibly detailed miniature depictions of various stories were charming, but a dozen trips would push the limits of even the most ardent Disney fan. In the end, it had proven to be a false lead—as Beth had so efficiently pointed out to them later.

His head snapped up. Beth. Beth always did have a clear head on her shoulders. Had enough time passed? Would he dare call her and ask for her help?

The sound of a honking horn brought him out of his musing. He shook his head as he continued on his way. "Hi, Beth. Sorry about the gun. I was just kidding. Say, I was wondering if you could look at this drawing and tell me what it means." He chuckled to himself. *Yeah, that would go over well.*

His cell phone chirped. He recognized the sound as the one he had assigned to Kimberly's phone number. As he came to a stop at the next red light, he answered and gave a cheery, "Hello."

Kimberly, speaking in a very low tone, was so brief that it hardly sounded like her at all. "Lance, you could please meet us at Disneyland? Please? At the Main Street Train Station steps. Can you make it soon?" She sounded like she was almost desperate.

Lance asked, "Are you all right?"

He could hear a cough and she muttered the word "Daniel" in the middle of the cough. "Sorry, I have something in my throat."

"Do you need help?" Lance wasn't sure whether he should be concerned or amused.

Her tone then became louder, more formal, "Yes, thank you. That will be nice, Mr. Brentwood. Say, two-thirty?"

Now Lance was intrigued. She obviously needed something from him, but it seemed like she was either unwilling or unable to talk freely. He thought it sounded like it was because she was with Daniel Crain. "I am about fifteen minutes away from the Park. I'll see you there."

He heard the phone disconnect without another word. "This should be interesting," he said out loud as the light changed and he made a right turn onto Harbor Boulevard.

Lance, leaning against the black railing that wound up the brick staircase to the Main Street Train Station, didn't notice the two girls who were walking back and forth in front of him, trying to get his attention. Still being deep in thought about the shields as well as the mysterious phone call from Kimberly, he barely noticed their presence, let alone their obvious attempts to get him to notice them.

"You sure can pick 'em, Brentwood," Daniel said, almost sneering at him as he and Kimberly approached.

At the confused looked on Lance's face, Daniel pointed toward the two girls who had now resorted to taking pictures of Lance. "Pick what?" he asked, oblivious to the attention he was drawing.

"Leave him alone, Daniel," Kimberly muttered to him.

On seeing the beautiful Kimberly walk up to Lance, the two girls heaved a heavy sigh and looked around for their next possible conquest. Daniel, trying to make eyes at them, earned a disgusted, "Eww," as they hurried off.

Her back now to Daniel, Kimberly faced Lance. He could tell from her facial expressions that she wasn't able to freely say what she wanted to say. "Lance, thank you for coming so quickly. I was hoping you would be able to join us." At the word 'us', she rolled her eyes. She hadn't wanted Daniel along—that much was obvious.

Daniel's attention starting to wane from the retreating girls, turned back to them. "Can we get on with this? It is illegal, you know."

"Shh!" Kimberly hissed. "Not so loud. It's for my father, Daniel. I thought you would honor him with his last request." Turning back to Lance, she rolled her eyes again. She could see that Lance was trying to hold back a smile. Linking her arm in Lance's, she led him through the Town Square, walking past the flagpole, and headed up Main Street. Daniel had to hurry to keep up, grumbling all the way. "Well, what Daniel said so inelegantly was true. What I am going to ask you to help me with is, sort of, illegal," she explained, lowering her voice. "If you say no, I'll understand." She gripped his arm tighter. Lance could tell she was fighting some other emotions along with the disgust at Daniel, for whatever reason.

"What is it you would like me to do?"

Kimberly paused before speaking again, her head down. Her voice was filled with grief when she spoke. "As you know, the last time I saw you was when my father died suddenly. I've…I've been trying to deal with that ever since. We knew his heart would give out on him eventually. We just didn't think it would be so soon…." She had to pause to gain control over her quivering voice.

When she was able to talk again, she told Lance, "Anyway, he had specific instructions for me to carry out. He wanted to be cremated."

Lance pulled up short. "Cremated?" He was surprised. "I thought he would want to be, you know, placed with Walt...," he added, lowering his voice so only she could hear him.

Kimberly tugged his arm for him to keep walking. "No, that was what *I* wanted," she told him. "But, he was happy with this life. It was enough for him." Kimberly broke off, swamped by the emotions that flooded through her. It might have been enough for her father, but it wasn't for her.

Lance thought he understood what she was feeling and patted her hand in comfort. "Everyone has the right to choose," he told her kindly.

"I know. I know. It's just so hard to accept when there might be another option." She took a deep, cleansing breath. "I've been going over and over this ever since it happened, and I have to honor his requests. Which is why I am here," as she led them through the wooden fortress that marked the entrance to Frontierland. As they continued walking, she pulled a small black vial out of her purse and showed it to Lance.

"What's that?"

"The old man," Daniel chuckled as he strode next to her. "Or, what's left of him."

"Let it go," Kimberly told Lance when she felt him tense up. It wouldn't do to have a fistfight break out right now. "He is right. This is part of my father's ashes. He spent so much of his life and energies here at the Park, building and protecting it, that he wanted to rest here, in the end."

Lance was touched by the thought. "I can see how that is fitting. But, as Daniel said earlier, it is illegal."

"So, is the security guard Lance going to stop us, or will he help us?" Kimberly stopped in front of the rafts that took guests over to Tom Sawyer's Island and looked up into his brown eyes.

"I believe security guard Lance is off duty. And...I would be honored to help you," he told her in a kind and gentle voice. "Just tell me what you'd like me to do."

"Just dump it in the River," Daniel chimed in.

Lance tensed up again. Kimberly got a tighter grasp on his arm. "I'd rather do it my way, Daniel, if you don't mind. Lance will accompany me over to the Island. I want you to stay here and call me if any of the security guards come this way. Can you do that for me, Daniel?"

They could tell he was gearing up to argue with them. He didn't like being left out of the loop and didn't want them to have time to talk without him being present. But, he couldn't think of any good reason to say no. With a disgusted nod, Daniel strode over to a bench and sat down. "But you'd better be back in ten minutes or I go public," he called out to them.

Lance and Kimberly joined the dozen people on the next raft over to the island. Kimberly felt she had to apologize for Daniel. "In his defense, he has been very supportive since dad died. I don't know if I would have thought of eating if he hadn't been there. He insisted on driving me here today. But when he knew I intended on calling you, he took on a completely different attitude. He doesn't think you are needed, that he should be the one doing everything my father used to do. He even dropped some vague reference about a white envelope—even though I don't know what he means or how he could possibly know something I don't. Is he referring to that final clue my father gave you?"

Lance nodded his head as the raft gently bumped against the wooden dock on Tom Sawyer's Island. They waited until almost all of the guests had gotten off. Seeing several people head toward the caves to the left, Kimberly decided to go in the opposite direction. She knew of a lovely wooded spot on the backside of the island, one that overlooked the site of the old Mine Train ride her father had loved so much. At the thought, she could feel her throat begin to tighten again.

Unaware of her distress, Lance continued her previous thought. "I don't see how he could know, either. You don't even know what I found. Do you?" he suddenly asked, wondering how far the War Room actually reached.

Kimberly briefly answered, "No," in a choked voice.

Remembering what she was about to do, Lance put a comforting arm around her shoulder. "I'm sorry," he told her. "How can I help?"

Kimberly led him to the edge of the island. The Mark Twain Steamboat had just passed by, the river water still churning from the large paddlewheel in the back. Two canoes full of guests had been waiting for the large ship to make the final sweeping turn back to her unloading dock. The canoes had to stay clear of the agitated water and that huge wooden paddlewheel. Behind Lance and Kimberly were two of the popular attractions of the Island—the pontoon bridge made up of large, floating barrels that made for a tricky, rocking passage, and the suspension bridge that was high off the ground and swayed with every step. Dozens of children were running back and forth over the two bridges and paid no attention to the two adults staring out over the water. There were a group of boys who appeared to be in an active game of hide-and-seek, the children intent in hiding among the many boulders, trees and passageways that made Tom Sawyer's Island a haven for kids.

When the canoes were finally able to continue their journey, Kimberly nodded to Lance. He glanced around for any adults that might be wandering by on that dusty trail. Seeing they were alone, he gave her the go-ahead. Sitting on her heels, Kimberly moved aside a round river rock nestled in a pretty stand of water grass and flowers. Opening the small lid of the vial, she poured its contents into the shallow depression left by the rock. "I love you, Daddy," she whispered as she put the rock back in place, tears streaming down her face.

Lance stood quietly behind her, moved by the gesture as well as its meaning. He hoped, when his time came, that someone would be as devoted to him and his wishes, and that he would be loved as much.

When she was ready, Kimberly stood. They

heard Mark Twain whistle right then, its two-whistle sound coming from its landing around the curve of the island. It was a lovely sound, one that Lance would now forever associate with the small ceremony he had just witnessed.

"Thank you for including me," Lance quietly told her.

As Kimberly looked up at him with her lovely green eyes, now clear and peaceful, she smiled at him. "I think he would have wanted you here. I was glad you could come."

Lance felt this was a special, defining moment for the two of them. Much of the distrust faded, as well as some of the lingering questions about intentions and reasons. He felt their relationship had just turned an important corner.

Now he just needed to get rid of Daniel Crain for the day.

Once Kimberly was done with the ashes, Lance knew she needed to get away from the Park for a while. He suggested a favorite restaurant of his in the historical section of town. Good food, good atmosphere, and he knew they would take his problematic credit card with no problem.

Kimberly now dismissed Daniel, telling him she would see him back at the house later. Eyes narrowed, he watched them walk away. He wasn't going to be put off that easily. He hadn't made any headway in figuring out what those items in Lance's apartment meant, and he just knew those two would discuss it fully.

Knowing where Lance had parked his Jag,

Daniel made his way back to the Cadillac. Moving the car within eyesight of the Jag, he waited there to see where they would go.

Sassy's Old Towne Café was a very popular place. Home of the best filet mignon in town, it also catered to the younger crowd with gourmet salads, organic French fries, and an imported beer selection that rivaled any restaurant in the county. The décor was relaxed California Surf; beach scenes with lots of flowers and palm trees were painted on the walls by local talent.

Lance was greeted warmly by the owner, Steve. "Ah, Mr. Brentwood. Delighted to see you again. Will you be dining with us tonight?"

The two men shook hands. "Steve, this is Ms. Waldron."

Steve's sharp blue eyes quickly appraised her beauty while gallantly kissing the back of her hand. "Enchanté," he murmured over her fingers.

"Merci," she beamed at him.

Lance rescued Kimberly's hand from Steve's eager grasp. "Steve.... Steve? You can drop the formalities. We're all friends here," Lance told him with a grin.

Bedazzled, Steve backed up against the entry podium. "Ah, cool. So, what's been happening, Lance?" he asked as he grabbed a couple of thick leather-bound menus and lead them to a quiet table in the corner. "Haven't seen you in a while."

Lance looked at Kimberly and then back to Steve. "Oh, we have a little project we are working on. It's been keeping us busy."

Purposely misunderstanding, Steve smiled broadly, his blond eyebrows rising a little. "Awesome. Hope that works out for you." He seemed to be following Kimberly's every move.

"Down, boy," Lance muttered good-naturedly to him as he accepted the menu.

Taking it all well, Steve chuckled and asked, "Can I bring the lady a drink? And your usual Single Malt, Lagavulin?" Just then he turned his attention to the entry door. There seemed to be a bit of a commotion going on over there. Glancing over, Lance saw what appeared to be Daniel trying to push his way in. He was pointing at them and giving the hostess a very difficult time. "You know that joker?" Steve asked Lance as Daniel strode to the table and pulled up a chair.

"Yeah. Let it go, Steve," Lance said to him as he and Kimberly exchanged a look.

Daniel was all smiles. "This is a cute little dump. I'm glad I saw your Jag out front, Lance. Didn't want to have to eat all by myself again tonight." Since Steve was still hovering protectively over them, Daniel thought he had better add, "You don't mind, do you, Lance?"

Steve's Nordic ancestry was bubbling to the surface. He would have loved to grab a broadsword and gotten rid of this obnoxious lout. He looked to Lance for direction.

Kimberly smoothly took over. "It's all right, Daniel. We weren't sure you would want to join us. Lance and I had some business to discuss and didn't want you to get bored."

Steve hid a grin. *You little liar!* he thought to

himself. "I'll send over your drinks," he told them, walking off, wondering yet again where Lance found all these beauties. They needed to start hanging out again.

When Steve came back to take their order, Kimberly decided on the California Dreaming Salad which had romaine lettuce garnished with figs, blue cheese, walnuts, dried apricots, and a raspberry vinaigrette. Lance decided to have the Cajun Salmon. Daniel figured it was time to show them that he was not a man to be trifled with. As Steve held his pencil ready, Daniel started in.

"Do you serve anything else but beer here?"

"We have a full bar, sir," Steve answered, stressing the last word so Lance and Kimberly could tell he had mentally substituted another, less desirable word in its place.

Oblivious, Daniel forged right on ahead, "Good. I want a good Scotch. Not just any old stuff. Do you have Dewars?"

"But of course," Steve muttered between his teeth. "Will that be all?"

Daniel threw him a nasty look. "I'm not done yet. I have to make sure you do it right. I want the bartender to make it as a Martini, up, naked. You do understand what that means, don't you?" He gave a smug look to Kimberly. Without waiting for Steve to say anything, Daniel continued, "It means I want a martini glass chilled in ice. Then the Scotch should be poured into a shaker with a scoop of shaved ice. Shake it vigorously for approximately thirty seconds until the Scotch is cold, but not diluted by the ice. I hate it when that happens. Then pour the Scotch into the cold martini glass. See? Simple. Naked means NO vermouth, just Dewars Scotch. Lance, I know you drink Scotch, but you pay far too much for that Single Malt. I drink blends and save a bundle, and when you order it this way it tastes the same as Single Malt. You should try it. Or would you rather have an Appletini?" he snickered. Laughing alone at his joke, he made a show of collecting himself, "Oh, gosh, that's funny! Now, for dinner I want the filet mignon. But I would prefer you to handpick a good one. And don't try to pass off some other cut like an eye of the round and try and tell me it's a filet. I can tell the difference, you know. I want it two inches thick, wrapped with bacon, and have your cook prepare it medium rare. Not what you tell me is medium rare. I want it pink in the middle. Not red, not brown, but pink. You know what pink means, don't you? If you want *me* to explain it to the cook, I can. Most cooks overcook their meat and if it comes overcooked I *will* send it back to re-do it. The top should be seared in a crisscross pattern. I want the juices sealed inside, not running out all over the plate. And don't overdo it with the spices. I just want salt and pepper on it. Got that? Just salt and pepper. Oh, and you'd better bring me a new bottle of A1. I can already tell I'm going to need it."

Lance could see Steve's fingers tightening on the pencil. He was afraid it would snap. "Daniel, they know how to do filets here. It is one of their signature dishes."

Daniel waved him off in what he thought was a suave manner. "Oh, all dives say that. I don't want to have to send it back after the first bite."

He looked at Kimberly and shook his head sadly, "That happens so many times, you know."

Steve was ready for him. "I'll tell you what. I will go in the back and *personally* hold your filet over a flaming match until it is seared *just right* for you. How does that sound?"

They could see that Daniel was actually considering that as a viable option. Lance grabbed up all their menus and gave them back to Steve, saying, "Thank you, Steve. I know you will take good care of us."

With a wink at Kimberly, who was desperately trying not to laugh, Steve drawled, "Exactly!" as he disappeared to put in their orders. Kimberly heard him mutter something under his breath. It sounded as though it might have been 'arm hole,' but she didn't think so. She lowered her eyes and pretended to look for something in her purse until she could compose herself.

When Lance tapped her leg with his foot under the table, Kimberly looked over at him with a questioning look in her eyes. Saying nothing, he just gave her a knowing look. They knew they would have to be careful in what they discussed with Daniel there staring at them. Any mention of Columbia or Lance's finds would have to be vague. He would go over all the details with Kimberly when they were alone.

Daniel, wanting them to get on with it, started the ball rolling. "So, Lance, was your trip to Columbia successful? I haven't heard the details yet."

Lance swallowed a curse. *Of course you haven't heard details. We aren't going to give you any....* Then his head snapped up. How did Daniel even know about his trip? He hadn't had time to even mention it to Kimberly yet. His eyes narrowed. Perhaps she knew all along where he had to go, and had discussed it with Daniel.... No, that couldn't be it. She acted like she could barely stand to be in the same room with the man. She wouldn't discuss something as important as the next clue.... Lance then remembered the odd things in his apartment, the chair being out of place and the pictures moved on his bed. Had Daniel been in his apartment? *Why that dirty....*

Kimberly waited for Lance to say something. Looking at him, she could see a variety of emotions playing across his handsome face—and none of them pleasant. After squeezing some fresh lime juice into her water, Kimberly took a sip to stall for time. She had to be careful how she worded things. She didn't want Daniel to know she was as much in the dark as he. She wasn't even sure Lance had been on any trip, let alone one to Columbia. But, since Lance hadn't corrected Daniel's assumption, she ran with that idea, "It was and it wasn't successful, Daniel. I believe Lance found what he needed, but we still have to figure out all the details. It seems to be very complex. We aren't actually sure what was meant." She looked over at Lance and got a surreptitious nod in return. She could tell he knew what she was doing.

"Like what? I would be glad to assist again," Daniel told her as he looked around for Steve and his drink.

Again? Lance repeated, mumbling to himself.

When have you helped yet?

Kimberly knew she needed to diffuse the moment. She did have an idea. "You know, I just had a brainstorm! Daniel, give me a twenty dollar bill! I saw this trick in a movie and I think it might work here!"

Daniel hesitated. He wasn't sure if he had twenty dollars in his wallet. That wouldn't look good…. "Oh, here you go," when he found it nestled in among the ones.

Kimberly took the twenty, and then looked back and forth at the two men. "Oh, please, just go on chatting. I don't know if this will work and don't want you staring at me. I have to remember how to do this."

When the two men reluctantly turned away from her as she started folding the money, they more or less just glared at each other. Steve brought their drinks, and watched a moment over Kimberly's shoulder. He walked off with a huge smile on his face.

After taking five minutes to work with the twenty, she sat back with a beaming face.

"That's it!" she declared.

When the men eagerly turned to her, they expected an answer to their latest mystery. She held out her hand to them and they leaned forward to see what secrets were revealed in the folded twenty dollar bill.

"It's a frog," Lance said flatly.

"It's not just a frog!" she replied brightly. "If you push in its hind legs, it jumps!" She looked back and forth to the two men who looked less than amused. "What? Oh, you thought I meant the clue?" Kimberly frowned, shaking her head. "Nope, sorry.... I got nothing." She sat back in her chair with a wicked grin on her face as she pocketed Daniel's last twenty.

"Wow, dinner and a show," Lance finally grinned as he took a sip of his single malt Lagavulin.

Without another word, Lance decided not to mention anything else about the Columbian trip and his discovery of the crests. After Daniel excused himself to go to the men's room, Lance told Kimberly about his suspicion that Daniel had broken into his apartment. When she was going to try and stick up for him, he asked her how Daniel could possibly know where he had gone.

When she had no reasonable answer, he said no more and let it sink in. By the time Daniel returned to the table, Lance and Kimberly just talked about minor things going on around Disneyland: Some changes to Tom Sawyer's Island that were coming up and needed to be analyzed and watched; a new direction for the Fantasyland Theater; an upcoming new design for the Monorails.

Daniel, getting bored and disgusted that he was not learning anything helpful for his own plans, ate his filet in welcomed silence. He didn't dare comment on how each bite melted in his mouth and was superb when compared to what he usually ate. When he spotted a chance to jump into the ongoing conversation about changes in the Park, he decided to show off his brilliant vision for the Park's future—with himself at the helm. "Those changes you mention are cute, like adding a Princess station in Fantasyland. But the Park really needs a defining hand at the wheel. It needs to move into the twenty-first century."

Not really wanting to hear what he had to say, Kimberly still felt she needed to be polite anyway. "What did you have in mind, Daniel? Sounds like you have put some thought into this."

Daniel sat straighter in his chair and smirked. "Well, working as closely with your father as I did...."

You were the chauffeur, Daniel..., both Kimberly and Lance thought at the same time.

"...I could see some big mistakes he had made. No offense, Kimberly," he added quickly as her eyes narrowed in anger. "It's obvious that a younger viewpoint is needed. Take the Pirates ride, for instance. It's like what? A hundred years old? It's time for that boring old ride to be torn down and something exciting put in. Like a high-voltage roller coaster! Bring in the mobs of teenagers and give them something exciting. Same with that Small World ride. And most of Fantasyland, now that I think about it. I mean, who wants to go on stuff like that any more?" Ignoring the looks he was being given, Daniel was warmed up and just kept on going. "I would even consider a full-service sports bar in New Orleans Square. Serving girls in tight shirts.... You know where I'm talking about...where all those boring bands play. Nobody likes Dixieland music any more. There could be a whole range of alcohol available. None of that Dole Whip pineapple junk.... And get rid of the security guards. No offense, Lance, but, really, who wants them breathing down their necks day and night? Every time I turn around I see a security guard."

Kimberly looked to Lance to see if he wanted to jump in here. Seeing Lance eye the steak knife, she decided to take over. "Well, those are some interesting observations, Daniel. But what about Walt's vision of Disneyland being a family park? There has to be rides and attractions for all age groups."

Daniel waved her off. "Walt's gone. It's time for a new direction."

"You don't think Walt's ideals and concepts are valid any longer?" Lance wanted to know.

Daniel shook his head back and forth as he stuffed another bite of potatoes au gratin in his mouth. "They were cute in his day, but times change. Disneyland is sitting on a prime piece of real estate. Another line of reasoning would be to think of what could be done with that!"

"But Daniel, the real estate is prime *because* Disneyland is sitting on it. Didn't you think of that?"

"Doesn't matter. Chicken. Egg. Same thing. The possibilities for change and profit are endless, that's what I am saying...."

Steve came back to their table at that moment, and that ended Daniel's wild dissertation. Kimberly could have hugged Steve for interrupting as Daniel's ideas and plans were almost making her ill. She could now tell he had learned nothing from all the time he had spent with her father. At Steve's inquiry, dessert was declined by all. And, as Daniel looked down to try and wipe away a stain on his slacks, Lance quickly whispered to Steve for separate checks. Steve bit his lip and retained the formal demeanor he had lapsed back into with the other customers. "As you wish, sir."

Steve returned with two leather-bound folders. "Your checks, sirs and Madame."

With a straight face, Lance handed a white-faced Daniel his portion of the bill. "There ya go, buddy." Lance then pulled the chair out for Kimberly as they said good-bye to Steve, handed him the origami frog, and walked out without a backwards glance.

Kimberly asked Lance to stay once they arrived at the mansion. Not wanting to make a rash decision, she asked him again about his suspicion of Daniel breaking into his apartment. Lance repeated what he had said earlier. "It can't be anything else, Kimberly. He couldn't have known by any other means. He's not that sharp."

She had to smile at that. She certainly couldn't argue the point. Kimberly gave a sigh and looked away for a moment. "He is a relative," she said in a resigned voice.

"I still don't see how you can possibly be related," observed Lance with a shake of his head.

"Father used to say the same thing," she smiled at the memory. "But," she stressed, coming to the issue at hand, "I can't have someone close to me who does things like breaking and entering."

Lance's eyes got wide. That was exactly

what he and Adam had done in San Francisco. And possibly Marceline…. He wasn't sure where she was going with this.

"I am finding more and more reasons to part company with Daniel. What we are involved in is just too important to not be able to trust someone. And, what he said at dinner about his plans for Disneyland just made my blood run cold." She stopped and rubbed her arms.

Not sure of his standing, Lance said nothing, waiting to let her finish her thoughts.

She looked directly at Lance. "I want Daniel gone from here, but I don't know that I can do it alone. With your legal training from Harvard, how do you suggest I proceed?"

Lance was just glad she wasn't talking about him being gone from there…. "I'm not sure. Do you have any agreement with Daniel in writing? Did your father?"

She shook her head. "Not that I know of. It was all done more as a favor than a lasting, life-time job."

"Does he own anything here? Car? His part of the house?"

"Heavens, no. He's given a healthy salary that he seems to blow through pretty quickly. I don't know on what…. He doesn't seem to have any friends."

"Do you think he has any idea of the scope of your father's work? Any real idea of the value?" Lance wanted to know.

Kimberly had to think on that. "He probably knows there is a lot of money 'somewhere' that keeps this house and the equipment running. He doesn't know about Walt, thank heavens."

"Do you think he could be bought out?"

Kimberly pursed her lips and looked away. That might work. Someone as greedy as Daniel would always go for a nice, big paycheck. "Perhaps," she answered slowly.

"Then I suggest you draw up a two-week notice with severance pay for Daniel. I will sign it as a witness. Make three copies—one for him, one for you, and one given to the real lawyer your father used, just in case."

"Just in case what, Lance?"

"Just in case he doesn't take the news very well."

"Well, we can be assured of that, but we don't have a 'real' lawyer, as you said. We are anonymous, if you remember."

"Clergy? Police you have worked with? Security guard?"

She shook her head negative for each suggestion. "Hmm, then I guess I will keep the third copy," Lance suggested, frowning. He didn't see that part going over very well with Daniel, either.

"Will you help me draw up the two-week notice? I'd appreciate the correct wordage."

"I'd also recommend getting a locksmith out here tonight and changing out all the doors. It is easy enough to change the keypad on the garage. Are you emotionally attached to the Cadillac?"

That surprised her. "Not exactly. Why?"

"Throw that in the package. It goes with the exalted image he has of himself. I'd give him cash, not a check. It is too easy to forge checks nowadays."

She moved to the phonebook and looked up an all-night locksmith. "When do you think I should give him the notice?" as the phone rang in her ear.

"Right after the locks are changed and he can't get into the house. When the two weeks are up, change the locks over the garage."

She nodded her understanding and made arrangements with the locksmith.

His face red with rage, Daniel re-read the notice that he had found pinned to his front door. "She can't do this to me!" he yelled at the paper. "I'll knock some sense into that empty head of hers! It's that idiot Brentwood," he claimed as he read Lance's signature on the bottom, both as witness of the document and as the quasi lawyer who advised the document.

He counted out the thousands of dollars that were contained in the thick envelope. Jamming the money into a desk drawer, he knew he would keep it—and the car.

And his rightful job. It was his job; he earned it.

He stormed to the mansion and found, to his dismay, his key no longer worked. Eyes narrowed, he tried to get into the garage. No success there, either. The little idiot had locked him out! When he went back to pound on the door, it was opened by a stranger—a huge stranger.

"Good evening," he said pleasantly. "I am Kevin, Ms. Waldron's bodyguard. You must be Daniel Crain." Kevin pointed a huge fist at Daniel, who, he noticed, was admirably white of face. "You are requested to leave this premise. You have thirteen days left. I suggest you begin packing. Or I will do it for you. Have a pleasant night." Kevin closed the door with a quiet click.

Daniel shakily walked back to his rooms. He looked at the signatures on the bottom of his notice and smiled an evil smirk, his bravado coming back. "Well, Brentwood, you know what Shakespeare said…'the first thing we do, let's kill all the lawyers'."

Switzerland – 1958

The filming of *Third Man on the Mountain* was going extremely well. Walt had even found a local choir to sing for the meadow shot. Rested and refreshed, he marveled at the beautiful scenery—especially the mountain at the center of the movie—the Matterhorn. Arms folded, he studied the tall, snow-covered peak. *I want one*, he told himself. *It could cover that ugly center pylon of the Skyway ride. Yes, that would work perfectly!*

Always looking for antiques and artifacts for his showpiece Disneyland, Walt and Lillian seemed to find their way to every small shop in every town they visited. Walt would be delighted to find some small, some not so small, items 'that would look perfect for the Snow White Ride,' or 'that would fit perfectly in the Dry Goods Store in

Frontierland.'

As the idea of a snow-covered mountain in Orange County germinated from a cover-up for one ride into a full-blown attraction of its own, Walt's mind turned to the 'set decoration' process. It can't just be a mountain—there has to be some kind of a story around it as well. In honor of the Swiss heritage of the real Matterhorn, there should be decorations depicting the nation of Switzerland. Through his knowledge of history, Walt knew each member state of Switzerland had its own flag and those flags could be placed throughout the attraction's site as shields like a coat-of-arms. Each ride in Fantasyland had its own shield, so that would do for continuity.

Walt found souvenirs of the flags he wanted in a quaint store in the town of Zermatt which is located in the canton of Valaise, overlooked by the Matterhorn. Just as they were leaving the shop, Walt spied something back in a darkened corner. It looked like a drawing of a wolf.

"Just a minute," he told Lillian, who was used to his attention darting here and there. "You go ahead to the hotel. I want to check something else out."

Even before the little bell over the door was tinkling that Lillian had exited into the bright Alpine day, Walt had already pulled out his new find. Shaped like a typical coat-of-arms—flat on the top and its rounded sides tapering to a point at the bottom, it was approximately twenty inches wide and twenty-four inches tall. The dark blue background offset the off-white shape of a wolf in the foreground. Above the standing wolf were three off-white stars. Ever since Columbia and the mystery at El Lobo, Walt had been intrigued with wolves. He took his find to the front desk that served as a cashier's table.

"What can you tell me about this?" he asked the clerk who had recognized her famous visitor.

"I'm sorry, Mr. Disney, but I really don't know. It came in with a load of goods from different estate sales around the area."

"Any way of tracking down the owner?"

She shook her head as she looked at the large shield. "No, sorry. It is not that old of a piece, so it could be a reproduction. There's no way for me to know. Did you see the other shield that came with it? The colors of the other piece make a nice contrast to this one."

Walt went back to the corner where he found the wolf. Off to the side was the other shield. It was not as interesting to him with the three songbirds and crosses that decorated the face. Yet, she was right—it was a complimentary piece to his wolf shield. "I'll take them both," he told the clerk. "Can you have them shipped to me in the States?"

"Of course," she beamed at him, pulling a camera out of the ancient desk. "May I take a picture of you with the wolf shield for our store? I can tell that it intrigues you."

Used to this request from his fans around the world, Walt gave a broad smile as she snapped a couple of pictures with her little camera.

"Say, why don't you send me a copy of that picture when you send the shields? I'd love to have one."

This pleased the clerk. "I'd be happy to, Mister Disney. Can I interest you in a suit of armor?"

2002

"**W**ow. So you really did go to Columbia?" Kimberly was asking Lance as she looked over the clue and the drawings he had found. "Are you sure about how Daniel learned about your trip? Are you sure he broke in here?" she asked one last time.

It was the next day and Lance had driven her to his apartment. He felt they would have had Daniel hovering over them if they stayed at the mansion. Kimberly had settled onto his sofa after a cursory glance around his small place. Knowing where he had come from, knowing what he had lost, Lance was prepared to be embarrassed by her assessment of his current situation. He was grateful when she curled up comfortably on his sofa and pulled a silken pillow into her lap.

"That had me baffled, too," Lance admitted, sitting in the matching side chair. "I certainly had no intention of even mentioning it to him. I thought you might have said something, but you had no idea about any of this, right?"

She slowly shook her head as she thought. "No, I didn't. Honestly, I was too wrapped up with my father's death.... No, I'm all right," she stopped when Lance made a move to come and sit by her, smiling warmly at his concern. "I had to make the arrangements and there were faxes coming in from the Park that I needed to handle. They don't know that the power has shifted to me. As I think you know, everything that is done is done anonymously. The faxes are impersonal. The telephone has a voice diffuser on it so it is impossible to know who is talking—even to the point of not knowing if it is a man or a woman." She gave a small smile here. "And that helps right now with my father gone. I have a feeling my power would disappear if they knew the truth. All they know now is that they must follow the last word—and the last word was my father."

Lance was getting the bigger picture now. "So you do know the location of the rest of the Hidden Mickeys? Is that what was on the holographic map I saw?"

"Yes and no. No, I'm not trying to put you off," she hurriedly told him when the look on his face said he didn't believe her. "There is more to those dots you saw than just being answers to clues. Yes, some are answers. But, they are also points of interest to Walt that cannot be moved or changed—points that will be revealed at a later time in the future. So, every change that is talked about at Disneyland has to be analyzed to see if it does or does not impact those points. Some changes that were going to be made were stopped and shelved with no explanation. That is how much power my father had. And how much power his successor, or successors, will have."

She stopped talking and let that information sink in with Lance. He had to know the extent of what he was getting into before he went any further. From all she had to do since her father died, she could see now that she would need help in handling the assignment. That much was clear to her. But, she wanted a willing partner, and one with the same vision of the future as she. She still wondered if Lance would be the one.

And, she still wondered what she would do if he was not the one. With all Lance knew, Kimberly still had to keep Walt safe. Daniel, she thought, would probably pull the plug and sell out to the highest bidder. What would Lance do with the seemingly endless power and wealth that would be his? Did she really know enough about him yet?

"You're studying me," Lance broke into her thoughts. "And you're frowning. That can't be good."

She smiled a little and looked down at the paper in her hands. "There's a lot at stake here."

"And not just the clue in your hand, either. Right?"

Her shoulder-length hair bobbed as she nodded. "You are right. There is a lot at stake. I'm in an interesting position, to say the least. I do want to explain one part of it, though. I think you realize my father and I didn't agree on his assessment of my ability to control everything...that he would need a successor that would not be me...."

When she broke off, Lance nodded, saying nothing.

"Well," she continued, punching the pillow, "I appreciate my father's concerns about my future and wanting me to have what he considered a normal family life. I want that, too. But," she stressed, "I have been in this my whole life." Her gesture took in the clue and the prizes, but it also, Lance realized, included the War Room and the Guardianship. "If I can't replace my father, then I at least want to be able to work with the person who does succeed him."

"If that person turns out to be me, it would mean that we would have to work closely together. Day and night," Lance stressed, staring steadily into her eyes. He allowed himself one small grin. "Do you think you can do that?"

Her eyes got wide at his suggestion, never leaving his. His smile enlarged, taking over his entire face. She kept her voice steady, cool. "Oh, I think I can resist your many charms, Mr. Brentwood."

The confidence in his smile faded. "Oh." *That didn't go so well*, he thought to himself.

Kimberly had to turn her eyes away from the full force of his smile. She dropped them to the pillow in her lap and plucked at a loose thread. *This is going to be harder than I thought.*

To lighten the mood, Lance indicated her feet tucked up under her on the sofa. "You said you were in a difficult position. I'd say you are in a very comfortable position, if you ask me."

"Well, I could use another pillow," she kidded, and then ducked to the right as one was thrown at her from the chair. Kimberly reached out and caught the pillow on the fly. "Yes, that's much better! Thanks," she added, placing the pillow behind her back.

"Any time. So, are you going to help me with the clue or are you going to continue ripping my pillows apart? Do I have to invite Daniel over to get some actual work done?"

Pushing the loose threads into the hole she had made, Kimberly wrinkled her pretty nose at the suggestion of Daniel and let out a sigh. Daniel was another problem that she would need to solve. He too knew a great deal about her father's work; not enough to know about Walt and the power he had left in her father's capable hands, but enough to know there was something big going on.

Lance held up the drawing of the three shields. "So, getting back to work, does this look familiar to you at all?"

Kimberly lightly bit her lip. "Yes and no." She gave a little laugh. "I seem to be saying that a lot lately!" Kimberly eyed the shields with a discerning eye, but had that faraway look of someone trying to draw from a long-ago memory that was just beyond their mental grasp. She refocused on the three shields then added, "But, yes, they do look familiar. I just don't know why or where I've seen them."

"From my previous experience with figuring out the clues, I think we can eliminate the first shield of France on the left. Walt specifically wrote that we don't have to go to France, so I vote to ignore that one. It might be included just because, wherever this is located, there are the three shields together. The clue also isolates and identifies the wolf in the one on the right. I think that needs to be our focus."

"Is there some royalty in times past who was known as a wolf? You know, like Richard the Lionhearted of England."

Lance looked at the large map of Disneyland that he had tacked up on the wall—just like Adam had done in their first search. "Well, I would have thought the research librarian would have found something like that. It would have been in the history books."

"You are probably right." She followed his glance to the map. "Maybe it is just something Disney came up with and we are supposed to recognize it. It might be hidden in plain sight, like your treasure room on Pirates," Kimberly said, referring to the popular treasure cave inside the ride at Disneyland.

Lance nodded in agreement. "That's the genius of the man—he could come up with something like that and make it work!" Lance looked out the window of his living room, not really seeing the large jacaranda tree in full bloom just outside, his mind deep in thought. He then added, looking at the map again, "And, of course, the problem lies in the fact that we are *not* geniuses like Walt." Lance raised his eyes back to Kimberly, and then amended, "Well, at least *I'm* not...which makes the hunt—and decipherment—of each clue probably more difficult." Lance sat back down in his leather recliner across from the couch with a sigh.

"'Decipherment'?" Kimberly repeated, with a grin. "Who said you're not a genius?"

"Ha ha, very funny," Lance scoffed. "I do know a few words that have more than one syllable."

"I'm just kidding you, Lance," Kimberly said

with a soft smile that made him want to be kidded a lot more by her. She tossed a pillow back at him. "Actually, I think you are incredibly smart."

"Well," Lance gave a sigh, wrapping his arms around the pillow. "At least someone thinks so. Certainly my former friends and family members probably wouldn't agree with your sentiments."

Her light mood dissipated with his words. She realized he said it in a half-joking way, but also realized it was something that affected him quite deeply. Her voice soft, Kimberly told him, "Someday, I hope you tell me about your parents...and your life. I know so little about you, other than what my father saw—and shared with me—when you and Adam first discovered the diary."

"Well, when I do, I hope you won't disown me," Lance replied, thinking to himself, *Like they all did.*

"I doubt it, Lance," Kimberly smiled, ending the discussion and then drawing her attention to the paper of the three shields that Lance had handed her earlier. "You think we need to go back to Disneyland and look around for this...wolf shield?" Kimberly asked.

"I know there is a coat-of-arms over at Toad Hall," Lance remembered, thinking of the popular Fantasyland ride, Mr. Toad's Wild Ride and the hectic coat-of-arms over the entryway. "We could start there."

Kimberly glanced at her watch. "How about if we get an early start tomorrow morning? I have some things I need to finish up today."

Lance agreed. "Are you working tomorrow?

I've been gone so long I don't know if I still have a job."

Kimberly smiled, "Oh, you do. It's been taken care of. Amazing what a little phone call can do. You are on 'executive leave' for an 'indeterminate' amount of time. You see? I know some big words, too!"

That earned a big grin from Lance. "Why, Miss Waldron, you little dickens! I think I like knowing someone on the inside like that!"

"Don't let it go to your pretty little head," she told him with an evil smile. "I can also get you fired!"

Lance threw back his head and gave a hearty laugh. "Let me drive you home before you change your pretty little mind."

"Before we get going, I need to turn in a report to Administration," Kimberly told Lance when they entered the Park through the employee entrance. The pair turned left after they emerged from the underpass that went under the train trestle and followed a sidewalk that ran along the Disney University building. This was where the new cast member training took place, as well as much of the overall administration of Disney management, as it applied to Disneyland's operations.

"Follow me," Kimberly motioned as she held open a glass double-door entrance in the middle of the building. "You probably have not been in this part of the building," she added as they followed a long and fairly wide, door-less hallway.

"Actually, I remember seeing this part when I

was hired. It wasn't that long ago," Lance recalled, remembering how he hired into the park after he and Adam had discovered Walt Disney's lost diary and he believed having access to the park would serve them well—and that he needed a source of income, since his father had cut out his trust fund receipts.

"Ah, yes. You're right. They do take new employees through here on their first day of orientation," Kimberly remembered.

As they continued down the hallway, there were framed, acrylic displays spaced about three feet apart. Each contained a collage of pictures depicting rides, shows, and other memorable events that occurred each year since Disneyland opened. There were more than forty-five such displays; Lance and Kimberly could see the degree of sophistication the displays took on as they moved from the more historic depictions to more current. If they had had more leisurely time, Lance would have liked to have lingered and looked at what was hanging there.

As it was, he was more concentrated with the subtly seductive sway of Kimberly's hips as she walked slightly in front of him leading him to her destination. He heard her give a sharp gasp, as without warning, she suddenly stopped and he ran into her.

She waved off his muttered "sorry", and pointed at one of the pictures on the wall. It was in the 1958-1959 display showing the construction of the Matterhorn Mountain, the Submarine Voyage, and the Monorail that were the main rides of that expansion.

"Look at that, Lance," Kimberly said, pointing to a black and white picture of Walt standing with a warm Tyrolean hat on his head. The shot of Walt looked to be in a dim antique shop; he was standing next to a counter...holding a shield. Lanced leaned forward and looked at the old picture. It was then he saw what Kimberly had recognized: The wolf shield in the drawing he and Wolf had found hidden in Columbia. Standing side by side, Kimberly and Lance looked below the picture where a small, brass plate read, "Zermatt, Switzerland—1958."

After a moment of silence to digest the image, Lance broke in and asked, "So, do we have to go to Switzerland?" Kimberly looked up from the picture and looked at Lance.

"You do know how to ski, don't you?" Lance asked with a grin on his lips.

Before Kimberly could reply, the door to Administrations opened and a long-time supervisor, George, came out. He nodded to Kimberly and looked at Lance as if he should know who he was, but just couldn't place him. "Hi there, Kimberly," he muttered as he tried to go around them.

"Hi George!" Kimberly greeted the older gentleman. Before George got a few steps past them, she called out to him again. "Hey, George."

Surprised by the call, he stopped and turned around. "Yeah?"

Kimberly moved a step toward the supervisor and said, "George, maybe you can help us here." She threw Lance a quick look to see if it was all right. At his subtle nod, she pointed at the picture of Walt. "Would you, by chance, know the location of this wolf shield that Walt is holding?"

George peered down at the picture and then walked away. They thought he was just going to leave, as if he hadn't heard her question. But, he stopped at another section of the wall of pictures. "Come over here," he called them. He pointed at a picture in the 1962-1963 section. It was obviously a 'before and after' picture of the Sleeping Beauty Castle. The 'before' half of the picture was the famous picture of Walt walking through the back of the Castle right before opening day. George indicated a section of the Castle above Walt's head. It was the plain face of the balcony under the three high arched windows, the picture taken from the Fantasyland side of the Castle. The 'after' picture showed the same balcony— only this time there were three shields in place on the face of the balcony. The third shield to the right was their wolf shield!

Kimberly gave a delighted shriek of joy, one that made the usually-sour George light up. "Glad I could help," he muttered as he turned and continued his interrupted journey.

"Oh my god! I see that every day when I work as a princess in Fantasyland! No wonder it looked familiar to me!"

"I know! How can you be so dense?" Lance kidded her, obviously enjoying the sight of her dazzling smile.

"Hey, Brentwood, you didn't know where it was either! And how long have you worked here? Forty years?"

They both laughed as Kimberly slipped her arm around his and said, "Let's go see Walt's wolf!"

They stood below the pink balcony and looked up. The crowds coming and going through the Castle parted around them, some pausing to see what was capturing the attention of the two people in the way. When the ones who paused didn't see anything different or noteworthy, they shrugged and went on their way.

"Does our shield look like it sticks out further than the other two?" Lance wanted to know, ignoring the few people still looking up with them.

"Could be," she squinted; the sun was cresting in the south where its brightness formed a silhouette outline of the castle turrets and rooftops. "Do you think we need to find if there is something that might be hidden behind it?"

Lance rubbed his chin. "Or inside it," he suggested, thinking out loud. "One of our clues was hidden inside a fake rafter," Lance said, remembering one of the clues found with Adam in the garage of Walt's old house. "If Adam hadn't been a General Contractor, I don't know if we would have found that one. It blended in so well."

"Then I think we need to get a closer look."

Lance grinned over at her. "You bring a ladder with you?"

"No, but I have an idea," she told him as she started walking through the shadowed interior of the Castle, heading toward the drawbridge. "Tell me, Lance, how do you look in tights?"

"I don't," he said stiffly.

Kimberly just laughed and led him backstage.

Moments later, Daniel Crain looked up at the backside of the Castle. "Ah, so that's where the old man meant. It's nice to have them doing all the work for me!" He chuckled at his own joke and blended back into the shadows of the exit leading to Tomorrowland. "Now all I have to do is wait."

CHAPTER 6

"**N**o!" Lance repeated even more heatedly, folding his arms in an obstinate gesture. "It's…it's just wrong!"

Kimberly looked at the costume she was holding out to the increasingly-stubborn Lance. "What? It's a perfectly lovely costume. Brad wears it all the time. He doesn't have a problem with it."

"Then let Brad wear it. And feathers? Oh, come on now!"

"And I thought you were secure in your masculinity," she teased. "It's only one feather."

His arms tightened against his chest where he had folded them. "I am secure. I could give you a list…never mind," as her fair eyebrows shot up. "I simply refuse to look like an idiot."

"Lance, unless you have another suggestion, I know this plan of mine will work. I dress up as Cinderella, you dress up as Prince Charming. We walk through the Castle, go upstairs through a secret passageway, and exit out on the balcony. We wave at the guests below, pretend to waltz a couple of steps.... You do know how to waltz, don't you?" she broke off, prolonging the teasing as long as she could.

He rolled his eyes. "Of course I do. You don't attend cotillions in Boston without knowing how to waltz," he huffed.

Her green eyes sparkled. "I'll ask you about the cotillions later," she promised. "After we waltz, I drop my shawl over the wolf, and you do what you need to do with it. Simple."

He stared at her. "You aren't going to give this up, are you?"

She held out the princely costume to him. "You'll look dashing."

Lance grabbed the clothes out of her hands. "I always look dashing," he sniffed as he headed for the men's changing room, hoping there was no one there who knew him—especially his Security partner, Wolf. He would never hear the end of it if Wolf was there.

The crowds parted as the royal couple swept past them. Kimberly had to keep hissing for Lance to smile as she daintily held up one side of her blue princess dress with her sparkling gloved hand. Dressed in dark blue tights, brown knee-high boots, and a white doublet with a golden cross on the front of it, Lance had to keep blowing the dark blue feather out of his face as it dropped from the flat velvet cap on his head. They stopped every few hundred feet to allow guests to take pictures. The guests were so excited, especially the women who came across the pair. They hardly ever got to see Prince Charming. And such a handsome one, at that!

Lance finally got into the spirit of the moment when he was asked by a darling little girl to sign her autograph book. He had to change the 'L' into a wide flowing 'P' when he remembered how he was supposed to sign the books. He actually felt the relief flow off Kimberly when he started acting in a princely fashion. He hadn't realized how difficult he was making it for her.

"This way," she whispered when they were at the back of the Castle again. "We'll be right back," she brightly told the guests who were still waiting for pictures. Kimberly led the way into a Cast Member's Only door. As they entered a small portico, Kimberly pointed toward the corner of the closet-sized room. "There's a stairway over here." She took his hand when the door closed, shutting off their light. There was a small fluorescent bulb under the first step of the stairway but it offered very little contrast once the door was shut.

"Glad you know where you are going," Lance muttered, his eyes taking a while to adjust in the blackness. He felt her fingers in his hand and, once again, enjoyed the touch of her even if it was encased in a light blue, elbow-length glove. Kimberly lead the way to the stairs, but the narrow passageway up to the balcony only allowed one at a time up the stairs. "Watch your step and stay close," Kimberly advised, letting go of his hand and moving up the stairs ahead of him. Lance reached forward in the darkness for her, his hand finding the small of her back. Feeling his hand just above the bustle that was part of her elaborate costume, Kimberly added, "Uh, not too close, Mr. Brentwood."

"Hey, you said to stay close," Lance reminded her with a little laugh.

"Okay, but be careful…it can be very dangerous in here," Kimberly warned, trying to sound menacing.

"Maybe I should hold on with both hands," Lance joked as he matched her step for step.

"Don't push your luck, mister," Kimberly told him, reaching behind herself for his hand. "Here, just hold my hand."

Kimberly led the way a few more steps and then stopped on a landing. Lance was able to join her as there was room for both of them. Another fluorescent bulb lit the floor. A muted green exit sign was hung above a door. "We don't use the balcony very often. The guests prefer us down at their level for pictures. But, we used to use it for shows a few years back." She paused and then added, "It is going to be bright out there when I open the door. You ready?"

Lance was enjoying just hearing her voice in the darkness. Without visual distractions, he was noticing her tone more acutely. He wanted to continue listening to her in this dark, almost tranquil room. Begrudgingly, Lance quit protesting her plan and said, "Yep, ready if you are."

They squinted at the brightness when Kimberly opened the outer door, Lance bringing his hand up over his eyes, shielded himself from the instant illumination. They were on a walkway that covered the entire back edge of the Castle. Kimberly led them to the balcony. From the noise rising from the ground level, they could tell that they had been spotted right away. For the guests below, this was something different and the royal pair soon had a large crowd watching. Lance found himself in an unfamiliar panic. It was not just from having to wear the embarrassing tights and feathered hat, but also from being exposed to the masses on a raised balcony that made him feel like he was on stage with the sun as their spotlight.

"Dance with me," Kimberly whispered, wondering why Lance was standing there looking like a deer in the headlights. She held out a dainty hand almost right in his face. It only took Lance the count of two before realizing what Kimberly was asking of him.

She was pleasantly surprised when Lance gave her a courtly bow at his waist. With his left arm tucked behind his back and holding her left arm up in the air with his right hand, he led her through a classic waltz step that covered most of the walkway, ending back at the balcony. When they stopped and faced the guests, a large round of applause went up.

The two took a bow and waved goodbye to the observers below. Lance had timed it so that, when they finished their dance, they were standing in the middle of the balcony, directly behind the three shields that were attached just below the balcony ledge. As people below began to disperse, Kimberly let her shawl down off her shoulders and laid it over her arm, resting it on the edge of the balcony rail. She moved it over to cover the far right crest, the one that had the wolf depicted on its shield.

Lance took his cue and reached down over the rail to grasp the shawl. To the crowd below, it must have caught on something sharp, because Prince Charming had a terrible time getting Cinderella's shawl loose. Lance was able to wrap the shield in the shawl and used it as cover to lift the piece off of its heavy mounting hooks. The two-foot tall shield slid easily off the pins, but Lance had to lift it up a good four inches before it slipped free. When he suddenly ducked down behind the edge of the balcony, out of sight of the guests below, the shield was securely in his hands. As he worked on retrieving whatever secret the shield held, Kimberly covered for him by waving and calling greetings to the little girls below.

"Got it!" Lance whispered as he stood from his hidden position. Using the shawl once more as a distraction, he slid the shield back down over the rail and carefully back onto its hooks, the whole process not taking more than thirty seconds.

"That was quick," Kimberly said as Lance stood up and handed her the abused shawl in princely, dramatic style.

"Yeah, well, I almost dropped it," Lance whispered through a clenched-teeth smile.

"The clue?"

"No, the shield."

"Oh, dear," Kimberly said thinking about the horror if that had occurred. "Let's not knock out anyone below. This might be hard enough to explain as it is."

"It's fine. Everything is as if we never touched the shield."

"Okay. Well, just keep smiling and let's get off the Castle. This isn't exactly an authorized appearance, you know," she told him through clenched teeth of her own. "You ready to go?"

"Any time you are, Princess," Lance said, walking a little gingerly. Seeing how he was walking, Kimberly thought he might have pulled a muscle or something leaning over the rail and lifting the crest. Lance leaned into Kimberly's ear and whispered, "You could have gotten me a costume with pockets, you know."

"Where is it?"

"You don't want to know," he told her with a grin.

"Charming," she told him.

"Always. Let us be gone. Our admiring subjects await."

"Don't get lost in the role," Kimberly muttered as they exited the balcony and headed for the stairway back to the ground level.

It had taken Kimberly and Lance almost a full hour to work their way through the delighted fans. They gamely posed for numerous photos again, all the time basically walking backwards toward the backstage area where they would be able to change clothes again and head home. To make sure they had the least time backstage and the least possible chance of running into someone who might know they really weren't supposed to be there, they aimed for the Cast Member's Only door that was nearest to the changing rooms. And that meant more time with the guests.

Lance was very conscious of the plastic capsule hidden underneath his clothes. He had to be careful how he walked and was unable to bend over to have his picture taken with the little Princes and Princesses. This, however, proved not to be much of a discouragement to the moms who were more than happy to throw an arm around the handsome Prince Charming and pose for their own picture. Lance heard quite a few comments like: "Just a minute, honey. Mommy's busy."

When they were finally backstage, Lance leaned wearily against the closed door. "How do you stand that day after day?" he asked Kimberly.

"Stand what?"

He closed his open mouth and just smiled at her. "Never mind. I'll meet you back here after you change, and we'll head to my place to check this out."

Kimberly's eyes were sparkling with excitement. She had to literally remind herself not to bounce up and down and clap her hands. They were still aware of the fact that they had made an unscheduled appearance and had basically ransacked part of the Castle—all of which was probably recorded for posterity in numerous cameras and camcorders. That probably wouldn't go over very well with The Powers That Be should those pictures come to light. So, they needed to play it cool until they were safely off the Park's property. Kimberly just grinned broadly and gave Lance a nod in agreement. Sweeping the hem of her blue gown up into her hands, she turned and ran up the steps to the dressing rooms. Lance had a vision of glass slippers and sparkling stockings as she disappeared from his view. Then, remembering his own predicament, he hurried into the men's changing room. With the hidden capsule, the tights were not only embarrassing, but now they were uncomfortable.

When they returned to Lance's apartment, Kimberly watched impatiently as he worked on opening the narrow capsule he had retrieved from behind the wolf shield. Right by his side, she reached out occasionally as if to do it herself; only to smile and pull her hand back.

"So, exactly where was this hidden?" she asked after a few moments.

Lance looked at her funny. "Behind…the…wolf…shield…," he slowly answered.

She playfully swatted his arm. "No, I mean in your costume."

"You *really* don't want to know."

"Eww."

"You asked," he mumbled, as he tried the seal again. This capsule was much narrower than the others had been. It had been nestled into the back of the shield, almost a second backing for it. Painted the same color as the front of the shield, the blending had been perfect. If Lance hadn't known what to look for, he probably would have just passed it by. Thinking about the timeline as he worked, he didn't know for sure when the shields had been placed on the Castle. In the famous photograph of Walt walking through the back of the Castle moments before Opening Day, there were three empty places for the shields that would come later. Lance figured it was some time in the 1960's that the shields were all put into place, including the more famous one on the front of the Castle.

Lance had taken the first animation cel he had found in Columbia out of his small safe and put it on his coffee table along with the clues. He could tell Kimberly was excited to be in on this find and subsequent unveiling of the next clue. He was silently tormenting her by pretending to have a very difficult time getting this capsule to pop open. Watching her reactions out of the corner of his eye, he could tell she was about to grab it from his inept hands and gnaw the end off herself if she had to. When she gave another impatient groan at an ineffectual turn of the end cap, Lance decided to end her misery and easily pulled the cap off.

She delightedly pounded on his shoulders and leaned closer to see what was inside. "What is it? What is it?" she asked, leaning even closer.

Lance, who was enjoying her nearness, teased, "Well, if you would like to climb into my lap, you might see it better."

Deciding to jump over the bait, she nudged his arm again. "Now, don't get fresh, Brentwood! What does it say? Is that another page out of Walt's diary? Can I see it?"

Lance was enjoying her enthusiasm. "You're a lot more fun than Adam was. After we did our 'breaking and entering' at the warehouse in San

Francisco, I got a lecture on honesty," he teased.

She gave him an adorable pout. "We didn't break and enter," she reasoned, "we just waltzed and borrowed! Completely different."

Lance gave a full-throated laugh. His arm moved to give her a hug, but he pulled it back. He still wasn't sure where all this was leading and didn't want to misstep and ruin things. He pretended like he was talking to a judge at their trial, "Yes, Your Honor. 'Waltzing and Borrowing' is a completely legal maneuver. If you will refer to Section 40, Line 14 of the 'Waltz/Borrow Law of 1942', you will see that we were completely within our rights as citizens…. Yeah, I can see that going over very well. So, what does our next clue say…assuming that is another clue. It looks like all the others we have come across."

"Maybe it's a good thing you didn't take the Bar," she kidded back, glossing over any wrongdoing they may have committed. She was having too much fun to worry about that now. Examining the ragged, yellowed piece of paper, she told him, "Yes, this has to be the next clue. Listen to this: **'The 'African Queen' wasn't shot on Manhattan or Catalina. Too many elephants…. Look for El Lobo'.**"

Also inside the grey capsule, along with the clue, they found a small animation cel. Kimberly and Lance now looked at it very closely, each of them frowning.

"I don't remember that scene," Lance commented as he handed the cel back to Kimberly.

"I don't either. Perhaps it's a conceptual drawing that wasn't actually used in the filming of

The Jungle Book. Wasn't that the last animated film Walt worked on before he passed away?"

Lance made a clicking sound with his tongue. "Wow, wouldn't that be something if this was the last thing drawn by Walt?"

Kimberly looked from the newest cel to the one Lance had found in Columbia—the Evil Queen's Heart box. "Two hearts," she murmured. "I wonder if that's significant."

The new cel was a drawing of the villain Kaa, the hypnotic snake from the animated film *The Jungle Book*. His lower body was wrapped around a tree branch with the jungle drawn in as a background. His upper body was off the branch of the tree and formed a large heart. There were no other characters in the shot.

"This is a strange scene," Lance wondered out loud. "Kaa wasn't exactly a loving character."

"Well, what all do we have here to work with? *The Jungle Book*, *The African Queen*, elephants, a snake, El Lobo again, and two islands, Manhattan and Catalina—one of each side of the United States. And maybe another heart," Kimberly counted off.

"I'm going to see what I can find out about the movie *The African Queen*. I know Bogart and Hepburn starred in it, but maybe we need to know where it was filmed," Lance suggested, going over to his computer.

Going online, Lance brought up various sites dedicated to the classic movie. Among the various tidbits of information, he quickly learned that a lot of the movie had been filmed in Uganda and Zaire in Africa, but about half was filmed on a man-made river in a studio in England as a protection for the actors. There were some scenes shot also in Turkey. "Oh, that reminds me…," he broke off.

Thinking it was some revelation about the clue, Kimberly eagerly looked over. "Yes? What?"

"Turkey. We didn't have lunch. I'm starved!"

"Lunch!" she exclaimed, surprised. "How can you think about food at a time like this? We need to figure this out!"

"But I'm hungry."

"You're always hungry," she observed with a grin. "Keep working! We already have England and Africa to cover, and *The Jungle Book* took place in India. Now you're adding Turkey to the list. That's a pretty broad spectrum."

Muttering to himself about slave drivers and starving to death, Lance cleared the search engine on his computer. "I'm going to try something different. I want to see if there is any tie to the movie *The African Queen* and Walt himself. He had to have put it in the clue for a reason."

He brought up a different search engine and typed in his request. "Nope. Nope. Nope. Gosh, I thought I had a brilliant idea. Wait…. Bingo! Look at this, Kimberly."

She came over and leaned over his shoulder to see his computer screen. He closed his eyes briefly as the scent of her subtle perfume washed over him. *Down boy*, he told himself yet again. *You have work to do.* "Look at the seventh entry down. 'One of the head designers frequently used the movie *The African Queen* as inspiration for the Disneyland attraction, *The Jungle Cruise'*."

"Okay, now that you mention it, I do recall the first boats were designed to look like the one in the movie. But what about the Manhattan and Catalina references? Is there any mention of that?"

Lance kept reading and then went back to try a different search. "No, I can't find anything relating to either Disneyland or the Jungle Cruise. But Walt did mention elephants. The majority of the elephants were added to the Jungle Cruise around 1964. That would fit in our timeframe for the clues."

"How in the world did you remember that little tidbit? Did you just read it?" Kimberly wanted to know.

Lance was still engrossed in his search. "No, not now. But, I must have read it at some point in time. If I read it, I will remember it."

"Fascinating," she murmured, "I'll have to remember that…. There has to be something from either the movie or the ride that relates to those islands. Do you know anyone who works on the ride who might know for sure—someone who wouldn't ask too many questions?"

Lance thought for a minute. His face broke into a wide smile. "Drew. Drew Briggs. You know him? He's been around forever. If anyone would know something about the Jungle Cruise, it would be Drew. I wouldn't be a bit surprised to learn he had even ridden in the 'Disneyland Rambler'! I'll give him a call…. He's probably forgotten I dated his sister by now…. Lovely little red-head," Lance muttered as he looked for his phone book in his middle desk drawer.

"What in the world is a 'Disneyland Rambler'? I've never heard of that," Kimberly stated as she perched on the edge of Lance's desk.

"You've never heard of the Rambler? I thought for sure your father would have told you about it." Lance finally found the address book buried under a sheaf of papers in his drawer. He hoped Kimberly wouldn't notice it was what would commonly be referred to as 'A Little Black Book.' He tucked it off to the side as he turned to answer her, his gaze falling on the pink tips of her toes peeking out of her sandals.

Kimberly gave a little smile as she saw his attention waver and his eyes started to travel up her leg. "Rambler? Hello!"

Unabashed at getting caught, Lance threw her a wide grin as he leaned back in his leather chair and told her the story of the 'Disneyland Rambler.'

February 8, 1955

Earthmovers and huge excavation buckets were hard at work, gouging deep trenches and holes in the dry soil of Anaheim. With the tires alone being higher than the men working near them, the machinery looked like fierce prehistoric beasts, crisscrossing back and forth across the sandy soil. One lone palm tree, only the top few feet showing above a tall berm of dirt, seemed to magically float across the skyline, the flatbed truck transporting the tree unseen behind a huge wall of dirt.

A camera crew was set up in the bottom of the excavated riverbed; a large camera mounted on a tripod faced west where a dust-covered American Motors Rambler station wagon sat.

"This is our latest progress report from the beautiful region of Southern California. We are ahead of schedule and making good progress," Walt Disney reported with a wry smile, proud of not just what was taking place around him with the massive excavation and sculpting the river bottom and shorelines, but proud of the surroundings that soon would encompass his vision, foresight and imagination. Much like his many years of acting out unseen stories to his animators back at the Disney studios, conveying what he saw in his mind's eye, Disney now was sharing his future with the world through the magic of Television.

Disney held out his arm in a sweeping motion, while holding a microphone in the other. "You can see how the earthmovers are scooping out rivers and lakes, literally transforming this area into a Tahitian setting fit for the embarkation of Disneyland guests on a wonderful excursion through Nature's Secret World.

"Let's climb on board our personal transport—our very own Rambler Cross Country."

The four-door station wagon began its journey down a wide trench dug into the soil, traveling over a raised trail that would later become the guide rail for the boats that would follow. A few trees were seen on the high sides of the trench as the car made its bouncing way along the dry riverbed.

"The first part of our magical journey will be these beautiful floating tropical gardens. You might not see them with your eyes just yet, but if you close your eyes and use your imagination, you will begin to see the flora and color that exists in tropical river valleys. As we go around this wide turn, we are now in Central and South America. See the bright flowers and birds that line the banks of the river on each side? This next sweeping turn heads us into the Caribbean, right into the heart of the everglades. These dry banks of dirt become a mangrove swamp with the help of your imagination. You can just see how it is infested with alligators."

The television cameras show viewers at home eager alligators slipping into the dark waters, noses up as they approach nearer and nearer. Jaws snapping, the clip now shows three alligators on a circular track going around in a pool of water. In a voice-over, Disney's voice is heard, "Made of plastic and steel, these life-like creatures are ready to menace unwary guests."

The television transmission goes back to showing Disney in the Rambler, making a left hand turn along the dry river bottom. "One more turn and we go to Africa with birds calling from the treetops. Hear that noise? This is elephant country!"

A baby elephant is shown playfully squirting water over its own head as the mother hovers protectively nearby.

The show shifts to a backstage warehouse where a full size elephant stood on a wooden platform. Disney continues the narration: "As we can see, this huge bull elephant in our studio is a perfect match for the *True-Life Adventure* scene. Our artists are hard at work to make this big fellow identical to his real life companions!

"Our Rambler is now approaching the makings of a waterfall." The camera pans to a slightly taller load of dirt that is being formed to the right of the station wagon, with a large backhoe building up its sides. "It may look like just a mound of dirt, but, with the use of our working model, we can see how beautiful it will be with the cascading water—all 4000 gallons a minute of it!

"We now turn onto the Congo River, the Zambezi, and Lake Tanganyika. See the lions stalking prey and the animals of the Serengeti Plain? Watch how the elegant giraffe bends down to eat the topmost branches of that tree. Now you can see how seamlessly the real blends into the plastic model! as it bends down to nibble on some plastic leaves.

"This is Zulu Land, a forbidden and dangerous territory where we will sail past a cannibal village," Disney pauses, then points to a flat area on the port side of the Rambler. "See that clearing? That will be the natives' village as they celebrate the kill of a lion! This dry waterbed we are seeing will become the marshy home of the huge hippopotamus. Look how lifelike our models are as they are being tested in that huge pool." A large metal pool of water three feet deep was now being shown; a family of hippos moving higher and lower at the water's surface could be seen, water cascading over their bodies as they emerged before sinking down again. "Now they are sinking out of our sight, ready to spring again at the next boat!"

The car continued its journey, weaving a little, avoiding some potholes in the sandy bottom. "We are now at Lake Victoria, headquarters of the Nile. Our Rambler is now actually sailing under what will become a swinging bridge and an overhanging rock formation that will support the flowing waters of the waterfall we had passed in front of earlier."

The scene shifted again to a small striped-canopy boat as it made its tentative way under the waterfall. Water cascaded over the top, split into three streams by huge boulders on the top of the fall.

"Hang on tight now. The Rambler gets rough running the rapids through this narrow gorge. It might look like barren piles of dirt, but imagine the white water rushing past our boat as we navigate the treacherous waters!

"As we make this last turn, we now emerge into the quiet waters of the International Dock. After disembarking, we invite you to wander through the tropical bazaar and find exotic plants and curios from around the world."

Models of shops and restaurants are then shown, lining a busy shopping bazaar along the edge of the river. The arched dome of the Bazaar seems to offer guests cool shade from the bright sun outside. Pastel-colored buildings draw the eye and excite the adventurer's mind.

Walt turned to the camera, "What will we find inside?" With a wink, Disney smiled and finished

with, "You will have to wait until this summer to
find out!"

CHAPTER 7

It felt weird to be heading for the regular line to ride the Jungle Cruise. Kimberly and Lance joined the other guests in the queue, weaving back and forth within the waiting area, between the metal bars that were expertly designed to look like bamboo that kept the anxious guests in orderly rows. Since both of them worked in the Park, they could have simply walked into the ride's backstage area…if they had been wearing their respective costumes. However, Kimberly was wearing comfortable white shorts, a beige tank top that framed her lovely shoulders and striking figure, and equally comfortable sandals. Her looks were not lost on Lance; his eyes seldom left hers. For the first time, he saw Kimberly for what she truly was: a beautiful…no, a stunningly beautiful woman. His eyes softened more each time he looked at her. Kimberly was no longer what she had been to him: his captor's daughter. Even though he had never really been kept at the mansion against his will, his memories of seeing her father holding a chrome-plated Magnum pointed at his head was something that was not soon forgotten. It had taken him this long to not only recognize and trust the man's intent, but equally, it took him this much time to trust his daughter. His desire to trust her was overtaking his desire to suspect her intentions.

Standing next to Kimberly here in line for the Jungle Cruise, Lance was feeling other internal desires surface as well.

"When you and Wolf discovered the capsule at El Lobo, where exactly did you find it?" she was asking him, forcing Lance out of his thoughts regarding Kimberly and her feminine virtues.

"Hmm? The what? Oh, it was buried down a ways under a layer of dirt and rocks. It was hidden well enough to protect it from any random discovery," Lance told her, thinking back to the find he and Wolf had made and comparing it to the different finds he and Adam had made a few months earlier.

The line moved a number of steps forward before stopping again near the steps that led to the upper level of the queue that was not needed with the lighter-than-usual crowd at the Park that day. They could hear the hornbill bird squawk in the rafters of the upper queue. Kimberly stopped abruptly and turned around to face Lance. Lance, who had been thinking about the capsule and the WED that had been carved into the rock formation, didn't see that she had stopped and he bumped into her.

"Oh! Sorry, Kimberly. I seem to be doing that a lot," he muttered, moving back a step.

Kimberly smiled, enjoying the fact that, for

once, he seemed totally disarmed. "Don't worry, Lance," she teasingly said with a smile. "I don't get mad. I get even."

Lance's eyes lit up. *Let the games begin*, flashed through his mind. He gave a laugh. "And how do you propose you will 'get even'?"

"Oh, I have my ways," was her mysterious reply as the line again moved forward.

Lance watched her turn and take several steps, now being more focused on Kimberly than anything else. He watched her long, tan legs move a number of paces before he followed suit.

When the line stopped again, Lance got back to their task at hand, speaking a little quieter considering the people all around them. "According to the map Drew got for me, the Jungle Cruise does have two islands. For as long as he can remember, they have been affectionately called Manhattan and Catalina by the cast members. These two islands separate the mainland from the internal ride elements. Drew told me that the rock formation behind Bertha, the elephant in the waterfall, is on the mainland side. I don't remember seeing anything on the other side of the river as we pass the elephant bathing pool." He paused, thinking about the few times he had ridden the Jungle Cruise. He had many friends who worked the ride; Drew being one of the 'lifers' as cast members would label those who had made a career out of working at Disneyland. "I guess because of all the action and the way the boat turns away from the elephant pool, most people probably never even look out the other side of the boat."

Kimberly nodded. "I guess we had better

take a better look this time. Maybe we can request to sit in the back."

The line split in two and their side of the queue headed toward the back of the freshly-emptied boat that had noisily motored up from the unloading dock about fifty feet to their left. The skipper was busy loading two blank bullets into his gun as the guests starting piling onboard. Both Kimberly and Lance were looking at everything around them with a different type of scrutiny than the other guests boarding with them. Attention to details and the fear of missing something vital kept both of them very alert.

As their boat, the *Kissimmee Kate*, motored off into the waiting, misty jungle, the guests were encouraged to "wave good-bye to the people left on the dock. You may never see them again.... Now sit back and enjoy the three exciting days and six enchanting nights of our journey on the deepest, most dangerous rivers known to man; you women are safe enough...." Lance and Kimberly paid little attention as the humorous spiel continued. They were busy looking at both sides of the river. The side off to the right was approaching the queue for the Indiana Jones ride and was pretty open to public view. The other side of the river—the long narrow side of the island called Manhattan—held tropical flowers, huge butterflies, and a loud Toucan bird. The skipper was asking everyone if they wanted to see the first sign of danger. He then used his hand-held mike to point to their right at a brown wooden plank with the word "Danger" stenciled over the face.

Lance nudged Kimberly as they sat 'cheek to

cheek' on the wooden seats that lined the gunnels of the boat. "Dangerous," he whispered in a menacing but mocking tone. "Are you scared, Kimberly?" he asked, his lips close to her ear.

Kimberly turned from scanning Manhattan's shoreline, her lips only inches from his. "Should I be scared?"

"Absolutely," he stated with a grin.   He nudged her again, adding, "Hey, pay attention."

Kimberly felt her face smile and was very aware of Lance's hip pressing against hers in the tightly-packed Jungle Cruise boat.

The boat slowly made its way past the ruins of an ancient Cambodian temple, "built by ancient Cambodians. And don't worry about that Bengal tiger. They can jump over forty feet. We are only twenty feet away, so he will just sail right over us. Oh, look," as a small crocodile surfaced next to the boat, "keep your fingers inside the boat. Remember: Ginger snaps!"

As they approached the elephant bathing pool—"It's all right to take pictures. They all have their trunks on."—Lance and Kimberly paid no attention to the right side of the boat where all the animatronic elephants were happily playing in the water. They were turned in the opposite direction of the other guests, scouring the foliage for anything that might resemble a rock mound in the shape of a wolf. Showing she was still aware of her surroundings, Kimberly suddenly giggled as the skipper continued his spiel. There was a lone elephant away from the main pool and he was currently squirting water out of his trunk directly in front of the approaching boat. Just as the boat's bow entered the streaming water and threatened the front passengers, the water stopped and the elephant slowly sank in the green water. Suddenly coming up again, trunk pointed at the boat, the skipper hollered into the microphone, "He's coming up again! Get down, get down! I'm not kidding! I'm not kidding." The elephant apparently had forgotten to reload as the boat continued on its way dry. "Okay, I'm kidding," the skipper told them. When a loud explosion was heard and a huge geyser of water erupted from the middle of the river only a few yards in front of their approaching boat, the skipper exclaimed, "Oooh, that looks dangerous. Let's get closer!"

There were thick bamboo trunks lining the opposite side of the river from where the elephants were. Ferns and palms of various sizes filled in much of the space between the vertical shafts of bamboo that formed a perforated wall that guarded the edge of the river from what lay deeper. A veil of mist enveloped the slow-moving boat, casting the ride in a mysterious, humid pall of vapor.

Just as the boat approached a ruined base camp overrun by chimps who had managed to flip a truck over on its top— "Oh, look, they got the Jeep to turn over" —Kimberly raised her hand just under Lance's face, pointing. "Look, Lance, quick!" she whispered. Through the narrow gap in the bamboo, a gap that was not completely filled in by other shrubbery and trees, a gray rock formation was just barely visible. Through the dense vegetation, the two could make out a dark gray edifice. Standing maybe ten feet tall, it appeared the rock mound was approximately twenty feet into the encroaching jungle. "Do you think that's our El Lobo?" she whispered, her hand dropping unconsciously to Lance's thigh.

Lance leaned toward the middle of the boat, squinting, trying to see through the mist and through sporadic shafts of sunlight finding openings in the canopy of foliage above. The *Kissimmee Kate* continued to follow the curve of the river, heading toward Schweitzer Falls— "named after that famous African explorer Dr. Falls. Don't worry. We'll go over that later." —For a single moment, a larger opening revealed a structure. "I can't tell for sure," Lance replied in hushed excitement. "What do you think? Do we need to ride again?"

"Rats!" she exclaimed as the glimpse disappeared from their view. "I should have brought a camera. Why didn't you remind me?"

"Didn't think of it," Lance shrugged. "Well, let's just ride this one out, and go again."

The boat continued past the jungle veldt scene—"Oh, look! That pride of lions is guarding that sleeping zebra. How sweet. He must be dead tired."—Lance was very aware of her hand that was now resting in her own lap. "So," he started with a slight resignation in his voice, "if that was our El Lobo, how do we get over there?"

The skipper's voice drowned out what Kimberly was going to reply. "Now we are entering a pool of hippopotami. They are only dangerous if they wiggle their ears, submerge under water, and blow bubbles…which is what all of them seem to be doing," as their boat rocked back and forth through the hippo pool. Just then, the skipper fired two shots at a charging hippo—"Don't worry. I wasn't aiming at him. I got the one in the trees…"—the boat turned another wide curve in the river. "Now we are entering headhunter country. It's a terrible place to beheaded…." Everyone's attention in the boat was turned to the clearing of thatched huts and native dancers who were chanting as some of them danced in a tribal circle. "I know their language. Let's see if I can translate for you…." The skipper stopped the boat and leaned forward, intently listening to the chanting. "Uh huh," he muttered, nodding, "uh huh…. Okay, I see…uh huh…. Nope, can't understand a word." With a push of the throttle, the *Kissimmee Kate* surged forward and the passengers were warned of a possible ambush on the right side of the boat. Within seconds, natives armed with spears rose up and threatened them from the left side of the boat.

As Kimberly smiled at the spear-throwing noises the skipper was making into the microphone, Lance excitedly tapped her leg. "Look to the right of the spear guys…. See that hut? Look just behind it. Look at that rocky thing. Quick!"

Turning fast in her seat, Kimberly almost knocked Lance in the face with her elbow.

"Is that what you mean by 'getting even'," he kidded, leaning backwards away from her.

Kimberly ignored his question. "I think I saw something!" she quietly told Lance when she turned back around to sit normally, her eyes shining with excitement. "I think there was something else back there. It was too thick to see clearly. Could it be another El Lobo? Do you think there are two of them? Doesn't that huge bull elephant stand behind those bamboo trees?"

Lance wasn't sure which question to answer first. He counted off on his fingers, "I don't know. Maybe. And, yes, I think so."

Kimberly laughed at his reply. The skipper then announced that they were seeing a sight seldom seen by man: "The Backside of Water, or, as we like to call it—O2H." The boat slid underneath Schweitzer Falls and headed up the Amazon River. Soon the launch was surrounded by churning water and mechanical piranhas went whirling past the boat. The *Kissimmee Kate* made a brief stop next to Trader Sam, the Head Salesman of the Jungle, who hopefully held out a display of shrunken heads toward the boatload of people. The skipper told the guests that he had gone to Sam's for dinner the other night. He remarked to Sam that his wife made a wonderful stew. Sam replied sadly, "Yes, and I'm going to miss her."

Realizing they were getting close to the end of the ride, Lance again voiced his concern about being able to check out either of the possible El Lobos.

Kimberly nodded, recognizing the difficulty of the situation. The first formation they spotted appeared to be on an inside section of the island. However, this lower Manhattan Island was itself directly across from the loading and unloading docks. The upper, smaller Catalina Island with the second possible site, held the African bull elephant and the attacking natives and was out of sight from the mainland. The two islands were separated by a narrow stretch of land and a shallow stream that moved water from one side of the ride to the other, a means of which, Lance had been told, to keep the river flowing in the direction that the boats travel, thus cutting down on the amount of fuel used to motor each launch.

The boat finished its trip by pulling up alongside the unloading dock. "Those of you on the dock side will be helped out by the front of the boat. Those of you on the water side will be helped out by the rear.....of the boat....rear of the boat. Sorry. Unfortunate pause.... Be sure to mind your head and watch your step. But, if you miss your step and hit your head, watch your language.... There are children everywhere!"

"Think they would just let us ride around again?"

Kimberly gave a laugh. "That hasn't happened since I was six! Come on, let's get back in line."

Lance looked over at the Bengal Barbecue. He could smell the tangy aroma of barbecued ribs wafting on the slight breeze. "Lunch?" he asked hopefully.

"Don't make me hurt you!" Kimberly teased, pushing him between the shoulder blades and aiming him toward the tall, boathouse entrance of the ride.

A gray-colored statue sat on the left bank of the river depicting a huge elephant, his trunk held in his hand. "And on your left is Ganesha, the Elephant God, Honorary Preserver of the Sacred Bathing Pool of the Elephants, Guider of all Mystical Beings. And on your right," pointing at an equally large statue of a seated, smiling monkey god holding out a glistening ruby to the passing boat, "is Bob."

Their skipper continued her spiel, pointing out various types of trees and plants by simply pointing at them. As they neared the overrun camp, Lance and Kimberly both turned to scan the opposite bank of the river.

This time, knowing exactly where to look, Kimberly could see what might be described as the 'mouth' of the formation, a rock shape that resembled what Lance had described to her as El Lobo: a wolf-like head with an open mouth that jutted out to the side with smaller, jagged rocks forming what looked a lot like fangs.

"That has to be it," Kimberly whispered, slapping Lance's thigh in confirmation, now looking directly into his eyes as their angle of observation changed and the rock shape was swallowed up again by the foliage around it.

Lance agreed with her. "Yeah, it was a little easier to spot when we knew where to look. Did you see the way the head seemed to be looking right at us? The one in Columbia was just like that. Amazing!"

"So, do you think they will just take us back to the dock now?" she kidded as the boat swept past Schweitzer Falls.

Lance laughed and leaned back, putting his arm behind her on the railing. "Probably not directly, but that's okay. We saw what we needed to see."

Indicating the animal on the left bank, they were informed, "This is the gigantic African Bull Elephant. You can tell by his sloping forehead, huge tusks, and large ears," as the boat glided past the huge animal. "And for those of you with a short-attention span," the skipper told them, now pointing to the right side of the boat, "this is the gigantic African Bull Elephant. You can tell by his sloping forehead, huge tusks, and large ears." The identical twin of the first elephant nodded his head and shook his ears as they went by.

"Now we are in the African Veldt. Our zebras are so old they are still in black and white! There are some gazelles, some giraffes, some lions. Hmm, I don't know what those are. They must be gnu."

As their launch approached the native village, a large painted canoe bobbed in the water. It was filled with sun-bleached skulls. "And here we see an example of native Arts and Crafts. That's Art on top, and the Craft family below!"

Nearing the attacking natives again, Lance and Kimberly became alert, trying to make sure of what they spotted the first time. Zeroed in now, they could make out another open mouth pointing up toward the riverbank through a narrow opening in the trees.

When they pulled up to the unloading dock they were told, "I'd like all of you to exit the boat the same way you came on—pushing, shoving, screaming, scratching, shouting, biting. For those of you who enjoyed the trip, my name is Suzi. For those of you who didn't enjoy the trip, names really aren't important, are they?"

As Lance stood, following Kimberly off the boat, he paused for a moment, looking over the top of the loading dock to where Tarzan's Treehouse stood tall and branched out over part of the Indiana Jones ride queue. He moved toward the exit where Kimberly waited for him under the "Escaping Passengers" exit sign, near the kiosk that sold jungle-themed merchandise and fresh fruit.

"Well, at least we know we have two possible locations. That's good, isn't it?" Kimberly commented as Lance came up to her side. She could see that Lance was thinking about something else. "What is it?" she asked as he moved toward the souvenir stand behind her.

A toy-filled game machine with a crane inside was being manipulated by a young boy trying to capture a stuffed monkey from dozens in the base of the glassed-in enclosure. Lance watched as the crane was positioned over monkey, the steel tips of the claw dropping and closing over the head and ears of the bright red animal.

"I think I have a plan!"

"Kimberly, it is too dangerous. The answer is no!" Lance stressed after taking a sip of iced tea from the tall glass he was holding. They were sitting across from each other at the large hardwood table in the expansive kitchen of Kimberly's house. On the table between them was a large, unfolded souvenir map of Disneyland.

Kimberly frowned as she looked up from the

map. "Lance, I am involved in this as much as you…if not more!" she exclaimed. Her eyes didn't have a pleading look in them but a determined glare. "I *am* going with you."

"But this could get us fired," Lance bluntly pointed out, hoping the possible outcome of what he proposed to do would deter her. To drive the point home more clearly, he amended, "It could get YOU fired."

"It doesn't matter. I have an intimate relationship with this…this…" Kimberly paused, trying to think of the best word to describe what had been her life. "Situation," she ended, shaking her head at the inadequacy of the word. "My father may not have lived long enough to make the decision about your…umm, qualifications for this quest and all the ramifications that go along with it," she explained, then, putting her hands on the table, she leaned over the map to bring her face closer to Lance's, she added resolutely, "But I have."

Lance looked into her eyes, searching for more. He broke eye contact first, looking down, unseeing, at the map. There was something else he needed to ask. "Why didn't your father tell you more about what was going on?" Lance finally asked. It was a question he had wanted to ask her many times since her father died. However, each time the question had come to mind, it had never seemed appropriate to ask something that might be too personal.

"Honestly, Lance," sitting back down, Kimberly sighed, the fire in her eyes dying. "I don't know." She shook her head slowly, thinking back. "He had his reasons, certainly. We did discuss my future. Argued, really. My feeling was that he didn't want me burdened with the same lifetime commitment that he had chosen…or that had chosen him, I guess." Kimberly's eyes looked far away. Lance could tell she was likely thinking about moments in her life with her father. He knew now that her mother had passed away when she was a baby, so Kimberly's only memories were with him. As she got older, she had thought it peculiar that he had never tried to date again, or settle down with another woman. She certainly had seen the interested glances that had been thrown his way by numerous ladies over the years. Recalling when she was a teenager, she began to see her father as secretive, elusive, and, at times, simply gone. One minute he would be in the house, and the next minute she could not find him anywhere. She called it his 'vanishing act,' and he passed off his infrequent vanishings as simply being in a different part of the large mansion they shared. It wasn't until her twentieth birthday that her father began to reveal to her his lot in life; how they had managed to secure such a lavish house; how they never seemed to be short of money; and, tragically, how his heart was failing him day by day. And yet, she had never seen her father work a day in his life. While it didn't seem to be such an unfortunate or arduous 'lot in life,' there always seemed to be a weight on her father. He had seemed very frugal and resourceful, literally teaching his only child through his actions—and very few words—that everything worth having was worth working hard to obtain.

It wasn't until she was older still that she

learned that he was "The Guardian." But, to this day, she had never been under the Pirates ride to actually see where Walt was being kept. She had only seen the room through the video monitors that her father had kept faithful sentry over for the last forty years in his secret War Room, as he had always called it.

Lance interrupted her thoughts. "Well, it would appear your father was intent on keeping something very safe," he said, leaning back against the chair. "After seeing the machine with Walt inside, I always assumed that HE was the secret." Lance paused, frowning. "Which, I guess, in and of itself, is indeed a BIG secret." He let himself lean forward again, back to the table, grabbing his nearly-empty glass. Tilting back his head, he finished off his tea, letting the ice cubes clink against his lips before setting the glass down on the edge of the table. He looked directly into Kimberly's eyes. "But I can't help believing that there is something going on here that is deeper, more significant, and, perhaps, more elusive than even knowing this secret of where Walt is."

"Yes," she affirmed. "Yes, and that's why I need to go with you, Lance. You and I might not be the only two living people that know about Walt, but we are probably the only ones who realize there must be something more significant than just his discovery." Kimberly frowned for a moment. "I just wish we knew what that 'something more' was that we are searching for."

"What about Crain?" Lance asked, saying his name as if it left a bad taste in his mouth. "Didn't your father reveal anything to him? I mean, how long has Daniel been his...what, assistant? He carries himself as if he has the full assurance of stepping into your father's shoes."

Kimberly scrunched up her nose. "Daniel Crain...is my uncle."

That caught Lance by surprise. "Really."

Kimberly nodded. "Yep. My mother's brother. Remember I told you we were related?"

"Yeah, I remember, but I thought you were kidding."

"Unfortunately, no, I wasn't. Actually, Daniel is my only living relative. When Mom died, he asked Dad for a job, so he reluctantly made Daniel his chauffer and gave him a suite of rooms over the garage. You know—close but not too close."

Lance thought for a minute. "That would explain why he has the run of the house and considers himself the 'Heir Apparent.' You don't seem to like him very much," Lance observed, and then added, "Heck, I don't like him very much."

"He is...hmmm, how should I put this? A pest? No, he is an annoying pest," she amended.

Lance grinned. "That seems an apt description. I would have to agree."

"I don't know," she sighed. "I never got the idea that Dad completely trusted him or really considered Daniel a viable candidate. For instance, he never allowed Daniel into the War Room. I just think Dad felt he owed it to my mother after she died...to take him in. But, then, Dad didn't really trust anyone." She paused for a moment and pursed her lips in frustration. "Heck, he didn't even trust me totally. Look at everything I don't know about what's going on!"

Lance shook his head. "I don't know if it was from a lack of trust or from a sincere desire to protect you…. But, it all leads me to believe that there is something far more complex at stake here…something that is so important that your father felt he couldn't even tell you about it." As Lance got up and walked around to her side of the table, he pointed to the map. "And whatever that complication is will become either more complicated or less once we find what is out there on the Jungle Cruise." His finger jabbed at the illustration of the ride on the unfolded map.

"And, like I said, I am going with you," stated Kimberly, poking the map right where Lance's finger had been.

Lance took a deep breath while slowly shaking his head. He let out that breath in a resigned exhale. "Kimberly…," he paused, looking away from her insistent, stubborn look. "Okay, okay." He thought back to what he, Beth and Adam had done following Walt's clues not so long ago. "I remember what Walt had written in his diary: *Two heads are better than one*…. Okay, we will do this together."

Kimberly said nothing, but let the expression on her face reveal her feelings.

On seeing her satisfied smile, Lance added, "Besides, I do believe I will need someone to help me carry out what I am planning to do. And I certainly do not want to ask Crain."

The following day, Lance went to an Army-Navy surplus store in Fullerton to purchase the items he had written down on a notepad. Going over the list yet again, he hoped he hadn't forgotten anything. He also hoped the two of them would not be faced with some situation that he had not anticipated.

The next morning, Lance picked Kimberly up at her house and drove her to Disneyland. Both of them had shifts to work; they had made shift-changes with a couple of fellow cast members so they would be able to be on stage, or working, at the same time. Kimberly was again going to be Belle from *Beauty and the Beast* during her shift. Lance was glad to be back at work and was on what was commonly called Fox Patrol—a plain-clothes, undercover position to observe people who might be inclined to shoplift in some of the stores where such activity regularly occurred and to look for pick-pockets who sometimes see the Park as valuable hunting grounds.

Walking together toward Disneyland's Harbor House, the small building that held the cast member's time cards and where the employees needed to flash their ID's to the security guard stationed at the entrance, Kimberly felt her heartbeat speed up as they got closer. Even though she had passed through the security checkpoint hundreds of times over the last couple of years working at the Park, this time was different—she had an ulterior motive. True, she was coming in to work a normal eight hour shift, but she—and Lance—were also coming in to do something that would most likely get them fired. And her father was no longer there to fix it for her. There was a lot at stake.

"I think we should hold hands," Lance suggested as they crossed the short-term parking entrance next to the Park that separated the employee parking area from the employee entrance. Kimberly looked at Lance with a 'what-on-earth-for?' expression.

"Really, Kimberly. I think it will make us look less suspicious—especially with me carrying my backpack."

"Okay," she reluctantly agreed. At the moment, she was more mindful of her hand feeling clammy due to the tension building in her mind than the idea of just holding Lance's hand. She held her right hand out and Lance slipped his hand into hers, interlocking his fingers with hers as if the two were a romantically-involved couple. Kimberly felt a sudden sense of security in the simple grasp of his hand, the feeling that she wasn't in this all alone. She looked down at their hands for a moment and then looked up at Lance's face.

Unlike what she felt she must look like—'guilty' was the term that was echoing in her head—Lance, on the other hand, looked completely at ease as they stepped over the curb in front of the landing where the security guard was looking over employee identification cards.

"Hey, Paul," Lance greeted, letting go of Kimberly's hand to offer a casual salute to the security guard who was standing at the entrance to Harbor House. Lance reached his left hand into his back pocket and pulled out his wallet, flipping easily to his Disneyland ID card in a clear plastic holder opposite his driver's license.

"What's up, Lance?" Paul returned with a smile, barely glancing at Lance's ID card. Kimberly had her card out and drew a broader grin from the security guard. Lance had positioned Kimberly between him and the guard for two reasons: One, her position would better shield his backpack from the guard's notice. Two, with Kimberly's good looks, Lance was sure that Paul would be eyeing her more than him. Kimberly had worn a pair of white corduroy shorts, a pale blue button-down, sleeveless blouse, and tennis shoes with low-cut socks that accentuated her long, tan legs. Lance smiled smugly to himself as Paul gave Kimberly a second, more lingering look. Lance had prepared some sandwiches and chips along with some granola bars that topped the large zippered section of his backpack, just in case the guard wanted to check the contents of the bag. It was only purely random that the guards would inspect employee bags, and such checks were cursory at best. The main contraband smuggled into the Park by a tiny minority of workers was alcohol. However, because of the zero tolerance for such actions by the Park Administration, such attempts by workers were a good example of Russian roulette; anyone caught with alcohol was immediately terminated.

Lance had timed their entrance into Harbor House so that they were in front of a group of other employees coming in to work. Lance figured Paul would need to move his attention quickly from them to checking the ID's of those coming in behind them. He was correct as Paul gave no notice to his backpack and was already busy with the new arrivals as Lance and Kimberly moved down the walkway to the Harbor House entrance door.

Kimberly let out an audible sigh, an obvious release from holding her breath, once they were safely in the timecard room, moving to their respective sections where their individual timecards would be. A handful of other cast members were moving in the opposite direction, clocking out after their own late-night shifts. Most of these individuals were maintenance or janitorial staff members who spend most of the early morning hours working at getting the Park ready for a new day of guests—from painting to washing walkways to gardening to replacing burnt-out light bulbs. It took literally an army to maintain Disneyland to the standards Walt's legacy would demand.

"That was easy," Lance proclaimed with a grin when Kimberly joined him again. He had felt the tension in her hand when they had approached the security checkpoint. Lance's other excursions with Adam and, later, with Beth when they had originally searched for Walt's clues had seasoned Lance for such situations. Not to mention that he was naturally very easy-going and very little seemed to faze his demeanor.

"Maybe for you! My heart is still pounding!" exclaimed Kimberly, holding her hand to her chest.

Lance resisted asking her if he could feel her heart pounding too. In fact, something about Kimberly was making Lance act like a true gentleman. Maybe this was how Adam felt all the time, Lance thought to himself as he waited for Kimberly to punch her timecard in ahead of him. Lance was normally gallant to the ladies, but...there was something special about Kimberly that made him hold his tongue where he might have been suggestively teasing. His mother would have definitely approved.

Together they walked down the sloping walkway that took workers under the train trestle of the Disneyland Railroad, the large steam train that circled the Park...the same train that Adam had jumped from in one of the caves along the loop that had held one of Walt's capsules left decades before. Walking under the train track marked an invisible point of reference that most employees recognized as the point that they were now officially IN Disneyland. For many, it was the very spot where they went from being 'employees' to becoming 'cast members'...a label that dated back to Walt Disney and his intention of Disneyland being a 'show' and that all his employees were indeed 'cast members' of that show.

As they came up from the dip under the tracks, Lance turned to Kimberly. "You are doing great. Don't worry about a thing," Lance smiled at her. It was his best and most sincere smile. And, at that moment, one he didn't have to fake. "I am really glad you are doing this with me." He paused, wanting to say more, but hesitating. "Have a great day being Belle. I'll meet you after work in the Inn Between." The Inn Between was one of the two full-service cast member restaurants inside Disneyland. It was situated literally between the 'off-stage' portions of Disneyland with cast member locker rooms and many of the main administration offices—places that few Disney-land guests were allowed to see—and the 'on-stage' portion of Disneyland. Hence the name Inn Between.

"Okay, Lance. Thanks." Kimberly smiled back at Lance. She was still thinking about his hand that she had been holding as they crossed to the entrance of Harbor House. "See you at dinner."

Kimberly turned to go upstairs into the women's locker room. Lance was still standing at the base of the stairs watching her. Feeling his eyes on her, Kimberly turned back to him. "What!?"

"Oh, well, it's just that the real adventure is still to come!"

"Thanks for reminding me."

"Not a problem. That's why I am here."

Kimberly shook her head. "What am I getting myself into?" she asked out loud with a resigned laugh and moved on up the stairs.

Lance smiled back at her and turned toward the men's locker room just adjacent to the women's. He was still thinking about Kimberly and looked down at his left hand, flexing his fingers for a moment, the memory of holding her hand still fresh in his mind.

"What am I getting myself into?" he murmured out loud to himself, adjusting the straps of his heavy backpack.

Lance, now waiting in his street clothes just outside the Inn Between entrance, had seen Kimberly heading toward the restaurant from the locker rooms. He waited as she walked up to the curved, dark green canvas awning that identified the entrance. The restaurant was next to the building that housed the Star Tours ride. The eatery had been there for well over forty years and had been remodeled and redecorated dozens of times over the course of its history. But, the food had always remained extremely reasonable for the cast members and actually had a good variety of items for nearly every palate.

It was just after eight p.m. and the evening crowd inside was light. Dozens of empty tables filled the room and two televisions with closed-captioning were on, one showing a baseball game, the other a nightly news program.

"How was your day, Belle?" he asked. He had even walked over to Fantasyland during his breaks to watch her interact with the guests, mainly children, from a distance. With her lovely gold, off-the-shoulder gown and her brown-haired wig, Kimberly was indeed a striking Belle. He noticed this time that her character was not just appealing to the kids who lined up for pictures and autographs. Lance had smiled when he noticed how many of the dads were not too shy about getting their picture taken with the lovely Kimberly, even to the point of forgetting to include their own children in the picture!

"It was just a beast," she kidded, playing off the cliché of the movie title, as Lance held the door open for her. They quickly ordered dinner with Lance gallantly paying for both meals. They found a quiet table away from the televisions and the few employees who were also eating a late dinner.

"Well, eat up," Lance told her as he took a sip of the hot coffee he had gotten for himself. "Tonight will be a long night."

Kimberly took a dainty bite of the pasta she had ordered. "You haven't exactly described the whole plan to me. Just what exactly will we be doing later tonight?"

"Well," Lance started, "have you seen the movie *Cliff Hanger*?"

"Stallone?" she asked, trying to remember if that was the actor who starred in it.

"Yep."

"If I remember, they did a lot of mountain climbing with ropes."

Lance smiled. "That they did."

CHAPTER 8

The Park didn't close until midnight. After dinner, Lance and Kimberly went to clock out, but instead of heading to the parking lot, they blended in with employees coming on for their night shifts and returned to the backstage area of the Park.

Leaving his backpack in his locker, Lance and Kimberly reentered the Park, this time as guests. They just strolled along the beautifully manicured gardens at the Hub in front of Sleeping Beauty's Castle, taking in the late sunset that cast a warm glow against the pastel-colored storefronts that lined Main Street, and enjoying the sights and sounds of people around them, just like everyone else was doing.

Lance did have a destination in mind. "I think I need to see something," he told her as they walked through the arched entrance to Adventureland. They then passed the Enchanted Tiki Room, a show that Kimberly had many fond memories of as a child; the South Pacific-themed attraction that featured singing birds, flowers and even tiki poles. It always made her think of the few family vacations taken with her father, once to Hawaii and once to the Cook Islands…places she would later learn had more to do with Walt Disney than just being family getaways.

A large group of people exiting the Tiki Room forced everyone to walk closer together within that narrow walkway. Lance squeezed in closer to Kimberly for a moment, his arm pressing against her side, as they slowed within the slew of people trying to disperse to other areas of the Park. He didn't seem to pay any attention to the physical contact, but Kimberly was very much aware of his arm brushing against her.

"Where are we headed, Lance?" she asked as the crowd finally thinned and they were now walking freely past the Jungle Cruise. Kimberly began to mentally drift back to when they were sitting 'cheek to cheek' on those wooden seats of those little boats, close enough to feel the physical heat radiate from one another. Lance's answer brought her out of her daydream.

"I want to see Tarzan's Treehouse," he explained, pointing up ahead of them to the incredibly large simulated tree that originally had been the home of the Swiss Family Robinson clan and built after the popular Disney film of the same name.

Gone was the *Swisska Polka* that was the featured song of the Treehouse. Before, the song had easily permeated the area around the Treehouse, often creating a subconscious beat in the heads of those who strolled through the surrounding areas of the Pirates of the Caribbean and the

Jungle Cruise. Now relegated to dim background music, the polka played occasionally on a gramophone set up in the lower area of the Treehouse. The attraction was now themed to match a more-recent animated feature, *Tarzan*.

"The Treehouse? I thought we needed to get to the Jungle Cruise."

"We do," Lance told her as he led her by the arm to the side of the walkway just before reaching the entrance stairs to the Treehouse, out of the stream of traffic. "Unfortunately," he quietly explained, "the island section of the Jungle Cruise that we need to get to is across the ride's river flume…a flume that is about three feet deep in the middle. While I suspect you would look fabulous all wet, I don't think we want to be explaining to anyone why we are both soaking wet."

Kimberly slightly blushed at his smiling comment of how she might look in wet clothes, but she recovered quickly and nodded. "So, what do you suggest as an alternative to getting wet?"

"I'll tell you once we are up in the Treehouse."

It was past midnight when Lance had returned to his locker to retrieve his backpack. Kimberly met him once again at the entrance to the Inn Between again. She had put on a dark windbreaker over her blouse, even though the summer night—or early morning as it had become—was most pleasant.

"Ready?" Lance asked her, opening up the opportunity for her to back out of the plan.

"I think so," was the reply, her eyes revealing

some trepidation.

Lance took her by the shoulders and looked into her eyes. "Kimberly, we don't have to do this."

She looked down at her feet for a moment, and then brought her eyes up to his. "Actually, yes, we do."

His smile was to encourage her. "Everything will be all right."

She gave a wan smile back, keeping silent. *I hope so*, she thought to herself. *I hope so*.

Directly across from the backstage location of the Inn Between was the entrance to Adventureland. Between these two points was the Central Plaza of the north Main Street Hub, the part of the Park where guests would decide which Land they would explore. Lance and Kimberly walked casually across the hub toward Adventureland. With the Park now closed, a large number of guests who had stayed until the very last minute of the normal operating hours were heading south down Main Street; many families with children in strollers who were sound asleep, teenagers holding hands, kids with Mickey balloons…and there they were, Lance and Kimberly walking diagonally across the Hub against the flow of guests who were heading for the exit.

As they entered Adventureland, they passed the safari-themed gift shops opposite the Jungle Cruise exit gate. There was a handful of guests still busy picking out last minute souvenirs while cast members were getting the stores ready for inventory, straightening merchandise, or moving misplaced items to their proper places.

After passing the silent queue area for the

Jungle Cruise, the two reached the Treehouse where Lance looked up at the angle of the large, simulated branches that hung well out from the massive trunk. From his research, Lance knew the incredibly life-like tree was made out of six tons of steel, over a hundred cubic yards of concrete artistically contoured and etched to look just like bark, branches and limbs, and over 300,000 handmade vinyl leaves and blossoms. The Treehouse was now illuminated by the ancient-looking lanterns that lined the wooden walkways that were built into the attraction to allow guests to move fairly easily up and down the one hundred thirty-three stair-steps.

Looking up through the leaves, Lance could see one of the huts that was one of the rooms of the Treehouse. It was shaped like the bow of a ship with two extending arms, transoms from a sea-going vessel, which held a small lifeboat off to the side of the hut. Higher up, more out of sight from the ground, was the second of the three huts. This one was positioned well out from the main core of the tree and literally sat over the edge of the narrow entrance queue to the neighboring Indiana Jones attraction. As they walked past Indy's truck parked in the viewing area, Lance could now see the dark green, and now silent, water of the Jungle Cruise. Looking up he also spotted some lights coming from inside one of the open-air windows of the hut, and just then he got an idea.

"Follow me," he whispered, conspiratorially.

He had seen that the front, main stair entrance to the Treehouse was blocked off for the night. Sitting literally in the middle of the Adventureland walkway, it was in open view. The exit to the attraction, however, was back off to the left, with its flagstone walkways and bubbling stream that fed into the Jungle Cruise river at some point. The exit had a fence surrounding it to deter people from sneaking into the attraction after the front had been closed off un-ceremonially by a large trashcan set inside the turnstile. While it was effective in keeping the children from darting in late at night, it now proved to be a deterrent to the two adults who wanted to do just that.

Lance and Kimberly followed the fence around to where it melded with a wall that both marked the beginning of New Orleans Square and housed the Pirates of the Caribbean attraction. He found a place where the wall could be climbed with minimal difficulty. The decorative iron bars that connected the fence to the wall would become a foot hold. Peering through the fencing, he could see a relatively flat area of shredded bark that would soften a landing from the top of the fence. Looking around again, he noticed that they were now in what Security commonly called a 'shadow zone'—an area of the Park that was not lit at night. Shadow zones were popular areas for amorous couples who wanted to spend some 'quality time' together without people easily seeing them. Lance gave a brief grin. His partner and fellow security guard, Wolf, could always ferret out these couples! It was like Wolf had a sixth sense.

"Here," Lance set his backpack down and motioned for Kimberly. "I'm going to give you a boost. Put your hands on the wall where the fence is attached to it. Lift your leg over the top and drop down into that flat area." After a last look around to make sure no one was close by, he linked his fingers together.

Kimberly didn't reveal her uncertainty. She just put her left hand on the top of the fence and her right hand on Lance's shoulder. She hesitated for a moment. "How about you? How are you going to get over?"

"Don't worry," he winked at her. "I think I've got it figured out."

Kimberly shrugged her shoulders and put her right foot in Lance's hands. He easily boosted her so she was able to throw her left leg over the top of the iron fence. She moved her right hand off Lance and braced herself on the wall with it. In one fluid motion, she swung herself over the top of the fence and dropped lightly to the ground with a soft thud. She landed with her feet close together and didn't even have to grab the fence for balance.

Watching her through the fence, Lance was surprised. "You should have been a gymnast," he whispered, after seeing her land. He almost expected her to raise her arms up as he had seen Olympians do after sticking a similar landing.

"I did take two years of gymnastics as a kid," she said with a hint of pride.

"Hmmm, I'll have to remember that," Lance chuckled.

After again checking for any passers-by, Lance handed his backpack over the fence. He then grabbed the top of the fence with one hand, the top of the wall with his other, and put a foot on the little foothold he had spotted. "Heads up," he softly called. "I'm coming over." He heard Kimberly take a couple of steps back. Pushing with his one foot, he used his hands and arms to lift himself with one easy move, launched his feet over the fence like a pummel horse competitor, and landed nearly in the exact footprints left by Kimberly. Unlike Kimberly, Lance took the opportunity to show off a little by raising his hands as he landed.

"Three years gymnastics," he whispered to her as she handed him the backpack.

Adjusting the straps across his back, she replied with just a gentle touch of sarcasm, "I'm suitably impressed with your strength and agility."

Lance laughed quietly, not completely sure if she was truly impressed or just making fun of him. "Thanks. I honestly didn't think my gymnastic training would have adult applications.... I guess I was wrong!"

The two of them glanced through the fence one last time for any observers. Not only was it extremely dark in this portion of Disneyland, but traditionally, this was often the most quiet part of the Park even before closing.

Since the exit of the Treehouse was at a higher elevation than the walkway through Adventureland, they now could use the rockwork of the retaining wall to climb into that section. Wading through ferns and flowers and careful not to step on any of the plants, they easily hopped over the narrow, bubbling stream. Lance helped Kimberly over the wood-rail fence that marked the guests' boundary leading into the laboratory section the Treehouse on ground level. Here, during the day, kids could find pots and pans to bang with metal spoons, ropes to climb that would make Sabor the Leopard scream high above, and plenty of hiding places to avoid their parents. As they walked past the kitchen area and its silent gramophone, they came to the first—or actually, the last—landing of stairs in the Treehouse since they had entered through the exit portion of the walk-through attraction. Once they got up to this small section of stairs that was well hidden behind the massive tree trunk, they would now be out in the open, so to speak, and visible from below should anyone be there to look upwards.

"Crawl through this section," Lance whispered, kneeling down. "The rails should hide us until we reach that hut, but take it slow and easy."

Following suit, Kimberly followed him across the twenty feet or so of the wooden planks, being very careful not to scrape their feet.

They were now at the lowest hut, completely protected on all sides by a lovely thatched porch. Inside were two sections—the ship's wheel sitting in a dark-paned window with various nautically-themed knickknacks, and the hut itself which held the figures of Jane and Tarzan as she was sketching him. During the day, a large animation pad on the back wall would show the sketch using an image from a hidden projector as it progressed until it was a full image of Tarzan.

"We need to get up there," Lance pointed, helping Kimberly to her feet. He pointed to the next, even higher hut. There was more cover up there, both from all the leaves of the tree and the sheer height of where they would be. It would now be easier traveling for them.

She followed his pointing finger. "Isn't that the master bedroom?" Kimberly asked. Even in the darkness Lance could make out a look of suspicion on her face.

"Well, as a matter of fact, it is," Lance admitted. "It is also the closest place to the Jungle Cruise."

"Uh huh…."

"Really, Kimberly," Lance said, spreading his arms. "Oh, come on…you think….?"

She folded her arms over her chest. "I know you, Lance."

"You know the old Lance."

She relented a little. "Well, you have been a total gentleman," Kimberly admitted, then added under her breath, "so far."

"I guess you will just have to trust me."

"Famous last words," she said, putting her hands on his hips and turning him around away from her. She gave a little shove toward the next flight of stairs. "Just keep moving, Tarzan."

"Yes, Jane."

As they continued their climb, they came to an observation platform. Pausing for a minute, secure in the abundance of leaves and tree limbs around them, they could see a nearly-full moon cresting over the top of the Pirates of the Caribbean building, past the black Jolly Roger flag blowing in the slight breeze. They could easily make out the tall masts of the Columbia Sailing Ship in its dock at Fowler's Harbor to the west and the outline of the red rocks of Big Thunder Mountain to the north. If it wasn't for the fact that what they were doing could get them fired, or the unanswered questions in their minds about what they might find, Lance and Kimberly would otherwise have recognized the night as simply a beautiful, balmy Southern California night.

Turning away from the sight, intent on their mission, they came to the second hut, the main room that once had been the master bedroom of the Mother and Father of the *Swiss Family Robinson*. Now it was home to a touching scene of the baby Tarzan being held by his adoptive mother, the gorilla Kala, as they watched scenes of his life play on a movie screen.

The topmost hut was depicted as being in ruins with the rouge leopard Sabor perched in the bamboo rafters and ready to pounce on anyone who came near. Lance knew there was no room in that hut to hide, and, besides, it was too far away from where they needed to be.

Lance set down his backpack as Kimberly looked over the scene. He reached in through the narrow window and bamboo bars that kept people from getting inside the hut. He found what he was looking for: a special latch that had a secret release button. While a lock could have been installed for the maintenance workers to use when having to clean or service the equipment in the hut, the use of such devices were more advantageous since using locks would have required dozens of keys for all the workers who would need access. Using a secret button that was hidden on a flat back portion of the door, guests, in all likelihood, would not even realize there was an access door, let alone a means with which to open it. With a click, the latch was released and the frame holding the bamboo shafts over the top of the window now swung open like a door.

"I'm impressed. You know any other secrets?" Kimberly asked as he began to step up and over the sill of the window.

"Well," Lance began, between grunts in trying to get his leg over and through the window. It was way too small for his six-foot-two-inch frame to squeeze through. "I have a feeling that when this is all over, you will probably know more about me than my own mother and father."

Kimberly, seeing the problem he was having, grabbed his foot and shoved him through the window opening.

He tumbled into the hut with a small thud. Being so high in the tree and surrounded by concrete and vinyl, they hoped the sound wouldn't carry too far.

Before Kimberly could start climbing over the sill, Lance suddenly saw through the loosely-fitting floor boards of the hut a bright beam of light that flickered somewhere below them.

"Get down on the plank!" Lance hissed from inside the hut. "Scrunch up as close as you can on that platform in front of here. Hurry!"

They could see the light shining on the opposite side of the tree from where they were, being tracked back and forth in a search pattern and was now coming toward the higher part of the Treehouse. The beam would flicker as it was caught between branches and leaves, and they could barely make out the outline of the person who was shining the light along the various walkways and stairs.

It was a strong bluish-white beam, one Lance immediately recognized as a standard Security issue Mag light—a four-cell rechargeable one that Lance would carry on his person when he was working as a closing shift guard.

The light was coming toward them now; Lance could barely see through the bamboo walls of the hut. He had already closed the window when he first spotted the light shining below them. Outside the hut, Kimberly lay motionless, afraid to move, even to breathe.

The beam followed the planks right to where Kimberly lay, moving along the far edge of the platform toward the edge that dropped into the Indy ride below. She watched in fear as the white light slowly edged along the floor. Pulling her body in tight so no part of her would be visible around the corner of the platform, she saw the light edge even closer to the tips of her shoes.

The light was now within inches of her shoe and then started a slow sweep back in the direction from which it came. Apparently the guard didn't want to make that last, high climb to the topmost hut. When the light was no longer visible, Kimberly sagged in relief and allowed herself to slowly exhale the breath she had been holding.

The two silently remained motionless for another two minutes. Kimberly finally took a hesitant peek over the edge of the platform, through the rails and could see that guard now moving inside the FastPass area for Indy. He then headed through the queue area and across the dock of the Jungle Cruise.

Slowly Kimberly stood up, her legs trembling and her heart still pounding. As she leaned into the window, she looked down at Lance who was now sitting up against the far wall with a big grin on his face. He unlatched the lock again and motioned for her to quickly come in through the window. He scooted over to where Kala and the baby Tarzan were as she leaned in and tried to step over the open frame. Lance took hold of her hand to help, but her toe caught on the bottom edge of the railing as she tried to clear her foot. Losing her balance, Kimberly fell forward against Lance who put out his other hand and caught her. The momentum caused him to fall backwards onto the thin carpet inside the hut, pulling her on top of him as he fell to cushion her fall.

Lance let out a grunt as the force of her body landed on his stomach. Kimberly, still scared of being heard or discovered, lay motionless on top of him, her hands still interlocked with his, her face buried in the crook of his neck.

Suddenly, she started to giggle, her body trembling as she lay on top of Lance.

"Shh!" Lance warned, and then suddenly started to giggle himself at the predicament they found themselves in. After the tense moments with that security guard before and now laying in that awkward position, they found themselves having a difficult time containing their emotions.

Kimberly lifted her face from Lance's neck and looked at his contorted face from just a few inches away. Air was slipping out of Lance's mouth as he tried to refrain from laughing. Kimberly let go of his hand and covered his mouth, which didn't help him at all from trying not to laugh. She was now laughing through her nose, trying desperately not to make any sound. Lance took his now-free hand and put his finger on Kimberly's lips.

In that moment, as Lance looked at Kimberly in the darkness, his laughing subsided and he just stared. He was very aware of her hand on his mouth and his finger against her lips and her body lying on top of him.

Kimberly felt herself being drawn into Lance's mesmerizing eyes. Her giggling stopped.

Suddenly, she rolled to her side, off of Lance and onto her knees. Her voice was a little strained. "Okay…what is your plan from here on out?" she asked as she felt her cheeks flush and heard her heart pound in her chest.

Their sudden change in position surprised Lance. A look of hurt passed over his face. Then, remembering why they were there, he recovered and quickly got to his feet, clearing his throat. "Well, since maintenance works on the ride from closing to about three a.m., I guess we sit up here and wait." Lance reached behind him for his backpack and unzipped the top, larger pocket. "I've got dinner, Madame." He glanced at his Rolex—one of his last luxury items he hadn't had to sell yet. The time was twelve-fifty in the morning. "I mean breakfast," he clarified with a grin.

Kimberly was suddenly very hungry. Perhaps from nerves. Perhaps from the raw emotion she had just felt. She was glad to have something to do with her hands. Lance handed her one of the two ham sandwiches he had packed. The sandwiches had been on top of a frozen Blue Ice bag, now no longer frozen but still cold. He reached into a side pocket and pulled out a thermos that matched the backpack.

"Thanks," Kimberly said as he handed her a sandwich. "I'm starving."

"If you don't mind sharing my germs," started Lance. He then paused while thinking about her lips again. "I've got some iced tea and one cup...well, minus the ice now," he amended after peering into the cup.

After a couple of minutes of silence while they ate and shared the one cup, Kimberly had a question as she handed the cup back to Lance. "So, what happens after maintenance wraps up at three?"

"Do you know what a zip line is?"

The question surprised her. It wasn't what she expected. "Yes. I rode one in Jamaica when my dad and I took a cruise together."

Lance lifted his eyebrow. "Really? For some reason I can't picture your father taking time off for anything, let alone a Caribbean cruise."

Kimberly smiled, remembering the trip. "Well, it was for my twentieth birthday. In fact, it was on that cruise that my father told me about Walt and about his role as the Guardian."

"Wow," he muttered, pouring more tea in the cup and holding it out to her. "How did you take that wee bit of news?"

"It was a relief in some ways," she admitted, taking the cup. She took a sip, pausing, as she looked over the rim of the cup. "I knew something was...different about Dad. You can't hide from family something like what my father has done for forty years and not raise some questions." Kimberly paused again, thinking.

Lance remained quiet as she sorted out her thoughts. He could see her eyes in the dim lights that were part of the Treehouse lighting system. It was a soft glow that permeated through the windows of the hut. It wasn't enough light to illuminate any colors in the small room, but Lance could see the emotions in Kimberly's eyes.

"I had no idea of the magnitude of what he was doing, of course. He filled me in only to the point of his relationship with Walt back in the early 1960's. You see, Dad had been working on some experimental cryogenics with some partners I never knew. He left the business when Walt Disney approached him with his incredible idea," Kimberly explained. "Dad told me that he was hired as a 'sub-contractor'." She gave a small smile as she looked at Lance. "Yeah, he wasn't really a sub-contractor working for WED Enterprises. He answered only to Walt and all the managers of Disneyland knew that Dad was not to be questioned the few times he appeared at the Park during the construction of New Orleans Square."

The pieces were starting to fall into place for Lance now. He nodded his understanding. "So your dad was able to install the subterranean machine in the Park under the guise of being part of the project Walt had designed and was building."

"And all the tanks that he figured he would need for a long time in...hibernation."

"How long did he plan for the tanks to keep Walt suspended?" Lance wanted to know.

"Dad said he estimated seventy-five years, provided everything worked correctly." Kimberly took another bite of her sandwich. "He was able to monitor everything from the house. So far, from what I understand, most everything has been working exactly the way my father designed it to work. There are back-up systems in place, too, just in case there is a loss of power to the Park."

She could tell Lance was impressed.

Lance thought back to the night he discovered Walt—the night Kimberly's father pointed a gun at him. That seemed a lifetime ago. "You should have seen my face when I looked in that contraption and saw Walt's face staring back at me," he said with a small laugh.

"I'll bet."

"Of course, you don't want to know what I was thinking when your dad pointed that .44 Magnum at my forehead!"

"Ah, Lance, I am so sorry." Kimberly was sincerely upset by what he must have been put through.

He waved her off. "No, no. It was...." He paused, and looked away. "I guess you could call it karma that someone else had a gun pointed at me," thinking back to when he had pulled a gun on his two best friends. *Former best friends*, he corrected to himself.

"Well, I know that if you weren't there when my dad died, you wouldn't have known to open that envelope." Kimberly stopped. "In fact," she added, "I honestly don't know what I would have done if Dad had just told me that something was missed along the way. I know one thing, though. I would not have trusted Daniel Crain." She shook her head. "I honestly would not put anything past him, uncle or no uncle. He just creeps me out."

Lance poured the last of the tea and held it out.

"No, go ahead. I'm fine," Kimberly said, holding up her hand. She didn't want to have to try and sneak into a Ladies Room any time soon....

Lance took the final sip. "Well," as he wiped his lips with the back of his hand, "all I know is that I've gone from feeling like I had missed the boat to now becoming the captain." He smiled, even as he secretly hoped he was not becoming captain of the *Titanic*. He brushed off the thought and then looked at Kimberly. "I'm glad we are on this little adventure together."

Kimberly could feel her heart skip a beat. She didn't say it, but she was glad too.

As it approached three in the morning, Kimberly awoke, startled at her unfamiliar surroundings. She had fallen asleep after the sandwich she had eaten, and was even more startled to look up into the face of Lance...finding his lap had been her pillow.

"Where...What?" Kimberly said groggily, lifting her head from his thigh.

"Good morning, Sleeping Beauty," Lance said, smiling as she got up half way, leaning on her outstretched arm. "Good timing, too. It is just after three a.m. and we have a lot of work to do."

Kimberly sat up and rubbed her eyes. She felt like she had sandpaper on the inside of each eyelid. "I guess I fell asleep."

"It's fine. You needed the rest and I guess I was a reasonable facsimile of a pillow," Lance replied, smiling at the sleepy look that was etched across her face. *Dang, she looks good at three in the morning,* Lance thought to himself.

"I assume we are still undiscovered?"

"Yes, and it is very quiet on the western front."

Kimberly looked toward Jungle Cruise. "I believe that is the south eastern front."

Lance chuckled. "That's why I brought you along. I'd probably end up on the roof of Pirates of the Caribbean if it weren't for you."

"I try."

Lance quietly went out the window of the hut, slipped on the backpack being held out by Kimberly, and walked around toward the back of the platform where a large, sturdy branch, at least eighteen inches in diameter, jutted out from under the foundation of the elevated hut. The branch, obviously a large camouflaged scaffolding structure for that section of the tree, was in turn supported by a vertical column of vines that was designed to conceal a steel shaft running straight down to the ground. He went over the rail that surrounded the walkway of hut and stood on the branch. Overhead he found small branches that he could grasp for balance as he walked toward the outer portion of the tree. There was a fairly large opening that allowed him to have a clear view over the middle part of Indiana Jones queue area and into part of the Jungle Cruise.

Kimberly waited and watched at the rail, keeping a lookout for anyone who might be walking below the tree. They were both well-protected from sight by the darkness as well as the layers of branches and leaves that went out in all directions below them. It was sound that was their enemy now.

Lance moved to the section of the branch that he felt was far enough out for what he had in mind. The branch had tapered down to about ten inches in diameter and Lance could have gone out a few more feet. However, that position where he stopped offered a clear shot to a large Magnolia tree opposite them. The tree was directly across the Indy queue area and the Jungle Cruise River after the boats had left the loading dock and headed into the so-called 'uncharted territory' of the ride. The tree he picked out was at the edge of the Manhattan Island portion of the Jungle Cruise ride. Lance worked his way down into a sitting position, straddling the branch between both legs. He slowly pulled the backpack off his shoulders and was able to rest it next to him by putting the straps through another sturdy branch that poked out of the one he was sitting on.

Unzipping the top pocket where their sandwiches had been stashed, Lance pulled out an aluminum shoulder bracket that looked like a futuristic rifle stock. Reaching back into the pack, he brought out a sleek, black, metal barrel that he screwed into the stock, making the contraption resemble an underwater spear-gun. Lance attached a black strap to both ends of the gun and placed the device around his neck.

Reaching into the pack again, Lance pulled out a pointed arrow-shaped spear that was about an inch in diameter and about a foot-and-a-half long. Lance tested the device by pushing the tip of it against a branch next to him. With a muted zinging sound, the arrow sprung open and three foot-long arms branched out from the tip, forming a grappling hook. Satisfied, he pushed the three barbs back into their nesting position on the arrow. He lifted the rifle-portion of the weapon from his chest and lined up the arrow on the barrel of the rifle where a narrow, metal eye-hook that was part of the arrow lined up with a channel along the top of the rifle. Lance slid the arrow into the barrel until it clicked into a locked position.

Fascinated, Kimberly watched from the back rail of the hut as Lance fished out a coil of wire that was held together by twist-ties. Carefully, he undid the ties and attached one end of the wire to the eye hook that extended just above the guide channel of the barrel. A spring-loaded carabiner attached to one end of the wire fit into the eye-hook of the arrow. Lance made sure the length of wire was untangled in its spool and then attached the other end of the wire to an anchor hook he put around a tree branch in front of him. When he was satisfied with his work, he looked back at Kimberly who offered a silent "good luck" by flashing him crossed fingers.

Lance nodded back and then leaned a little to his right. Through a gap in the branches, he had a clear view of a large Magnolia tree he had picked out earlier that was about thirty-five feet away, across the Jungle Cruise river. He knew he had fifty feet of cable which looked liked it would be plenty of excess to reach the tree. He reached into the backpack one last time and came up with a four-inch-long CO_2 canister; the inch-wide, smoothly polished aluminum cylinder was then slipped into a slot on the rifle directly behind the barrel of the gun. With a short sound of air escaping at the connection point, Lance pushed the canister into the gun and pulled up on a small locking bar that hinged up and over the back of the cylinder.

While the CO_2 cartridge had the capability of about six shots, Lance decided he had to do this in one attempt. He gauged the distance to a large Magnolia tree with its good supply of branches offering plenty of attachment points for the grappling hook once it hit and released. He also liked the tree since it was well up off the ground and would make the zip line across the river at a declined angle.

Looking one last time far below him and across the Jungle Cruise river, he saw no one near enough to hear either him or the hook land. The cable wire that lay in front of him was given one final check before he lifted the rifle up toward his target. Lance locked his ankles around the branch he was sitting on for a firm foundation. Worse than missing his target, falling from forty feet up would certainly ruin his day.

Now ready to fire, Lance counted his heartbeats and in-between a heartbeat, pulled the trigger. With a quick, half of a second explosive release of air, the arrow launched from the rifle on a straight line cleanly through the opening in the tree. The cable in front of Lance spooled out fast, looking as if he had just hooked a large barracuda. The arching arrow, pulling the line along, landed in the middle of the Magnolia tree with a slight rustle of leaves and a muted thud as the arrow hit solid wood. An instant later, Lance could hear the prongs release.

"Yes!" Lance whispered to himself, seeing the arrow disappear within the array of branches across the river.

Kimberly unconsciously had been holding her breath as she watched what Lance was doing. Her fingernails dug into the wooden rail. As he pulled back on the slack of the cable, only then did she let her breath out and relax her hands.

Pulling the cable taut, he tested the steadfastness of the hook in the branches. After disengaging the rifle stock from the barrel and setting them back into the pack, he then twisted his body around and located a separate branch above his head where he could re-wrap the cable. Because the tree he was in was actually made of concrete and steel, he wasn't concerned about the stability of this end of the cable anchor. It was the living Magnolia tree that he hoped would be strong enough, especially wherever the hook had landed. Lance found what he liked in the way of a reinforced branch above him and took the end of the cable and threaded it around the branch twice. When he had the cable as firm as he could manually pull it, he used a small ratchet to pull the cable even tighter, which dug the grappling hook on the other end even deeper into whatever branches it had settled around. He held his hand around the ratchet so that he could muffle the clicking noise the device created with each up and down movement. In a short while, the cable went from being a loose, sagging wire to a taut, frozen rope that stretched from Lance down at a thirty-degree angle toward the Jungle Cruise island.

When he was satisfied with his creation, he whispered to Kimberly, "I need you here," signaling her with his hand.

As she gingerly made her way over the rail and followed the wide branch toward him, Lance reached into his backpack and took out a small pulley device—a dark gray rectangular object that had a hook on the bottom and two wheels sandwiched between the two dark pieces of aluminum. With a snap, the device opened up and Lance placed the wheels over the cable before snapping the two ends back together, encircling the device on the cable.

He took out a small wooden handle with an eye bolt drilled through the center of it. He hooked the eye bolt onto the hook at the bottom of the pulley as Kimberly came up behind him. He reached into the bag one more time and pulled out a small gardening spade that he placed in his back pocket.

"I need you to stay here when I zip across the river," he whispered, gripping the wooden handle and testing the pulley by pulling it soundlessly back and forth across the cable. "When I get back I will need you to look below to see if anyone is around the base of the Tree House. I won't be able to see over the tall berm of bushes separating the Indy queue area and the river."

Somewhat disappointed, Kimberly nodded, wishing she could go with him to search the island and El Lobo. "Okay. But hurry, Lance."

Lance smiled. He looked relaxed, as if he were going for a short walk. "I'll be right back." He turned around but then felt a tap on his shoulder. He turned back to Kimberly with an inquisitive look on his face.

"Good luck…break a leg…pull a hamstring….whatever it is they say before you do something like this," Kimberly smiled, looking into his eyes. She then leaned in and kissed him on his lips. A short, sweet—and for Lance—a completely unexpected first kiss. As Lanced looked at her, he secretly was hoping that it would not be their last kiss.

Lance grinned even broader and nodded. He then leaned out over the branch, hanging onto the handle connected to the pulley over his head. Slowly letting his weight move from the branch to his hands holding the handle, he tested how far the cable would sag under his weight. He was pleased to see that it only dropped about eight inches when his weight was finally fully onto the cable. He used his foot to hold his position against a lower branch. Without a word, Lance released the branch and let gravity take over. The downward slope of the cable made the first ten feet flash by. He lifted his legs up as high as he could so he would clear the branches below the opening of the tree. Soon he was free and gliding directly over the river of Jungle Cruise. As he approached the tree, the slight sag of the cable went below the anchor point, enough so Lance would slow down as he approached the Magnolia tree. With a slight whoosh, Lance hit the leaves of the Magnolia and used his legs to brace the abrupt end against the lower branches and trunk of the huge tree.

Being careful not to sprain his ankle, Lance compressed against the tree with his legs, turning his head to avoid a group of branches that poked out from below the cable. He was a good five feet above the ground when he grabbed a lower branch and swung himself from the handle to the ground. Quickly kneeling down into a tight ball, bringing his knees up to his chest and holding there for just a moment, he paused to hear any approaching voices in the distance. After a minute, he pushed himself up and swept some leaves off the front of his black sweatshirt. Lance looked back up along the cable to where he could make out Kimberly on the branch from where he launched himself.

Lance flashed her an "A-Okay" sign and then looked around for a path to the other side of the is-land. Kimberly gave him a wave and watched him vanish into the bushes.

Even though it was dark, Kimberly felt both visible and vulnerable—if not perilous—standing out on that large branch. There was nothing she could do from there for Lance, and, besides, she could not see past the large Magnolia tree that Lance had used.

Kimberly knew it would probably be longer than the "be right back" Lance had promised her.

She knew Lance would have to negotiate the trek across the small, but dense, jungle, cross the connected islands, find both El Lobos, search for something he hoped would still be hidden there after forty-plus years, and make it back…all without being caught or discovered.

Instead of wistfully scanning the side of the river where Lance entered, Kimberly climbed back over the rail of the hut that she and Lance had hid out in earlier. She climbed back through the hinged window and made herself as comfortable as she could on the thin carpeted floor of the hut. She closed her eyes and listened for any noise that might signal Lance's return.

Or someone else's.

Lance found a surprisingly well-marked trail that led in the direction he believed he needed to go. He had a hand-drawn map of the ride, basically showing the shape of the river, the two islands that make up the interior of the looped river—Manhattan and Catalina—and simple descriptions of various attractions along the ride. There was no description of the trail or where it went, nor was there any depiction of the rock formation in either location they had spotted. Lance believed one of those places had to be where the clue was directing him. This ambiguity was actually a good thing, in Lance's mind. For something to have been left virtually alone for all this time, it would have to be something nearly forgotten, lost.

According to the map, Lance had landed on Manhattan, near the Cambodian Shrine and sunken ruins where a large, animated Bengal tiger stood snarling at the passing boats. However, with the entire ride's animation turned off, the tiger, along with all the ride's mechanical creatures would be motionless—in 'suspended animation'— Lance playfully thought. The first location they had spotted would be down the narrow strip of island toward the attraction's entrance. Just in case there was a worker somewhere in the queue area for the Indiana Jones attraction, Lance headed to the opposite side of Manhattan, across the river from where he remembered seeing the baboons and the wrecked campsite. The going was slow as the underbrush was thick. He could tell no one had been through that section of the island in a long time. There was no path, no signs, and no footprints.

Sticking near the riverbank, Lance could see well enough. When the river started to make the bend toward the now-silent Schweitzer Falls, he headed into the thicket of vines and tree trunks. Reaching into his pocket, he pulled out his small Mag light when he found the rock formation. "Hello, beautiful!" he muttered as he shone the light over the open mouth of the smaller El Lobo. Careful to look over every inch of the rocks, Lance was disappointed when he could not spot any carved WED. He double-checked the base of the man-made rock, pulled leaves and dirt away from the edges, looked inside the wolf-like jaw and all along the top of the structure.

"Going to make me work for it, huh, Walt?" Lance grinned, undeterred as he decided to move on to the next formation he and Kimberly had spotted.

He knew he needed to get to the point of the island across from where Schweitzer Falls was located. He would then climb over the rocks that make up the Falls and then climb down opposite the second island, Catalina.

Once he got to the end of Manhattan, it was obvious that he was going to have to get wet—something he had kidded Kimberly about. "Now it's *really* too bad she didn't come," he smiled to himself. Not taking the time to grouse about it, Lance sat down on the grassy spit of land and started removing his shoes, socks, and pants. With a resigned sigh, he entered the dark green water. Surprised to find the water was quite warm, Lance concluded that the dark coloring of the water retained the heat from the sun during the day much better than if it had not been colored at all. As he moved from ankle-deep water to a depth well past his knees in just a few steps, he kept holding his clothes higher and higher as he approached the center of the river. He had thought it was only about three feet deep. It was more like five feet. When the water reached his chest, the bottom of the river flattened out. Lance knew there would have to be a rail of some sort for the track that kept each of the Jungle Cruise boats in the middle of the river. As expected, he felt a raised bar with his bare foot, a bar that seemed about eight inches off the floor of the river. Carefully stepping over the rail, he continued moving across, passing the mid-point of the river.

Once on the other side, he started to get dressed again, but hesitated. Was there a connecting piece of land? He gave a loud groan. "Idiot. It's called Catalina *Island* for a reason...." He decided to only put his shoes on at this point wondering how he might have to explain his current condition should someone discover him only wearing a shirt, boxers and shoes! Immediately, Lance found the traces of a trail that led in the direction he wanted. It had to be a maintenance trail since it ended at a small clearing that contained large pumps and other large valves that Lance concluded must control the flow of water over Schweitzer Falls.

There were steps that were built within the concrete rockwork that formed the back of the Falls. Those steps, in turn, led up to the top where a second set of steps, probably only used to service the outflow tubes filling the small basin where the water fills up before going over the fifteen-foot wide fall, were located. Lance looked at his watch; it read 4:10 a.m. At this hour, the pumps were off and there was only some standing water at the top of the falls when he climbed up to take a look. There were stepping stones in the small basin and Lance cautiously stepped on each as he crossed over the top of Schweitzer Falls. In the darkness he missed one of the stones that had a worn—but unmistakable—WED chiseled into its face. In fact, if he had been looking carefully enough in the right places, he would have spotted two other WED carvings, both of them worn from age and the elements; one was in the first step that lead to the top of the Falls and one was farther back on a well-camouflaged rock face that also featured an arrow that was pointing in the exact direction Lance had been following to the El Lobo formation.

Reaching the other side of Schweitzer Falls, there were similar steps down to the soil from the top. These seemed to have been neglected with little use as there was ample growth of vines and plants that surrounded and nearly blocked the steps leading down. Lance plied through the foliage and came down onto the ground on a nearly non-descript path that led to the water's edge. With another deep sigh, he sat down and again removed his shoes. He didn't bother rolling his soggy sweatshirt any higher. He didn't think it could possibly get any wetter than it already was.

Stopping near the attacking natives, who were now in the 'down' position, Lance again looked at the map he had gotten from his friend Drew. He realized why the Catalina side of the ride did not have a clearly defined path: almost all of the animation around this part of the ride was on the mainland side. Only some natives and non-animated animals were on this side and needed only periodic attention; mainly gardening so the surrounding jungle doesn't swallow the elements completely; in addition, all those animations were at the edge of the island and probably more easily accessible by maintenance skiffs and boats.

This might explain why it was hard to spot the second El Lobo. Lance thought it might have been a more important part of the ride when Walt was in charge. More of the sophisticated animation was developed later when the technology improved. Anything on this part of the ride may have literally been left alone, forgotten, in favor of the newer ride elements that occupied the mainland side of the ride—the side viewed by the guests and most easily serviced by maintenance. Lance understood this since it would cost more and be a logistical nightmare bringing huge power and control cables under the river to the isolated island. It would be much easier to keep the technical elements on the mainland side where power and all the wiring and hydraulic cables that controlled the animation would be easier to maintain.

Folding the map after once again using it for a reference, he slipped it into his shirt pocket. It was much darker on this island as there was literally no lighting filtering through the trees as there had been on the Manhattan side which was much closer to the lights of the Park. He pulled out his miniature Mag flashlight and twisted the glass lens. A bright, narrow beam emerged, and Lance could see that there was a path, albeit not as well traversed as the one he had been following before the Falls.

Before he continued his search, Lance wanted to check out one more thing he had spotted when they had ridden through the attraction: There was a thatched hut behind the attacking natives. Knowing his fellow cast members as well as he did, he wanted to see if anything was inside the hut. Cast members were known to have a bizarre sense of humor. There have been plenty of Mouse ears sitting atop animatronic jungle animals or pirates over the years. Since he was already there, he thought he might as well take a look. The grass and thatch hut stood a little over seven feet tall and had a woven grass curtain to close off the interior. The curtain was hardly necessary considering how dense the jungle was that surrounded it. Pushing aside the grass curtain and waiting a moment to see if anything scurried past his feet, Lance shined his light into the darkness of the hut. He was surprised when the light illuminated a pile of clothes. Grinning wickedly, Lance entered the hut, eager to see what was hidden there. His surprised look faded as his flashlight revealed that the pile of clothes was a Security uniform, complete with hat and shoes and utility belt. "So, who has been hiding out on me?" he wondered. "How come I miss all the fun parties?"

The uniform, from what little he could see of it, was different from his own. The colors were off, for one thing. He couldn't tell if it was an older uniform, a style that wasn't used any longer. Lance was going to search the clothes to see if the owner's identifying nametag was still attached to the shirt. But, he held back, hesitant. The clothes were folded too neatly to be the cast-offs of some energetic party. No, they looked like they were there for a reason—one that Lance could not comprehend at the moment—but for a definite reason, nonetheless. He decided to leave them be, out of respect for whomever had left them But...if they were remnants of some Jungle party, he sincerely hoped he and Kimberly would be invited to the next one.

Emerging from the hut, and still thinking about the uniform he had found, Lance followed the meager trail. He poked through some of the tall bamboo that now lined the shore and could see the outline of the huge African Bull Elephant that stood about eight and a half feet tall at the shoulder. He grinned as part of the skipper's spiel came to his mind: "The second most-feared animal in the jungle. And if you look on the opposite bank, you will see THE most-feared animal in the jungle—his mother-in-law," as the skipper would point at an identical elephant on the other side of the river.

Weaving his way between ferns, bushes, and exotic plants that Lance knew were not indigenous to the Southern California climate, he nearly ran headfirst into the gray rock edifice that he had been trying to find. With his flashlight in his mouth, Lance had lit the way while using both hands to spread the limbs of a full willow tree away. Carefully looking down at his feet as he walked, he nearly hit his head on the overhanging rock that formed the rough mouth of the wolf-mound El Lobo.

"Well, there you are. Your twin on Manhattan says hello, by the way," Lance kidded, shining his light at the rocks that formed the teeth of the beast. Even surrounded by lush foliage, he noted the strong resemblance of this El Lobo to the one In Columbia where he and Wolf had discovered Walt's capsule.

Immediately, Lance pushed his way around to the side of the rock mound, looking first for letters that would be engraved in the stone, assuming Walt would have created a similar hiding place as he had for the clue found in Columbia. The flashlight beam followed along the base of the rock, revealing a large accumulation of pine needles, dead fern leaves and other plant remnants. Using his foot to pull some of these away along the back portion of the mound, it was there that Lance suddenly felt his heart start pounding.

WED

It was much more clearly engraved in the rock, although it was well hidden by the debris that had been pulled away.

Now he again wished Kimberly could be with him. He would have enjoyed sharing the discovery with her as he had done when they climbed the steps of the castle and found the shield. He chuckled to himself, thinking that he was glad he didn't have to wear tights this time.

Taking out the small gardening spade that he had carried across the water, he raked the leaves along the base of the rock, forming a small clearing of moist soil. He took a breath, thinking for a moment that he wished Wolf was here to do the digging. Either that, or go to Maintenance and 'borrow' a backhoe....

After about three minutes of easy digging, Lance had a hole about two feet in diameter. When it reached about eight inches deep, he started hoping it would not need to be another eight inches as the ground was getting much harder and more compact the deeper down he dug.

Near the base of an overgrown Bird of Paradise plant, he expanded the hole another foot to his right. It was there that he hit something other than soft soil.

Quickly digging in, Lance felt around with the

tip of the small shovel and then shined his flash-light into the hole. There, against the black back-drop of fertile soil, the light clearly illuminated something plastic and gray.

At 4:50 a.m., Kimberly awoke suddenly, again disorientated from her location and the time of morning. Her back stiff from lying on the hard floor on her side, she tried to push herself up on her arm, rubbing her eyes with her hand. She quickly realized something and looked down at the glowing dial of her watch. *How long was I asleep?* Kimberly panicked, trying to read the hands. As best she could, she calculated that her partner had been gone for well over an hour.

More importantly, she realized that Lance was still nowhere in sight.

Quickly going out of the hut's window, she glanced around in the darkness for any flashlights and listened for any voices. The Park was prob-ably the quietest she had ever experienced. Kim-berly walked around the outer planking and climbed over the rail and carefully walked along the branch to where the cable which Lance had zoomed across was still attached to the large branch.

Panic took hold of her when she realized that the cable now hung loosely, the length of it limply lying across the branches, its end disappearing at the edge of the Jungle Cruise river. *Had some-one discovered the line and cut it?* Kimberly thought to herself, wondering how Lance was going to get back across the river.

Just then she heard a sound from behind her. In her state of panic, she wheeled around on the branch and lost her balance. A hand shot out and grabbed her by the waist.

"You really need to be more careful when you are climbing trees, Jane," Lance kidded, pulling Kimberly up to him with one arm, his other hand holding a tall branch.

Kimberly's eyes were huge. Lance pulled her in next to him, her hips and chest pressing up against his. He could feel her heart pounding in her chest.

"Happy to see your long-lost partner?" he asked with a devastating smile.

"Oh my god," Kimberly was able to gasp between breaths; she wrapped her arm around Lance and just looked at him, not even noticing the top half of him was soaking wet and the bottom half only slightly soggy.

"Not sure if this is the right time or not," Lance murmured, and then pulled Kimberly tighter against himself. He moved his lips to hers and kissed her with a firm, consuming kiss. He felt her body tremble; the combination of panic, breathlessness and now this seemed…surreal to Kimberly. He pulled back after a moment, still clutching her around the small of her back. He looked deeply into her eyes, searching for anything…a mutual response, rejection, anything.

"Not the right time, huh?" Lance asked, still looking into her stunned eyes.

Kimberly took a deep breath, looking as deeply into Lance's eyes as he was looking into hers. "I can't think of a better time," she uttered in a breathless whisper and reached up to Lance's head and pulled his mouth to hers.

After reeling in the slack cable and stashing all the equipment in his backpack, Lance and Kimberly returned to their little hut. Reaching into his back pocket under the illumination of the flashlight Kimberly held, he pulled out the latest find. She cupped her hand around the lighted end, muting the brightness with her fingers.

"Was it hard to locate?" Kimberly asked, her voice an excited, whisper.

"Well, you know there were two El Lobo's," he reminded her. "And, of course, it had to be at the second formation we saw that I finally located after crossing over the top of Schweitzer Falls." Lance left off the part about having to cross the river in his boxer shorts.

Kimberly looked at the capsule he held in his hand. It was larger than the one they found behind the crest on the back side of Sleeping Beauty's Castle.

"This is like the capsules we found before," Lance explained to her as the beam from the flashlight played over the dark gray capsule, its outer plastic covering weathered from being underground for over forty years. It was probably the only time, he thought, that he was glad plastic didn't biodegrade quickly over time.

"I can imagine what it was like to find the first clue," Kimberly smiled, her eyes big with anticipation.

"Until we actually unearthed the first clue

under Walt's Dreaming Tree, I don't think Adam nor I really believed it was all real," Lance said, with a look of regret at the memory of what he had done to his friend: his selfishness and greed had turned him into a monster. His memories of the discoveries they had made followed by his insane attempt to capture the Disney cache for himself still weighed heavy on his mind.

She couldn't help but see the gloomy look in his eyes, the dejection. "Lance, don't be too hard on yourself," she told him.

"I don't think Adam or Beth will ever see me as anything other than the idiot—no, the greedy fool—that I let myself become." Lance shook his head in disgust, dropping his hands to his lap, the capsule forgotten momentarily.

"I think you will earn their trust again," she assured him, taking his chin in her hand. She then added, "Just as you have earned my trust." Kimberly leaned into Lance and kissed him softly once again on the lips. He responded after a moment, kissing her back as he softly caressed her cheek.

"Thank you…," Lance replied, bringing his eyes to hers before adding, "for everything."

Emotion flooding through her, Kimberly gave Lance another kiss and said, "You're welcome." After a wordless pause, Kimberly looked down at the capsule in Lance's hands. She put her hand on his and raised it up. "Now, Tarzan, are you going to open Walt's treasure or should I?"

With a Tarzan-like grunt, Lance responded and turned the sealing cap of the capsule. When it wouldn't budge, he tapped it on the floor of the tree house a few times. This time they heard something different—there was the sound of something moving inside the capsule, hitting against the plastic. Lance thought it sounded metallic. Hoping he hadn't broken something important, he tried the end cap again. This time, the cap creaked a quarter inch as Lance grimaced, putting all of his strength into the effort. The end cap moved another inch, and, with a couple more grunts, Lance finally had the capsule open.

"**W**hat the heck does that mean?" Kimberly asked with a quizzical look on her face.

"Let me read it again. **'Is the Heart the WINDOW to the soul? "Caring and Giving Come from the Heart" Two WEDs are better than one!'**" Lance reread the clue penned in Walt Disney's own handwriting on the now-familiar yellowed paper torn from the original diary. "I...," he started, and then finished with a shrug, "I have no idea."

Setting down the clue, Lance looked at the treasures he found inside with the paper: A small brass key and three animation cels that they had immediately recognized as scenes from *Alice in Wonderland*. Each clear plastic sheet, separated by a layer of wax-like paper, had an animated drawing of a playing card along with a character from the animated feature film: The White Rabbit holding a large gold watch in one, the Cheshire Cat—grinning ear-to-ear—in another, and finally Alice herself in her blue and white pinafore dress. Pocketing the key for safekeeping, Lance held the eight-by-nine inch cels up to the flashlight Kimberly still held. He could even see odd-looking production codes, sets of letters, which were printed along the bottom of each cel.

"What is similar in each of these?" he suddenly asked the fascinated Kimberly with a knowing tone in his voice.

She looked from one cel to the other, and then smiled at the discovery. "The cards."

Lance nodded. There was an ace of hearts in the cel with the rabbit, an ace of clubs next to the cat, and Alice was seen standing next to a giant five of diamonds.

"Knowing the way Walt devised all the previous clues, these cels and the clue itself are probably all somehow related," Lance said, and then added, "I just don't know how yet." He fished the key out of his pocket. It looked very old with intricate engraving around the uniquely-shaped teeth. "Plus, there is the added twist of finding something that requires this key to open."

Kimberly tried to stifle a yawn. The excitement followed by the revelation of the clues and the sudden confusion as to their meaning, not to mention the fact that the two had been up for well over twenty-four hours straight after working their normal shifts the day before, was taking its toll on her.

"I saw that," Lance grinned and immediately started to yawn himself. "Great. Now you have me doing it! Come over here," he invited, taking her hand and pulling her next to him. "It's been a long day. We have, what, about three hours before the park opens?" Lance looked at his watch which read 5:25 a.m. "Let's knock off for the morning, relax and then when the first crowds come into the Park, we will simply walk out of the Treehouse like everyone else and head home."

Before he had even finished his sentence, Kimberly had moved her head to his shoulder and closed her eyes. Lance smiled as he looked down at her tired but angelic face.

Within two minutes, he, too, was sound asleep.

"**M**ommy! Look!" a little boy said pointing through the bamboo rails of the window of the tree house hut. "Is that Tarzan and Jane? They look funny."

Lance opened one eye at the irritating commotion, stared at the freckled little red-head boy and now his mother who was staring through the window, her mouth wide open in shock.

"Come on, Mikey," the mother called out after seeing the couple asleep on the floor of the Tarzan Treehouse, dragging him away from the window. "Let's go ride Jungle Cruise. Now!"

Lance was now fully awake. He had fallen asleep against the side wall of the hut where he had been sitting earlier. Kimberly now had her head on his thigh, her blond hair splayed out over his leg. He nudged her shoulder.

"Kimberly….Kimberly, wake up."

Raising her head, the green eyes opened slowly. Pushing herself up onto her hands, she turned her stiff neck toward Lance's direction. Their precarious situation became instantly apparent to her. "Oh, my god," Kimberly panicked.

"What time is it, Lance?"

Lance started getting up from the floor. "It's after nine," he groaned, pain shooting through his stiff legs as he got to his feet. He reached down to help her up off of the floor. Glancing out the window, he could see more people coming down the stairs toward the hut.

"We'd better get going before someone else sees us and calls security."

Lance replaced the diary page and the animation cels inside the gray capsule, zipped them securely out of sight in one of the pockets of his backpack, and stepped out the window. He held the window frame open for Kimberly and helped her over the short wall just before a young family came off the steps and onto the landing around the other side of the hut. Quickly, Lance and Kimberly shuffled down the steps, went across the bottom landing and, with a sigh of relief, exited the Treehouse into a growing number of guests who were just starting their day at Disneyland.

CHAPTER 9

Once they escaped from Disneyland with the capsule secure, Lance drove straight to Kimberly's house. The drive had been one of companionable silence for the most part. As Lance listened to some classical music on his radio, Kimberly leaned back into the corner of her seat in the Jag, quickly falling into a tranquil nap until they reached the house. Sending her off to her bedroom, he collapsed on the couch in the living room and instantly fell asleep.

The next morning, Lance was quite surprised to learn that, in their exhaustion and excitement, they had slept for nearly twenty hours. Glancing up the stairs, he wondered why it still so quiet. He had expected Kimberly to come bouncing downstairs, eager to begin the day. But, instead, he was greeted with silence. Tiptoeing up the first flight, he found Kimberly's door slightly ajar. Tapping lightly, there was no response. He gave the heavy oak door a push and debated on the wisdom of actually looking into her bedroom. His natural curiosity overcame the propriety of the situation. Lance peeked in, spotting Kimberly on her bed as she was curled around a body-length pillow, still sleeping soundly.

Lance leaned against the door jam for a moment, simply taking in the sight of Kimberly in that moment of quiet solitude. He couldn't wait to spend more time with her but, seeing her in such a disarming position on the bed—still wearing the shorts and blouse she had worn the day before—Lance enjoyed just watching her as she slept.

Knowing her a little better, as he now did, he knew she was getting more and more excited by the search they were on, perhaps more so than he, since this was all so new to her; but he also knew that she was stressed. He pondered on all that she was going through. A lot had happened in a short period of time: Her father had brought a stranger into their home and declared that he might be the next Guardian. Her father had suddenly died from his heart problem. She had the emotional tasks of privately interring him next to her mother at Forest Lawn and then illegally spreading some of his ashes as he had requested. There was the ongoing pressure being exerted by her uncle, Daniel Crain, to be her father's successor. She had started proceedings to have Daniel removed from her property and her life. They had to locate and retrieve two clues hidden within Disneyland with the chance of being caught—and God knows what the consequences of that could have been. Yet, the intensity of those situations, and the subsequent success they so far had enjoyed, seemed to be creating an emotional bond between them. To Lance, it was a bond that was as unique as it was potent and he sincerely hoped it would not end as quickly as it had begun.

Never had he been so drawn to a woman. No, it wasn't just the physical attraction—though he could not deny the sensual, yet innocent allure Kimberly's entire being seemed to radiate. It seemed a lifetime ago that he was chasing—and catching—potential 'conquests.' Kimberly presented a challenge that he had never before encountered in a woman. He seriously felt that he had experienced an emotional epiphany. And his concern for Kimberly was not just sensitive, but truly sincere. On top of such emotions, Lance thought about the night they had just spent in the Treehouse. While it was innocent and innocuous—certainly as harmless as anyone could describe spending a night hiding out at Disneyland could possibly be—Lance also had the memory of her kiss still on his mind and on his lips.

Looking away from studying her lying there in bed, he gave a small smile. He liked the kissing part just fine. And, he had the feeling she liked it just fine, too. Quietly shutting her door, he walked back downstairs to the kitchen.

Two hours later, awakening to the smell of bacon sizzling in the kitchen, Kimberly was momentarily transported back in time. Feeling like she was her father's little girl again, she used to awaken on Saturday mornings to the smell of bacon and the delight of knowing she didn't have to go to school. Treading silently down the stairs, Kimberly peered into the kitchen and smiled as she spied Lance frying up some bacon and eggs. He had bread propped up in the toaster, ready to toast, and two glasses of orange juice sitting on the table.

Realizing that she had fallen asleep in the same clothes she had worn the entire day and night before and had not showered for more than twenty-four hours, she felt the immediate need to clean up before announcing her presence. After a quick shower, she fixed her hair, and slipped into a little summer dress that matched her current emotional state: Flirty.

Throughout her life, Kimberly had led a sheltered existence. Her father protected her, to the point of arranging dates for her; his deep-seated fear of who might discover their 'Family Secret' made such situations unavoidable. Yet, Kimberly made her father's decisions easier as her interest in boys was not only minimal, but her greater quest for knowledge and information seemed to dictate her interests. While many a boy at the exclusive and private school in Orange she attended paid her many a compliment, her shy personality made her appear aloof—if not disinterested—in any of them.

When she turned twenty, the cruise that her father arranged for them—one of the few vacations of any duration—introduced her to the feelings of intimacy and even romance. For some reason, the combination of being on a ship, cut off from the world and cut off from her father's responsibilities, plus the tropical romantic setting—

brilliant sunsets across infinite ocean horizons, enticing music and exotic foods—all made her discover and explore a different side of her personality that she hadn't even known was inside of her.

It was while she washed her hair, letting the soothing aloe fragrance of her bodywash clear her mind, that Kimberly remembered those romantic feelings she had first experienced on that cruise ten years earlier. She felt a tug at her heart as she thought about Antonio. Handsome Antonio. Leaning against the side of the shower, she let the warm memories flow over her, mixing with the warm water flowing from the showerhead. She hadn't thought about him in years. Antonio was one of the officers that she had met while dining at the Captain's Table. His offer to go dancing after dinner had been shyly, yet eagerly accepted. It was in one of the smaller lounges, a more private and intimate setting for dancing and talking. They had found a lot in common as they talked over a bottle of fine Italian wine that Antonio had brought from his cabin. Their dancing continued into the small hours of the morning, extending down the Esplanade and into the moonlit night overlooking the ever-moving ocean, her hair a halo of silver in the moonlight. That was when they had kissed for the first time—a kiss as soft and warm as the tropical breeze surrounding them. Antonio promised to meet her again the following evening after he had finished his duties. It was a heavenly week for Kimberly, torn at the end by the inevitable pain of parting that they had both known was coming. Still, the remembrance of their special passion was there, safe and warm in her memory.

What that cruise had done for her when she was twenty, she now realized Lance was doing for her at thirty. And, even though she missed her father so very much, she also felt a compelling sense of freedom that she had never felt before.

"Well, if it isn't Julia Child in my very own house!" Kimberly kidded as she strode into the kitchen, stopping at the large granite-topped island in the middle of the room, resting her hands on the cool, smooth countertop. Lance, holding a spatula in one hand and a pan with a folded omelet in the other, turned from the stove and nearly dropped the spatula upon seeing her.

For a moment, he could only stare at Kimberly, the spatula dangling at his fingertips. The sun radiating in through the large bay windows that surrounded the kitchen angled across Kimberly like a spotlight. The radiance of Kimberly's blond hair accented her tan arms and legs, all of which were visible and beautifully framed within the thin straps, simple bodice and short, flared hem of the white dress with pastel flowers faintly printed over the material. Kimberly's figure was definitely noticed by Lance, too. Recovering his voice, he replied with a high-pitched French accent, "Your breakfast will be done in a moment, my dear."

Kimberly laughed. "I hope your cooking is better than your accent!" She noticed a strand of his brown hair had fallen across his forehead as he was cooking breakfast. Walking up to him, she reached out a tentative hand toward his face. Some of her latent shyness rushed through her and she started to lower her fingers. At his inquisitive look, she mentally told herself to *knock it off*, and reached back and smoothed his errant hair back in place. His warm smile made her stomach flutter. And she knew it wasn't from being ravenously hungry. "You're going to spoil me," she finally said, indicating the fine meal he had taken the effort to prepare for her.

Lance had to turn back to the cooking food which was in serious danger of burning if he didn't snap out of his trance. "Well, we all could use a little spoiling now and then."

"Now and then, huh? So, I shouldn't get used to this, is that what you're telling me?" She had snitched a piece of bacon from the ones drying on a paper towel. "Where is Kevin, by the way?"

Lance tried to swat her hand with the back of the spatula, but she had been too quick. "I gave him the morning off. It's just you and me."

"Well, I guess we will just have to get by the best we can! Shall I set the table? Where do you want to eat? Here or in the dining room?"

Lance looked back at her, a little surprised. "Dining room? That's a little too formal for my tastes for breakfast. Have you been talking to my mother?" he added with a grin.

Kimberly appeared to be deep in thought. "Your mother? Hmmm, not a bad idea. She might be able to give me some wonderful insights into your soul!"

Lance gave a fake shudder. "Let's not and just say we did…."

With a twinkling laugh, Kimberly took out some woven placemats from the pantry and set an intimate table for two at the family table.

It was one of the most enjoyable breakfasts Lance had ever had. And, Kimberly discovered that the food was indeed much better than his accent.

"So, have you been up all morning thinking about the clue?" Kimberly asked, wiping the corner of her mouth with a cloth napkin.

"Yes. I even spent time on the Internet this morning, looking up and cross-referencing the clues with anything Walt had done or that might be remotely connected to him in any way."

"Nothing yet, I assume?"

"Nada. Zilch," Lance replied, finishing a bite of his omelet.

"Well, it has to connect somehow," Kimberly thought out loud as she pushed her chair out from the table and walked over to Lance. Without thinking, she leaned down and kissed him.

"Thank you for a wonderful breakfast," she said after pulling her lips from his. She gazed into his eyes, and Lance noticed that something was different. There was a sparkle in her green eyes indicative of someone who was very excited about life. He had not seen that in her eyes before.

"What do I get if I fix lunch and dinner too?" asked Lance with a smile.

"Don't get greedy, Brentwood," Kimberly replied with a laugh as she picked up their plates and started cleaning up.

"I'll do that," Lance offered. "Why don't you have a go with the clues while I clean up the kitchen. Then I'll head home to get cleaned up and changed. I have a feeling we have quite a lot of work ahead of us."

"Okay," Kimberly said slowly. "But please don't be gone too long." Her laughter faded as a worried look seeped into her eyes.

"Keep the alarm on," Lance advised, seeing the sparkle suddenly vanish, knowing what she was thinking. "I don't think Crain will be coming around here since we changed the locks and alarm codes. Besides, you gave him plenty of money. It was more than fair. Hopefully he will find a nice place to stay and figure out what he is going to do with his life."

"I know…," Kimberly was hesitant, not wanting to say her fears out loud.

"Kimberly, listen, I don't trust him either. But, I'm sure if he thinks about it, he is getting a lot from you…and your father," Lance said, leaning back against the kitchen chair.

"I guess so," Kimberly sighed, the look of concern still visible.

"I'll be quick," Lance promised, getting up from the table as he started loading the dishwasher and clearing the stove. "I want you to relax and enjoy the rest of the morning. After all we went through at Disneyland, you deserve a little R and R."

Kimberly smiled at that. She walked over to Lance who was rinsing off a plate at the sink. She stood behind him and wrapped her arms around his waist, pulling him against her. "You make me feel very safe," she whispered into his ear.

Lance turned his head and silently kissed her cheek.

It was six o'clock that evening when Lance tossed his Disney research book aside. He and Kimberly had been cloistered in her father's office, searching every book, magazine, and Internet site that would have been remotely associated with hearts, windows and Disney.

"I'm going stir crazy," Lance said, rubbing his eyes and his temples. They had only taken the time to stop for a quick lunch of frozen lasagna popped into the microwave and some iced tea. Comparing notes, they were discussing and then dismissing items as they found each new lead led to a dead end.

Her golden head shot up at his sudden voice. Deeply into the hunt, she was sitting in front of the computer, trying to research the 'heart' portion of their last clue. The 1948 movie *So Dear to My Heart* kept coming up, but she could find no correlation between the movie and the rest of the clue. She was getting very frustrated and actually welcomed Lance's distraction—whatever it was. "Yes?" she slowly drawled out.

"Let's go grab dinner. I'm starving."

Kimberly readily agreed, feeling her stomach rumble again. After setting the alarm and locking up the mansion, they headed off to El Torido, a Mexican restaurant in Anaheim that was a regular eating and drinking joint for many Disneyland cast members after they finished their shifts at the

Park. Both Kimberly and Lance knew several patrons, stopping to chat with a few of them. They
spotted a private booth near the back of the place
and sat down.

"How about a margarita?" Lance asked Kimberly as she looked over the menu.

"Sounds good right about now," Kimberly
said. Chips and salsa were promptly delivered to
their table and drink orders taken.

Kimberly dove into the chips with gusto.
"Mmm, this is so good," she mumbled between
bites, munching on a salted chip dipped into the
mild red salsa. Their server delivered their Mar-
garitas in cute little glasses shaped like cactus.
Taking her glass, she licked a little salt from the
edge, and sipped the frozen lime-colored mixture.

Televisions were mounted in each of the four
corners of the back room where they were seated.
Lance took his drink, sipped through a narrow
straw and glanced up at the screen behind Kimberly. A basketball game was being featured on
ESPN; however, when the commercial came on,
the closed-caption told viewers, "What happens in
Vegas stays in Vegas."

Lance got an idea.

"Uh, Kimberly," Lance started, bringing his
brown eyes to meet hers.

"Uh Lance," Kimberly repeated, mimicking
Lance's serious tone. The tequila in the margarita
was taking effect on Kimberly; her empty stomach
was no match for the alcohol. It took an extra effort on her part just to keep from giggling at him.

"I'm thinking we need a break from this whole
adventure," Lance said, taking a chip and dipping

it in the small bowl of salsa. He caught Kimberly's concerned look. "No, really, hear me out." Lance knew that all this clue-hunting and discovery was new and quite exciting for her. Yet, at the same time, understanding the frustration of what they were experiencing with the lack of progress on the current clue and the difficulty they were having with Daniel Crain, and coming on the heels of her father's death, Lance felt they needed to simply get away.

"I'm listening," Kimberly said.

"I have a proposition for you."

Her eyebrows shot up at the word he had chosen. "Oh?" as her eyes narrowed. "How intriguing."

He grinned at the look on her face. "You haven't even heard it yet."

She sat back in her chair and folded her arms over her chest. "Any time anyone uses the word 'proposition,' it has to be intriguing."

"I think we need a break," explained Lance.

"From each other?" Kimberly asked incredulously, not understanding the direction Lance was taking. She tried not to reveal her disappointment.

"No! No…not that at all," Lance said in a consoling tone. "No, in fact, just the opposite," Lance held his breath before telling her the rest of his idea. "I am proposing the idea of taking you to Las Vegas."

This wasn't what she had expected. "Las Vegas? What would we do there?"

Get married. The immediate thought flashed through Lance's mind like a thunder bolt. It stunned him. His mouth fell open into an 'O' and then he snapped it shut. *Where did that come from?* he thought to himself as his heart started pounding.

Kimberly saw his mouth open to answer her, and then it inexplicably closed. The oddest look crossed over his face that was now ashen. "Are you all right?" she asked, reaching across the table to put her smooth hand on his.

His eyes, which had been staring at the wall behind their booth all this time, darted back to her face. He looked over her delicate features and his glance stopped on her red lips. Those lips curled into a confused smile. "Are you all right?" they repeated.

A sudden warmth infused Lance. His heart stopped pounding. His shoulders visibly relaxed. A look of contentment overshadowed the look of complete astonishment that had been there moments earlier. Color flooded back into his white face. "Yes, everything is fine," he managed to say at last. "Perfect, actually."

"Glad to hear it…. Wow, a proposition to take me to Las Vegas." Kimberly was thinking over the possibilities. "But, it doesn't seem to fit anything that Walt has us searching for."

"No. You are right. I wasn't thinking of a trip there for research or anything," Lance clarified, and then thought about what 'anything' might include. He hurriedly added, "I was wondering if you would like to take a break and go to dinner and a show with me. I think we both could use the diversion."

Kimberly thought about his offer. "Lance, I've never even been to Las Vegas," she confided, a little embarrassed at the fact that she had, in fact, not even been outside of California very many times.

Lance looked at her with a slightly stunned expression. "Really?"

Kimberly shook her head. "I really haven't been to very many places in my life," she quietly explained, still embarrassed at what she perceived was a shortcoming on her part.

Lance now clearly understood. It would have been very difficult for her father to absolve his responsibilities long enough to travel…with or without Kimberly. He felt another tug on his emotional strings and he felt he would very much like to show her more of the world that he knew and share new discoveries together.

"Well, then it's decided," Lance declared with an adamant hand-slap on the table. "Tomorrow we lock everything up, set the alarm on the house, fill up the tank on my Jag and head north on I-15." Lance paused. An awkward moment passed between them and he then offered a meek, "Okay?"

Kimberly, taking another sip of her margarita, was thoughtful. She didn't want to reveal her excitement.

Lance watched her eyes; Kimberly's were glued on his. "Is that a yes?" Lance asked, leaning forward toward her.

Kimberly pushed her glass away. Licking her fingertip, she ran her wet finger around the salted edge of her margarita glass and then licked the granules off her finger. "You had me at proposition." She then gave him a stunning smile.

Looking at her, Lance couldn't suppress a

laugh.

"I think the diversion is just what we need. We can get away from town and have a change of scenery. Enjoy some good food and a good show," Lance called out to Kimberly who was in her bathroom. "I know of a chick singer you would probably like," he teased, "You know—all that mushy romantic ballad crap." Lance bent over to pick up her day bag. "Geez, what have you got packed in here…a set of weights?" he grumbled, carrying the bag from her room.

"I packed a couple books on Disney that I thought we could read on the way to Vegas," Kimberly called to him as she checked herself in the bathroom mirror. She had minimal blush and no other makeup on. There was a sparkle in her eyes as she anticipated the chance to spend more time with Lance. Her pulse automatically quickened as she pictured the two of them going to a romantic restaurant and show. *A real date with Lance*, she thought to herself. She wore a layered, fly-away camisole halter top and a pair of white jeans. Cute and just a little daring, especially for her, Kimberly thought, liking the look she saw in the mirror. "And what do you mean 'mushy, romantic ballad crap'?" Kimberly, hands on her hips, stopped in the arched opening of her bathroom, facing Lance.

Lance looked up at her as he put the strap of her suitcase over his shoulder. "Wow," he mumbled appreciatively, catching sight of her. Clearing his throat, he added, "Oh, I mean, mushy, romantic, ballads that everyone loves," he amended with a chuckle.

"That's better," Kimberly said with a smile. "You know, we could always look for some twangy, my-dog-died country crap for you, if you prefer."

"No, no, that's fine," he laughed, holding up his hands in a mock surrender. "Ready?" Lance asked.

"I guess so," Kimberly replied vaguely, looking around to see if she missed anything.

"Then, let's go," Lance said, reaching out to her with his hand.

She took his hand and then pulled him back toward her. "Kiss me first."

Lance looked into her beautiful eyes, wanting nothing more than to kiss her lips. He had remained a little reserved up to now, not sure if Kimberly was on the same romantic page as he. But, he also knew how to play hard to get. "What do I get if I kiss you?" he asked, his head tilted to the side and the essence of a grin etched on his lips.

"If you kiss me," Kimberly said, pausing for effect, "I'll let you drive my car to Vegas."

"You have a car?" Lance asked, not even thinking that she owned a car.

"Of course I have a car!" she retorted, dropping her hands from his. "How do you think I get back and forth to work?"

"Broom?" he offered.

"Oh, you will pay for that, Mr. Brentwood! You can just forget about my request for a kiss."

"You've been holding out on me," Lance mumbled as he slowly walked around her car.

"Well, I needed a little something to zip around town in. Daddy thought this would be cute."

"Cute…," Lance repeated, unable to believe the word she was using to describe her car, as he ran his fingers over the two-tone beige and green Connolly leather bucket seats. "Cute?"

"You're repeating yourself," she grinned as she tied a scarf over her hair and slipped into the driver's seat. "You coming?"

As the twelve-cylinder engine roared to life, Lance hurried around to the passenger door. Resisting the urge to vault over the door frame, he sedately opened the door instead.

As he settled into the plush leather, Kimberly gave a knowing laugh. "You wanted to jump in, didn't you?"

Lance was running his hands lovingly over the burlwood interior of the cockpit. "Did it show?"

"Oh, yeah! I actually did once when no one was looking," she admitted with a grin. "Just about killed myself on the shifter."

Her 2000 Aston Martin DB7 Vantage Volante backed out of the four-car garage and slid to a stop as the garage door slowly lowered. Kimberly was about to slap it into drive when Daniel came running down the stairs that led to his suite over the garage. He positioned himself in front of the car so she couldn't just drive off without first running him down. Daniel was wise enough to recognize that she would very much like to run him over....

"Hey, Kimberly, Lance," he tried to say pleasantly. "Where are you going in such a hurry?"

"Out to lunch," Lance answered brusquely.

"Wonderful! I was hoping you would ask. Let's just let bygones be bygones and forget that silly notice you gave me. Why don't we take the Caddy and I'll drive?" He was attempting to sound anything but whiney.

Kimberly revved the engine, making him jump back. "Sorry, Daniel. I'm afraid it will be just Lance and me today. We have some things to discuss. And, you only have a few days left."

Daniel could see there would be no arguing with the little hussy. He gave a smile that looked anything but sincere. "Well, it was worth a try. Ha ha. You two kids run along and have a good time. We'll talk later."

"Yes, we will," Kimberly muttered as she slipped the car into first and smoked the tires, showering Daniel with gravel from the driveway.

Daniel watched until her car made the first turn in the drive. He ran to the small carport off to the side of the garage where his Cadillac now sat. Jumping into the driver's seat of the dusty car, Daniel jerked it into reverse. "Two can play that little game, Missy," he spat out. "Let's just see where you and that slummer are going this time."

He had no trouble spotting the metallic racing-green Aston Martin as Kimberly navigated the twists and turns heading down the hill. Keeping a reasonable distance behind them, he was relying on the fact that they wouldn't expect to be followed. He was surprised when she headed for the 91 freeway, and even more surprised about a mile later when she merged onto the 57, heading north. Fifteen miles further, she merged onto Interstate 15 and sped over to the fast lane. "What the…," he muttered, narrowly avoiding a semi and weaving in and out of the lanes to get into a better position to watch them. "Vegas? Is that where the idiots are going?" He glanced at the gas tank and was relieved to see it read three-quarters full. If that was where they were heading, he had plenty of gas to get there. "What could they possibly find in Vegas? I thought everything was at that stupid amusement park. This had better be worth it," he groused, switching on the radio to keep himself entertained during the long drive.

  As Daniel Crain hung his elbow out the window of the Cadillac feeling the dry desert air mix with the cold refrigerated air blowing out the multiple vents of the Caddy, he wondered what in the world Las Vegas had to do with Walt Disney. He was following the Aston Martin from varying distances, coming closer when there were off ramps approaching, further back when the desert stretched for dozens of miles. In the event they pulled off in some isolated town or took Highway 395 north out of Barstow or stopped in Baker, Daniel just wanted to make sure he didn't lose sight of them. He came close to losing them when they pulled over in Barstow and Lance took over the driving. Daniel knew if they got into Vegas without him, it would be next to impossible to find them without knowing where they were headed.

Crain watched as the Aston Martin passed the little used—but famous—Zzyzx off-ramp, the last alphabetical listing of any North American landmark; he could see that the little sports car was not slowing up and he knew that not much lay between Zzyzx and the next town of Jean, another fifty-five miles ahead. Daniel now allowed his Caddy to drift back about three miles, confident that they were indeed headed to the gambling capital of the world.

However, he had no idea what their ultimate destination might be.

"Hey, I like that song," Kimberly protested as she reached for the radio dial.

"I thought you were asleep," Lance apologized, glancing over at Kimberly as she hunted for the station that had been playing a song by Boston.

"I was, until you decided to ride the 'wake-up' ruts in the side of the road for a mile."

"Sorry, I was just thinking about the clue again," admitted Lance a little sheepishly. "And it wasn't for a mile…it was only about three seconds."

"That's okay," Kimberly waved him off, finding the song 'More than a Feeling' on the radio. "Sorry I haven't been much of a driving companion," she added, leaning toward Lance whose hair was blowing softly in the wind that trailed over the windshield and into the convertible.

"That's alright. I know you needed some rest, considering what the past week has been like for you."

Kimberly smiled at Lance, enthralled for the moment by that cute dimple he had on his right cheek. She was content in his presence. It was an emotion she was surprised to find herself feeling. Only a month earlier was when she had learned what little she knew about him from her father. Kimberly had immediately felt that she could never trust—let alone fall for someone like Lance. She had labeled him 'Hollywood' in her mind; she saw herself as the complete opposite to that label. If he was the Film-Making Capital of the World, Hollywood, then she saw herself as some quiet, sleepy little town.

Yet, now she knew a different side to this incredibly good looking man.

And she found her heart racing when he looked at her.

"I guess I haven't been getting enough sleep lately," Kimberly admitted, taking a deep breath then stretched her arms over her head, letting the wind blow through her fingers for the sheer enjoyment of the feeling. Lance watched her out of the corner of his eye. He found difficulty keeping his eyes on the road.

"How much further?" Kimberly asked, glancing out the windshield and seeing the stretch of asphalt vanish in a shimmering mirage miles ahead. She could see the little casino-town of Jean poking out of the glistening haze that radiated from the hot desert floor.

Lance couldn't resist. "Are we there yet? Man, can I picture you as a child!" He broke off the teasing at the look on her face. "I'm just kidding. You were probably precocious.... In answer to your question, we are about fifty miles outside Vegas right now," Lance told her. "That is Jean up ahead. Need to stop for a bathroom break or something to eat?" Lance knew that there was a couple of fast food stops in Jean as well as an Outlet Mall.

"Nope, I'm good." She suddenly chuckled and shook her head.

"What?" Lance asked, intrigued by the unknown reason for her levity.

She turned her smiling face to his. "Oh, I just had a sudden random memory pop up. This trip of ours reminded me of a date I once went on."

"Should I be jealous?" was his light question.

"Hmm, I'll let you figure that out. Let's see, I had to have been about seventeen or eighteen. He was so dreamy! He worked the canoes...."

"What is it about those canoe guides?" Lance broke in, disbelieving. "They always have all the girls waiting for them when they get off work. I do not get it."

"Then transfer to the canoes and you'll find out!"

Lance scoffed at her idea. "Naw, too much work. Go on with your story."

"Todd was his name. That's right, it was Todd. Gosh, I haven't thought about him in years."

"Glad I could help," Lance good-naturedly groused.

"Now, don't get frumpy. Let me finish," she laughed. "We decided to go for a drive one day. We got on I-5 and just started driving south, talking the whole time, not really paying attention to where we were. I swear Dad must have been tracking me with GPS or LoJack or something. We got all the way to San Diego when suddenly two highway patrol cars pulled up behind us, lights flashing! Scared the bejeebers out of Todd. Well, out of me, too. We didn't know what was going on. They made us pull off the freeway and checked our IDs and all. One of them went back to his car and made a call. Guess who? My dad! I guess I was getting way too far away from my usual habits and he was worried that something had happened to me and I was being taken to Mexico. Guess whose date ended right then?" She laughed again. "Yeah, Todd turned us right around and drove straight back to the house. Never saw him again. Well, I never dated him again. I saw him in the Park now and then. He avoided me every time!"

"And I remind you of the studly Todd? The buff canoe guide?"

Kimberly made a show of looking him up and down as he drove. "Well, Todd did have brown hair...."

Lance slapped the steering wheel. "There you go! Spitting image."

"Actually," she drawled out, "this whole adventure reminds me of the studly Todd. Jumping in the car and driving somewhere new. Wind blowing through my hair. Handsome man driving my car.... The whole thing."

"Ah, so know we know studly Todd is also handsome. I think I should find him and beat him up."

"Poor Todd. He was pretty shook up! I was

mad at my dad for weeks…. Say, do you need to stop?" Kimberly asked realizing Lance had been driving since they left Barstow, at least two hours ago.

"No, I'm doing fine. Relax and we should be checking in…," Lance looked at his watch and then at the speedometer which read eighty-three mph, "in about thirty-three minutes."

"Checking in?" Kimberly asked. She didn't even ask Lance about where they would be staying. Or *how* they would be staying…. She felt her heart start pounding. "Uh, Lance, where *are* we staying? And how many rooms?"

Lance gave an understanding smile, knowing exactly what Kimberly was thinking. "Hey, I'm nothing if not a true gentleman. We are staying in a two-bedroom suite on the Strip at the Luxor."

Kimberly thought about how that sentence could be turned around. Then she smiled, thankful that Lance was not assuming anything. She didn't know what the 'Luxor' was. But it didn't matter to her at this point.

Reassured, she leaned in and kissed his dimple. "I trust you."

Lance gave a little laugh. "And…I…trust…you," he said, accenting each word as he cupped her chin in his fingers.

Kimberly was almost giddy with excitement as the Aston Martin cruised down the Strip. Alternately looking out one side of the convertible and then the other, Kimberly saw landmark hotels…colossal structures that she had only seen in postcards and on television. Like Disneyland, each resort hotel offered guests a world of fantasy; unlike the world Disney had created, however, each one of these worlds was often a jarring sense of contradicting themes. Nothing really tied one hotel to the next; from Medieval themes to Egyptian, from the skyline of New York to the fabled Emerald City, Las Vegas was a city in perpetual competition; each resort vying for each tourist's particular imagination—as well as each tourist's last dollar.

Outside the glitz of the Strip, unseen to most guests was another form of conflicting chaos. Just as Disneyland had built a berm that separated the Park from the outside world, Vegas had its own berm of parking structures and freeway sound barriers that blocked the view of a small portion of the city with its run-down homes with metal bars protecting each window, and residents who sat on beat-up couches or ripped-out bench seats from old cars, drinking cheap beer. As the saying goes, 'What happens in Vegas stays in Vegas'. But to Lance, who had been to Las Vegas many times, he always thought the saying should have been, 'What you lose in Vegas is lost forever'.

Yet, here where money has produced multiple havens of man-made fountains and high-rise steel, glass and concrete hotels, Kimberly only saw the world that the architects and the visionaries wanted the people with money to see.

"**W**ow," was all Kimberly seemed able to say over and over, seeing one mega hotel after another as Lance drove slowly through the congested Las Vegas Boulevard. "Is that a roller-coaster going around that hotel?"

Lance glanced to his left and saw the 'Manhattan Express' rocketing down a steep hill at the New York, New York hotel. "Yep." A moment later, the a speeding coaster was moving through a cork-screw section of the track that was elevated above the entrance to the hotel and the screams emanating from the riders could be heard over the honking horns and other sounds on the busy street.

"Want to do some shopping before we check in?" Lance asked her, checking his watch. They had an hour to kill before they could officially check in at the Luxor.

"Sure," Kimberly readily replied. "I can't imagine what shopping must be like here. Is there a mall around?"

Lance laughed. "I'll take you to the most decadent mall I know."

Making a left turn into Caesar's Palace, he pulled into the parking garage in the back. After a series of left turns, he found a level with some empty parking spots near double glass doors that had a large gold sign above them that read 'The Forum Shops.'

"Should we put the top up on my car?" Kimberly asked as they pulled into the parking space, wondering on the wisdom of leaving her convertible open. There were people everywhere and she was a little concerned about her car.

"Well, you'll have to show me how to pull up the top," Lance told her. "Every convertible is different, you know.... Why are you looking at me funny?"

Kimberly had an odd smile on her face. "Yeah, it is pretty tricky," she nodded as she pushed a button on the console, right next to the shifter. With a soft hum, the top started lifting and quickly settled in place.

Lance took it well. He laughed as he opened his door and went around to assist Kimberly out of the car. "Are you ready to follow me down the rabbit hole, Alice?" Lance invited, locking the car with a remote and taking her hand as he led her to the glass doors and the elevators that would take them down to the luxurious casino and equally opulent Forum Shops.

Behind them, they were unaware of headlights reflecting off those closing glass doors—the headlights of a car moving very slowly through the parking structure. It pulled into a nearby empty stall and the lights were quickly extinguished.

Sensory overload was the term coming to Kimberly's mind. The casino they entered was magnificent; an understatement, really, where it appeared that money was no object when it came to building and decorating the casino. As they passed through the entrance to the Forum Shops, beautiful boutiques designed to resemble a Roman city, were lined one after another; fountains, columns, gold-painted statues, and a dome-shaped ceiling that had lights emitted from hidden projectors that conveyed a perpetual purple dusk-like sky where pink clouds actually moved slowly across the fictional skyline. It felt like dusk even at one-thirty in the afternoon.

"I've never seen anything like this." Kimberly was in awe as they walked along the marbled floors.

He held her hand as they visited various shops; elegant and sparkling retail outlets that sold everything from clothing to toys, from perfume to electronics.

Lance soon found that Kimberly was like her father—frugal. She enjoyed everything she saw, but was hesitant to try anything on or to purchase something that caught her eye. Yet, Lance was finally able to convince her to buy a beautiful soft pink dress that was marked down from $250 to $94.99. It flowed in appealing and flattering lines when she emerged from the dressing room, pirouetting in front of a full-length three-sided mirror. Lance had applauded the dress and the pleased smile he saw upon Kimberly's face.

"It's you," Lance said simply.

"Oh, I've never owned anything like it," Kimberly grinned, adjusting the straps on her shoulders and looking herself over in the mirror. Her blond hair fell gracefully over her shoulders. "I feel so…pink," Kimberly laughed, watching the mid-length hem dancing around her thighs.

Lance smiled, feeling very pleased with himself.

Waiting for Kimberly just outside the doors of the shop, Lance watched people pass by. He spied a magic shop two doors down and on the other side of the Mall from where he stood.

As he stepped back into the clothing shop, he called out, "Kimberly?" The saleswoman who had patiently helped Kimberly try on the dress was folding the lovely creation neatly into a box. "I'm going to be over at the magic shop right across the way," Lance pointed in the right direction.

"Okay. I'm almost done here."

Lance turned and headed out across the mall. Back home, his tennis partner, Mike, was an avid amateur magician in addition to being a great tennis instructor and player. Many a time after a tennis match, Mike would astound opponents with slight of hand and card tricks. Lance thought a little magical gift, like a book or a new trick, might be fun to give his friend.

Lance was always impressed with such feats of dexterity and manipulation by his friend and other magicians he'd seen perform. Through the shop window he watched as a small crowd amassed in front of the counter. The clerk, obviously a magician himself, made a playing card magically float, spin and fly around the spectators. Lance smiled, knowing the secret of that trick. Even as the secret had been revealed to him years ago, he still enjoyed watching a professional execute the effect, and seeing the resulting look of awe the visual trick inspired on those who watched.

Lance continued to watch as the magician finished his trick and the crowd began to disperse, many of whom were still talking about what they had seen as they exited the shop. A few stragglers were begging him to perform the trick again. The magician, well trained in both the performance of such magic as well as making sales, convinced two young boys to "invest" in purchasing that magic trick for themselves.

Just as he was about to enter the shop and look around, Lance noticed the shop address on the upper corner of the large plate glass window he had been looking through. He tilted his head at the numbers, each one being spelled out with playing cards that overlapped each other as if in a fan. The letters before the numbered cards said 'Magic Masters', the name of the shop.

Kimberly came up beside him, her package under her arm.

"I didn't know you liked magic," she told him, looking inside the shop. A number of people milled about the displays, books, and counters that housed interesting magical devices.

"Uh, Kim," Lance said, his voice distracted. Kimberly had never heard him call her that. "Does the shop address look familiar to you?"

Kimberly looked up and saw the numbers two, seven, and three displayed as fanned cards, a diamond, spade and hearts representing the suits.

At first she was going to say "No," but then it came to her. "The cards on the animation cels," Kimberly gasped, putting her free hand on his shoulder as he turned to face her.

They looked at each other for a moment and instantly said at the same time, "Walt's clue!"

They laughed at their simultaneous remark.

"You don't think it could be an address Walt might be trying to tell us?" Kimberly asked.

Eyes bright, Lance was looking back at the numbers, smiling. "Perhaps, Kimberly. Perhaps."

Forgotten were the remainder of the shops, the intermittent show held in the middle of the mall every hour on the hour, and even the reason they were in Vegas—relaxation.

Lance and Kimberly made a beeline back to the parking garage.

"Since the break-in, I didn't want to leave the animation cels or the clue at my place," Lance told her as they speed-walked to the car. He cast a sideways glance at Kimberly next to him. "I also thought we might need something to pass the time in the hotel room."

Kimberly looked over at Lance with a gleam in her eye. "What, you didn't want to play cards or watch television in the room?"

"Nah…. But I did have other interests in mind."

They reached the car and Lance opened the trunk then closed it quickly, not taking anything out.

"What is it?" Kimberly asked.

"Too dark in the parking garage to look at the cels the way we need to," Lance said, thinking about what he wanted to do with them. "Let's go to the hotel, check in and then let's look at the cels in the quiet…." Lance looked around the shadowed parking structure, then finished, "and in the security of our room."

Kimberly agreed as the two jumped in the car.

After exiting the parking structure and turning right, they headed back down the Strip the way they had come earlier. The Luxor Hotel was back another mile.

After waiting for traffic to let up for a moment, Lance chirped the tires and gunned the small car into traffic and made it without any cars honking at him.

Less than a minute later, a black Cadillac pulled out into the rush of traffic.

Lance tossed their two bags onto his king-sized bed and sat down. Kimberly sat next to him as he pulled the briefcase onto his lap.

Where sitting on a bed in a hotel room with Lance might have otherwise been awkward for Kimberly, or at least dangerously exciting, she did-n't have anything on her mind more than what Lance had in the briefcase.

"Why didn't we think of this before?" he asked her.

"Think of what?" Kimberly was confused, not sure what he was referring to. She figured Lance thought that the playing cards on the animated cels might represent an address. But, an address number without a street or even city would be pretty hard to determine…if the cards represented a numbered address at all.

"I think these three cels are hiding something else," Lance explained, pushing the little tabs to open the case with a loud clack. Propping open the lid and pulling out a manila folder, he handed the folder to Kimberly while he set the case on the floor at their feet.

Kimberly held the folder on her lap and opened it, pointing the opening toward Lance. He pulled out the three clear plastic sheets and held them up in front of him, spread between his hands. Besides the colored animated playing cards and the characters from *Alice in Wonderland* on each eight by nine-inch clear plastic sheet, there was something else; centered along the bottom of each sheet was a set of hand-written letters. When Lance had originally examined the sheets, he thought the letters identified the production position of each cel—where each particular sheet fell within the tens of thousands of cels that would need to be produced for a full-length animated motion picture. Other thoughts that had entered his head were that they were identification markings for music and/or dialogue that would be recorded later after an entire scene had been drawn. He hadn't given the random letters much thought.

That was until he saw the playing-card address at the magic shop.

"See these letters?" Lance asked Kimberly, pointing to the handwritten letters along the bottom of each frame.

Kimberly nodded, looking at the letters which seemed to have no meaning.

The first sheet had the letters M N   T E U, the second sheet read, A __   R T S; the third sheet had, I S E __   A

"Do you think those could be abbreviations for something?" Kimberly wondered, pointing at the letters on the first page. "Like 'minute' or 'miniature' or something?"

"Well, that's what I thought at first, too," Lance told her. "Then I thought it stood for initials of animators responsible for drawing each page or markings for dialogue and music that would be added later."

"So that magic shop didn't make you think of an address with these playing cards on each sheet, like these, then?" Kimberly pointed to the three different playing cards depicted on the three cels.

"Not at all," Lance told her with a sly smile forming on his lips. Kimberly looked at him and slapped his shoulder playfully.

"What!? Tell me what you know!" Kimberly demanded with a laugh, her eyes wide and expectant.

Lance took his time, not because he was trying to drive Kimberly mad, but because he wasn't one hundred percent sure that he was correct.

He started to explain. "The address on the magic shop had three cards fanned out, like a magician holding a deck of cards out for a spectator to choose one." Lance paused. As if to clarify his last sentence, he added, "I have a friend who does some excellent card tricks."

"I don't care about some magician friend of yours!" Kimberly laughingly shouted. "What is it about that address?"

"Well, you see, the cards were overlapped." Lance held the three plastic sheets so that the ace, which was drawn in the left-middle of the sheet, was on the bottom. The next sheet, the three of hearts, was drawn nearly in the middle. The last sheet, which had the two of spades being drawn slightly on the right-middle of its sheet, Lance put on top of the others. He held the sheets out like three cards fanned out. Instead of saying something like, "here pick a card," he took the three sheets and held them up toward the window where the afternoon sun was still bright.

"Watch." Lance lined the three sheets up together. The way the cards were drawn looked just like the cards that were on the magic shop…fanned apart but overlapping.

"I still don't get it," Kimberly murmured with her eyebrows pinched together looking intently at the cards on the sheets.

"It isn't the cards," Lance said with a sly, knowing grin. "Look at the letters."

With a gasp, Kimberly now saw exactly what Lance saw.

"I can't believe we didn't see it before!" exclaimed Kimberly, her hand covering her mouth.

"It was right there all along," Lance shook his head, looking at the three sheets he held together in his hand. "But, like Walt's other clues, it required not just a little work…." He paused, thinking back to what Walt had written in the diary he and Adam had found. He smiled oddly. "It all started with a moose, you know."

"Daddy used to say that, too. I was never exactly sure what it meant."

"Walt had written it in his diary, and then he explained about the cartoon it referred to. The moral of the story was to choose your friends wisely and that two heads were better than one."

"But, I didn't come up with anything, you did," Kimberly pointed out, somewhat deflated.

"I would never have seen that magic shop, its address, and the layered cards had *you* and I not come here together," Lance told her, emphasizing his point by holding Kimberly's chin in his fingers. He leaned in and gave her a soft kiss. "Well, it all started now!" he murmured, gazing into her eyes.

Kimberly smiled, excited by what they had just discovered and the emotions she felt when Lance kissed her. Lance reached over to the dresser in front of them, setting the cels down. Turning to Kimberly again, he said, "And Kimberly, I *really* like working with you. You're a lot more fun than Adam." He then kissed her again hard and long. Kimberly's fingers reached up and ran through Lance's thick hair as she kissed him back.

On the dresser, the three cels sat neatly together. Along the bottom of the three pages, the letters that had been an enigma just moments before now fell in a straight line together.

MAIN STREET USA

Lance and Kimberly now had a street name to go with the numbers.

CHAPTER 10

As tempting as it was to check out of the hotel, hop in the Aston Martin and test the reliability of her radar detector as they sped back to Anaheim, they decided instead to celebrate their discovery more sedately by going out to dinner. Lance figured that if the clue, provided it was where they thought it was, had been hidden there for over forty years, it could wait another twenty-four hours for them to begin their search. Actually, Lance decided, the two of them were celebrating more than just solving of latest clue. They were celebrating themselves.

Both Kimberly and Lance had been almost exuberant with the discovery of the coded address along the bottom of the three animated cels that Walt had left behind. What was perhaps equally exciting was the relationship that they both felt was growing; a relationship that was now built on mutual trust and mutual respect—even though it had begun with the two of them being thrown together by mysterious and bizarre circumstances.

They decided to dress up a little with Kimberly modeling her new dress for Lance as he finished shaving in front of his bathroom mirror in their suite. Afterward, he had put on tailored pants, an off-white shirt with an amber brown tie that blended with his eyes, topped off by a very nice woven sport coat.

As Kimberly was putting the finishing touches on her hair, Lance knocked and then walked into her room and softly kissed her exposed neck, sending shivering goose bumps over her arms and neck. Happy with that reaction, he kissed her again once they were in the elevator that took them down to the enormous lobby of the Luxor. When the valet brought around the Aston Martin, Lance popped open the door for Kimberly and kissed her one more time as she settled into her seat. As Lance pulled away to shut her door, Kimberly pulled on Lance's arm, pulling him back to her lips.

"I think I'm enjoying this," Kimberly whispered breathlessly.

Lance remained close to her face. "I have never enjoyed kissing anyone as much as I do you," Lance truthfully told her, then sealed his remark with one final kiss before closing her door.

"Where are you taking me?" Kimberly asked, finding it harder and harder to keep her eyes off his handsome face. She was seeing his attractiveness differently than she had before and wanted to memorize every curve and shape that made up Lance Brentwood.

"I'm taking you to the top," Lance told her with a sly smile.

Kimberly looked at him quizzically. She was expecting something like "Italian" or some exotic restaurant name that she had never even heard of before.

Instead of explaining further, Lance simply pointed. Up ahead, as they drove north on Las Vegas Boulevard, Kimberly followed the line from his pointing finger.

A gasp escaped Kimberly's lips when she saw that his finger was pointing at the tallest structure in the southwest: The Stratosphere Hotel. Kimberly looked back at Lance. "Is there really a restaurant up there?" she asked a little tentatively. While she had no problem flying in an airplane or climbing out onto a branch in the Treehouse at Disneyland, she had never been up in a building so tall and so narrow…let alone to have dinner at such a location.

"Not only is there a restaurant, there is also a roller coaster up there," he teased as they approached the needle-like structure that rose almost twelve-hundred feet above Downtown Las Vegas. "That is, if you're game."

"Uh, no way, Lance."

Lance smiled at the look of shock on her face. "Don't worry," he assured her with a laugh. "Even I won't go on that one!"

As Lance drove past Sahara Avenue, making the curve into Downtown, Kimberly craned her neck in looking up at the towering structure that was just ahead, to their left. She had no idea what it must be like to look out from such a height and see the sights of Las Vegas so far below.

The Top of the World restaurant, located

below the observation deck near the top of the towering structure, revolved 360 degrees every hour, giving patrons undeniably the best views of the valley. The twinkling lights far below now stretched all the way to the slopes of Mt. Charleston to the west and to the mountains that bordered the Lake Mead recreational area and the Valley of Fire to the east.

"To Walt," Lance said as he was holding a glass of 1985 French Bordeaux just after the waiter had opened and poured the two glasses and left to turn in their orders.

Kimberly was smiling. In fact, she felt that her smile was now a permanent fixture on her face. "Yes, to Walt," Kimberly responded. Their eyes met and words, at that point, were totally unnecessary. They sipped their wine, feeling the intoxication of their feelings mix with the wine, the view and subtle music that permeated within the room adding additional ambiance.

"Main Street, USA…," Lance said, thinking about the clue for the hundredth time since they cleaned up, changed and drove downtown.

"At least we know where we need to start looking next," Kimberly agreed as salads were placed on the table in front of them.

"Each store on Main Street at Disneyland is supposed to have an address," Lance told her as he took a bite of his Caesar's Salad, remembering the clue for the Penny Arcade and finally seeing the address on either side of the arcade sign. "I know at least some of shops have three-digit addresses," he added, savoring flavor of the dressing that had just a hint of anchovies mixed in.

Kimberly nodded, finishing a small fork full of salad. She took a sip of wine as she thought. "If a clue is in one of the shops on Main Street, I wonder where he could have hidden it. We have to consider that all of the shops have gone through significant renovations over the last forty years since Walt...," Kimberly paused not really knowing what word to use to describe Walt's resting place.

"Went into hiding?" Lance finished for her with a smile. She nodded, wiping the corner of her mouth with the cloth napkin on her lap. He continued, saying, "Yeah, I thought of that possibility too." Lance angled his chair to the side of the table and turned his face toward the dramatic sights, but he wasn't really focused on anything but his thoughts. "I hope that *whatever* is supposed to be there hasn't unwittingly been removed by some construction crew." Lance turned back to the table and looked at Kimberly again, adding, "You know, Kimberly, what Walt is sending us to find might very well be at the bottom of a landfill."

"Oh, that would be a shame." Kimberly's smile faded.

Lance saw the disappointment etched across her face. To him, it felt as if the sun was being obscured by a fogbank. "However," he reminded her, "I have to say that up to this point, every clue that Walt left had been so thoughtfully worked out that each one of them had been preserved...you know, left unmoved and undetected. It could have been a combination of Walt's and your father's efforts." Lance saw a look of hope come back to Kimberly's eyes. He then added, "I don't see why this one would be any different."

"Well, I guess there is only one way to find out," Kimberly grinned as the waiter came and refreshed their wine glasses.

Lance had something else he wanted to tell her. He waited for the server to return the bottle to the table and then assure them their dinner would be right out. When the waiter turned to attend another table, Lance took a deep breath and reached out to take Kimberly's hands in his. "Kimberly," Lance started in a soft, serious voice, "regardless of what we find…or don't find," Lance paused and interlocked his fingers with hers. He brought his eyes up from the joined hands and looked into her eyes as if he was searching for an answer to a question he hadn't asked yet. "I don't want to lose you. I *can't* lose you."

Kimberly was stunned by his words. She felt tears of happiness form in her eyes. Never had she felt such emotion in her life.

"I don't ever want to lose you, either, Lance."

Instead of catching a show as they had intended, Lance and Kimberly decided to drive down the Strip to the Hard Rock Casino.

"I want to show you a really good time," he told her as he pulled into the Casino's valet parking area. The valet helped Kimberly out of the Aston Martin and Lance was given a card in exchange for his keys.

"You already have," Kimberly replied as

Lance walked around the car to the curb where she waited. Kimberly slid her arm through his and gave him a light kiss on his cheek. The brown-vested man holding their keys smiled as he looked at the couple, his gaze lingering on the stunning blond. He thanked Lance with a slight bow and offered a "Have a great evening," before slipping in behind the wheel.

Unseen by either Lance or Kimberly was a black Cadillac that had pulled into the short-term registration parking zone, lights off and motor idling.

The pool area of the Hard Rock Casino was restricted to adults only, with an eclectic gathering of people dressed in everything from hand-beaded cocktail dresses to string bikinis. A DJ played music in front of a well-lit dance floor; a number of couples were dancing to the heavy beat permeating from the surround sound system. The tropical flora of the entire pool area was complemented by waterfalls, large rock formations, intimate coves and the huge pool itself that literally wove around the three-acre grounds like a maze.

As they stood taking in the sights, a cocktail waitress, dressed in a bright reddish-orange bikini top and matching sarong-covered bottom, walked up to Lance and Kimberly. They ordered the 'drink of the night'—an appropriately-named drink called Caribbean Kiss. Containing dark rum mixed with Kahlua and Amaretto and had a ring of brown sugar around the rim of the glass, it was as sweet as it was potent.

"There is an empty cabana over there," the waitress pointed out to them. She gave them a knowing smile as she handed them their drinks from a small tray held on the palm of her hand.

Lance took a sip and followed where she was pointing. He could see there was indeed a very private curtained cabana, with an oversized, stuffed lounge chair for two.

"Thank you very much," Lance replied as he took out a fifty dollar bill from his pocket and paid the attractive brunette. "Keep the change." Lance took Kimberly's hand and the two walked around the lighted edge of the pool and over to the cabana where they could sit facing the middle of the pool. Except for some mood lighting that highlighted the tropical plants around the cabana, the interior of the ten-by-ten canvas covered cabana was intimately dark.

Lance adjusted the back of the lounge so that it was tilted up more and took off his jacket. Mindful of the fluttering hem of her dress, Kimberly took her place on one side, Lance on the other.

They settled back against the comfortable cushions as Lance remarked with a contented sigh, "Doesn't get much better than this!" He took Kimberly's hand in his and they interlocked their fingers.

"Thank you for all of this," Kimberly shyly told him after a long, slow sip of her drink.

Lance smiled. "I did this for both of us. We both needed the break," he told her, squeezing her hand as he leaned over for a kiss.

Just then, Kimberly's face went slack.

"What is it? What's wrong? I was just going

to kiss you," Lance drew back when he saw her eyes widen and her mouth open as if she were going to scream. It wasn't the usual reaction she had to his kisses.

"I...I swear I just saw my uncle Daniel over there behind those trees," Kimberly pointed after shakily setting her glass down on the small table next to the lounge.

"What?!" Lance asked incredulously. "No way. Crain...here?" He thought about it for a half second. "Wait here." He set his glass down and bolted from the lounge. Circling around the pool, he ran toward a small grove of palm trees that were protected by a hedge of manicured shrubs.

As Lance darted around the cluster of trees, Kimberly sat up on her lounge, afraid to move.

Lance double-checked all the areas around that part of the pool but found no Daniel. He even walked up the secluded path that lead back to the crowded area of the pool. He passed several couples, one of which he asked if they had seen a brown-haired man skulking around the area. Their answer was a surprised no as they said they hadn't. They had just come from the bar on the other side of the pool.

Lance returned to Kimberly who was still sitting where he had left her, unconsciously trembling. "I didn't see him," Lance explained as he sat next to her on her side of the lounge. Both looked out over the gardens, their eyes scanning.

"I could have sworn it was him, Lance," Kimberly insisted, trying to validate herself.

"I believe you. I honestly believe you," Lance replied, putting his arm around her. Kimberly tilted her head onto Lance's shoulder as he rocked slowly back and forth. "I wouldn't put it past the idiot to follow us here," Lance quietly remarked. "But if it really was him, *why* would he go to such an extreme?"

"I don't know," Kimberly answered, miserable. "I just know that I don't trust him."

"Yeah, me either."

"Can we go, Lance?" Kimberly looked up into his face. She felt he might be upset with her for their having to leave such a wonderful evening, but she just could not put her mind at ease now.

"Absolutely," Lance immediately responded as he stood up, taking Kimberly's hand.

"I hope you aren't too disappointed," Kimberly dropped her eyes as she turned to face him. "I…I just have to get out of here. Whether or not it was him, he has me spooked now."

"Regardless of who you saw, I want you safe and I want us to be happy," Lance told her, kissing her forehead. "There will be other evenings. I promise."

Relieved by his understanding, Kimberly turned her head and laid it on Lance's chest. He could feel her heart beating rapidly as he held her. He knew she had seen something that really scared her. And he certainly wouldn't put it past Daniel Crain to have followed them.

What made Lance most nervous was the possibility that it really was Crain who Kimberly saw. If he had followed them all the way to Las Vegas, Lance knew he must be desperate. And, from his own history, Lance knew a desperate man could do things…. He shook his head at the thought. He had better not take any chances. He had to get Kimberly away from there.

Leaving their unfinished drinks in the cabana, they quickly exited the Hard Rock Casino. Lance presented the valet with his card and the Aston Martin was quickly driven around the curved entrance and came to a screeching halt at the curb in front of them.

Lance tipped the attendant who held open Kimberly's door and couldn't help but notice the trailing gaze of the young man watching her. *Yes, she is beautiful, isn't she*, Lance thought to himself as he shoved the shift lever into gear and pulled out of the hotel driveway.

Wanting nothing more than to get back to the Luxor, Lance wanted Kimberly feeling safe and back at a relaxed state of mind. He could see, as she sat in her bucket seat, that she was sitting very upright, her still-worried eyes were darting across the windshield.

Lance took her hand as they entered Harmon Avenue, turning right away from the Strip. Lance, checking his rear-view mirror several times just to make sure they weren't being followed, passed the first signal at Koval Lane and turned right onto Paradise Road. There was far less traffic on Paradise, a street that paralleled Las Vegas Boulevard. Heading south, they passed through a more residential area of Las Vegas, one that certainly did not resemble the name of the street.

Stepping up his pace, he moved into the right lane where he made a right turn on the green arrow onto Tropicana Avenue. At the next signal, Lance had to slow down. It looked like there was a major accident ahead on Tropicana. All traffic was being diverted to the left onto Koval Lane.

"Dang, if the police don't have more lights on their cars than the hotels," Lance commented with a laugh, looking at all the pulsating blue and red lights on at least three police cars, two paramedic vehicles and a fire truck.

The street was literally ablaze with lights. Kimberly looked out her side of the car as Lance followed the traffic onto Koval Lane.

"Looks like a pretty bad accident," Kimberly told him as she saw two cars surrounded by a shroud of glass on the asphalt. Angled the way they were, Kimberly couldn't make out what kind of vehicles were involved in the wreck. As Lance finished the turn, she saw from a different angle that one car was black; it was imbedded into the side of what she could now see was a large truck, one with a jacked-up body sitting on large wheels. The front windshield of the car had a large hole in the driver's side. Not a good sign, Kimberly grimaced as she turned her head from the sight of the wreckage as they continued driving down Koval.

What Kimberly hadn't seen was the emblem on the black car; it was the gold laurel wreath of a Cadillac.

Koval Lane made a bend to the right and then to the left before making another right toward Las Vegas Boulevard.

"You all right, Kimberly?" Lance asked. She had been silent for quite a while, which told him that she was still troubled.

"Yes, I'm fine," Kimberly remarked automatically, her mind still centered on the accident they just passed. There was something about it that made her think of déjà vu. She shook her head in frustration and turned to look at Lance. "I'm just...." Suddenly, Kimberly shrieked as she saw a car careening over toward Lance's side of the Aston Martin. "Look out, Lance!" Kimberly screamed, grabbing the front dash of the car.

At her warning, Lance's head jerked to his left just in time to see the car sliding toward him. He punched the gas pedal, knowing her car can do zero-to-sixty in five seconds. The V-12 roared into action, throwing their heads back as the car started to pull away. With a sickening grind, they still heard—and felt—an impact as the other car glanced into their rear bumper. Had they stayed in place, Lance would have been T-boned.

"Dang!" Lance yelled as he yanked the wheel to the right. The rack-and-pinion steering responded instantly. Swerving away from the impact, and still accelerating, Lance could see there were no cars parked along the side of the road where he had slid. Mind racing as fast as the car, he stayed in the designated bicycle lane, glad that the late night hour didn't encourage too many night riders. Glancing in the rearview mirror, he wanted to see what happened to the other car. But, no headlights could be seen.

Even though the Aston Martin had been going only about thirty miles per hour at the time of the impact, they were now doing almost sixty. Still seeing only darkness behind their car, Lance felt it was safe to pull over. He applied the brakes to slow them down to a more reasonable speed and then pulled over to regroup and check the damage to Kimberly's car. "The other car had to be a drunk driver," Lance was thinking out loud, assuming that the man—or woman—must have panicked, slammed on their brakes and headed in a different direction away from their actions. As he reached over to open the door, he was shocked to see headlights suddenly glaring in his side mirror and coming at them again. "What the…!" Lance yelled at the mirror, seeing how rapidly the other car was nearing them.

Kimberly turned and saw it too. She yelled, "Lance look out!"

Pushing the start button, the engine immediately roared to life. Lance jammed it into gear and swerved back into the lane, accelerating full throttle. He could see he was quickly coming up on a van in the slower of the two lanes. Lance had less than one second to make a decision—slam on the brakes or gun it.

He chose the latter and yanked the wheel quickly to the left, narrowly missing the rear bumper of a mini-van in front of him. Lance then quickly straightened the wheel avoiding the honking on-coming traffic without losing control of the fine sports car.

When he heard the horns behind him, Lance took the chance of looking in the rear view mirror once again. Apparently the mini-van had been forced off the road by the other car. It was then that he truly was unnerved.

Gaining speed, even though the other car

was again bearing down on them, he could make out that it was a large black Cadillac. And he was shocked to see that it was being driven by Daniel Crain.

Lance didn't have the time or the inclination to share that bit of information with Kimberly at that moment. Instead he was looking for a way out of a very dangerous situation and yet still managing to drive at over sixty miles per hour in a thirty-five zone.

Looking forward, Lance saw a yellow sign on the side of the road with a black arrow making a ninety-degree right turn, showing the road curved that way up ahead. Lance now knew that he had the edge.

"Hang on, darling," he managed to call to Kimberly who was white-faced, but silent.

In the moment it took Lance to see the sign and talk to Kimberly, the Cadillac roared up behind them, banging twice into their already-damaged rear bumper. The force caused Lance to jerk the wheel to the left toward on-coming traffic as Kimberly gave a whimper, closing her eyes. Regaining control of his steering wheel, Lance took a chance and gunned the engine faster. Pulling away from the Caddy for a brief moment was all he needed. Sensing that Crain was intent on pushing the Aston Martin across the road into the heavy on-coming traffic, Lance moved into the center turn lane, then hit the brakes as he turned the wheel hard to the right. As expected, the sports car went into a sideways slide for about twenty feet. Lance then slammed his foot back onto the accelerator and he turned deftly to correct his slide. Immediately the wheels stopped skidding, grabbed pavement, and he regained full control as the road turned sharply to the right.

Luckily, there were no cars directly in front of the Aston Martin as Lance retained control of the speeding vehicle and applied the brakes in short pulses.

Kimberly was holding on to the door handle and the bottom of her seat the whole time, too afraid to even scream.

As Lance anticipated, the very heavy Cadillac could not negotiate the hard right turn at the speed that it was traveling. Slowing down, both Lance and Kimberly whipped their heads around as they watched the black car skid uncontrolled across two lanes of traffic. Four cars in the eastbound lanes saw the headlights and what was happening and slammed on their brakes in time. In what seemed like slow motion, the Cadillac continued to slide sideways across the street, tires billowing white smoke.

In another second, the Caddy hit the curb, its left side wheels bent sideways. The car's momentum carried it over the curb where it then slammed into a light pole and a fire hydrant, neither object slowing the big car down much. In a spray of sparks from the undercarriage dragging on the ground, the car went sideways into the back corner of an empty video store taking out a huge chunk of the building's graffiti-covered stucco before coming to a full stop. The back half of the Cadillac was buried in the debris.

Lance had slowed down enough to see that there was no explosion or fire as he feared might occur.

"Shouldn't we stop?" Kimberly asked as Lance turned onto a side street before coming to Las Vegas Boulevard. He made another right turn into a dark cul-de-sac and pulled over to the curb.

"Kimberly," Lance started, breathing hard as he turned off the lights and killed the engine. "That car was a big, black Cadillac." Lance saw the association already being made by Kimberly. He knew there hadn't been time for her to recognize the car or the driver. She more than likely had had her eyes closed during the event.

"You mean it was Daniel?" Kimberly whispered, her hand on her mouth.

"Yes. I saw him in the rear-view mirror."

Kimberly didn't say anything. She was willing her heart to stop pounding in her chest.

"At first I thought it was a drunk...that was until he came after us again," Lance explained, rubbing his temples. "I don't know if he was hurt or not," he said picturing the fleeting image of the crash. "And, to be perfectly honest, I don't really care if he was. I just hope no one else was hurt by his stupidity."

Kimberly was thoughtful for a moment. "If he had anything to drink...and, knowing Daniel like I do, he probably had a few beers to give him the courage to try what he had just tried."

"I was thinking that too." Lance said as he reached out to stroke her arm. He now found that his hands were shaking from the experience.

"If we are lucky, he will be taken in for drunk driving. It looks like there may have been quite a few witnesses." Kimberly was just hopeful he wouldn't be able to come after them again.

"And if we are unlucky, someone may have gotten our license plate."

Kimberly pondered that for a moment. Then she remembered something. "Lance, my car doesn't have plates!" She pointed to the paper taped to the inside of the front windshield. "It's a temporary license tag they give you until your personalized plates come in."

"I didn't know you ordered plates." Lance said with a grin, glad for a diversion, any diversion. "What did you order, 'Belle' or 'Princess'?"

"Very funny. I ordered 'Wishful'," Kimberly told him.

"How appropriate," Lance smiled as he nodded.

Kimberly's small smile faded and she became serious again. "Lance? I really want to go home now."

"Back to the Luxor?"

"No, home home. Can we please go *now*?"

Lance gave her an understanding pat on the arm. "Sure, sweetheart. Of course we can. I already have the cels in my briefcase in the trunk. Let's just go get the rest of our stuff and then we'll hit the road." He could feel her body quivering as nerves were taking over.

"No, I want to go now. I...I don't care about those clothes. I want to be safe in my own home...with you," she added shyly, trying to will her body to keep from shaking.

Without another word, Lance leaned over to give her a reassuring kiss. Starting the car, he headed for I-15 and home.

"It turned out to be an unlucky night tonight in Las Vegas for Cadillac as there were two major accidents that tied up traffic in both directions on the Strip in the popular gambling Mecca. What made the two unrelated accidents bizarre was that they both involved last year's 2001 black Cadillacs.

"As we can see in the news feed, officers on the scene in the first two-car wreck had to use the Jaws of Life to extricate the driver. The driver of that Cadillac was then taken by ambulance to the hospital with severe injuries.

"By the time emergency personnel arrived at the scene of the second accident site, as seen here, the driver of this Cadillac had fled the scene. Witnesses reported the car had been speeding down Koval Lane; some speculated it was chasing an unidentified green sports car.

"Veering across two lanes of oncoming traffic, the black Cadillac hit a telephone pole and a fire hydrant before slamming into an empty video store. Lady Luck was on the side of the oncoming cars as all of them were able to avoid the accident.

"As we can see from this footage, it is amazing the unknown driver was able to walk away from the accident. It will take a little more than a paint job to fix up this car.

"Police are still looking for the driver of that second Caddy. If you have any information, please call the number on the screen.

"Now, in other local news...."

The television was clicked off. Kimberly stared at the black screen. "He got away? How could he have gotten out of that mess? Where is he?"

Lance could tell she was still in shock from their horrible evening. After sleeping most of the way home, he had hoped she would have awakened in a calmer frame of mind. Now that they knew Daniel was still out there, he could see that this wouldn't be the case.

"I'm going to call Kevin over for the rest of the night. Until we know where your uncle is, I don't want you left alone. Okay?" he asked when she just sat on the sofa, staring.

"Yes, that's fine," was her automatic response. "Maybe he can't get out of Vegas."

Lance knew now was not the time to pretend to misunderstand her and ask if she meant Kevin. He put an arm around her shoulder and drew her next to him. "Kevin will be here in fifteen minutes. He saw the newscast, too. I'll stay until the house is safely locked and you are good. Okay?"

"Yes, that's fine."

Lance just sat with her until the doorbell rang, causing Kimberly to jump. "It's just Kevin," he assured her. "You stay here. I'll let him in."

"Yes, that's fine."

The two men talked briefly at the door, their voices low. They both now knew they had an injured, desperate, dangerous man on their hands. Kevin would stay at the house until this matter was solved—one way or the other. Lance would be with Kimberly any time she needed to leave the house. They would both make sure she was never alone.

Finding a prescription for a mild sleeping pill in one of the bathrooms, Lance persuaded her to take half a tablet. First she made him promise he too would stay in the house. At her frightened look, he knew he would promise her anything.

He also realized it would be a couple of days before they could begin searching Main Street to see if their discovery was indeed correct. He hoped their next search would be a good distraction for her. Perhaps finding the next step in the hunt would take her mind off things.

Looking at her finally sleeping, at last peaceful, he came to another realization: He would forego the entire quest if he had to just to make sure she was safe and secure.

CHAPTER 11

Like two robbers casing the perimeter of a bank, Kimberly and Lance moved down Main Street with purpose in their step. Unlike the thousands of guests excitedly moving toward various destinations within the Park, taking in all that Disneyland offered the senses, these two were focused only on the few addresses that were written above some of the shop doors.

"I still can't figure out why a street with so many buildings has so few addresses!" Lance grumbled.

Kimberly gave the arm she was holding a squeeze. "My, someone is anxious!"

"Yes, I am," he admitted with a big, contagious grin. "You can't fool me, either, Missy. I know you are just as excited as I…. Hey, didn't we just go past this number again?"

"The Blue Ribbon Bakery is number 201— and, no, we don't have time to get something to eat. We just had lunch a couple of hours ago…."

"I wasn't…."

"Yes, you were."

"Fine." Lance gave a dramatic sigh as they turned to retrace their steps to the other address they had just seen. "Let me starve to death. You'll miss me, you know." He grinned to himself when she unconsciously held his arm tighter. "Here, look. The Crystal Arcade is number 107."

"Well, we now know the building we are looking for is between these two. Since the Bakery's number starts with a two, our building has to be in the same block as the Arcade. There aren't that many storefronts. Want to look for the sign in the window instead?"

Looking upwards at the windows that lined the second stories of the different buildings, Lance cracked, "And that's why you make the big bucks!"

"Just keep reading, Brentwood."

Many windows on Main Street had what looked like an advertisement painted on them. They were actually honors for the person or persons named—a thank you for years of service or dedication to Disneyland or to Walt Disney himself. The windows were presented to the honoree with much ceremony.

"And there we are! Look," he pointed at one of a brick building's identical four windows moments later. "Wow, you were actually right about Walt's use of the word 'WINDOW' being written all in caps in the clue—that it literally referred to a window. It all makes sense," he concluded, nodding his head as he looked up at the window. "The window, the phrase, the coded address, like all of his clues, each part had a connected meaning."

As Kimberly had anticipated, that part of

Walt's clue, **'Caring and Giving Come from the Heart'** was printed in bold black letters, made more prominent by the lace curtain that backed the window. Beige and white striped awnings shaded not only the upper windows, but also the large plate glass window that allowed passers-by to look inside the brick building.

"That has to be the right shop, but I don't see any address," Kimberly indicated the New Century Timepieces store. They were halfway down Main Street, just past the Crystal Arcade.

"Well," Lance told her in a low voice as the two of them stood on the busy sidewalk looking up at the clock shop, "If Walt is destined to return to see the future fruits of his labors someday, it would seem apropos that he would hide a clue in a watch shop."

"But what about the other phrase, 'Two WEDs are better than one'?" she wondered, thinking about the last part of the clue Walt had written on the diary page.

"It looks like a play on words to me. Part of Walt's original instructions was 'Two heads are better than one'," Lance reasoned, taking Kimberly's hand. "We have to assume, since nearly every clue we have found had the letters WED positioned as a reference point to where the clue was hidden, that there must be two sets of WED letters somewhere. Hopefully here," he indicated the shop with a tilt of his chin.

Kimberly thought about that for a moment. She could only agree with Lance's reasoning.

"Let's go see if we can find a pair of WEDs. Want to start out here?"

Lance and Kimberly went up the storefront window, looking carefully at the edges of the frames, and even the pillars that held up the awnings shading the angled front door. The store sat on the corner of the small side street halfway down Main Street and there were two windows facing Main Street and two facing the small cul-de-sac that formed the intersection halfway between the Main Street entrance hub and the north hub that led to all the other areas of the Park. The Carnation Cafe with its outdoor tables shaded in the Carnation-trademark red and white striped umbrellas was right next to them in the cul-de-sac. Lance thought about the incredible croissant sandwiches they served inside and his stomach began to growl. Knowing Kimberly wouldn't want to stop for a snack now that they had just found their destination, he ignored the persistent rumblings.

Not knowing what they were looking for, the couple made sure they didn't miss anything. Concentrating on finding the telltale WEDs, they ran their fingers along the window sills; they ran their hands up and down the shop's heavily painted outside walls. Several guests watched the two of them, curious; it looked like they were either inspectors or two people who had somehow lost a contact lens that they expected to find somehow attached to the wall or windows.

One young child even asked, "Whatcha doing, mister?"

Lance's head jerked in the direction of the question and looked down at the ten- or eleven-year old boy, for the first time considering what their actions probably looked like to the child—and everyone else walking by. "Uh, why, we are Magic Kingdom Inspectors, young man," Lance told him in an 'official' voice. "We make sure that every inch of the Kingdom is magical for little kids."

The kid tilted his head at Lance with a look that said, 'What do I look like, stupid?' "Yeah, uh huh," the kid muttered before moving on with his older sister and parents.

"Well, 'inspector'… the kid really bought that line!" Kimberly kidded him with a laugh.

"Hey, what can I say? I panicked!" Lance admitted, holding out his hands. "I think it was that same kid who followed us from Marceline," he added, thinking back to the first trip he and Adam had taken to the town in which Walt grew up. He and Adam had become paranoid when a similar young lad had made it his business to see what the two of them had been digging up around Walt's 'Dreaming Tree'. Lance turned back toward the building. "Besides, imagine what it must look like we are doing."

She glanced around at the few people who were still watching the 'show' they were presenting. "Very true," she replied, turning red.

"Did you find anything yet?" Lance asked, ignoring the watchers who were now getting bored by the inaction of the 'performers.' Waiting them out, he knew they would move on very soon.

In reality, neither Lance nor Kimberly expected to find anything too much out in the open. Anything out on the street would have eventually been seen by some of the tens of thousands of guests that passed by that point each day. Yet, both felt it was still important to look over every inch of the store. They knew they had the right place…and they certainly didn't want to miss Walt's reference point.

"I haven't found anything yet. I'd bet that whatever Walt left behind is going to be inside and somewhere that's not going to be easy to find," Kimberly voiced same thing Lance was thinking. Regardless, she was relieved when the other people around them continued on their ways.

"I tend to agree with you on that," Lance said as he looked inside the store through the open door. Glancing one last time at the nearby Carnation Café, he tried, "However, before we go in, how about a snack first?"

"If we find the clue, I'll take you to dinner afterwards," Kimberly promised, taking his arm and leading him through the door.

"And if we don't?"

"I guess you are going to be a lot thinner."

"**U**p until 1970, this building was the Upjohn-sponsored drug store," the man who looked to be in his late fifties and wearing a watch-maker's apron told them from behind a beautiful glass counter displaying watches of various makes. After a casual glance around the shop, Lance and Kimberly had approached the cast member to see what they could learn about the shop.

"So, this watch store wasn't here while Walt was alive?" Kimberly asked.

The man took off took off a pair of magnifying glasses he had perched on his balding head. A nametag identified the man as Jeffery. Kimberly didn't think he looked like a Jeffery.

"No. As a matter of fact, my dad was working for Upjohn Pharmacy when Walt signed the company on to be the sponsor of the store," Jeffery explained, smiling at the memory. "I was only about, oh, seven or so when my dad came to work at Disneyland as a cast member back then," he added. "I thought that was the coolest thing in the whole world."

"So you were here while Walt was alive?" Lance wanted to know.

"Yep. In fact, I met him several times back then...although, to be honest, I don't remember much about the man." Before continuing, the man looked around the store to see if he was needed. A co-worker was arranging a display in the corner near the front entrance. There were not a lot of customers browsing; it was early in the day and most guests were busy heading to various rides. The majority of shopping was done later in the day or in the evening right before leaving the Park.

Satisfied that he had some time, Jeffery continued. "I do have a lot of fond memories hanging out with my pop here, though. I used to sit on a big stool they had for the pharmacist that worked behind the counter over there," pointing to the opposite wall where two glass counters now ran the length of the room from wall to wall. There was a three-foot gap between the two counters so cast members could get behind them in order to open the display and withdraw items for guests.

"I'll bet that was a kick," Lance said with a smile. He would have bet that a lot of kids who lived in the area dreamed about working at Disneyland.

"You guys from around here?" Jeffery asked.

"Actually, we both work here," Kimberly told him. "I'm in entertainment as a Character. Lance is in Security."

"Hey, that's why you both look a little familiar!"

"Probably," Kimberly acknowledged. "I'm usually in a brown wig as Belle."

"And, even though it's been a while, I've been on Fox Patrol on Main Street a number of times," Lance added.

Jeffery snapped his fingers. "That's where I remember you," he said, pointing to Lance. "In fact, wasn't it you about six months ago who caught a pick-pocket who was working Main Street? Wasn't it the same guy who also stole one of our really expensive pocket watches right from this counter?"

"Yes. In fact, that was how we knew he was a pick-pocket. He had a dozen wallets on him when we searched him after I observed him lifting the watch from the counter when one of your guys had turned his back."

Lance loved working Fox Patrol as he got to dress like a tourist, to the point of wearing black socks with sandals and Bermuda shorts. It was a nice change-of-pace from the usual security uniform, hat and hard shoes he normally wore for a regular shift.

"Hey, want to see some pictures of me with Walt?" Jeffery suddenly changed the subject, his voice light and excited, revealing how much it would mean to him.

"You actually have a picture of you with Walt?" Lance was impressed.

"A couple, actually. Dad would make a big deal out of it whenever Walt walked into the store."

"Wow, those have to be treasured pictures," Kimberly said.

Suddenly, Lance thought about what the man had just said. "Did Walt come in very often?"

"Actually, yes, he did," Jeffery nodded, thinking back. "I remember my dad saying that Walt must have really liked the store because he dropped in so often…more than the other shops, I think."

"Really," Lance said slowly, letting the information sink in. "You have that picture here? Of you and Walt?"

"Sure, I've got a copy here and the original at home. I work here full time. Been here for almost twenty-five years," Jeffery told them proudly. He then turned to his co-worker. "Hey, Grant, I'm going in the back for a second."

Grant, a younger worker than Jeffery, but with even less hair, nodded. "I got it covered. Kinda slow right now."

"Thanks," he replied as he signaled for Lance and Kimberly to follow him through a door in the back of the room.

"Here is one of them," Jeffery proudly said, pulling a thin-framed eight-by-ten black-and-white picture from the wall above a desk that was cluttered with papers. "That's my dad," he told them, pointing a finger to a spitting-image of himself. The man in the picture was standing on one side of a tall stool on which a young Jeffery was sitting. Walt was on the other side with an arm around the young boy. Walt had hunched over so his head was about the same height as Jeffery's, his grey, thin mustache above Disney's trademark smile.

Mounted on the wall above and behind the boy was an old-time telephone with its crank on one side and the receiver connected by a black cord to the other side. Lance remembered seeing some phones just like it over in the General Store located just across Main Street.

"Wasn't there a phone or two just like that one over in the General Store?" Lance asked, pointing to the wooden, rectangular box in the background of the picture.

Jeffery gave a little chuckle. "You remember those, too? Yeah, there are a couple of them still there. There used to be a couple others, this one here…," He stopped and paused. "Oh yeah, there was another one in the Magic Shop, too," he added with a snap of his fingers.

Lance smiled at the joint memory. Kimberly had no idea what either man was talking about.

"What? Were they actual phones to call out on?" she wondered out loud.

"No, no. Not at all. The phones had a recording of old 'party line' where an operator would come in and interrupt a conversation. The others would be on the line talking over each other, you know, like arguing about the price of eggs or which girl was seeing which boy," Lance explained, turning to Kimberly. "It was part of the atmosphere of the buildings they were in."

"Probably just like in the twenties, in Marceline, where Walt grew up," Jeffery added.

Kimberly nodded, having heard about 'party lines' from her Grandmother who grew up in rural Iowa as a little girl.

"Walt used to love to walk over and pretend he was talking on the phone," the cast member smiled. "He even carved his initials in that phone saying, 'This is my special phone when I need to get information'," Jeffery chuckled. Only the Boss could get away with carving up anything!

Suddenly, Lance and Kimberly felt the hair on their arms stand straight up.

"His initials…as in W. E. D.?" Lance repeated slowly, spelling out the letters.

"Yeah. On the side of the box," Jeffery explained. "They were carved, I think, right under a keyhole, if I remember right, which I think I do," he winked at Kimberly.

Lance looked over at Kimberly. Together they lipped the words, 'The key.'

"And….where might that phone be today?" Lance tried to keep the excitement out of his voice, choosing his words carefully.

"Funny you should ask. My dad was told that the phone was never to be removed," Jeffery said as he put the picture back on a nail in the wall. "However, because the theme of the building changed when this went from a drug store to a watch shop…," Jeffery waved an arm around, indicating what the store was now, "The phone was removed."

"What?!" Kimberly almost shouted, sounding much more dismayed than she should over what was a seemingly normal, routine occurrence at the

Park. Jeffery looked at her funny.

"What Kimberly means," Lance countered smoothly, "is that we are looking for historical changes that have been made since Walt...um, died," Lance offered as an explanation.

"Ah! So, you guys are working on something historical pertaining to Walt?" Jeffery asked, sensing their interest.

Lance nodded, glad the man had skipped over her inappropriate response. "Yes. Actually, we are co-authoring a book on Disney," he came up with at that moment. "More specifically, on everything that has changed since Walt passed." Kimberly looked relieved when Lance covered for her and just let him keep talking. "So, naturally, we are upset that the phone was taken away," Lance said, pointing back to the framed picture.

"Oh, I didn't say it was taken away," Jeffery corrected Lance. "I just said it was removed. Removed from inside the guest area.... I guess I should have mentioned that."

Lance and Kimberly looked at each other with a renewed sense of hope that they could see mirrored in each other's eyes.

"Sounds like you both would really enjoy seeing the old phone." Kimberly and Lance nodded in unison. "Well, right this way then," as Jeffery lead the two deeper into the narrow office. "By the way, what did you say your names were?" he asked as he took out a small ring of keys out of his apron pocket.

"Oh, sorry. We didn't introduce ourselves. I'm Lance, and this is my friend, Kimberly."

"Good to meet you, good to meet you both.

I've always been interested in all things 'Walt'."
Jeffery suddenly added, "Hey, maybe you can
mention me in your book!"

"Absolutely!" Lance replied immediately.

"All right!" Jeffery smiled as he opened a door
in the office near the back. It was on the opposite
wall from the desk they had just been standing beside.

"This is just a storage area for displays," Jeffery was almost apologetic as he opened the door
into the cluttered, unadorned room. He reached
up above the door and pulled on a chain. A light
clicked on overhead, illuminating a very small six-
by-six closet. "We don't keep anything of value in
here," he added. A few boxes labeled with various
display manufacturers sat stacked up along the
back and right side walls. On the left side, attached to the wall, was the old crank phone that
they had seen in the picture with young Jeffery.

"Of course, I guess you could say that the
phone is valuable," Jeffery amended, a little nostalgic in his voice.

Lance and Kimberly looked at the phone with
a different kind of awe. "You say that this is the
same phone that was in the picture?" Lance
wanted to make sure.

"Sure is. And look here," Jeffery pointed
along the bottom edge of the phone. In deeply cut
letters, Kimberly and Lance found what they had
been looking for: three very meaningful letters,

W E D

"Do you know when Walt would have engraved those letters?" Kimberly asked, running
her fingers across the quarter-inch deep letters.

The carving was a little worn because of time and oxidation of the wood. And, because of their location, the letters were nearly invisible to anyone not knowing or caring to look for them.

"I remember my dad saying something about the letters not too long before Walt passed away," Jeffery answered her.

Thinking about something else, Lance added, "I'm surprised the phone has never been stolen by some employee over the years." He knew how some of the seasoned employees would take little things from the rides they worked when they were quitting…little souvenirs of the Park. Some would become treasured mementos within their family; others would instantly be listed on some online auction to be sold to the highest bidder. He thought about the canoe paddle Wolf had once smuggled out for him and smiled to himself. He had it mounted on the wall over his television just like a fishing trophy.

"Well, look back here," Jeffery instructed as he stepped into the small closet. Lance and Kimberly squeezed in with the man. On the sides and top of the telephone were heavy brass brackets, presumably screwed into the wall studs with long screws. However, the top of each screw had been filed flat, giving no means to remove the screws. "As you can see, someone made sure the phone could not be removed," Jeffery nodded sagely, crossing his hands over his chest.

Lance looked at Kimberly who mouthed a single word: 'Dad.'

She moved back as far as she could without actually leaving the small room to allow Lance more space to examine the phone. He picked up the earpiece of the phone, the part that was connected to a black, braided cord leading to the side of the phone. He held it to his ear, half expecting to hear Walt Disney's voice come booming through the black, cylindrical speaker, telling him something like, "Congratulations! You have found my phone and your next clue!" However, only silence greeted his ear.

"Yeah, it never got plugged back in, I guess," the cast member broke in, thinking Lance was waiting to hear the old party line recorded conversations that they had just been talking about a couple of minutes earlier.

Lance smiled and let him think what he wanted.

As Lance was replacing the earpiece, a voice called out. "Hey, Jeff, can you give me a hand out here?" Grant had shouted through the office door.

"Sure, be right there," Jeffery called back.

Lance thought quickly. "Is it all right if we stay in here for a moment and take a couple pictures of the phone? They would make a great addition to our book."

"Sure. No problem," Jeffery answered as he slowly squeezed past Kimberly. It seemed to be taking him a long time to get by her. "I'll be out in front. Just come on out when you are done and I'll lock up in a few minutes."

"Okay, thanks!" Kimberly said with a sweet smile, telling herself not to make a scene. "We would like to take a picture of you in front of the store entrance, too, if that's okay?"

"Sure! I'd love to do that."

Jeffery left the office and headed back out in front. Before he was gone, Lance had his hand in his pocket and was fingering the key that Walt had left them. When Lance had first spotted the key-hole on the side of the box and felt the size of the key in his pocket, it looked just right to him. But, it wasn't until they were finally alone that he could try it out. He was about to fit it into the keyhole when Kimberly interrupted him.

"Wait, let me have your camera first," Kimberly held out her hand to Lance.

The hand holding the key dropped. "What camera?"

"The one you told him we were going use to take pictures."

Lance looked momentarily confused. "I didn't bring a camera. Why would I bring a camera?"

"But you just told…."

Lance gave her a broad grin and turned back to the old-fashioned telephone.

"Next time, fill me in on the details ahead of time, okay?" Her attention reverted to what Lance was doing as she watched his efforts, her heart speeding up. "Think this is it?" she asked, holding her breath.

"Gotta be," Lance muttered, trying to push the key into the slot. At first it didn't go in at all. "Ah, come on, Walt. Quit teasing us!" Then he turned the key upside down and it slid easily into the machined keyhole. He turned the key and an audible *click* could be heard inside the phone. Below the rectangular box, a hinged door fell open along the bottom. Bending down, Lance saw that the little wooden door was cut nearly perfectly and it became the flat bottom of the phone box when it was closed. Attached to the door was a pocket that was formed by a small leather-like pouch neatly nailed to the inside of the door.

Smiling at the discovery, Lance looked up at Kimberly for a moment.

"Hurry, Lance!" Kimberly whispered, gesturing with her hands. "We are only supposed to be taking pictures!"

He nodded and reached into the pocket. Inside was a small yellowed envelope. Not taking time to open it, he stashed it inside his pants pocket and then bent down to look further up inside the opening. "Nope, nothing else. Wait a minute." Reaching up inside the phone, Lance pulled out a strand of loose wires. "Look at this!" The wires had been cut. Presumably, they ran some recording device that played the party line conversations. He felt around again and felt nothing out of the ordinary. No cels, no capsules, no plastic boxes.

Pushing the wires back in place, he shut the door and turned the key. The locking mechanism was pretty solid as the door shut with a deep clicking sound. Lance momentarily marveled at the seamless joint where the door met the edges of the phone box. In the next moment, Jeffery walked back in.

Standing back up, Lance acted like he was inspecting the detail of the phone. Luckily the keyhole was on the side away from where Jeffery was standing.

"Get some shots?" Jeffery asked.

"Shots?... Oh, yeah, thanks. This is so cool!"

Lance gushed to pull the attention away from his non-existent camera, running his hand along the edge as if he was feeling the texture of the wood. Kimberly watched out of the corner of her eye as his fingers grasped the key still in the keyhole and pulled it out in one deft move. At the same time, Lance used a little diversion. "You know, you are just the man to ask: What is this keyhole on the side for?" he pointed.

As he moved to the side, Jeffery turned to look at the phone. Lance took that moment to drop the key into his pocket.

"Oh that. No one knows. We assumed it must be to work on the insides of the phone…some sort of release for the front panel, I suppose," Jeffery scratched his head after running a finger over the small keyhole. "The box feels so dang solid, though. I know a few of us tried to pick the lock a long time ago," he admitted with a self-conscious chuckle. "Now don't go adding that to your book! But, anyway, since the old phone isn't even plugged in any more, I doubt that it's even worth the effort to try and figure out where the key might be…if it even exists anymore!"

Lance gave a little knowing grin to Kimberly before patting Jeffery on the shoulder. "Hey, what's your last name…you know, for the book?" as he let Kimberly lead the way out. He knew Jeffery would most likely be admiring her charming figure from the back as they walked out of the office.

"Oh, its Winchester…you know, like the rifle," Jeffery told him as they moved out of the office and back into the main store.

"No relationship, huh?" Lance asked.

"Ha.... No, Dad was into pills not bullets, I'm afraid."

Suddenly, Kimberly took Lance's arm and said, "Oh, no, Lance. We're late to meet with the guy in the Disney Archives."

"Oh gosh, you're right, Kimberly," Lance pretended to look at his watch. "Sorry, but we gotta run, Jeffery. Thanks for showing us the picture of you and Walt. That's a keeper. We need to run over to Administration and meet that guy, uh...Smythe, right, Kimberly?"

"Yeah, that was his name. Nice meeting you!" she smiled sweetly, shaking Jeffery's hand.

"You, too." Totally smitten by Kimberly's beauty and hating to see her leave, he gave a silent sigh. *If I were just twenty years younger....* He looked at Lance and then silently added, *I still wouldn't have a chance!*

Lance tugged at her hand as he went out the door. Through the window, Jeffery watched as the two looked back, gave him a wave, and then dashed up Main Street toward the cast members' entrance near Tomorrowland.

Going back behind the counter, Jeffery took out a soft cloth from his apron pocket and started wiping the already clean counters. Suddenly he remembered something:

"Dang, those guys forgot to take my picture!"

"**W**hat does it say?!" Kimberly begged Lance as they sat down on a shaded bench around the corner from Star Tours. Further back in this area were restrooms and a first aid station. When they first left the Timepieces shop, Lance had planned on heading to the Central Plaza at the north end of Main Street. This hub was home to beautifully manicured trees, flower gardens and shrubs, and bronze sculptures of various Disney characters sitting on identical beige pillars. In the middle, appropriately staged on a large, four-foot-high pedestal was a nearly life-size bronze sculpture of Walt Disney holding hands with his most famous character, Mickey Mouse. Benches lined the inside planters facing this statue, but, as Lance knew, this section was extremely popular for guests to either sit and relax or to take pictures of Walt with the elegant Sleeping Beauty Castle as the backdrop—too popular an area for what Lance and Kimberly needed to do. In choosing their current location, Lance did think it appropriate—or at least symbolic—that they reveal the next clue at least nearby Walt's bronze gaze.

Seeing her eagerness, he gave a sly smile as he slowly pulled the old envelope from his pants pocket. "Curious, eh?" Lance asked teasingly, only to be rewarded by a playful slap on the shoulder.

"Okay, okay," he conceded, turning the envelope over in his hands. Nothing was written on either side. He could feel that was something more than just paper inside. "Feels like another key is inside," Lance told her as he slipped his finger under the sealed triangle on the back of the envelope. Since the glue was so old, the folded side of the envelope parted easily. He stopped and held the envelope out to his partner. "I want you to do the honors."

"Me?" It took Kimberly all of two seconds before she carefully, almost with reverence, took the opened envelope from Lance. "Oh my gosh. I can't believe how fast my heart is pounding in my chest!"

He could understand what she was feeling. Even though he had been through it so many times, he now marveled at his own relative calm.

Delicately sliding her fingers into the opening, she first slid out a folded piece of paper. Reaching back in, she found a bright brass key, larger than the key Lance had just used and obviously made for a more sophisticated lock. Handing Lance the key, Kimberly opened the note as she leaned in closer to Lance, and, in a low, soft voice, began to read out loud:

"If you have found this final clue and key, then I know you have done several things to make you worthy of what you will discover next.

"First off, you must have chosen your friends wisely. I could never have been as successful as I was without my brother Roy, or all the individuals who have contributed to my dreams and visions. It is highly unlikely you were able to have successfully followed all my clues without a partner or two of your own.

"Second, I know that you have been persistent. I always said, 'Keep moving forward'; even during all my setbacks I knew that the end would not only justify the means, but it would validate my beliefs. I'm sure many of the quests I sent you on tested your resolve as well as your ability to 'think

on your feet.'

"Finally, I know that you have a deep interest in my life's work…as well as my life in general, or else you wouldn't have made all the effort to have gotten this far. The reason I threw in a few distant places was to test your desire, your will, to follow through come what may. Only someone who truly wanted to discover my 'legacy' would have the will to follow all the clues I placed along your journey. Congratulations to you! I hope you will not be disappointed in what I have bestowed upon you and what it entails.

"I'm dying; at least that is what my doctor says. But, since you have found my 'other' treasure, then you know what I put into place before death took away my final breath.

*"This last clue is important—well, they all were! Ha ha. However, the final place I want you to go is very important to me, as you will soon find out. And, if you are where I think you should be after finding this here envelope and key, then I can tell you that you are very, very close. **Pull up a chair and use this key to open the door that was only open for six months on Main Street. In fact, you don't have to be a 'Wizard' to know which door this might be. It isn't hidden. In fact, like almost everything else was, it is in plain sight.***

"Find the door. Use the key. See your future in the heart. I saw mine!"

While Kimberly had been reading, Lance had been following along over her shoulder. Once she finished, he settled back on the bench next to her, looking intently at the sculpture of Walt and Mickey over in the Hub. Turning the key over and over in his fingers, he had a conscious realization that the last fingers to have touched this key were probably Walt Disney's.

"So, it sounds like we are close?" Lance asked, turning his gaze back to Kimberly.

Very excited and, at the same time, intrigued by the fact that they must indeed be close to whatever final 'treasure' Walt was alluding to, Kimberly's gaze was unfocused as the Omnibus pulled up nearby, allowing a dozen passengers to disembark. "I guess so," she answered, distracted as her voice trailed off in thought. She turned back to Lance. "What do you think he meant, 'See your future in the heart'?"

"I don't know. Could be anything. Maybe he's got some sort of crystal ball hidden away in there, one in the shape of a heart."

"We seem to have found a lot of hearts in this search. Or maybe it's a figurative statement, like 'trust your heart' or 'follow your heart'," Kimberly reasoned.

"Well, that makes a lot more sense than my crystal ball theory," Lance admitted with a grin. "I guess we won't know until we find out where this key goes," Lance said, holding the key up between them by his fingertips.

Looking at the key, she smiled. "Let's go find Walt's door."

"I think the best place to start is at the beginning of Main Street...and then work our way up to the Hub," Lance said as they stood up from the bench, carefully placing the envelope and key deep in his pocket.

It was already well past midday and a large number of guests were still entering the Park, dispersing from Main Street like a colorful mass of ants leaving the small opening of an ant hill.

"Let's avoid the crowd on Main Street by going backstage," Kimberly offered.

"Great idea," knowing how hard it is to move against the flow of so many people, he agreed, and then added, "We can come out all the way down next to the Main Street Bank and work our way back up to here."

Hand in hand, the couple moved toward the cast members' entrance next to the First Aid station. Beyond their door was the Inn Between Restaurant where they had eaten just before spending the night in the Treehouse. As they walked past the restaurant, Lance squeezed her hand. "Seems like a lifetime ago since we met and then slept with Tarzan...," Lance trailed, off thinking about all that they had experienced together in the last four weeks.

Thinking her own thoughts, Kimberly remained silent, giving his hand a light squeeze.

Veering to the right after they passed the restaurant, they came to a large parking area with most of the spaces reserved for those who worked in the Administration offices to their left. Following a walkway that paralleled Main Street, they knew the backs of the various Main Street shops were to their right.

"I wonder what we are going to find," Kimberly said, her statement being more rhetorical than actually expecting an answer.

"I wonder what effect this all will have on our future, if any," Lance answered her with his own rhetoric.

"Well, I do know that my life has already been changed drastically over the past few weeks," Kimberly told him as they reached a canopied break area where several costumed cast members were eating lunch or talking with fellow employees.

Looking at his companion, Lance thought she probably meant her losing her dad, dealing with firing Daniel, and all. But he hoped that, in there somewhere, she was also relating her comment to their relationship, too.

As if reading his mind, she tugged on his hand and pulled him to a stop. "I'm talking about us, Lance."

Looking deeply into her eyes, he had a serious, sincere look on his face. "I was hoping that I figured in your life, somehow."

She smiled. "I know it has only been a month…and certainly we were brought together under some very extreme conditions," Kimberly acknowledged, shrugging her shoulders. "But, you know? I honestly feel like I've known you a long time."

"You do? Me, too. But I also know there is a great deal we still don't know about each other," Lance added, touched by her words.

"Yes," she agreed, slowly drawing out the 's' on the word. She tried to put her feelings into words. "You know that feeling you get when you are looking forward to doing something? I remember looking forward to that first cruise with my dad." Kimberly broke off and smiled at the memory. "I had no idea what to expect or what I would be doing or what I would be seeing. But, mostly I was so excited because I was going somewhere with my dad and I knew that the trip with him would be an adventure. And it was, in more ways than one."

Lance smiled as he thought back on his recent trips with his friends Adam and Beth.

But she wasn't finished with her explanation. Shyly reaching out, she took both his hands in hers. "Well, I feel like that now—with you."

Looking down at their entwined fingers, he had never before felt the kind of electricity that seemed to pass between them every time they touched. "I want that adventure, too." Lance pulled her into his arms and felt that intense desire build as they kissed.

Across the way, seated under the break area canopy, a couple of security guards snickered and yelled out, "Hey, Lance, get a room!"

With a groan, the couple reluctantly ended their kiss. Turning red, Kimberly buried her face in Lance's chest.

"You guys are just jealous," Lance called over with a grin as he took Kimberly's hand. He led her toward the long, narrow passage that went to the cast members' entryway just outside of the entrance tunnel near the Main Gate. The two security guards, obviously friends of Lance, whistled at him as they vanished into the corridor. Both men were indeed very jealous.

"Okay, so right or left?" Lance asked Kimberly as they emerged onto Main Street's Town Square. Before they could decide, Lance told her, "Hold on a sec. Let's go over here for a minute," and led her over to the brass, engraved plate at the base of the tall, silver flagpole. Paying his respects, he looked at the words that were etched there for all time: The Opening Day speech that Walt Disney had given when he opened the Park on July 17th, 1955.

"I always get goose bumps when I read those words," Kimberly admitted, looking down at the plaque that was surrounded by beautifully manicured flower beds.

"You should have seen Adam and me when we first found Walt's diary," Lance grinned. "Walt had written out that part of the speech on the first page."

Kimberly was lost in her own thoughts and memories. "Doesn't this all seem a little surreal?" she asked as she looked up from the plaque and gazed down Main Street at the Castle and then back to Lance. "Honestly, don't you ever step back and wonder if this is all some kind of dream?"

Lance took her hand. "If it is a dream, I honestly don't *ever* want to wake up."

Blushing at his words and the look he was giving her, she whispered, "Me neither."

They decided to cover the right side of Main Street first, walking very slowly along the sidewalk that fronted the shops on the Street. They passed the beautiful white and gold Opera House where the *Disney Story* was playing daily inside. There was no locked door to be found, in plain sight or otherwise. Almost all of the doors that were on Main Street were entrances to the various shops.

"I can't imagine a door leading to some…chamber, or whatever, existing here on Main Street without someone knowing about it," Lance pondered as they passed the Magic Shoppe. Five steps led up to a closed door next to the Shoppe, but they could see books and souvenirs through the windows. The huge, brightly colored marquee of the Main Street Cinema was next, proclaiming it was showing *Steamboat Willie*, the first animated cartoon with sound. Two more quaint shops followed as they slowly walked down the street. To passersby, it would look as though they were doing some serious window shopping, which, under normal circumstances, they would have been doing.

Their steps paused as they walked under the blue awning of the Disneyana shop. There was a flight of stairs between the Disneyana shop and the store whose banner proclaimed 'Canned Goods' and 'Spices.' "Lance," Kimberly whispered, "There's a door up there! Go try the key!"

Positioning her in front of the stairs, Lance stood behind her on the first step. Not seeing any attention thrown their way, he took another tentative step upwards. Kimberly turned to look into the window, moving away from the stairs. Now out of sight from the street, Lance turned and hurried up the stairs. Whether he turned it up or down, the key didn't fit the locked door he found at the top of the stairs. In fact, the door and the lock both looked as if they were used with some regularity. The lock was clean and had signs of lubrication; the hinges did not have the look of forty years of disuse. A little disappointed, Lance moved down the stairs and returned to street level.

"Nope," was his brief answer to her inquisitive, eager eyes.

While Kimberly displayed a subtle look of disappointment, something had already told her this was not *the* door. After putting her arm in Lance's, she led the way back up Main Street. "Then, let us continue."

A few more shops brought them to the first corner and the large Market House that had proudly occupied that spot since Opening Day. It was in here that the working Party Line telephones still entertained the guests. Sitting next to a beautiful, intricately detailed potbellied stove was an old-fashioned checkerboard sitting on top of a cracker barrel, two wooden chairs waiting for the next two players.

Crossing the small side street that led to the daily-use lockers, the large, curved entrance to the Disney Clothiers, Ltd. greeted them. A popular place for the singing group The Dapper Dans to stand and entertain the guests, the wide doors now had only customers going in and out. What looked like another storefront turned out to be another entrance into the popular clothing store.

The next building used to be the home of a greeting card store, but had no outstanding features to make them pause.

The sparkling window display of the Crystal Arts shop dazzled their eyes as they paused to admire the goods. Hand-blown glass figurines, faceted crystal, and imported glass from different countries all vied for attention. "See anything you like?" Lance suddenly asked, as Kimberly had come to a full stop.

"I'm sorry. I got distracted," she admitted, thinking he was intent on continuing their search.

"No, it's all right. They have some beautiful things in here. Did you see that huge blue Chech vas up in the corner?" he pointed. Standing eighteen inches tall, rimmed in gold, the vas was adorned with handcrafted porcelain flowers and leaves, and twisting veins of twenty-four karat gold wound around the flowers. It was stunning.

"Wow, that is beautiful. It looks like they have a lot of matching pieces, too. Didn't they used to have a glassblower in here?"

Lance nodded. "I never saw him, but I heard that it was pretty fascinating to watch him create a castle out of melted threads of glass."

Next was the narrow, three-story-tall Silhouette Studio. Small black examples of their work sat in oval frames in the one window of the shop. Inside, the artist was hard at work.

Lance was about to ask her if she wanted her likeness made for posterity, when her clasp on his arm tightened. "Lance?" She sounded distracted, far away.

"What?" He was still watching the makings of

a child's face appear on a screen inside the little studio.

"What did the clue say about chairs?"

Concerned by her abstract voice, he turned from the shop. "What?"

"The clue...what did it say about chairs? I can't remember."

Lance recited from memory: "It said 'Pull up a chair and use this key to open the door that was only open for six months on Main Street. In fact, you don't have to be a 'Wizard' to know which door this might be. It isn't hidden. In fact, like almost everything else was, it is in plain sight.' Why do you ask? Would you like to look at it again?" He was getting concerned as she had gone pale.

She pointed at the next storefront. "Chairs," was all she said.

Next, up a short flight of three steps, was an inviting railed porch having three wooden chairs bolted to the wooden deck. Shaded by a filigreed balcony overhead, it was a pleasant, restful place to take a break and watch the crowds as they walked up and down Main Street. In fact, two guests were doing just that as Kimberly and Lance stood looking at the porch. There was no sign over the door, no address. The two windows and the pane of glass in the door were all backed by a white lace panel that effectively blocked whatever was inside the little building.

"Do you think this is where he meant?" she whispered.

Lance looked up the street. There were only a couple more shops before the end building which was the large Photo Supply Company.

They would have to start down the west side of Main Street, but, from their trip to find the Time-pieces shop, he knew there were no chairs on that side of the street. His heart started beating a little faster. "I think you are right!" he told her.

"What do you think we should do? There are people here," she indicated with a tilt of her head.

Lance grinned. "Yeah, they are everywhere! I wonder why?"

That broke her out of her serious, whispering mode. "Ok, ok, I get it! What do you want to do?"

"I don't suppose you could pull off a dead faint, have me carry you up the steps and ask them to run and fetch help?"

She just looked at him. "I do hope you're joking."

"Yeah, you do look really heavy," he kidded. "No, no, don't hurt me!" he laughed, throwing his hands up in mock surrender. "There was another part of the clue, the part about the Wizard. Do you think we should first find out what that means?"

Kimberly then looked across the street and down a block to where the New Century Time-pieces shop was. "We could go ask Jeffery. I'd bet he'd know."

"Yeah, but, he's probably still waiting for us to take his picture."

"True, that won't work. How about if we pick a fight and make it so uncomfortable the people on the porch will leave?"

Lance gave a laugh. "I don't think I could make an argument with you look convincing. I'd rather kiss you than argue with you."

"Well, maybe if we did *that* long enough they

would get uncomfortable enough to leave."

He raised his eyebrows. "Is that an offer, Ms. Waldron?"

She cleared her throat to cover her embarrassment. She should have known he would be willing to try that suggestion. Funny, she found herself thinking she would be willing to try, too. Instead, Kimberly suggested, "Why don't you take me to eat and we'll talk about our *various* options."

"If you insist. Dinner does sound great right now!" Lance said as he took her arm in his and started walking toward Adventureland. Lance was thinking the Blue Bayou would be an ideal restaurant to take Kimberly.

"Where are you taking me? Club 33?"

Lance whistled. "I wish! I'm not a member. I was heading for the Blue Bayou. Their jambalaya is really good."

Smiling to herself, Kimberly let Lance lead them into New Orleans Square. When they approached the busy entrance of the popular restaurant, she motioned for him to give her a moment. Thinking she needed to use the Ladies Room, he stepped back across the street next to where the artists were drawing caricatures. Instead, she went to the small door right next to the Blue Bayou's entrance. Surprised, he watched as she pushed an intercom button located under a brass cover plate. Opposite the brass plate was an oval mirror framed in bronze. The mirror had the number 33 beautifully etched in frosted emerald green and white. There was a small speaker above the button with a card slot that looked like the kind that opened a hotel room.

"You sly devil," Lance grinned, walking up to Kimberly. It had just dawned on him that, of course she and her father would have access to the most exclusive dinner club in the west! "I should have known," he said as they heard a voice come through the speaker.

"Waldron, Kimberly. Number 9865," Kimberly spoke into the intercom.

After a brief moment, the voice in the speaker came back. "Welcome back, Miss Waldron. Please come through." A buzz was followed by an audible 'click' as the pale green door opened automatically in front of them.

Kimberly smiled at Lance. It was one of the rare times in their short relationship that she was able to one-up Lance.

Behind them, Disneyland guests craned their necks to try and see inside that mysterious door as Lance and Kimberly walked inside. While many people had never heard of the famous Club 33, there were those around the door who knew about the exclusive club and stood there gawking at who they imagined where probably celebrities, or maybe very wealthy executives, entering the restaurant.

"This is so cool," Lance told her as the door shut behind him. "I haven't been here in years!" He was now in a small foyer with polished cherry wood walls and large, inlayed mirrors on one side and expensive crushed velvet wallpaper in a deep burgundy that nearly matched the woodwork on the other wall. The centerpiece of the lobby was an elegant antique English elevator that sat with its door open just ahead of them; its matching cherry wood walls were accented with black wire mesh so people could see in or out of the elevator. The reception desk was to their immediate right as they stood in the center of the black and white marble tile floor. The carpeted stairway that wrapped around the elevator shaft featured gold-framed pictures depicting the early Jazz era that grew out of New Orleans.

"Good afternoon, Miss Waldron," a hostess wearing a conservative-looking, black French-maid-style costume greeted the couple.

"Hello," Kimberly said. "I know I don't have a reservation, but I wondered if there would be an opening for two of us for dinner?"

"Absolutely," the hostess replied immediately without even looking at her reservation book to see if they were full or not. Lance felt a sense of certainty that if Kimberly—or her father before her—wanted to eat at the Club, they would not be refused.

The tuxedoed maitre d' was seen coming down the stairs. "Robert, could you show Miss Waldron and her guest to the Disney Room, please?"

"Of course, Cynthia," Robert told the hostess, then, turning to the couple he asked, "Would you prefer the lift or the stairs?"

Kimberly looked at Lance, already knowing what his choice would be.

"Oh, by all means, let's ride!" Lance said with a grin.

Once Lance had raided the dessert table for the third time, it appeared he was finally full and content. Kimberly watched as the last bite of the crème Brule disappeared into his smiling mouth.

"Where do you put all that?" she marveled. "If I ate that much I would be as big as a horse."

Sitting back in his seat, he gave a contented sigh as he patted his flat stomach. "I don't know. I've always had a healthy appetite. Thanks for a great dinner, by the way. This was a wonderful surprise."

Their server, Russell, quietly placed a leather-bound check on the edge of the table between them. Kimberly shook her head as Lance reached for it. Signing her name, she handed it back to the server. Expecting a credit card, Russell was going to say something, but then he glanced at the name on the bill. Not having served her before he hadn't recognized the face, but he certainly recognized the name. A knowing smile crossed his face. "A pleasure having you here, Ms. Waldron. Come back any time," he told her.

"Thank you, Russell. The Lobster Bisque was wonderful. Would you please give our compliments to the chef?"

"I'd be happy to. Anything else I can get for you? After-dinner aperitif? Another cocktail?"

"No, no, that's fine." Kimberly was going to let him go, but she remembered something. "Russell, how long have you been working here?"

Wondering if he did something wrong, the server hesitated, quickly thinking back on the dinner he had just served. "Umm, five, six years," he told her.

Kimberly continued, "We were wondering if you knew much about the history of the Park. I know you are well-versed in the history of Club 33," as Russell nodded, "but what about Main Street, for instance. Was there a store that used a wizard as a decoration, or in the name?"

Now realizing he wasn't in trouble, Russell relaxed, leaning against the chair at the empty table next to theirs. "A wizard, you say? No, I can't think of anything except the Magic Shoppe, but I don't think they had a wizard in there…. You know who might know?" he said with a snap of his fingers, "Robert, the maitre d'. I think he and God went to school together. He's been here forever. Want me to ask?"

"Would you, please?" Kimberly turned on her brightest smile. She hadn't been hanging around Lance so long and learned nothing! "Is Robert still here?"

"Yeah, yeah, you stay here and enjoy the view. I'll go ask. He's back in the lobby," Russell hurriedly told her. "Here, have a pen!" As he rushed off, Russell dropped one of the popular souvenirs from the exclusive restaurant on the table. It was a black pen with the famous gold crest and 33 on it.

With a grin, Lance pocketed the pen. "Good thinking," he remarked. "I was going to ask Russell, but he seemed too young."

Before Kimberly could reply, the server was back. "The Wonderful Wizard of Bras," he declared with a wide smile.

"Excuse me?"

With a quick laugh, Russell explained, "Yeah, that's what I said at first, too. But Robert said there used to be a store on Main Street called The Wonderful Wizard of Bras. It was only open for about five or six months. It actually was an intimate apparel store that featured, of all things, bras; hence the name," he said, with a self-conscious grin, not looking at Kimberly at the mention of the word 'bras'. He then continued, "Once that store closed, it was never used for anything else. He says that if you want to see the storefront, look for the porch and chairs. That's where it was."

Russell assumed the silence from the couple was their mulling over the information. In actuality, they were both stunned as they realized they had solved Walt's clue.

"Nothing is there anymore?" Lance finally asked.

"Nope. In fact, the area behind the window now is a small break area with lockers for employees."

This information was a disappointment for Lance and Kimberly. If a break area had been built behind the façade of that storefront, then there was a chance whatever may have been hidden there had been long since removed.

Russell sensed some bit of disappointment in the pair. "Is anything wrong, Miss Waldron?" he asked, confused at their change in expressions.

"Oh no, Russell," Kimberly said, quickly becoming aware that she and Lance must appear ungrateful for the information he had so helpfully provided.

The server was surprised and more than a little pleased when the lovely blond got up from her chair to give him a hug. "Thank you so much for a lovely dinner and the interesting information about the store," she told him.

"Uh, you're welcome," Russell replied, a little unsure whether he should hug her back...especially with her date sitting right there. He did the next best thing and gave Kimberly a one-arm hug, then added with a big grin, "Anything else I can do? Really?"

She smiled sweetly back, noting the slight pink color in his face. "No, thank you so much. We really need to get going, though."

Lance now stood and shook Russell's hand. "You've been a big help. Thanks." Offering his arm to Kimberly, they walked through the elegant restaurant and headed for the elevator to take them to the ground level.

Russell stood in the same place, watching her retreating steps, the grin still on his face.

"Lance, I think I have an idea," Kimberly told him as they exited the private door and emerged onto the busy Royal Street in New Orleans Square. "But, it might take some time to wait out. Would you be able to sit in one place for a long time?"

Obviously, she didn't know everything there was to know about her partner. Lance gave her a little grin. "I think I can sit for a while. What's your plan?"

As they continued walking together back to Main Street, they crossed over the pedestrian bridge that spanned the entryway to the Pirate ride and dropped down next to the Treehouse.

"Do you want to ride Indy first?" Lance asked hopefully as they walked past the popular ride.

With a groan, Kimberly answered, "On a full stomach? Oh, please, no! Maybe later?"

"Ok, what's your plan?"

"Well, we can't just walk up to the door and use our key. There are way too many people going by. Especially in broad daylight. I was thinking that we needed the cover of darkness."

"So far, so good."

They could hear two shots from the gun of a Jungle Cruise skipper as they walked around the line that had extended into the walkway. "What if," she continued, "we wait it out on the porch. I thought about how dark it is for the fireworks show. They turn off all the lights on Main Street."

"But the fireworks themselves are pretty bright," he pointed out.

"True, but they aren't constant. There are lulls in the blasts. You know, for the music and the narrator."

Lance gave her arm a squeeze. "Like I said, that's why you make the big bucks!"

The porch in question was now occupied by a different couple. Settled in, they seemed to be people-watching and gave Lance and Kimberly a friendly nod as they approached.

"Well, we can't sit and wait like I thought. Do you think it would be all right if we just went up and looked in the windows to see if we can see anything?" she quietly asked Lance, her back to the porch. There was the door on the far right of the porch with windows in the upper half and two windows behind the chairs where the couple was sitting and relaxing.

"Sure. People do it all the time. I remember on Haunted Mansion, while waiting in the queue area that went around the house, everyone would try to look into the windows through any opening in the shades to see what might be behind there. I think its natural curiosity to want to know what secrets are hidden behind various walls, doors and windows here."

Lance walked up to the porch and greeted the couple with a friendly, "Hello. Say, can you see anything behind these windows?"

"Nah," the man replied. "We tried that, too," he added as Lance peered along the edges of the glass. The windows were blocked with see-through lace curtains. The only problem was that all the windows also had a dark green window covering that was pulled down behind the lace and completely blocked the view.

However, along the right hand edge of the window nearest the door, he could just make out a bank of lockers along the wall on the right, just like Russell had said were in there. But then it dawned on Lance: the wall the lockers were up against ended on the left side of the door frame. From the small opening Lance was peaking in through, he could tell that the wall did not leave room for the door. There had to be something on the other side of the wall that was behind the door.

Giving a friendly nod to the people sitting on

the porch, Lance walked down the steps to rejoin Kimberly.

"There is a wall on this side of the door with lockers on it, just like Russell said," he explained to Kimberly, pointing toward the door. "I'm interested in the depth of the wall on the other side from the Silhouette Studio." Eyeballing a line between himself and the left hand side of the door, he stepped off a few paces along the sidewalk parallel to the front of the shops. Stopping when he was even with the left edge of the window of the Studio next door, he mumbled to himself, "Six steps, eighteen feet, give or take a foot."

Turning back to the puzzled Kimberly, he told her, "Wait here, I'll be right back." Lance jogged to the entrance of the Silhouette Studio. Watching through the store window, Kimberly could see Lance walking to the edge of the window then repeating the same pacing he had done on the sidewalk until he moved out of her view.

When he came jogging back outside, he told her with a grin, "The plot thickens."

"What? Tell me what you were doing!"

"Well, from where I estimated the locker wall was, there should be approximately eighteen feet from the window edge to the interior wall inside the Studio," Lance said.

"And?"

"And, unless my hanging around Adam the General Contractor for years was completely wasted, there was only thirteen feet from the window to the inside wall of the Silhouette place."

"Which means," Kimberly said the revelation of what Lance was saying sunk in, "there are about five feet unaccounted for between the two walls."

He nodded at her conclusion. "Assuming there are four to six inches of insulation, studs and plaster or drywall on each wall, there should be a corridor of three to four feet between the two walls…and," Lance turned back toward the porch and pointed at the innocuous door, "those three or four feet must lie directly behind that door."

Biding their time, Lance and Kimberly waited over an hour until the couple on the porch finally moved on to continue their day at the Park. Darkness was settling in and Main Street was a dazzling sight of white lights illuminating the storefronts and twinkling lights in all the trees. As they glanced toward Sleeping Beauty's Castle, they could see it was now glowing in spotlights of pink and white. It was a lovely time of the night.

With a look of triumph, Kimberly settled into one of the wooden chairs. "Now we can put our plan into action," she told Lance as he joined her. "Do you think you can sit it out and wait for the firework show in a couple of hours?"

Kimberly needn't have worried about Lance's abilities to remain still. He settled into his chair, stretching out his long legs, chin resting on his chest, and immediately fell asleep.

Looking at him, she made a disgusted little sound. "Now what am I supposed to do for the next few hours all by myself?"

Perhaps she should have come up with a more mutually beneficial plan….

After watching Lance sleep for about forty-five minutes, Kimberly awakened him. "I'm bored! Tell me what you were like growing up"

Stretching, he came out of the nap in his usual good humor. "I was very handsome," he told her without the trace of a smile.

"And modest, I can tell."

"Oh, extremely. I was proud of my humility, too."

She gave a light laugh. "Don't make me sorry I woke you up! Tell me a story. What did you like to do with your friends?"

"When I was a teenager in Boston, Kip Baker and I used to hang out at the Atrium Mall." Lance stretched out his legs, settling his hands on his stomach. Looking out across Main Street, watching the constant flow of people, he continued, "We would watch people walk by, just like this."

"Girls, you mean!" she smiled, enjoying the sound of his voice.

"Not *just* girls," was his honest reply. "We had a game we played…while we waited for girls to come by," Lance said with a big grin on his face, and then continued, "We would pick out a person or a couple, and make up a life-story about them. The more unbelievable the story, the more points we gave each other," he chuckled, thinking back. "I remember one guy who walked by and Kip made up a story about him saying he had murdered his family with an ax in Missouri. As the guy got past us, we looked at the back of his tee shirt and it said something like, 'Fastest Ax in the

Ozarks.' We just about freaked out."

Kimberly grinned, picturing the two teenagers coming up with imaginative stories about people they saw. She looked out over the sea of people and immediately could see how easy it could be to do the same. Turning to Lance, she asked, "What would you say about me?"

"What, you mean if we had seen you walking across the Mall?"

"Yes. What story would you have made up if you had seen me walking by?"

Lance thought about it. "Well, get up and walk down the sidewalk."

Good sport that she was, Kimberly got right up. "Okay. Save my chair." She moved down the steps and walked toward Tomorrowland. Turning, she started walking slowly back down the sidewalk toward the porch. As she got in front of Lance, she slowed down, tossed her hair in a flirty way, adding a little extra bounce in her step.

Lance leaned forward and whistled low as she passed.

A few people around Kimberly heard the whistle and gave Lance an offended frown, not aware of the situation.

She continued past the porch, and then turned around to bound back up the steps. "Well?" she asked, leaning over the arm of his chair, batting her eyelashes.

"Easy: Librarian, working six nights a week. Never been on a date. Still reads Nancy Drew mysteries. Likes the Partridge Family and secretly wishes she was Marsha Brady from the Brady Bunch."

"Oh, you are so bad!" she exclaimed, moving back over to her chair. Lance tried to take her hand, but she pretended to be disgusted with him.

"You see, that would have been what *Kip* would have said," Lance smoothly amended his story. "I guess you don't want to hear what *my* evaluation would have been?"

Kimberly eyed him with a look of mock contempt. "Sure. Try to bail yourself out."

"*I* would have said that you were a secret spy, working as a double agent for the KGB and the CIA. You can pick any lock faster than Houdini and are fluent in seven languages… including the language of love."

She couldn't help but laugh. "Wow. That's spooky! It's just like you know me!"

"Yeah, I'm that good."

Kimberly leaned toward Lance and gave him a lingering kiss. She slowly pulled away and whispered, "Yes you are. And modest, too!"

Main Street was packed from the train station all the way to the street in front of the Castle. The nightly fireworks show was extremely popular. Even more people poured in once the *Fantasmic!* show on the Frontierland River ended at 9:25.

Still secure in their chairs on the porch, the couple found out why the seats had been empty so close to show time—they wouldn't be able to see the fireworks because of the overhanging balcony above their heads.

The lights all along Main Street dimmed as an announcer told everyone the Fireworks Spectacular would begin in just five minutes. An excited buzz traveled down the length of the street as people tried to move into a more promising position. Elbow-to-elbow, the guests all found it was just easier to stand where they were and look up. It was fireworks, after all!

Once the show started, an appreciative roar of "Ooh" and "Aah" began. The brilliant colors flashed overhead and a deep *BOOM!* that was felt deep in their chests. Lasers cut through the smoke of the fireworks, turning it green and blue and red. A skull was seen projected on the Matterhorn.

Now standing near their target door, Lance whispered into Kimberly's ear. "You ready?"

Trying to lean out to see the next cascading waterfall of sparkles, she gave a short, "Oh, yeah," and turned her attention to their task at hand. "Sorry. They're just so beautiful!"

"Get ready," he whispered.

The lasers were crossing high over their heads, pinwheels of sparks turning on the spires of the Castle which was now a brilliant yellow. The music came to a crescendo as thirty geysers of sparkling fire erupted behind the Castle. When the geysers died down, the music slowed and the lasers went out. It was suddenly pitch black.

When the next overlapping rockets lit the sky, there were so many of them that it was as bright as if it were midday. The colors all blended into one another as the sparkles descended toward the now blue Castle.

Had anyone thought to look, they would have seen that the porch was now empty.

CHAPTER 12

As soon as the door clicked shut sounding like it automatically locked behind them, Lance felt Kimberly's hand seeking his back in the darkness that enveloped them. Occasional brilliant flashes of fireworks were barely visible through a small crack that Lance had missed a couple of hours earlier. The resulting *Boom* and the 'oohs' and 'ahhs' from the crowd were quite loud in the small space in which they found themselves.

Not knowing exactly what was around them, Kimberly kept her voice in a whisper. "Where are the lockers? I thought we would be in the locker area."

Pulling a small Mag flashlight from his pocket, Lance clicked it on, shielding the majority of the small beam with his hands. Kimberly could see his hand glowing red as he aimed the light toward the area the lockers should occupy. The light met only a blank dark wall.

"Perfect! They are on the other side of this wall," she heard Lance mutter as the feeble light crept upwards. "Follow me."

Her eyes adjusting to the darkness, she could now see Lance moving away from her. Putting her hand on his shoulder, she was surprised when he started walking up what had to be stairs. "What's that smell?" she whispered, resisting the urge to sneeze.

The light she saw rising up the stairs in front of her now dipped downwards toward her feet as Lance stopped. She saw a thick coat of dust on the narrow stairwell. As the light returned to the path in front of them, she saw how narrow it truly was. If she had moved her elbows slightly sideways, she would have been able to touch both sides at once.

"This place hasn't been visited in a long, long time," Lance told her. "Uh, do you like spiders?"

He could hear a soft chuckle behind him. "Why?"

"No…, she heard a loud smack on the wall as the light wavered up in front of her. "…reason," Lance finished. "I wonder if this stairway—and whatever is at the top—is on any blueprints," he said as he reached the top step. Here there was another small landing with a single door to the left of the landing. As Kimberly stepped up next to him, Lance knocked softly, more to see how solid the door was than expecting anyone to answer. "Hey Walt...we're home!" Lance called out in a loud whisper. He was rewarded with a light slap on the shoulder.

"Shhh," Kimberly giggled, still fearful that someone might hear them, even though they were probably within a section of Main Street that absolutely no one knew existed. And, with the finale of the firework show going on outside, he probably could have shouted at the top of his lungs and still have no one hear him.

"Okay, okay," Lance chuckled. "This is a steel door! Almost broke my knuckles when I knocked," he added as he shone his light around the door frame. "Hey, there is another lock here. Well, lookie that!"

Just above the round brass lock, there were three letters that Kimberly and Lance immediately recognized—**W E D**

"I would say we are in the right place," Kimberly excitedly whispered, seeing the letters.

Lance fished out of his pocket the same key that opened the door at the bottom of the stairs. "For some reason, I didn't expect another lock up here. Hope the same key opens it. Here, hold this," he said, handing the flashlight over his shoulder so she could shine it on the lock. "Well, sweetheart, this is it," he said, turning to Kimberly. They could hear the final explosions of the fireworks die down outside. Within minutes, masses of people would be streaming down Main Street toward the exit gates. There were probably people already in the chairs the couple had left vacant moments earlier, watching the streams of humanity as they flowed toward the Park's exit gates.

"Wait!" Kimberly told him as he turned and reached toward the lock. "This wouldn't be a booby trap, would it?" she asked, thinking about the gas that came out of the machine next to Walt that had knocked Lance unconscious.

"No way, not at this point." Lance sounded

sure of himself, at the same time silently thinking that he *hoped* he was right. However, he did take a moment and have her shine the light over the edges of the door, looking for telltale wires.

As she watched the light play over the door, Kimberly had a sense of familiarity wash over her. When her light stopped on the deadbolt once again, she suddenly remembered. "Lance, wait a minute. I just remembered something."

He sounded a little anxious. "Anything wrong?"

"No, no," as the light suddenly aimed up-wards, toward the ceiling.

"The lock is down here, sweetie," he kidded her.

He could hear the smile in her voice when she answered. "Look up there. See that round disc? That's a camera. This is that door on the monitor!"

"What monitor?"

"In Daddy's War Room. I don't know if you saw it or not, but there is one monitor that always shows a closed door. This is the door! That's why it looked familiar to me! Daddy was keeping watch on this room just like he did Walt's secret chamber."

Lance felt his heart rate speed up. "If you are right, then this has to be *it*. You think?"

The light aimed back at the deadbolt lock. "There's only one way to find out."

Fitting the key into the lock, Lance had to apply some force to make it turn. They were both surprised when they heard the sound of at least three heavy steel deadbolts retracting. As they struggled to pull the steel door open, they could feel and hear the vacuum as if the room had been sealed for a long, long time.

At first, their flashlight only illuminated the dust that slowly filtered down off the tops and sides of the door frame. Kimberly immediately thought of 'pixie dust' as the door swung open a little wider.

Lance gave a final pull on the massive door, opening it completely. As they stepped through over the ribbed sill, their narrow beam of light revealed nothing that Lance or Kimberly could have possibly imagined.

Like finding a long-lost Egyptian Pharaoh's tomb, Kimberly and Lance gazed open-mouthed into the narrow but relatively deep room. It felt as if they had climbed the stairs of an old house and had stumbled into Grandma's attic—a lifetime of memories salvaged from the thief of time.

The flashlight swung in a slow arc around the room. It revealed pictures hanging all over the walls; chests and cabinets neatly lined the far wall, sheet-covered boxes and unidentified objects piled in front of the furniture. What turned out to be a model of early Disneyland, at least six feet square, sat on a table in the corner enclosed within a dust-covered glass case. A number of audio-animatronic birds, presumably prototypes from the Enchanted Tiki Room, sat on a metal perch. It appeared they were at one time covered with another sheet but it had slid off the display. Kimberly moved the light down to the floor where they could see the sheet now lying in a small pile. Examining the birds, the beam of light revealed wires extending out of the base of the perch to some sort of remote-control box. Lance immediately recognized one bird sitting alone on a perch as "Jose". This red and orange parrot was the one that Walt Disney himself had operated in one of his Disneyland Television Specials as he demonstrated to the audience the realistic advances they had made in the field of robotics. Lance remembered reading that Disney Archives had been in search of that first audio-animatronics bird, but had never been able to find its location. Lance now understood why.

Feeling the wall near the door where they were still standing, he found a toggle that might be a light switch. He just hoped it was a light switch and not an alarm signal summoning another 'guardian' with a gun like Kimberly's father had been. "Shine the light over here," Lance requested.

"Think it is a light switch?" Kimberly asked, shining the light on the wall.

"I'm guessing that," Lance hesitated, his fingers waffling over the switch. "Should I?"

"There aren't any windows in the room, from what I could see with the flashlight. I think it's more like a vault than a room. What have we got to lose?"

Lance thought about that and came up with a few things they could lose; their lives being one of them, even though that was, at this point, an unlikely scenario.

Somewhat reluctantly, he pushed the old toggle switch up. Instead of a piercing alarm or red flashing security lights, a flicker of light was the only result; a pair of vintage light bulbs came to life, each in a protective fixture that resembled a kind of inverted brass funnel. There were two of them centered in the room's ceiling. Both light bulbs came on and cast the room in relatively bright amber light. Hurriedly, they both scanned for windows again to make sure they weren't inadvertently advertising the room's presence to the outside world. Seeing none, as Kimberly had surmised, they turned their attention to the contents.

It was then the full magnitude of the room became clear to Lance and Kimberly. They stood in silent awe of the sights that surrounded them.

It was a museum of everything Walt Disney.

There were shelves lined with books and what looked to be photo albums. They could see boxes stacked neatly against the back wall, each labeled in faded black ink with numeric numbers representing various years followed by short descriptions: Burbank Studio Office, Anaheim Facility, Florida EPCOT Ideas. There were other boxes with the names of Disney movies like *Snow White*, *Mary Poppins*, and *Fantasia*. A few boxes were labeled as either Clothes or Hats.

Lance felt like he had come upon the penultimate treasure trove of Disney memorabilia. Not wanting to open any of the boxes yet, he could only imagine the things collected from each location or from each movie. The monetary value of such collectibles and memorabilia would be staggering.

Near the center of the room sat a small, round wooden table. Sitting on a lace doily was a dusty glass dome, similar in size to what Lance remembered used to cover an old anniversary clock that his grandparents owned that kept time with a spinning weight on a metal wire that perpetually spun in one direction then the other, over and over. Before he could remove the dust to see what was inside the glass dome, Kimberly called him over.

"Lance, look over here," she said, clicking the flashlight off now that they had plenty of light. There was a pedestal standing near the entry door. Atop the small fixture was a notebook, like everything else in the room covered in dust. Lance slowly lifted the book. Tilting the thin, one-inch leather-bound journal, Lance gently blew the majority of dust off the cover. The word "Walt" was embossed in black letters upon the light-brown leather. Cracked with age and dry from lack of care, the book was fragile and obviously very old.

"What is it?" Kimberly asked as Lance gently opened the book.

"It looks like a journal, similar to the diary Adam had found in Walt's apartment."

Lance opened to the first page as Kimberly read aloud the words:

"Depending on who finds my little 'home away from home,' I hope for my sake, you will understand the purpose of this room and all that is in it.

"I trust that someday I will be able to return

to this room. I won't know if I will be able to re-member anything from my past. All that you see is here for one purpose: to help me know me. I've been told that, in theory, re-animation from a cryo-genic state often is like being born again. I want to make sure that, if I need to, I can re-educate myself so I can, perhaps, continue with my dreams and not be totally unaware of my past.

"First off, to whoever has managed to follow each of the clues I have left, let me thank you for being so diligent. I'm sure it was not an easy task to solve each clue and follow each hint I left be-hind. With the help of my two Guardians, I was able to create the means in which I could be left undisturbed, hopefully until such time as doctors or the medical industry could cure my cancer. Chances are I won't make it back. And, well, if that is the case, then so be it. It is hoped that peo-ple will remember me and those who helped me along the way. This room is a tribute to everyone who helped me bring to life all that I envisioned.

"Actually, there is so much more that I was unable to accomplish; so many dreams left only as dreams. I hope that my Florida project gets completed some day. Now that was a vision!

"I built Disneyland so that it would continue to grow and expand. As long as imagination is in the world, then indeed Disneyland will never be finished. There is a box in here—somewhere—with all the new ideas I have for my Park. Maybe someone will be able to continue building some of these ideas.

"In the meantime, I hope that you will be able to maintain this room for the purpose for which it

was intended. The reason I made this quest for the Hidden Mickey so intricate was because I didn't want the world clawing at my personal things. I figured that any individual diligent enough to find this room would also be diligent enough to protect it for me.

"Finally, I didn't want this quest to end without a reward. Yes, there is something of great value that I want you to have. In the middle of the room you should find a magnificent diamond heart. It is under a glass enclosure. Beyond the value of the diamond itself, I think you will find it has a value far beyond money itself. I know it will provide for your future as it did for mine. You must remember, though, that how you achieve your future is up to you! This point was stressed to me and I cannot stress that enough.

"In the meantime, feel free to look around. I don't know if much here will have any value to anyone except me. Yet, if there is anything you see that you might like to keep as a personal memento of your search, please feel free. Just don't take my hat! I'd really appreciate it if you could leave the rest of everything where I've put it, since it will help me someday, I hope.

"Until we meet again, remember always to keep moving forward.

"Walt Disney"

Kimberly wiped a tear from her eye as they looked at each other and, as one they turned toward the center of the room.

Lance used the sleeve of his jacket to wipe the heavy layer of dust off of the glass dome. Kneeling down, he and Kimberly looked inside. Hanging off of a Y-shaped brass stand was an antique-looking gold chain with a brilliant red, heart-shaped diamond that dangled several inches above its wooden base. The gem was backed by three small circlets of gold set in a very familiar shape. The simple, yet elegant setting looked to be very old. The chain itself was heavy yet beautiful with its intricate woven braiding of gold. It connected to the pendant at the top of the golden ears. Lance thought perhaps they were looking at truly the very first 'Hidden Mickey.'

"This is incredible, Lance," Kimberly whispered. "I'm almost afraid to touch it."

"Let me lift the dome off the base," Lance said as he put both his hands around the glass sides and lifted straight up, careful not to hit the exquisite piece of jewelry. With care, he set the glass covering on the table next to its base.

The two of them simply stared at the large diamond; now free of the dome, they could see the fiery gem without the distortion of the glass and dust. Catching the light in the room, rainbow sparkles shimmered off of the facets of the gem.

With great care, Lance took hold of the chain and carefully lifted the pendant off its stand. He let it dangle by his fingers at eye level so Kimberly could really examine it up close.

As he turned the heavy piece back and forth, he noticed the gold setting and wondered out loud, "That looks like a hidden mickey that you would find in the Park. Do you think Walt had this made? Wow, this red diamond is huge! Have you ever seen anything like it?" Lance asked her, realizing the stone looked to be about an inch wide and an inch tall.

She shook her head as she was nearly speechless. Reaching out to touch the gemstone, she let the pendant lay flat in her hand as Lance held the chain, her fingers closing over the stone. "I've never even se…." Her sentence was cut short. In only a split second, Kimberly felt as if she was seeing fireworks going off in her head. The bright light expanded and was followed by a vision. She was transfixed by the apparition:

In that moment, Kimberly saw herself in a wedding dress. The scene instantly shifted to a beach surrounded by blue waters and swaying palm trees. Before she could blink, she was at Disneyland, holding hands with a young, beautiful blond girl. Her own hair, she could now see, was gray as she walked arm in arm with someone…someone who was also seen in all the other images.

That someone was Lance.

"Kimberly, Kimberly!" Lance's voice called out to her sounding as if it was coming from far away.

At the sound of his voice, her hand jerked and the diamond fell from the palm of her hand. She watched as it swayed back and forth on its chain as it hung from Lance's fingertips.

"You were saying something about the pendant and then you just stopped. Are you okay?"

"Yes," was her hesitant reply. She reached out a tentative finger and touched the red diamond again. Her mind was filled with the unknown blond girl who looked to be around five years old. She jerked her hand back as if it was burned. Her eyes flying to Lance's face, she could only see concern there. He didn't see it? It was so real…. "Yes, I am fine. I think I just got some dust in my eyes or something. I sort of blanked out for a moment. Must be allergies with all this dust."

For some reason, she was afraid to reveal what she thought she had just seen to Lance. She needed some time to ponder all that had just happened in her mind. "I think we need to leave," Kimberly told him as the worried look on his face eased.

His worried look was replaced by an incredulous one. "What? But I want to look around."

Kimberly saw a small velvet box under the table where the pendant had been displayed. She reached down and took the box. "Here, put the pendant in here," Kimberly requested as she held the box out to Lance. She watched him let the pendant drop into the box, letting the chain spill from his fingers until it was all inside the velvet box. Kimberly then shut the lid. "This needs to come with us," as she took the box and fit it into her jacket's pocket.

As Lance looked around the room, he thought he understood what she meant, but wondered why she was acting a little odd. "You're right. This isn't our room. It's Walt's. There is nothing in here that we should disturb except this pendant. I think that is what Walt wanted to reward us—well, whoever found it—with."

"Yes." Kimberly was distracted, her mind still trying to grasp the visions she had just seen.

While they had been just fleeting glimpses, they were the most clearly seen 'dreams' she had ever had. They were so vivid, not abstract as with sleeping dreams. The whole episode had to have taken place in only a second or two of time. Yet, she felt as though she had seen a lifetime pass before her eyes…*her* lifetime.

"I think we should take the book and the pendant with us and leave the rest. We have the key. If we ever need to return, or if Walt needs to return, we can do just that," Lance suggested as he picked up the glass dome and placed it over the now empty display.

Looking around the room one last time, Lance knew that sometime in his future, he would return to this room. As he glanced over at Kimberly, he could see her blond hair almost glowing in the amber light. Lance came to another realization: he also knew he wanted to spend his life with one woman.

And that woman was Kimberly.

Going out of the door on the porch was far easier than going in. Lance had pulled aside a lower corner of the green shade behind the lace curtain and peeked out. The porch was now empty as the Park was clearing of guests. People were strolling past the porch now with the determination of making it out of the Park as quickly as possible.

Lance had one reminder for Kimberly, "I told Adam this when we were coming out of someplace where we shouldn't have been: Always act like you know what you are doing. People tend to believe you then. When I open the door, just walk out as if we did it every day. Okay?"

She just nodded, her mind still wrapped around the vision.

Stepping out onto the porch and shutting the door behind them, Lance used the key one last time to securely lock the door. Chatting as if he was continuing a conversation, he led her off of the porch and became part of the flow of the people leaving.

Once they reached Lance's car in the Employee lot, Kimberly allowed herself to relax. She pulled the small box from her pocket and opened the hinged lid. The gold chain had worked it way under the large red heart-shaped diamond. Now the pendant sat beautifully perched in the box; illuminated by the overhead light she had just turned on, the diamond again reflected sparkling beams of light.

"Do you think the pendant is why Walt used hearts in all his clues?" she pondered as she tilted the box to make the glistening light dance. She was afraid to touch the gemstone with her fingers; afraid of what it seemed to have done to her already. While the images were actually beautiful and comforting, the loss of consciousness—even for the briefest of moments—was disconcerting.

"I guess," Lance murmured, intent on his driving as he changed lanes and accelerated down Harbor Boulevard. "It sure seems to tie it all together," he added when traffic eased. He then became quiet for a moment. "But I'm not sure what Walt meant when he said the pendant had a value that was something beyond money itself."

Kimberly thought she knew.   But, her thoughts seemed too farfetched to say out loud. Even after experiencing what power she thought the pendant seemed to possess, it all seemed too fantastic and unbelievable to her. Kimberly closed the lid again and carefully set the velvet box onto the dashboard in front of her. "Well, I'm too tired to even think about the ramifications of what Walt did or did not mean." She closed her eyes.

Lance reached over and stroked her hair. A smile grew on Kimberly's lips as she drifted off. It was only a matter of moments before she began to dream about weddings, beaches and Lance Brentwood.

The next morning, Lance rose from one of the guest bedrooms and padded barefoot across the hardwood floors of the hallway. He knocked softly on Kimberly's bedroom door. Not hearing anything, he quietly opened the door. Entering, he found her still asleep on her bed, only a sheet covering the lower half of her. Sleeping in a tank top, Lance admired her smooth skin and the curves of her figure.

Slowly, Kimberly stirred, turning from her side onto her back, she stretched out her arms and opened her eyes. She didn't seem surprised to see Lance standing beside her bed. With a smile, she told him, "Morning. Come here," she invited, holding out her hand to Lance who came and sat down on the edge of her bed.

"Sweet dreams?" Lance asked.

Kimberly thought about her dreams as well as the dream she had had the night before while holding the pendant. "Very sweet. You?"

"Oh, you don't want to know," Lance said with a grin.

"Maybe I do," Kimberly responded.

"Someday I promise I'll share."

"I hope you will," Kimberly said, thinking how much his response sounded like a long term promise.

During breakfast, which Kimberly cooked, Lance brought up something he had thought about up until he had fallen asleep: "I wonder if we should have the pendant evaluated."

"You mean appraised?"

"Not necessarily appraised," he replied slowly, looking away. "From what I know about red diamonds, the largest heart shape on record is a little over one carat in size. This one is huge! I would guess it is well over twenty carats. I would just like to know a little more about it. I mean, the setting looks very old and, knowing Walt, the stone and the necklace probably have some sort of history to them."

Kimberly thought about this as she munched on an English muffin. She knew from her own experience that the stone possessed something far more powerful than anything monetary. It would not be advisable to have someone else look at— let alone touch—the pendant. "Perhaps," she hedged, finishing her muffin. "But, I'm not sure we should. After all, I doubt Walt had ever had it appraised. I'm sure there would have been some reference to it if he had. If it did end up having some fantastic history behind it, how would we explain how we got it? I mean, I have never even *heard* of a red diamond before, let alone seen one!"

Lance slowly nodded. "Well, let's put the pendant away for safe keeping and we can think more about it later. I'd like to go over the journal again and Walt's ideas on coming back. We should look through your father's notes to see what he was planning on doing."

They both sat silently as they finished their breakfast, thinking their own thoughts. However, outside the open kitchen window, their conversation was clearly overheard by a smiling man whose face was bandaged and who limped slightly as he moved quickly away from the house.

CHAPTER 13

"You have one last chance to give me the pendant, or I start taking little pieces out of that pretty face of yours," Daniel yelled at Kimberly, his scarred face pushing close to hers. He could see her eyes, wide with fear, returning again to the open door of the library. He gave a victorious chuckle. "Don't be expecting any grand rescue from that dumb bodyguard of yours. Kevin is out back investigating a small explosion."

"Is that what that was? I thought a jet went by overhead. What did you do?" she demanded, leaping out of the chair she had been sitting in, her temper warring against the fear of the knife he held in his damaged hand.

Daniel grabbed her arm as he could tell she was about to bolt around him. "No you don't, Missy," he yelled as he yanked her arm up behind her back, getting satisfaction from the grunt of pain that came from her clenched lips. "You know that ugly little white thing out back you were so fond of? I'm afraid it went boom."

She pulled against his grasp and was rewarded by another vicious yank on her arm. "My gazebo? You blew up my gazebo? That was a gift to my father from Walt. You know it was hand-made to look like the one in Marceline! How could you?"

"Oh, it was quite easy," he bragged, thinking he had accomplished something great. "It's amazing what you can buy over the Internet.... Now quit changing the subject. Where is that diamond?" he demanded, sliding the knife even closer to her face.

She backed away as far as the pain in her arm would allow. "I don't have it. It isn't here."

"Now why don't I believe you?"

"You know me, Daniel. You know I could never convincingly lie. Father always knew when I was lying, and so did you."

"Where is it, then?"

"Lance has it," she said in a quiet voice, dropping her eyes so he couldn't see that she was lying through her teeth.

"You gave a red diamond to Pretty Boy? How stupid are you!?" he yelled at her. "Do you have any idea how rare those are?"

"Oh, been doing a little research, Daniel?" she spat back at him.

"What, do you think I'm an idiot? Of course I did. Right after I heard you and Brentwood talking about it. Maybe you should have done a little yourself before giving it to that con artist. Do you really think you have a future with that loser? Your dad told me he turned on his own friends!"

Kimberly kept her voice low. "I know his history, Daniel. You don't need to lecture me. Anyway, you of all people should know that people can change."

"If you mean they can go from bad to worse, then you are correct. But I don't trust this guy. Never did. But, no, you never listen to family! You think you know everything. Well, I want that diamond. And I will get it. One way or the other. Then I'll deal with your stupid amusement park. And the little secret you have hidden away down there."

Kimberly gave a gasp. "You wouldn't dare! Don't you dare touch Walt! Let go of me!"

He gave her sore arm another yank. "Don't tell me what to do. You aren't in charge any more. I am. As I should have been all along. I finally got your father out of the picture. You cooperate, or you're next." He roughly pulled her over to a window overlooking the expansive back yard. He could see the bodyguard still poking around through the debris of the gazebo looking for the detonator. He knew Kevin wouldn't be there much longer. Now it was time to put his secondary plan into action. "I need you to make a call to the Park."

"I'm not doing anything you say! What do you mean you got my father out of the way?" she struggled against his grasp. "What did you do!?"

He waved off the shocked look on her face. "Seems there are certain teas someone with a heart condition shouldn't drink…. He should really have been more careful. And, yes, you are going to do what I say. If you don't go along, your dear Mr. Brentwood will have an unfortunate accident in that piece of crap he drives. You know how unreliable Jags are." Daniel started laughing at his own joke. It was a sick, desperate laugh that chilled Kimberly to the bone. She knew he meant every word. She also knew he was past the point of no return. He was desperate. He was dangerous. He had killed once and wouldn't hesitate to do it again to get what he wanted.

"What do you want me to do," she asked in a deceptively calm tone, trying to keep the hatred out of her voice. She didn't want him doing anything impulsive to her. She now had 'revenge' to add to her list of grievances against her uncle....

The pressure on her arm lessened and the knife lowered. "That's a good girl. You usually did listen to reason once a strong hand was shown."

I'll cut your heart out if you blink twice, she silently promised.

Daniel, misunderstanding her sudden smile, assumed she was compliant. "Call the Park and tell them to shut down Tom Sawyer's Island and leave one raft operational. And don't even try and tell me you don't have that power," he pulled her arm again as soon as she opened her mouth to protest.

"I understand. I need to get over to the phone, Daniel," as he tried to keep her from moving away from him.

"Oh, right. I knew that."

With a knife held in her face, Kimberly picked up the direct phone to the Park and pushed number two. When the phone was answered, she knew there was no need for any pleasantries. This was the Direct Order phone line with the voice-altering transmitter. "I need Tom Sawyer's Island shut down for the rest of the day. Leave one raft ready to use at the dock. Effective immediately. Thank you."

As Kimberly replaced the handset, she knew there would be another call being placed immediately within the Park system. In approximately fifteen minutes, the Island would be completely cleared of guests. She also knew there would be no questions and no one checking to see what was either needed or wrong.

"Now what?" she demanded. "And put away that stupid knife. You know you don't need it."

He started pushing her out of the library and toward the hallway leading to the garage. "You must think I am really stupid. I'm not about to get rid of the knife. I don't trust you any farther than I can throw you."

Yes, I do think you are stupid. I am just waiting….

"You are going to drive us to Disneyland, park in the regular lot, and enter the main gate just like any other loving family. No employee entrance. No message to any security guard. We are just going to blend in," as they entered the garage and he motioned for her to drive her car.

"Yeah, a knife held at my throat really blends in, Daniel," as she started the car, pretending to warm it up in hopes Kevin came looking for her.

"Don't worry about the knife. It will be aimed at your spine the whole time we are walking down that insipid Main Street.... Man, I'll be glad when the bulldozers finally take care of that eyesore.... One false step, one tiny word to any of your friends, and you get stuck straight into the spine. Then I go after Brentwood. Savvy?" He could barely refrain from laughing out loud. His plan was working brilliantly. He could tell she was putty in his hands. He figured it would be one hour, two tops, until he would get his hands on that diamond. And then the fun would begin.

Realizing they weren't moving yet, he yelled, "Quit stalling! Put this jelly bean in gear and get moving." By now Kevin would have found the cause of the explosion and would be on his way back to the house. Daniel knew he could manhandle Kimberly easily enough. Kevin was another problem. Kevin could break him in two like a matchstick.

With a silent sigh, Kimberly backed out of the garage and started down the hill, her mind spinning. Sooner or later Daniel would relax his vigilance. And she would be ready when he did.

It was a beautiful, sunny summer day in Anaheim. Disneyland was full of smiling faces, all heading in a myriad of directions to go on their next adventure. The Central Hub was newly decorated with bright flowers; the hanging pots of fuchsias a vivid pink against the green of the full trees all lined up behind the flowers.

Kimberly had more on her mind than the flowers as she was roughly led by the arm through the crowds of people. Daniel had clamped onto her arm from the moment her car stopped in its parking spot in the Mickey and Friends Lot. He didn't even let go of her arm when they went through the

Security checkpoint. He wasn't giving her any chance of either fleeing on foot or striking out at him.

Daniel led her under the thatched arch entry of Adventureland and they wound their way through the crowds in front of Indiana Jones. Kimberly gave a glance upwards as she passed under the boughs of the Treehouse, a small smile playing over her lips as she remembered the night she shared with Lance. They had gotten so close in such a short period of time. Then there had been that strange, wonderful vision…. Another yank on her arm brought her attention back to her hated uncle.

"You don't need to be so rough, Daniel," she quietly told him. "You're going to leave bruises if you don't stop that."

"I'll leave more than that if you don't shut up. I see a raft at the Landing. At least you got that right."

Kimberly gave a short sigh. *Yes, her instructions were always followed to the letter, as her father's had been. Rats.*

Daniel slowed their pace as they approached the Frontierland River. He wanted to see if there was anyone who appeared to be watching the raft. Satisfied after a quick look around, Daniel pushed her through the exit gate of the Raft ride. There didn't seem to be anyone giving them a second look. The closest people were the ones on the smoking dock, over by the Columbia's berth. There were no security guards hovering. It looked like they were free and clear. "Get on the raft and get back by engine, away from the entrance." He unhooked the leather ties that were holding the wooden raft to the dock. With a quick glance on the location of the Mark Twain and any approaching canoes, he flipped a couple of switches and the small engine roared to life, water shooting out from under the rudder. He let the force of the water being agitated by the engine slowly push them free of the dock. The task of getting clear of the dock was usually accomplished by a second cast member who pushed off, balancing from a precarious perch on the outermost pontoon of the raft. Daniel knew better than to ask Kimberly to help.

The raft took a rather awkward trip over to the Island. Daniel had learned how to drive the raft by questioning a friend of his who used to work there. He had never actually steered or docked one. He missed the landing dock by a few feet and had to back the raft into position. It banged heavily against the wooden dock, almost throwing them off their feet—much to the delight of several guests who were watching, wondering why the rafts were open now and only two people on them who were obviously not cast members. Some of them guessed the raft had been 'borrowed' by two guests and wished they had thought of it themselves. When the raft hit the landing, their attention drifted and they moved along. They had wanted to see the raft make the complete trip around the Island. This wasn't any fun to watch.

Once the engine was killed and the raft secured, Daniel motioned for Kimberly to get moving.

"Where are we going?" she wanted to know.

She was getting more worried. She knew the island was empty and no one would come back until they received the call for the Go Ahead. She knew Daniel wouldn't make the call. Kimberly then swallowed nervously as no one else knew she was there.

"Head for the Fort," she was told. Daniel was referring to Fort Wilderness, a stockade built out of twelve- to fourteen-foot tall logs, designed to look like real wooden stakes even to the pointed tips on top. It had been called the 'Last Outpost of Civilization' in years gone past, a favorite place for children of all ages to climb through and shoot imaginary rifles through the small slits high in the watchtowers.

"The Fort has been closed for years, Daniel. You should know that."

"I do know that, smart-aleck. That's why it is so perfect."

Kimberly felt a chill go through her. "Perfect for what?" she asked, trying to keep her voice from breaking.

"You won't be found for a long, long time. No, head to the back of the Fort," he told her, pushing her down a narrow dusty path toward the back of the island. "Head to the graveyard."

Kimberly stopped short, causing Daniel to run into her. He grabbed the knife out of his pocket. "Get moving!"

"Why do you want the graveyard?"

He could hear the fear in her voice. He gave her a twisted smile, one that looked even worse because of the damage the accident had done to his face. "Do what I say, or it will be your last stop.

There's a tunnel back there."

Kimberly's mind was turning. She had to get away from him, but he had already nicked her with the knife since they had landed on the island. She knew it wasn't an accident; it was a warning for her. Kimberly also knew which tunnel he meant. He was taking her to the exit of the old Escape Tunnel. The start of the tunnel was inside the Fort and had been a fun idea for children pretending to be attacked by savages. The tunnel itself was narrow, low and dark. There was no telling how long it had been since anyone had been in there. Once something was closed and locked up, it was generally forgotten. She could feel her heart start pounding.

"I'm sure it's locked, Daniel," she threw out there. "Can't we talk this through?"

Daniel was busy with the cell phone he had pulled out of his pocket with his free hand. "We're done talking...and it isn't locked. You aren't the only one with friends," he scoffed. "Stand over there," he pointed with the knife, indicating the low exit to the tunnel. He then blocked the only path with his body. "Hello? Is this Lance? Hey, buddy, this is Daniel. How are you?.... Now, now, no need to get nasty.... Say, I have something of yours that I would like to offer as an exchange.... Oh, I think you should be very interested in what I have to say.... Say hello," he jabbed the phone to Kimberly's face and nicked her arm again with the knife.

"Ouch! That's not necessary, Daniel.... Lance! Don't do anything he says...."

Daniel gave a laugh and put the phone back

to his ear. "You still there, Brentwood? Yeah, you'd better listen. Oh, she just cut herself with a knife, that's all. You know how clumsy she is…. Now, no need for unpleasantness. We're all friends here." Daniel gave a loud laugh. "Gosh, I'm funny! Say Lance, I want to make a trade with you. I'll give you Kimberly alive and you give me the red diamond…. No, no, no argument. I know you have it. You have, oh, say, half an hour to bring it to Tom Sawyer's Island. I'll meet you at the raft dock. If you come alone and bring me the diamond, I'll actually tell you where Kimberly is…. Half an hour, Brentwood, or I'll send a piece of Miss Waldron across the River on its own." Daniel snapped shut the phone and thrust it back in his pocket. He was still chuckling at his own cleverness. His humor died when he saw the look on Kimberly's face. "Wow, if looks could kill…."

"Then you would have been dead a long time ago, Daniel," she said through clenched teeth.

Daniel checked his watch. "Now, let's see how prompt your dearly beloved is."

"He's going to need more time than that."

"Don't give me any of your lip. I know how long it takes to drive here from his crappy apartment. I went through it often enough to know," he admitted with a huge grin.

Kimberly licked her dry lips. "The pendant isn't in Lance's apartment. It's at the mansion. It's been there all along."

Angry again, he waved the knife under her face. "You told me Lance had it."

Kimberly gave a little shrug. "I lied."

He looked at his watch again. "Then you will

pay the penalty if he doesn't get here in time." *Stupid girl...always messing with me.... I'll show her*, his mind urged him. Out loud, he said, "Let's see how my friend did. Try that door under there. Now!" he prompted by shoving her into the door.

Knowing he would use the knife again, she felt it was in her best interests to comply at this point. If his friends were as mindless as he was, perhaps they didn't—or couldn't—do what he asked of them. After all, the Fort had been closed a long time. Only a few key people would have access to these hidden tunnels. Buoyed by that hope, Kimberly felt her heart sink when the door swung open. A rush of stale air hit her in the face. No one had been in there for a long time. "Don't make me go in there, Daniel," she whispered. "I won't call out. I promise."

"'I won't call out. I promise'," he mocked in a shrill voice. "You must really think I'm stupid. That does remind me, though." He pulled out a long string of twine from his pocket. "Turn around and put your hands behind your back," he ordered. After she slowly complied, he secured her wrists so tightly she couldn't move them. Since her back was turned, she couldn't see that he now pulled out a long strip of material.

"You don't need...." The rest of what Kimberly was going to say was cut off when he roughly put the strip of cloth in her mouth, pulling it around to the back where he tied it behind her head, catching some of her hair in the knot. Her eyes started to water from the pain.

Rats, she inwardly complained to herself. *Should have kept my mouth shut.*

"Now you really won't call out. Get in the tunnel."

Kimberly had to bend over to fit in the fairly low exit. Darkness enveloped her as she stumbled forward, hoping she didn't bang her head on one of the unseen stalactites in the realistically-built cave. Unable to use her hands to steady herself, she found it easier to drop down on her knees. She gave a small, unheard scream when the door—her only source of light—was slammed shut behind her. She sank into a sitting position, tears filling her eyes, as drops of blood ran down the cuts on her abused arms.

Daniel guided the raft back over at the mainland before Lance arrived. He had to turn away guests who wanted to take their children over to the Island to play. They walked away wondering why that cast member was not in costume and very rude.

Lance was wide-eyed and breathless by the time he got to the Raft dock. He had to force himself to drive carefully and then not run through the Park, pushing people out of the way, to get to Frontierland. "Where is she?" Lance demanded once he got face-to-face with Daniel.

Daniel reached in his pocket and showed the point of the knife to Lance. Lance could see specks of red on the knife. He knew it was Kimberly's blood and he turned red with rage.

"If you hurt her in any way, I will kill you," Lance muttered to Daniel, low enough so he would not be overheard by anyone happening to be passing by.

Daniel took a step back from the intensity in Lance's eyes. He knew Lance was being perfectly honest. "Back off, playboy," Daniel tried to sound menacing, like he was in charge. But his voice quavered and that irritated him. "I'm in charge here, not you. If you want to see her alive again, you'll do what I say. Got that? Now, where is the diamond?"

"I want to know she's all right first."

"You don't have any bargaining chips, Brentwood. Show me the diamond. Now, or I walk and you try and find her on that island before she bleeds to death," he added as a last-minute thought to force Lance to comply. He wanted that diamond. The whereabouts of Kimberly was his only ace in the hole. But Lance didn't know that.

Lance realized he could call in the entire Security force to help him scour the island. But, there might be secret hiding places he didn't know about that Daniel did. If Kimberly was hurt as badly as Daniel was implying, it wasn't worth the risk. Look what he had found hidden under the Pirate ride that had been there untouched and undiscovered for thirty-six years.... He knew he had to go along with Daniel at this point.

Lance reached into his jacket pocket and pulled a velvet box out far enough for Daniel to see. "It's right here, Crain. Now take me to Kimberly!"

"Open it. I trust you just about as much as I trust her. Open it!"

Lance pulled apart the velvet sides of the small box. The sunlight caught on the facets inside and sent out a dazzling sparkle of red light. "See? It's here. Now take me to her."

"I could just take the diamond and leave," Daniel laughed. His smug smile faded when Lance showed no fear.

"And I could shoot you where you stand," was Lance's quiet response. He was rewarded by Daniel's eyes going wide with fear and hesitation. "You didn't say come unarmed, Daniel, only alone," Lance leaned closer to him and whispered.

"I don't believe you." Daniel was trying to force his bravado.

"Then I guess we're at a stand-off. Take me to Kimberly and you can have the diamond. I only want her." Lance swallowed when the words came out of his mouth. The words were true. He knew he would give Daniel every diamond in the world if Kimberly was safe and he had her in his arms. Nothing else mattered. He shoved the velvet box back in his pocket. "Take me there. Now."

"When I show you the girl, you will give me the diamond, and I bring the raft back here. Is that agreed? Gentlemen's agreement?"

Lance suddenly grinned. "Gentlemen's agreement? Why, of course."

The grin should have clued Daniel in. Lance didn't consider Daniel a gentleman....

"Get on the raft. I'll take us over. How you get back off the island is up to you," Daniel told him.

Lance just gave a curt nod in agreement. The time for words was over.

As the raft made its irregular course over to Tom Sawyer's Island one more time, a pair of sharp blue eyes was watching from the deck of the Columbia, berthed in Fowler's Harbor. The eyes narrowed as the two men left the raft and turned left, heading for the old Fort.

What was Lance up to now? He didn't look very happy.

Sitting in the darkness, Kimberly tried humming to relieve her nerves. Small, dark places had never been her favorite. She tried to keep down the choking fear that was crowding the edges of her mind. *Think, think, girl. What can you do?*

She had tried unsuccessfully to get her hands free. The pricks from the knife still smarted, but she thought the blood had stopped running down her arm. She knew Daniel had locked the door behind her. How long was this tunnel? What was at the other end of it? Did it go straight to the old Fort?

She got back onto her knees and began her slow advance through the tunnel. She could have stood and walked, but she was still mindful of the low-hanging rocks. Thankful there were no scurrying noises around her, she knew those noises would indicate that the tunnel was being occupied by something else.

The main tunnel twisted and turned, but there were no other smaller tunnels branching off like there were in the other caves on the Island. She came to the end of the tunnel, which she hoped was the entrance inside the Fort. Anything would be better than this dirty darkness. With some effort, she got turned around and got her hands around the handle. It, too, was locked. She held back a wave of panic and turned around again. Using her feet, she kicked at the door, giving a muffled yell of triumph when the second kick splintered the old door and fresh air and sunlight streamed into the tunnel.

Blinking from the bright light, she crawled out of the tunnel and stood up in the littered, but otherwise vacant, parade grounds of the old Fort Wilderness.

"She's in there," Daniel indicated the tunnel with the knife he had taken out of his pocket once they were out of sight of the mainland.

Lance looked up at the tall walls of the Fort. "What is this? The old escape tunnel?"

Pleased with himself, Daniel smiled and rocked back on his heels. "Yeah. Kinda ironic, isn't it?" He pulled out a key and threw it to Lance. He didn't want to have his back turned to the very angry man in front of him. "Unlock the door," he instructed. "Then, you first. I insist."

Worried about Kimberly, Lance didn't bother arguing. He still had the diamond and the assumption he might have brought a gun. Ducking down, he started making his way through the tunnel, using the light from the open door to see what was in front of him. Daniel came in after him.

"Kimberly?" Lance called out. "You all right?

Kimberly?"

The men could hear no movement except for their own. "I'm warning you, Daniel. Where is she?"

Daniel felt a moment of panic. She was supposed to be there, cowering in fear. *Where was she?* "I left her gagged right here in the opening. It's not my fault she didn't stay where she was told."

Lance bit back the angry words he was going to hurl at Daniel when he heard Kimberly had been gagged. There would be time later. He started moving through the tunnel. "I see more light up ahead."

"You do?" Daniel didn't know what to think. This wasn't part of his plan. He should have had the diamond by now and been on his way back to the Aston Martin and the mansion.

Lance emerged from the tunnel, blinking from the bright light. He was relieved to see her sitting on a bench in front of one of the old buildings. She jumped to her feet, swaying from having her hands tied behind her back. Lance ran up to her and caught her. "Are you all right? Why are your arms bloody!?" He pulled the gag out of her mouth and untied her hands.

"I'm okay, Lance, really," she whispered, leaning into him. "Just do what he says. Please? I just want to go home."

During this whispered exchange, Daniel silently came up behind them and smashed a rock down on the base of Lance's skull. His eyes stunned, Lance collapsed at Kimberly's feet without a word. She let out a small shriek and sank beside him. "What did you do that for!? We've done everything you said," she cried, running her fingers over Lance's head. She found a large, bleeding bump at the top of his neck. "You've hurt him really bad!"

Daniel just shrugged as he backed away from the hatred he saw in her eyes. "He said he had a gun. I was just making sure I was safe. Now, take the diamond out of his jacket pocket and throw it over here."

"You are despicable, Daniel," as she reached into Lance's jacket to find the box.

"Yeah, I'm really going to lose sleep over that one, Kimberly. Hurry up. I have plans to put into action," he motioned with the knife. "Enjoy your day at the Park. It will be one of the last. I have a plug to pull."

Her heart aching, Kimberly pulled out the velvet box and tossed it to Daniel. With a shout of triumph, he shoved it down his shirt and turned to head back to the escape tunnel. "Now, if you will excuse me, I will be on my way."

"I hope you rot in…."

"Now, now, Kimberly. You know how your father didn't approve of you talking that way." Daniel turned to go back the way they had come.

"Don't you mention my father! After what you did, you have no right to even speak his name!"

Ready to give her a smart remark, Daniel was stopped in his tracks by a sudden, unexpected noise over by the locked stockade gates. Thinking they were alone on the Island, both of them jerked their heads in that direction. They were stunned to see Wolf, dressed in his Security outfit, drop easily to the ground from one of the high watchtower windows. Eyes narrowed in anger, he walked slowly toward Daniel, his hands out from his sides. He looked like a gunslinger walking toward a shootout. "Is he okay?" he briefly asked Kimberly, indicating his partner Lance with a tilt of his chin.

"I…I think so," she told him, feeling the throb in Lance's neck. "His pulse is strong. I think he was just knocked out. Wolf! It was Daniel…he killed my father!"

"I know. He was poisoned. I have a Fort to clean up." He turned back to Daniel who was still rooted by shock in the same spot. "This is *my* turf," he snarled at Daniel.

"It was you! You were the inside man!" Ashen-faced, Daniel came to life and dove into the tunnel. They could see him scrambling forward like a crab as fast as he could. Wolf followed him into the tunnel, his eyes flashing and lips compressed into an angry line.

Daniel got to the end of the tunnel, but he knew he would never make it to the raft in time. He pulled the knife back out of his pocket and turned to wait for the security guard. He didn't have to wait long.

Wolf emerged from the tunnel and was faintly surprised to see Daniel standing there waiting for him. He wasn't surprised to see the knife in Daniel's hand. The knife didn't worry him at all.

Daniel held out his free hand in front of him. The red diamond pendant was dangling from his fingers by its chain. "I don't have an argument with you. I don't want the girl. I only want this.

Let me pass and nobody else gets hurt."

Wolf pulled up short when he saw the pendant in Daniel's hand. *How the heck did he get that?* His eyes never left the sparkling diamond. "You don't know what you've got."

Daniel smiled when the security guard stopped advancing toward him. It was a sick smile, a smile tinged with delusions. "I've got this knife and I've got this diamond. This knife is going to get me off this Island, and this diamond is going to make me rich."

"You think so?" Wolf asked him in a deceptively calm voice. He might have been discussing the possibility of rain.

With a confident laugh, Daniel swung the diamond up by its chain and caught the gem in his hand. "Absolut...."

Suddenly, Daniel grabbed his chest as he saw a flaming arrow pierce his heart. Looking down at the blood pouring out of the hole in his chest, he saw he was wearing some kind of a soldier's uniform. It was blue and there were gold buttons and gold trim like the old Calvary uniforms. He was surrounded by the sounds of a battle. Then, he realized he was in a canoe and it was rocking violently from side to side, heading toward a swirling vortex of lightning and water....

At the moment of Daniel's vision, Wolf pointed at him and snarled, "You have seen the future...and the future is now!" He emitted a roar and launched himself at the distracted, panicking man. The knife flew out of Daniel's hand as he was thrown to the ground. "This is my turf," Wolf told him again, grabbing the diamond from

Daniel's grasp and dragging him to his feet, shaking him like a rag doll as a fog suddenly enveloped the Island and a brilliant light flashed all around them.

When Lance came to, Kimberly told him about Wolf's sudden appearance. Lance managed a small smile. "That's my partner."

"Why is it foggy all of a sudden?" she asked, distracted. "We need to get you out of here, Lance. You need help. Can you walk?"

"Yeah, I think so. My head is killing me."

"At least Daniel hit the hardest part of you," Kimberly smiled. She was so relieved he was all right she was almost crying.

"Ha ha," as all Lance could manage as a comeback.

Kimberly led him over to the escape tunnel and entered ahead of him. Lance was slow, but he knew he had to get out of there. A moan of pain came from his white lips from time to time.

When they got near the exit, Kimberly heard what sounded like a howl and she was suddenly blinded by a brilliant light that came from just outside the tunnel. A sudden blast of wind blew her backwards, covering her with leaves and dirt. Then, the light and the wind stopped as quickly as they had started.

"What was that?" Lance asked as she fell back against him.

"I'm not sure. It came from outside," as she helped him out of the tunnel and they stood together in a close embrace, an embrace that was as much from emotion as it was to help Lance remain upright. Her mind was spinning. She wasn't sure what she had just seen and heard, never having witnessed Wolf's methods before. But, if that was what had just happened, it chilled her to the bone.

As Lance looked up toward the sky, trying to peer through the fog, the movement of his neck caused a sharp pain to course through his head. "Oww. Remind me not to do that again. Where are Wolf and Daniel? Wolf should have caught him by now."

"But Daniel had a knife, as the holes in my arm can testify," she muttered angrily, rubbing the red welts, recalling Lance wouldn't have any way of knowing what had just happened.

Lance gave a chuckle. It wasn't a mirthful chuckle. "I don't think Wolf cared about that knife."

"Lance, I had to give Daniel the pendant. He had it when he left. He is probably long gone by now. Maybe Wolf is still chasing him."

Lance held her tight. "I don't care about the diamond. We'll do fine without it. I just care about you. You're safe. That's all the reward I need."

They stood together for a moment longer, foreheads touching. That was enough for them. They had each other.

It was a moan from Lance that brought Kimberly back to the present—the uncertain present. "We need to get you back to the mainland. Daniel brought me over on a raft."

Lance tried to nod, but the movement still hurt too much. "Same here. I'm not sure how Wolf got here. There might be a canoe nearby." That was all he seemed capable of contributing when he lapsed into silence, grimacing from the pain.

Kimberly put his arm around her waist to help him along. Walking a few steps in the fog, she suddenly stopped. "Lance! That's Daniel's knife! Why is it there on the ground?"

"Dunno," Lance mumbled. "Bring it along. I might need it later," but he didn't tell Kimberly why. If need be, he had plans of his own.

"Come on, Lance. The raft dock is just down this path. You can make it," she encouraged, trying not to cry from either frustration, anger, or worry about Lance.

She led them around the front of the Fort. If that odd fog hadn't come in, they could have seen the canoe dock across from them and the Hungry Bear Restaurant. In their current predicament, she wondered if the fog was a blessing or a curse. Did they want help and have to explain the Whats and the Whys? Or could they manage to get Lance across on their own and not have the risk of exposure?

Kimberly stopped short when she reached the raft's landing dock. The raft Daniel had used was still there. A small utility canoe, usually hidden on the far side of the Hungry Bear Restaurant, was tied up next to the raft. That had to be the means Wolf used to get across the River. Hopefully Lance wouldn't notice and ask too many questions—ones she didn't want to have to answer.

Lance did notice. "That means they are still here on the Island. There is no other way to get off unless they swam, which is totally unnecessary with a raft and a canoe here."

Kimberly said nothing and tried to help Lance move toward the raft.

Still trying to work out the inconsistency, Lance attempted to shake his head no, but stopped. "No, we would have heard them. The Island isn't that wide. I have a feeling neither one of them would be silent right now."

Kimberly got him as far as a bench under one of the overhanging trees. "The fog is clearing," she observed.

"That's really weird. Well, if they aren't here and they couldn't have left, then where are they?"

For four days, Lance tried to reach Wolf to find out what happened on the Island. But Wolf never answered his phone and never showed up at work. It was as if he had disappeared off the face of the planet.

On the fifth day, there was a knock on the door of Lance's apartment. Kimberly answered the door and was surprised to see a bedraggled Wolf standing there. He looked as if he hadn't slept in days. It was Wolf's turn to be surprised when Kimberly threw her arms around his neck. "Oh, Wolf! I am so glad to see you!".... *Lance doesn't know*, she whispered.... "We were so worried! Lance! Wolf is here," she called, finally releasing Wolf just after he whispered back to her that 'all is well.'

Lance, the back of his neck still bandaged, came to shake hands with his Security partner. "Good to see you, man. Come on in."

He took a couple of steps inside. "I can't stay. I'm on my way to work," Wolf told them, looking back and forth at the two pairs of eyes staring at him. "I just came to tell you everything was taken care of."

Lance looked at Kimberly, not sure what he meant. "What is taken care of?"

"Daniel. He won't bother you ever again." At Lance's confused look, Wolf explained, "I...umm, convinced him to move far away. He won't be coming back."

Lance looked relieved. "For Kimberly's sake, I hope that's true. What about the pendant? Did you see what he did with it?"

Wolf shrugged one shoulder, knowing he couldn't reveal the truth that the pendant was back in his safe-keeping. He didn't like to lie to his best friend, but it couldn't be avoided. "I didn't see it. I have to go. Doka, Lance. Kimberly."

Lance clapped him on the shoulder. "Doka, Wolf."

Wolf gave a quick, meaningful glance to Kimberly. *It wasn't time yet for Lance to know.* They both nodded their heads once in understanding as he turned toward the door to leave.

As he closed the door behind Wolf, Lance gave a sigh and commented, "Well, I guess we'll never know."

Kimberly slipped her arm around his waist. "Know what?" She hoped he wasn't referring again to her uncle.

"What the power of the pendant was. Why it was so important to Walt."

Kimberly's mind flashed back to her vision—

still so real that she could almost touch it—of her holding the hand of a happy, smiling blond-haired little girl and standing with Lance. *How you get it is up to you*, Walt had written. "Hmm," she hesitated as the power of the vision took away her power of speech. "I only know the diamond was very beautiful," she told Lance when she could talk again. In her mind, she felt thankful that the red diamond heart was gone. While her vision was quite wonderful to her, it was also quite revealing of the diamond's power. That power, what it meant, was something she felt should not be in anyone's hands.

"Lance?"

"Hmmm?"

"Did I tell you today that I loved you?"

Lance smiled. "No, actually you didn't," pulling her into a full embrace.

She smiled back. "Oh, okay, then. Just checking."

CHAPTER 14

Lance, dressed in his Security uniform, stood quietly inside the exit of the Pirates of the Caribbean ride. His mouth was dry and his heart racing as he walked up the exit ramp into the dark interior of the ride. He quickly scanned the cos-tumed cast members who were intent at their jobs of loading and unloading guests. It was a busy summer day at the Park and he knew the line winding its way through the ramped queue out-side was long. None of the cast members gave him any heed; only a few disembarking female guests gave him a lingering look as they herded toward the exit and their next destination.

Lance didn't see these glances. If he had, they would have received just a vague smile. He had something on his mind that was bothering him. Still. It was eating at him and sometimes throbbed worse than that knot on the back of his head, a parting gift from Daniel Crain. He had to try and talk to Beth to see if she could ever forgive him. If she yelled at him or slapped him in the face, so be it. He deserved it. Maybe she needed closure, too. She didn't deserve what he had done to her. She should have her chance, her day in court as his lawyer friends would have said.

But knowing what you should do and knowing the possible outcomes don't make that first step any easier. He had made it into the exit of the ride she was currently working. But now he needed to take the next steps and actually find her to see if they could have a private moment together. He licked his dry lips and headed for the cast member at the podium who was overseeing the boats, making sure they were loaded properly and sent on their way.

Sabrina's eyes lit up when Lance strode up to her. She had been trying to catch his attention for about a year now. "Lance! Hold on a second, Sweetheart, don't move.... Diane, see that row three is left empty in the next boat for the handicap section. Thank you.... Now, Lance," she turned back to him with a broad grin, leaning forward a little over the top of the podium. "What can I do for you?"

Lance knew she wasn't talking about anything to do with Security. He gave her a half smile. "Nice to see you, Sabrina. How's Tom?"

Sabrina gave a pretty pout at the name of her current boyfriend. She'd easily dump him for Lance. She gave a shrug. "Hold on.... Cloe? There's a jacket left behind in row one. Could you grab it, please?.... Now, Lance, you were saying?"

"Say 'hi' to Tom for me," he smiled, seeing a look of disappointment pass over her pretty face.

"I am looking for someone, actually."

She wasn't giving up. "You found someone, actually."

"Actually," Lance drawled out, "I am looking for Beth Roberts. I thought she was working today." The calming effect that bantering with Sabrina had on him ended with his mentioning Beth's name. His heart started pounding again.

"Humpf," Sabrina sighed. "Beth? First Wolf comes looking for her and now you. Some things are just not fair. She's up in Dispatch," she indicated the upper booth with a tilt of her chin. "You can cross over after this next boat unloads."

Lance gave her a pat on the shoulder. "Thanks, Sabrina. Tom's a lucky man."

Sabrina watched him as he walked over to the edge of the dock. She looked as if she had no idea who Tom was.

Lance climbed the flight of wooden steps up to the Dispatch office. There was a bank of monitors on one wall, each showing a different part of the ride and the boats going through. The cast member in charge of Dispatch made sure everyone stayed safely seated and that no one was taking flash pictures. If there was any problem on the ride, Dispatch would be the first to know about it and respond accordingly, even to the point of shutting down the ride if necessary. Two of the walls had huge windows overlooking the Blue Bayou and the boats as they started on their journey.

He paused unseen in the doorway. Beth was

there, her back to him as she watched the monitors. She was muttering out loud to herself as another bright flash went off in the Ship Battle scene. Lance smiled. *That's my Beth!* he told himself.

Beth took the microphone in hand again and, watching the screen, she could see the person actually stand up in the flat-bottom boat to take a better picture of the *Wicked Wench*. "How many times do I have to tell you?" she muttered to herself before pressing the button on the microphone. "For your safety, please remain seated. And no flash photography!" she announced in a calm voice.

"What is it with you people!" she exclaimed to the monitor that showed the person was still standing and ready to take another picture as they sailed past the fort. She grabbed the microphone. "Please remain seated! Don't make me pull this car over!"

She gave a laugh of triumph when the man's head shot around, looking for the person who was watching him. He sat back down immediately. She could see the other guests in the boat start to applaud. "Idiot," she mumbled.

Lance started laughing. He wanted to go give her a hug, but held back. "Boy, Captain, I think you scared the bejeebers out of him!"

Beth startled in her chair, almost knocking it over in her surprise. She immediately recognized Lance's voice but hadn't known anyone was in the small room with her. "Oh my god. Lance," she whispered, regaining her composure and managing to go white at the same time.

He got nervous again and didn't know what to

do with his hands. He thrust them in his pockets. His mouth opened to say something and then closed again when he saw her eyes fill with tears. Lance gave a small shrug, unsure what to do next.

Beth didn't give him too many choices. She flung herself into his arms, hugging him.

His arms went around his lost friend. If they hugged any tighter, they would have gone right through each other.

"I'm so sorry," he started.

"I've missed you so much," she started at the same time.

"What?" they both laughed, breaking the tension.

"Crybaby," he teased, wiping a tear that ran down her cheek.

"Felon," she kidded back.

"Hold-out."

"Heartbreaker."

"Sweetheart."

"Hey, you're not playing right," she told him with a laugh, breaking the hug, and glancing back at the monitors. The man was still seated and his camera was not in sight. "Just a second," she told Lance, "and don't go anywhere. I think I need to yell at you or something…." Beth picked up the handset of the phone and called down to Sabrina. "Sabrina, when boat forty-two comes back, give everyone except the dark-haired guy in row four a readmission pass. Yeah, they deserve it…. Okay, back to you, Slick," as she turned her attention back to Lance.

He held his arms out to the sides and lifted his chin. "Go ahead. Take a free shot. You deserve it."

"Drama queen," she muttered, grinning broadly, folding her arms across her chest.

Lance opened one eye when he realized she wasn't going to take him up on his offer. He relaxed his stance and became serious. His heart started racing again. "Beth, I hope you know how sorry I am. I don't know what came over me that day with you and Adam.... Well, besides greed and desperation and an amazing amount of stupidity," he muttered more to himself than to Beth. "There's no excuse, really. I hope you can forgive me."

Beth's eyes filled with tears again. "You made me cry again."

"Obviously, Captain," he grinned.

That got her laughing and crying at the same time. "I have missed you so much. How did you get that bandage on your head, by the way?"

Lance grimaced and touched the thick pad gingerly. "Let's just say I got some sense knocked into me and leave it at that." He wasn't going to fill her in on all that he had been through lately, especially with Daniel Crain and the heart pendant. There were some things that would just have to remain between Kimberly and him.

"At least they hit the hardest part of you."

Lance rolled his eyes. "Why is that the first thing everyone says!?"

"Duh."

"So, I'm forgiven?" he asked, hopeful, sounding like a small child who broke his mom's favorite vase.

After a glance at the monitor bank, Beth

came into his arms again. He could hear the relief in her voice. "Of course, Frat Boy. I knew
something had to be very wrong for you to do that.
And, hopefully, it all got worked out?" It was more
of a question for Lance than a wishful statement.

He didn't miss the question. "Yes, I think it
has." His face darkened a little. "What about
Adam?"

Beth gave a sigh and walked back to her
chair at the monitor wall. She gave a cursory look
at all the images. Everyone was seated and there
were no blinding flashes going off. "Adam," she
repeated with another sigh. "That's a whole different ball game, Slick." She looked away, unseeing at the wall. She was still upset she couldn't
even bring up the subject of Lance to Adam yet.
"It is going to take some more time, I think." She
wasn't even sure if she had said that out loud or
just thought it to herself.

Lance just nodded. He knew Adam. When
Adam's trust was lost, it takes a long time—if
ever—to earn it again. "Well, then I will just have
to wait." He was discouraged, as he was hoping—even against the facts of Adam's personality—that it would somehow be over by now and
they could all go back to being friends. Well, he
had Beth back. That was a good start. He would-
n't give up on Adam. "Hey, I have some good
news for you, Captain. I'm getting married!"

He could always read Beth like a book. As
she silently sat there, stunned, he could see every
emotion play across her expressive face. Happiness. Surprise. Jealousy. Disappointment. Curiosity. And back to happiness. "Oh my god,

Lance! That's wonderful! Who is she? Anyone I know?" The shock and jealousy held her glued to the chair.

"Do you know Kimberly Waldron? She usually works as one of the princesses."

Beth's eyebrows went up in surprise. "Kimberly? Yes, I know of her. She's gorgeous, Lance. Wow. You're getting married. That's wonderful."

Lance smiled at the expression on her pretty face. "You looked stunned. Not happy for me."

Beth tried to control the look on her face. She should have known better. "Of course I am happy for you! My word, but it's you, Lance…. Well, you know what I mean…. All those girls…. And now you are getting married?…. Wow, I'm really messing this up, aren't I?" she asked sheepishly.

Lance's eyes softened. "She's really wonderful, Beth. I'd like you two to meet. I know you would be friends…." He broke off when he saw a small spark of the jealousy flit across her face again. Lance took the two steps over to her chair and picked up her hands. He softly told her, "You know I will always love you, Beth, as my very best friend. We've always had a special connection, but it never went beyond that…try as I might," he teased and was rewarded with a knowing smile from Beth. "Okay? I want you to be happy for me."

Beth let him pull her out of the chair. Her arms went around his waist again. "Of course I am happy for you. But, you know me. You're My Lance. I don't like sharing."

He looked into her upturned face. "You're still seeing Adam, aren't you?"

Her smile got warm as she thought about Adam and their relationship. She knew Adam was the only man she had ever wanted. She also knew Lance was aware of this and that made their easy flirtation fun. "Yes, we are doing well. He has some big secret project he is working on that he won't tell me about. He'll come around…eventually," she added with a sigh. "Can I come to the wedding? When is it? Where are you going on your honeymoon? When can I meet Kimberly?"

He held his hands up against the barrage of questions that he knew would be endless. "Hey, you and I both need to get back to work. We'll have you over some evening and talk. How does that sound?"

She gave him a last squeeze. "That sounds great. So, at least tell me when the wedding is."

"Saturday."

"Which Saturday?"

"This Saturday."

"Lance, that is only four days from now."

He smiled at the look on her face. "Yeah, I know. I wanted to give everyone plenty of time."

"'Plenty of time'," she slowly repeated, shaking her head. "Only you, Slick, only you could get away with that. You have asked the bride already, right?"

Lance pretended to be thinking. "Yeah, I think I mentioned something to her…. It will be one o'clock at the gazebo on the Hotel grounds. Wear something pretty."

"I always wear something pretty!…. Say, are you registered anywhere? Do you need anything?" she stumbled, knowing his reduced straights.

Thinking of the mansion, the trust fund from Walt, and especially the lovely bride herself, Lance just smiled. "I have everything I need. We're good. I just want you there!"

"I'll be there." She glanced at the monitors as a bright flash illuminated one of them. "Uh oh, I have another flasher in the Bar Scene." As he turned to go, Beth called him back. "Lance? Thanks for coming! You'll always be my Lance, you know."

His eyes got a little misty. "I love you, too, Beth."

Outlined in twinkling white lights and trailing greenery, the Disneyland Hotel's ornate white gazebo stood alone on a grassy section of grass. The stone walkway leading to the romantic setting was lined with white chairs and colorful flower arrangements. Friends of the bride and groom—mostly fellow cast members—filled the chairs and stood quietly in the background as the simple ceremony concluded.

The bride and groom had walked together arm-in-arm up to the gazebo where the justice of the peace stood waiting. Dressed in a column-style gown, its pearl studded bodice shimmering in the bright sunlight, the bride carried a single white long-stemmed rose. The groom looking elegant in a black, vested suit had been unable to take his eyes off his beautiful bride. Their first kiss as husband and wife continued until some laughs and whistles came from the on-lookers. As they turned to walk back down the aisle, all the Security force stood at attention and held out their Mag lights in a high salute as the couple walked underneath, pelted with rose petals from the women guests.

There was a reception area set up under white canopies a few steps over. As they sliced into the heart-encrusted wedding cake, Wolf called out for Lance to "leave some for the rest of us!"

When glasses were raised in tribute to the couple, Lance glanced over the champagne flutes. His glass stopped halfway to his lips. Adam was standing in the back with Beth, watching him. Beside them were John and Margaret, Adam's parents and practically second parents to Lance. Lance raised his glass to them as a thank you, smiling. Neither frowning nor smiling, Adam gave a single nod, and turning to his father, he and John headed to the Lost Bar across from the pool.

The first step, Lance told himself, smiling. He turned back to his bride.

This day was, now, officially perfect.

Kimberly marveled on how quickly the two-week cruise sped by. It was a wonderful adventure; their honeymoon was all that Kimberly anticipated and more. As they arrived back at the mansion, Wolf greeted them at the door. "All's well," was his entire report of the two weeks they were gone on their honeymoon.

Satisfied, Kimberly started to take some of her luggage upstairs. Lance, however, was still surprised to see his Security partner both at the Mansion and in some way connected to his new responsibilities.

"I don't understand," he began as Wolf picked up a small overnight bag and was ready to leave.

In her happiness over the past month, Kimberly had forgotten Lance wasn't up to speed on all the developments that had happened over the years and that she took for granted. Wolf and his role was one now-glaring omission. She called Wolf back from the door and asked if they could take a few minutes in the library to talk.

With a nod, Wolf set his bag near the door and followed them, content to let her take the lead in this.

Sitting close to Lance on the leather sofa, she seemed happy to have a hand on him, touching him. Still in the relaxed mood the cruise had set for them, she hoped to keep this information session with Lance on a good level. She wasn't sure how much he really knew about his partner.

"First, Wolf, thank you so much for watching the house and the activities for us while we were gone. We appreciate it very much." At his nod, she continued, "Lance, you should know that Wolf has worked with my father for many years and he has proven to be invaluable. Now he will be working with you and me as we continue my father's work."

Lance suddenly pointed at Wolf. "*You* are the second Guardian Walt wrote about?"

Kimberly continued. "Yes, he is also a Guardian. His role has been very special to us and greatly appreciated. You might remember when you were first brought here to our home that the question arose as to what would become of you if things didn't work out. As you yourself stated, you 'knew too much.' Well, that is where Wolf's position comes in. It is his sometimes unenviable job of having to protect what was put in place—by means known only to himself, my father...," she paused, and looked to Wolf for confirmation to continue. He gave a glance at Lance's serious face and nodded for her to proceed. "...and Walt. Wolf is indeed the other Guardian mentioned in the journal we found upstairs on Main Street."

When she became silent, Lance realized he needed to say something. But, he was stunned. How was this possible? How could Wolf know Walt? As far as he knew, he and Wolf were the same age. Weren't they? How could Walt have written about Wolf forty years ago? "I...," he broke off and shook his head, looking at his friend.

Wolf had the same stoic look on his face he usually wore. "Walt was a wonderful man," he stated quietly. "You would have enjoyed knowing him."

"I don't understand how that is possible. You should be an old man," he told Wolf. Becoming paranoid, he looked to Kimberly for confirmation. "And *you*? Did you know Walt, too?"

"No, no," she quickly said, placing a calming hand on his arm. "I am just like you. Wolf, even though I really don't understand it all myself, has a unique ability. He is able to, shall we say, *move* differently than we do."

"Move? That doesn't make sense. None of

this does," Lance concluded, sitting back against the sofa as he ran a hand through his hair.

When Wolf remained silent, Kimberly admitted again, "I don't understand the physics of it, the science. He shouldn't be able to travel like he does, but he does," she ended simply.

"When you had that showdown with Daniel Crain on the Island, I never did understand how you both got off the Island. The raft and the canoe were still there. I thought you must have swum for some odd reason. You didn't kill him, did you, and hide the body?" Lance had a small smile on his face as he said this, but he really wasn't kidding.

Wolf knew not to be insulted by his friend. "No, I do not remove threats by killing them."

"You told us you convinced Crain to move far away, that he would never be back to bother us." Lance paused, and then added, "Just where exactly is 'far away'?"

Wolf looked at Lance with a solemn stare. "Not so much 'where', but 'when' is a better description of what happened to Crain." Wolf thought he saw a flicker of understanding within the disbelief that Lance simply could not hide. "His future," Wolf paused, "is...how should I put this?" He rubbed his chin as he thought. "His future is now in...a very distant past."

Lance simply shook his head. His foundation in reality would not grasp the concept that Wolf was trying to explain. His eyes narrowed as he tried to work it all out in his churning mind. "Wolf, I need to know—what exactly did you do to Daniel Crain!?"

EPILOGUE

2042

Big Red, the Mark XII Monorail, glided silently past the entry to the Magic Kingdom. Hovering electromagnetically a foot above the rail, it had just come from its fourth stop at the Disneyland Hotel and was headed for the Tomorrowland Station. After picking up new passengers at the California Adventure Station and at the Paradise Pier Hotel, all the seats in the six cars were taken. Some new arrivals would be heading to the newly-opened apartments in the Sleeping Beauty Castle Towers; others would be eager to continue their adventures within the Park. A ten-year old boy sitting in the co-pilot seat pushed the horn button and energetically waved to the people on the moving walkways below.

The remodeled, larger Sleeping Beauty Castle with its furnished towers wasn't the only place

Park visitors could spend the night. After much popular demand, the Swiss Family Treehouse had returned to Adventureland. The three original huts were back in refurnished glory. The largest, most popular hut, the Main Bedroom that had belonged to Mother and Father in the 1960 film *Swiss Family Robinson,* was complete with its own lavatory with a 'tortoise-shell' sink and running water that was seemingly supplied by the large, turning waterwheel made out of realistic-looking bamboo. What most guests loved was the special tasseled pull-rope that hung over the opulent king-sized bed. Just like in the movie, guests could pull on the rope and have the thatched ceiling open on hidden levers. Lying in bed, in their own secluded privacy, the occupants could watch the 9:30 fireworks show with the music piped into hidden speakers.

The two smaller huts had been the boys' rooms in the movie. Now they were less opulent than the Main Bedroom, but more fun for visitors. The lower hut had a private waterfall slide that ended up in the pool below, guarded over by Ellie the baby elephant that would playfully squirt each rider as they curved along the bottom portion of the slide.

The uppermost hut had the best views. High above the Park, guests could sit on their own private wooden deck to watch the nighttime shows of *Fantasmic!* or even the interactive water show in California Adventure. The fireworks would be so close they could almost reach out to touch them.

One of the newer attractions that was visible from the upper hut was the Mine Train through Nature's Wonderland. Overlapping the Big Thunder rollercoaster that boasted a new 360-degree loop, guests could once again travel through the balancing rocks and colorful Rainbow Caverns in the backmost portion of Frontierland. At one point in the ride, the Big Thunder train would look as if it was going to crash right into the slower moving Mine Train. Seemingly coming out of nowhere, the Big Thunder train would screech out of a hidden cavern and race toward the other train. Then, at the last minute, Old Unfaithful Geyser would erupt and the Big Thunder cars would veer sharply away, narrowly avoiding disaster. Careening around the Bubbling Pots of Mud, the train would vanish down a steep incline, its passengers screaming in delight as they narrowly missed being crushed by an avalanche of rocks. The Mine Train would continue on its more sedate journey through Bear Country, Elk Meadow, and under the mist-water of Cascade Peaks, returning once more to Rainbow Ridge and its interactive displays of the Old West where kids of all ages could replicate gunfights and see a stunt show spectacular in the street just in front of the popular attraction.

Back on Main Street, a line had formed for the extremely popular Main Street Cinema. As original cartoons of Mickey Mouse played on the old-fashioned flat-screen televisions, guests could enter private booths that lined the walls—much like the old-time telephone booths, but ones that could comfortably accommodate a family of four. Each guest was given a special mouse-eared Virtual Reality headset that fit over their eyes and plugged into their ears. They would have a menu pop up on the screen in front of them. With the push of a button, they would be 'transported' into any attraction of Disneyland's history that they wanted to relive. Older guests especially loved to visit the Disneyland of their own childhood. They would be instantly seated in an Atomobile for their personal Adventure through Inner Space, or they would climb into a Skyway Cab for a roundtrip flight over Fantasyland, ending back at the Swiss chalet nestled up and behind the Storybook Land Canal Boats. The Mike Fink Keelboats could come alive for them once again, with Beth Roberts as their pilot. As they listened to her humorous spiel, they could turn their head in any direction and see Tom Sawyer's Island as it was way back in 1996 or further back when the surrounding trees did not hide the fort and when Native American shows could be seen in the nearby Village. The Country Bear Jamboree or the Carousel of Progress, the original Sleeping Beauty Walk-Through or the Submarine Voyage, America Sings or the Lion King Parade; they were all there in vivid virtual clarity.

The Jungle Cruise now offered two tracks for its passengers. Guests could take one track and be entertained by the skipper as he took them through the underground caverns and rivers of Middle Asia before emerging back into the bright light and continuing onto the rivers of Africa and South America.

The second track let the guests skipper their own boat. Bringing along as many guests as they wanted, the entertainment was theirs to provide.

Those who always felt 'they could do it better' now had the opportunity to do so. Riding along the original guiding track set in 1955 and timed so the boats never ran side-by-side, each track was immersed in the Jungle all their own. Considering the happy faces of the returning guests, each side was extremely popular.

Lance guided his granddaughter through the bricked arch of the entry tunnel, holding her hand, feeling her squeeze his hand tighter as she emerged onto Main Street. He smiled as he heard her sharp intake of breath as the grand view opened before her wide green eyes. The Castle, the shops, the people, all signified something fantastic to the little five-year-old.

They walked to the Town Square, toward the tall, shiny flagpole that stood upon its foundation among beautifully manicured flowers. The two stopped and gazed down the street. The trolley car was moving slowly toward the pink and white Castle, the clop-clop-clop of the Belgium horse's hooves easily heard over the sounds of the crowd. The muted honk of the Omnibus drew her excited attention as it started on its own electric journey down Main Street. A small group of guests were taking pictures of the *E.P. Ripley* steam train as it waited at the Depot for its next load of guests, sounding its whistle in hello. The sounds were as plentiful as the sights and smells.

Lance looked down at his granddaughter, smiling to himself, enjoying the emotional memory of the first time he had seen Disneyland.

Then, as he stood there, other memories of Disneyland came flooding back. Memories of good times with friends, exciting adventures, and romantic moments with a certain blond, green-eyed beauty. He looked toward the Fire House and the apartment in the upper story. The light was still burning bright in the window. He let the memories wash through him, delighted with each and every one. *Had it really been forty years?* he asked himself in wonderment. *It seemed like just yesterday.*

"Well, what do you think, Lilly?" Lance asked the wide-eyed, blond-haired little girl who excitedly tugged on his arm. Living out of the country with her parents, this was Lilly's first time visiting Disneyland.

"It's a dream!" was her breathless answer, not taking her eyes off the tall, golden spires of the Castle in the distance.

Lance smiled and looked over to his right. He could see a few inquisitive guests looking at the bronze plaque imbedded in the base of the flagpole.

Kneeling down to her level, Lance gave Lilly a kiss. "Stay here with Grandma, Lilly." He stood and whispered to his wife, Kimberly, "I'll be right back." Expecting this, she just nodded as he walked off toward the flagpole.

"Where's Papa going!? I wanna go with Papa!" Not wanting to miss anything, Lilly was getting worried.

Looking down at the little hand that was placed in her own, Kimberly suddenly felt her heart start to pound, her mouth forming an 'O'. It was a memory, a vision that came rushing back into her mind, one that she had had forty years ago not far away from where they now stood. She had forgotten about the vision that was given to her by the red diamond heart. Lance had never been told about it; it was too personal at the time she had received it. 'How you get there is up to you' had been written on the note from Walt. Things between Lance and her had been too new, too fresh then. How could she throw into the conversation, "Oh, by the way, I just saw myself holding the hand of a beautiful blond-haired little girl. She looked around five or six years old and she was *our* granddaughter. So, what would you like to do for dinner?" No, she had buried the vision deep in her heart, safe to take out and cherish whenever she wanted to see it again in her memories. But, time and reality came—as they always did—and she eventually forgot as her life with Lance started and found that this reality with him was so very wonderful and so very, very real. Now, forty years later, holding Lilly's hand, she saw the vision again. She and Lance had had three boys. The vision had remained deeply contained with nothing to prick at the memory. Now, she looked down at the little hand in hers and the eager, beautiful, concerned face that peered up into her own. The amazement on Kimberly's face faded into a loving smile at her granddaughter. This was the lovely child she had seen. Her future had come true.

"Thank you, Walt," she whispered to herself.

"Grandma?" Lilly repeated, pulling on her hand and pointing to the retreating back of Lance.

"It's okay, honey," Kimberly soothed her. "Papa has something he needs to do. Let's go say hi to Mickey at the Opera House."

Following her Grandmother's pointing finger, Lilly bounced up and down. "Is that the real Mickey!?"

With a laugh, Kimberly led her over toward the ornate white building. "Well, let's go ask him!"

As Lance slowly walked toward the plaque, the other guests moved on. A lone man stood there now, looking down at the raised letters. He moved his fingers over the bronze words, reading as he went. Seeing a red button just above the plaque, he pushed it and jumped back, startled.

A three-dimensional Walt Disney appeared in front of the flagpole. "To all who come to this happy place, welcome...," he began, Disney's familiar voice reciting the Opening Day Speech.

The older man leaned toward the transparent, but still somehow solid figure as the speech continued. He poked a finger through the apparition and began chuckling to himself.

Lance looked back toward his wife and Lilly, easily finding their shining blond heads in the crowd surrounding Mickey. He smiled contentedly. He thought of all the 'first times' Lilly would have today. The Matterhorn, the Jungle Cruise, Peter Pan, It's a Small World, Pirates of the Caribbean. Lance grinned at his own memories—especially of Pirates.

A young family moved near Lance. They were attempting to take a picture that would include all of them and have the Castle as the backdrop. Their hovering tripod wasn't cooperating. Lance offered to take the picture the old-fashioned way so they could all be in the shot. Appreciative of the offer, the young father handed the camera to Lance who told them, "On three, smile!"

When he handed the camera back, they got back on their Upright Transports and hummed down Main Street. Lance turned back to the older man who had activated the Opening Speech again. Walking all the way around the shimmering image of Walt, the man seemed impressed and amused at the same time.

"What do you think?" Lance asked the man as he came up beside him.

The man just rocked back on his heels and smiled at him, a twinkle in his eye. "Couldn't have said it better myself!" he told Lance, pushing his battered Fedora back off of his forehead.

Lance glanced once more at his wife who was busy pointing out something in the Disney Gallery's window to Lilly.

"You did well," Lance said, putting his hand on the man's shoulder. A little softer, he repeated, "You did real well, Walt!"

—THE END—

THANKS AND ACKNOWLEDGEMENTS TO:

KAYE MALINS AT THE WALT DISNEY HOMETOWN
MUSEUM IN MARCELINE, MISSOURI – FOR HER
CONTRIBUTIONS TO HISTORICAL RESEARCH
WWW.WALTDISNEYMUSEUM.ORG

AND ALSO TO OUR PROOFREADERS AND EDITORS:
MISTY AMODT
ALYSSA COLODNY
KARLA GALLAGHER, ENGLISH B.A.

WITH THE POPULARITY OF THE FIRST HIDDEN MICKEY BOOK, "SOMETIMES DEAD MEN DO TELL TALES!" THE HIDDEN MICKEY FAN CLUB WAS FORMED.

FAN CLUB MEMBERS GET MONTHLY E-MAIL NEWSLETTERS CONTAINING BEHIND-THE-SCENES ARTICLES WRITTEN BY VARIOUS PAST AND PRESENT CAST MEMBERS WITHIN THE DISNEY PARKS, AS WELL AS ADVANCE ANNOUNCEMENTS ON FUTURE BOOK SIGNINGS, SPECIAL EVENTS, AND SPECIAL OFFERS. IN ADDITION, FAN CLUB MEMBERS GET SPECIAL PUR-CHASE OPPORTUNITIES FOR THE NEXT HIDDEN MICKEY SERIES BOOKS AND MERCHANDISE BEFORE THEY ARE RELEASED TO THE PUBLIC.

JOIN THE HIDDEN MICKEY FAN CLUB:
www.HIDDENMICKEYBOOK.COM/fanclub

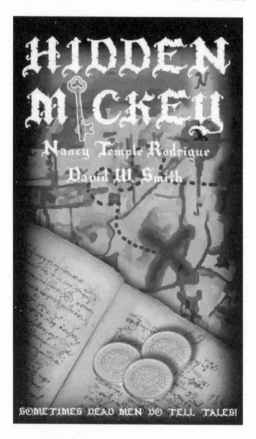

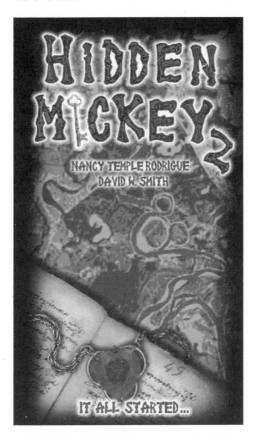

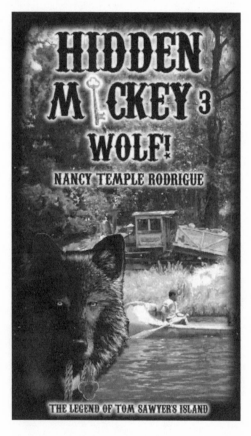

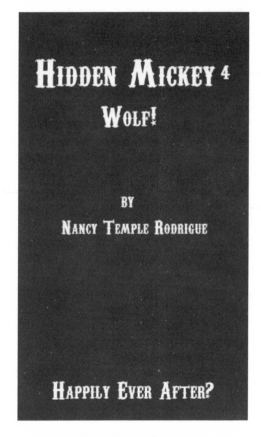

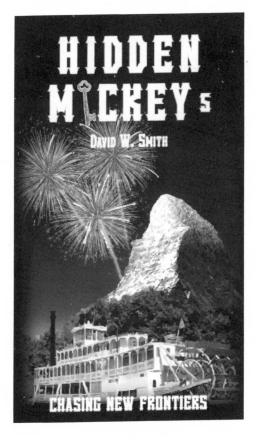

ABOUT THE AUTHORS

NANCY TEMPLE RODRIGUE

Nancy lives in the small town of Lompoc, California. Four of her ten grandchildren live nearby and she has enjoyed sharing the wonders of Disneyland with them. Besides writing, Nancy is an avid reader, enjoys knitting, crocheting, and showing her award-winning 1957 T-Bird at local car shows. She also enjoys tasting the wonderful wines in the wine regions in her area.

Writing about Disneyland comes easy for Nancy as she has been an avid Disney fan ever since she was 6 years old and went to Disneyland for the first time. Her novels show her admiration and respect for the man who started it all–Walt Disney. *Hidden Mickey: Sometimes Dead Men DO Tell Tales!* and this sequel *Hidden Mickey 2: It All Started...* are the first novels in the Hidden Mickey series. In these first two novels she was assisted by her co-author David W. Smith. Nancy has been writing for most of her life, mostly in the fiction and fantasy genre, so when Smith approached her with the idea of a story along the line of the movie National Treasure, but with connections to Walt Disney, she jumped at the opportunity write it with him. Following the sequel, *Hidden Mickey 2: It All Started....*, Smith recommended she author the next two novels in the series by herself to allow her to continue the fantasy element she had introduced in the sequel. She then authored *Hidden Mickey 3 Wolf!: The Legend of Tom Sawyer's Island* and *Hidden Mickey 4 Wolf!: Happily Ever After?* without Smith. Nancy also authored the romantic fantasy titled *The Fan Letter*.

Nancy actively participates in book signing and speaking events, and loves talking to people who enjoy her novels. www.Double-Rbooks.com has Nancy's blog where fans can learn where book signing event dates and locations are posted.

David W. Smith

Having worked at Disneyland in the late 1970's, Dave experienced first-hand the inner workings of the park and the many wonderful inspirations that were cultivated within the mind of Walt Disney. Dave always felt a special connection to Disneyland, growing up just a couple miles south of the park in Garden Grove and seeing it evolve and grow to what we now recognize as the worldwide destination resort it has become. Dave believes everyone who has ever had a dream can relate to Walt Disney s own dreams of "doing the impossible. While most of us never fulfill our dreams to the extent Walt did, we all can imagine just how he must have felt walking down Main Street, USA of Disneyland, taking in all that he had done. However, while most of us would have felt a sense of accomplishment, knowing Walt as we know him today, he, most likely, would have been thinking of something new or doing something better...instead of being satisfied his success. His saying, "Keep moving forward certainly kindles this spirit!

Dave Smith is the author of two tennis instructional books, TENNIS MASTERY and COACHING MASTERY and is the Senior Editor of the world's top-rated tennis website, TennisOne.com. While Dave has published more than 150 tennis articles over the past 9years, the HIDDEN MICKEY series is his first venture into writing novels. Dave has been a featured speaker at various tennis conferences, clubs and workshops. He owns Top Notch Tennis Academy in St. George, Utah.

Dave has been married over 20 years to Dr. Kerri N. Smith and has two children, Kyla Marie who is eleven and Keaton Bruce who is seven.

Hidden Mickey Merchandise Items

Hidden Mickey Mugs

Hidden Mickey Baseball Caps

Hidden Mickey Shirts

Hidden Mickey Jackets

Hidden Mickey Clocks

Hidden Mickey Specialty Items

The Limited Edition
Hidden Mickey Heart Pendant
Pendant Design by Nancy Rodrigue
Copyright © 2010 by Nancy Rodrigue

And Much More...
Available At:
www.HiddenMickeyBook.com